MW01165499

A FLASH IN THE PAN

The Story of the Crack Apprentice Jockey, Tommy Murray, During the Real Golden Age of Racing 1919

By

Donald Clare

A Flash in the Pan: The Story of the Crack Apprentice Jockey, Tommy Murray, During the Real Golden Age of Racing 1919

Author: Donald Clare

Original cover photos have been provided by the author. Cover artwork alteration by The Merlot Group.

Front Cover Photo: Official Winner's Circle photo, 1919 Kentucky Oaks.

Back Cover Photo: Cliff Robinson taking first place as Tommy Murray settles for second at Old Latonia in June 1919. The two were vying for the 1919 "Winningest Jockey" title.

ISBN: 978-0-9816123-7-9

Published by:

The Merlot Group, LLC, P.O. Box 302, Covington KY 41012-0302

(859) 743-1003, www.merlotgroup.com

DEDICATION

I dedicate this work to the memories of my grandmother, Virginia Conley Murray and her four children, my mother Virginia Murray Clare, my uncles, Tom and Dick Murray, and my aunt, Patricia Murray Vogelpohl. Their lives and times with my grandfather were full of difficulty, disappointment, struggle and sacrifice but they each persevered and endured and managed to reach pinnacles of success, despite my grandfather's plummet from fame. From them I have learned hard work, determination, endurance and fortitude. From him, I have learned hard work, determination, endurance and fortitude. What matters is how one applies these attributes to family, career, interpersonal relationships, and life.

(Grandpa) Tommy Murray in 1959 as a jockey valet at Churchill Downs

Jay Jay Jockey on Thoroughbred Higgens. Even the family pets have a little "jockey" in them.

(L-R) Robert Conley, Dick Conley, Jr., and Virginia Conley (Grandma Murray) in 1908 on 3rd Street in Covington

TOMMY MURRAY

Valet Tommy Murray at Ascot Park, 1951

Author's mother, Virginia Murray Clare, 1949

(L-R) Dick Murray, Patricia Murray Vogelpohl, and Tom Murray

Author's grandmother, Virginia Conley Murray, and his mother, Virginia Murray Clare

Tommy's wife Virginia and his two oldest children, Virginia and Tommy

Louisville 1950 – Tommy remained on the track up until his death in 1963. Tommy ended his career as a jockey valet, working at almost every racetrack in the U.S. Canada, Mexico, and Cuba

Lexington (Keenland) 1951 – Tommy, second from left, working as a jockey valet.

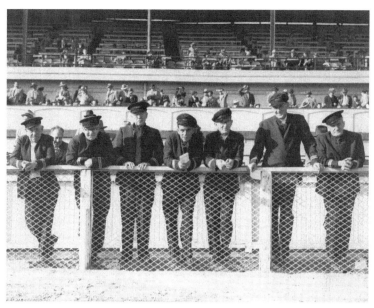

Louisville (Churchill) 1952 – Tommy, far right, working as a jockey valet.

ACKNOWLEDGEMENTS

The longer a project like this takes to complete, the more people there are to thank. There are those like my family to thank for not only the encouragement and support to take on such a project, but for the understanding they had and the sacrifices they made when I was not around for them. Eight years of research and writing and rewriting is eight years of absence and non-participation in the everyday family issues, happenings and togetherness, at least in a physical sense. Thank you, Sue, Callie, and Caitlyn for putting up with me and for recognizing and allowing me to pursue something I felt was important. Mere thank yous do not do justice for the love and gratitude I have for each one of you.

I thank my mother for telling me about Grandpa Murray when I was young and every time I would ask about him, despite the fact that "we don't talk about your grandfather." The hard feelings of the family toward him were made known to me early on, and I am sure they were legitimate feelings of abandonment and neglect but for a young child they were intriguing and exciting and became a source of pride and respect. Unfortunately, my mother died before I could really pick her brain as an adult. So I must thank James Claypool for his book, *The Tradition Continues*, which I purchased from him as a Christmas gift to my mother in 1997 and which I re-discovered in her estate after she died the next year full of handwritten notes and comments for me about my grandfather. At that point, this book project was born.

At first, all my research took place at the Keeneland Library on the campus of the historic and significant Keeneland Racetrack in Lexington. Special thanks to Kathy Shenck, the Executive Director, for all the help and assistance in the library's extensive collection of reference works, newspapers, copies of the *Daily Racing Form*, and collections of *The Thoroughbred Record*. She graciously led me to the proper resources day after day, making suggestions and instructing me in all things horseracing research. I thank her for letting me camp out on her library tables and surround myself in her books, right next to the copier, with my coffee and my lunch close by.

My long day-trips to Lexington soon ceased when, thanks to Kathy Caminiti, I learned about the Kentucky Department of Libraries and the *Daily Racing Form's* joint project of digitizing the collection on a web site and making it available to the public. This allowed me two full years of research from my home computer, at any time of day or night, saving me loads of gas money and sleep. It is a wonderful resource and a true blessing for those looking to research any horse race that had taken place at any track in the U.S., Canada, Mexico, and Cuba; along with news articles, editorials, trade news items, and other horse racing related topics. It served as a convenient and indispensible tool for my research, and I thank all involved in the creation of this valuable resource.

I have included an extensive bibliography at the end of this work to which I owe an immeasurable amount of gratitude for the extensive degree of general knowledge of the history of horseracing in America, the training of horses, the conditioning of jockeys, life on the track, everyday routines of training and racing, and the history of the horses, jockeys, trainers, and owners, all of which combined, accounts for what we enjoy today as the sport of Thoroughbred horseracing.

I want to thank Mr. Robert N. Elliston, President and C.E.O. of Turfway Park in Florence, Kentucky for allowing me to spend valuable research time on Turfway's backside and for allowing Sherry Pinson, Director of Communications, to take the time from several of her very full and busy days to allow me the experience and opportunity to visit and observe every aspect of the day-to-day goings-on at a major professional Thoroughbred racing facility and plant. It was through Sherry that I had the opportunity to meet and spend several other days with trainer Matt Kordenbrock and learn firsthand all that is involved in the operation; toils and dealings in running a successful stable from the perspective of someone actually 'playing in the dirt on the backside' which included, but was not limited to, early morning work outs, daily duties and chores, afternoon racing, and afternoon and evening routines and procedures in the barns, as well as the general day-by-day operation of a major race facility from the perspective of the administration all the way down to that of the general public and patrons of Thoroughbred horseracing.

A very special thank you goes out to my dear friend and fellow board member of the Rabbit Hash Historical Society, Shawn W. Masters, without whose encouragement, prodding, direction, suggestions, and assistance this work would still be just a dream. Because of him and his publishing company, The Merlot Group, with its competent, caring and professional staff, particularly Jerod Theobald, this dream is now a reality.

I cannot forget to thank Jannes Garbett for her years and years of friendship, encouragement, knowledge and love of history, and inspiration, not to mention her proofing and critiquing of the rough draft into the final product and a very special thank you to her for leading my elementary school-age daughters on their quest for knowledge and education that led them both on to post-graduate pursuits. I'd also like to send my appreciation to Mr. M.A. Alvarez of Kearneysville, W.V., whose father and grandfather were trainers at Oriental Park in Havana, Cuba, for sharing information he had about that track. Finally, I'd like to give a very special thank you to my recently "discovered" cousin, Jamie Johnson

Hunter, who enlightened me with photos and information about her uncle Harry Lunsford, who played such a big role in my grandfather's life.

I would also be remiss if I did not acknowledge my gratitude to nineteenth/twentieth century Boone County, Kentucky author John Uri Lloyd, from whom I "borrowed" the character Cupe and his masterful style and commanding reproduction of the nineteenth century black American Kentucky dialect and jargon. Thank you all from the bottom of my heart.

Knowing me, I am leaving people out who should also be included in this section. Please don't think ill of me, just pity my poor memory!

September, 2011
Rabbit Hash, Kentucky

PREFACE

I barely knew my grandfather, Tom Murray, but I definitely remember him and I have a lasting impression of him on my mind, considering the few times I was with him. It seems like it was always at a family picnic or family function, like a wedding, funeral, first communion, birthday, 4th of July, confirmation and things like that. He was a short little guy with leathery complexion, solidly built, and way over an ideal riding weight but he had a presence about him that commanded your attention - very charismatic, very alluring, and very noticeable, almost like a TV personality or movie star.

Grandpa was a jockey. I knew that when I was younger, but it didn't really have any important significance to me until I reached my midlife, when things like family lineage and family histories start to mean something to you. That is one of life's milestones which usually makes its appearance when it's too late, after everyone in the family who could have shared a wonderful oral history has passed on. There is so much I could have learned from my grandmother (his wife) and my mother (his oldest child) but I allowed those opportunities to slip away in favor of the pursuit of the milestones of youth and young adulthood. I find it fortunate to have remembered enough about grandpa and to have collected any and all records, research, and photos of him I could gather from the family.

Besides being a jockey, he was a very good one with lots of promise. In just his second year of professional riding (1919), he was the second winningest jockey in the nation for total number of wins. He also won the Kentucky Oaks that year, and rode (but did not place) in the Kentucky Derby the next year. Unfortunately, he peaked early on and was unable to keep pace with his early success, and eventually plummeted into a progressive spiral downhill skid as far as a spectacular career was concerned. In researching the material for this book, I have discovered that the career of Tommy Murray, the jockey, was much the same story as the career of Sir Barton, the very first Triple Crown winner in the history of American Thoroughbred racing for the same year of 1919. Of course, this was before there ever was such a thing called the Triple Crown. Perhaps they both could be described as being just "a flash in the pan" but using the same black powder muzzleloading rifle terminology, they both found their mark, and they found it with precision and a steady aim. They both possessed components of flint and steel. Too bad the two of them never hooked up. They would have made quite a team.

The year, 1919, was the banner year for both Tommy and for Sir Barton. Both were relative newcomers and unknowns to the sport. At least neither of them had made their mark yet in the public eye. Sir Barton went to the post at Churchill Downs for the 1919 Kentucky Derby as a maiden. His weight allowance of 110 pounds could easily have been met by Tommy's 98 pound frame at the time. By five lengths, Sir Barton won his maiden race, taking the early lead and never looking back, making the Kentucky Derby his very first career victory (Robertson, 1964). Sir Barton finished the season as the biggest money winner for 1919, and he accomplished this as a three-year-old. Out of thirteen starts, he won eight and took three seconds and two third places, accounting for his $88,250 in total winnings. However, lurking in the shadows and winning nine out of his ten total starts for the season, with a second place for the other, and winning a total amount of $83,325, was a two-year-old quickly becoming a household name. Man o' War was soon to extinguish the bright light of fame and popularity for Sir Barton, just once more proving the old adage about being in the right place at the right time.

Similarly, the year 1919 played out the same for Tommy. He began the year as an apprentice jockey under the tutelage of trainer and conditioner, Kay Spence, and climaxed his maiden year by winning the Kentucky Oaks on Lillian Shaw. According to his obituary in *The Thoroughbred Record*, Saturday, January 23, 1937:

KAY SPENCE LOSES FIGHT AGAINST PNEUMONIA

Arcadia, California, January 21---Sorrow was wide spread at the Santa Anita track Thursday morning when it was learned that Kay Spence, one of the best known horsemen on the American turf, was dead, victim of bronchial pneumonia.

"Mr. Spence, a native of Fairbury, Ill., who was in his late fifties, became ill a few days ago with a severe cold, which steadily grew worse. He was removed from his hotel to the hospital Wednesday, and although special nurses and doctors were engaged and an oxygen tent pressed into service nothing could stave off the inevitable.

"Mr. Spence had trained some of the great Thoroughbreds on the American turf, he formerly trained the Audley Farm Stable, among horses he handled then being the famous mare, Princess Doreen. He was training the horses of J.W. Marchbank at the time of his death.

"A few years ago, Mr. Spence decided to make his home in California and to that end purchased a ranch near Woodside, in the northern part of the state, where he intended to breed a few horses. He is survived by his wife.

"Kay Spence's name first appeared in the trainer records in 1912 and he was the leader for three consecutive years, 1918, 1919 and 1920. In all, he saddled 1,078 winners of $1,536,593 during twenty-five years of active participation in racing. Although he always had a large string of horses under his care, he found time to develop jockeys and in this work had no peer. Among the jockeys who had their preparation under him, were Harry Lunsford, Allen Aubechon, Tommy Murray, Herman Schutte, Grover Noell, Harry Stutts, William Kern, Robert Russell, Eddie Martin and Claude Hunt."

In the 1938 edition of *The American Racing Manual*, in "Necrology of the Turf in 1937", it was recorded: "Kay Spence, one of America's leading trainers, died in California early in 1937. He led the American trainers in 1918 and 1919, also tied for first place with A.C. Compton in 1920. In all, Spence trained the winners of 1,078 races and their total earning amounted to $1,536,593. In addition to being remarkably successful as trainer, Spence developed a number of first class jockeys. The best horses he handled were Princess Doreen, Gallant Knight, Hodge and Miss Joy."

In Tommy's case, peaking one's career at the very beginning sets a very difficult and demanding precedent for the years to follow. The stress and pressure placed on one's self to attain a higher level and reach a higher goal in subsequent years often times becomes the destructive force that obstructs and prevents its realization. That's what makes a jockey a "flash in the pan".

CHAPTER ONE

"I'm Gonna Be a Jockey"

Thomas Peter Murray was born on January 1, 1902 in Covington, Kentucky, to Martin Murray and Margaret Gavin Murray, both of whom were born in Ireland, immigrated to the U.S. and settled in a predominantly Irish neighborhood in Covington, Kentucky. They lived on Second Street all of their lives. They were members of St. Patrick's Catholic Church. Tommy was baptized there on Jan 12, 1902. He was the last of five children. Being raised an Irish Catholic in a predominantly Irish neighborhood of Covington, the son of an immigrant Irish laborer, really set the stage for his life story and it could have gone either way. But it went the way it did.

Tommy was the typical turn-of-the-century inner city street urchin, in his well worn knickers and wool cap; good natured, fun loving, inquisitive and mischievous; all clean and slick for Sunday morning mass, but getting into a fight on the way home. He had big ideas and big dreams. He wasn't about to spend the rest of his life on Second Street in Covington. He was going to be something. Like the other boys, he emulated his heroes and aspired to be just like them but he was too little and scrawny to be a professional ballplayer, like one of the Cincinnati Red Stockings, or one of the distinguished looking policemen walking their own beat everyday, or one of the sturdy Irish firemen on the many

Covington Fire Department Stations. No, he was going to be a jockey, just like the ones out at Latonia. He was going to ride for all the big stables and the famous owners and trainers, travel all over the world, and become very famous and very rich.

During the meetings at Latonia, Tommy would take the street car out to the track every day. It didn't matter if school was in or not, he would just leave at lunch time and head south. He would head straight to the stables and watch and learn the ways of track people. Eventually, they would talk to him and let him clean out a stall or help with other menial chores. He would tell them, "I'm going to be a jockey," and they would smile, or have some off color comment that would bring laughs from the others. It didn't matter. He had made up his mind and he would persevere, come hell or high water.

After a couple of seasons of hanging around the track and getting odd jobs which actually paid some decent money in his estimation, he began to localize his visits and stops at the stables of Kay Spence (Spence would soon become the leading trainer in the category of recorded wins in the industry for three consecutive years - 1918, 1919 and 1920 - and also trained the 1920s champion Princess Doreen). It seems there was a mutual attraction or interest or something between the two. Spence was always willing to hire Tommy for odd jobs and his people seemed to enjoy the kid hanging around. Tommy learned an awful lot from this bunch.

One day he got up the courage to tell Spence that he would like to ride his horses for him.

"You ever been on a horse, son?"

"Well sure I have Mr. Spence, plenty of them, right here at the track!"

"You ever exercised one, son?"

"Well, yes sir! I've walked plenty of 'em around the circle, and even out around the track, I have."

"You ever been up on one at a trot or a canter?"

"Well, I guess…No sir, I haven't but I know I can do it. Just ask your monkeys. They been teaching me. They'll tell you."

"Monkeys? Now where in the Sam Hill did you come up with that name, son?" Spence blurted.

"I dunno, sir," Tommy muttered apologetically. "Just heard it around the stables, that's all."

"And now just why do you think jockeys are called monkeys in the first place?"

"Um, because they're little and wiry and they can hang on to the reins like monkeys hang on to vines?"

"Ha, ha! That's a good one boy," Spence choked up in a deep belly laugh. "Naw, son," he continued. "It's cause of a fella named Tod Sloan, a squatty little short legged jockey who come up with his own kinda riding stance and style. His legs was so short, they had to raise his stirrups up so high that his knees actually brushed against his cheeks when he was riding and he leaned way over the horses withers and his back was perfectly in line with the horses. Couldn't use spurs all perched up like that, so he carried his bat in one hand and people said he looked just like a monkey on a stick. Funny part about it was he was winning big! Gave him better balance with the horse, less wind resistance, and better use of his hands right on the horse's neck. Now every jockey in the business rides like that."

"Wow, Mr. Spence! I thought jockeys always rode like that! At least every one I ever seen does."

"Nope, sonny. They used to ride like common cowboys up until the 1890s when Sloan come up with his style."

"Wow, that ain't that long ago," marveled Tommy.

"So, my monkeys been tellin' you how to be a jockey, eh?" Spence continued. "Have they told you how to actually win a race? 'Cause I'm not so sure any of them know how to do that part of it. Heh, heh!"

"No, Mr. Spence. Lunsford's been a teaching me, an' he's your best apprentice jockey. Ain't it so, Mr. Spence?"

"Well Tommy, you got me there. Let me talk to him so I can see what he thinks about things."

"Oh, thank you, Mr. Spence! Thank you! Harry'll tell you alright, he will! Yoohoo!"

Harry Lunsford was one of Kay Spence's apprentice jockeys. In American horseracing during the first quarter of the 20th century, good jockeys were in great demand. This was due mainly to the weight requirements that the rules of Thoroughbred racing dictated and regulated. It was the weight, and the constant maintenance of that ideal riding weight, which weeded out many young men from pursuing a career as a jockey. Once the weight criterion was met, then came the other necessary requirements of agility, strength, endurance, good hands, common sense, intelligence, quick thinking and decision making, dedication, and the willingness to put in long hours and grueling days. It meant traveling which was less than comfortable more times than not. Jockeys were usually stowed away in the horse car with the rest of the stable employees and always on the lookout for the railroad detectives so as not to be discovered. It meant being away from home and family for long periods of time, and during certain special family events, or family needs. The only means of communication with the family back home was letter writing and that was always slow - too slow for a homesick boy. Of course, the family could always keep track of you by following the tracks' racing page in the newspapers or in *The Daily Racing Form* but you had to run in the money - 1st, 2nd or 3rd - in order to get your name in the racing results. That was even more incentive to becoming a winning jockey. At least that way the folks back home could keep track of you.

In order to gain the status of jockey and be eligible to apply for and receive a jockey license, a young man had to serve an apprenticeship similar to what was required of other trades back in the day. The apprentice was always under the direction of the particular stable's trainer who took the boy under his wing. Harry Lunsford was already one of Spence's apprentices. Harry was also a Covington born-and-raised boy. Before he took an interest in the track and racing at the age of 13 years, he and his brother Guy sang together in Vaudeville shows in Covington. Harry got his first win as an apprentice jockey for Spence in 1917 in Havana, Cuba during the 1917 winter meeting.

Apprentice jockeys were also called "bug boys". This name originated from the asterisk which was placed next to the apprentice's name in the racing program and racing forms, thus designating the rider as an apprentice. Every horse having an apprentice jockey aboard received a weight allowance for that particular race. This allowance ranged from five to 10 pounds, depending on the rules set down at each track by the racing stewards. This meant that a horse that was handicapped to carry a certain number of pounds of weight could deduct the five, or seven, or 10 pounds allowed due to having an apprentice jockey. This weight allowance was instituted to make up for the new jockey's lack of experience in balance, handling, and the rigors and variables encountered in a hard fighting professional Thoroughbred race in which the high speed mass of muscle and momentum weighs in excess of 10 times more than the rider aboard attempting to direct things. The horse players liked the weight allowance because losing that much weight on a horse really increased that horse's chances of finishing in the money if the apprentice was a really good and promising jockey. So the bookies and the bettors always paid a little attention to the bug boys.

Harry did put in a good word for Tommy. A couple days later, Lunsford had Tommy up on one of Spence's nags (that was just one of the popular terms the jockeys used to affectionately refer to their mounts) leading Tommy around the barn and shed row, the whole time telling him what to do and not to do. He had him on a racing saddle, not a regular one and he made him keep his feet in the irons at all times, teaching him how to communicate with the horse just by shifting his weight and the forces applied on the stirrups. He hadn't even had a chance to hold the reins yet. Every morning of the meeting, Tommy was there, on the very first street car. He didn't even bother to attend the morning session of school any more. School just didn't even seem to fit into the equation while a meeting was in session. Margaret really didn't approve of this whole thing. She had been sickly over the past year and wanted to keep Tommy close by. The boy's father had died many years earlier and Tommy had taken on the role of the man of the house, at least in Margaret's eyes. Tommy's aspiration of becoming a jockey was the biggest topic of discussion every evening down at the corner pub, cattycorner to St. Patrick's Church. Everybody was pulling for young Tommy. They'd like to see him get away and make good and never have to put even one single day in at the foundry like his father did. Everybody blamed Martin's early death on his job. He died December 12, 1913, in his sixty-fifth year, when Tommy was just ten years old.

In her dreams every night, Margaret would argue her point with her late husband.

"But Martin, he's only fifteen years old. I don't want him down there with those hoodlums and gamblers and pick-pockets."

And then Martin's response to her would be, *"Margaret, please listen to me. He is not with gamblers and hoodlums and pick-pockets! They are all in the grandstands and around the betting rings. Tommy is in the background, back at the stables, and on the backside. He is far removed from the evils you worry about. Let him be. Let him go with his dream."*

And she would awaken each morning with tears in her eyes and these words on her lips: *"As you wish, Martin, as you wish."*

So it was. Tommy's training began in early 1917, when he was 15 years old. It was still his responsibility to clean stalls, make sure the bedding was clean and soft, with no hard stems or twigs. It was his duty to assist the grooms and curry the horses, feed them, and keep the water fresh, plus whatever else he was told to do. Sometimes he assisted Spence, the farrier, the exercise riders, and the veterinarian. He cleaned, brushed and oiled the tack, the saddles, riding boots and whatever else was assigned him. During the Spring Meeting of the Latonia Jockey Club in June and July, he began working so many hours for Mr. Spence's stables that he began living there at the stables, bedding down on the straw heaped in front of the stalls on one of his mother's coverlets she gave him.

When July 4th, and the last day of the Spring Meeting came around, Spence decided to keep most of his string boarded there at Latonia, while he chose a select few to ship to New York to Empire City. Since all racing in Canada was slated to cease August first, Spence decided to forego the several Canadian Meetings in favor of the Empire City Meeting. He would take Harry along and one or two grooms, and leave the rest of his crew at Latonia under the watch of a close cohort trainer who was remaining there to rest and condition his stable for the upcoming Fall Meeting. So far, from January 1, 1916 to June 23, 1917, the 90-pound Harry Lunsford had had only 13 mounts total, and had not yet broke his maiden. That simply meant that he had yet to place in the money as an apprentice jockey.

During this same time span, Roscoe Goose was the number one rider with a total of 757 mounts with 164 first place finishes, 126 seconds, and 132 third place finishes for a riding percentage of 0.22, the highest in the nation. C. Hunt, who was a regular rider for Kay Spence, was in fifth place with a percentage of 0.15, having collected 127 first place finishes, 121 seconds, and 128 third place scores out of a total of 837 mounts for that eighteen month time span. Willie Kelsay, who became good friends with Harry and eventually with Tommy, was in the eighth standing with a winning percentage of 0.14, having 74 first places, 83 seconds, and 71 thirds out of his 514 mounts. Spence wanted Harry to get lots of exposure to these boys to improve his riding skills, numbers, and confidence.

Spence left Tommy back at Latonia as the chief stable boy to care for his string and make sure they got the proper personal care, exercise, nutrition, and rest. Cleanliness, hygiene, foot care, and comfort were all important issues for him to oversee. Tommy took this charge very seriously and he carried out his duties flawlessly and to perfection.

Before Spence had returned to Latonia for the Fall Meeting, Tommy had been dealt a most devastating blow. In mid-September Margaret was struck down by the pandemic 1917-1918 Asian flu. She had been a stalwart caregiver in her neighborhood for other unfortunate victims of this fast spreading and devastating illness for many months before it enveloped her own well being. In all, it took the lives of between 10 and 20 million souls in a six-month period across the United States. That is one and a half times more deaths than those attributed to World War I over a four-year period. Margaret finally succumbed to pneumonia secondary to the influenza virus infection on Sept 23, 1917. She was only 51 years old.

Tommy was nearly devastated by his mother's death. He was essentially an orphan now, being the youngest sibling. His grown seven brothers and two sisters all had their own families and lives and jobs and Tommy had no intentions of hooking up with one of them, to be taken in and raised as an orphan brother. No sir! Tommy had his own loving family and it was firmly established and alive at Latonia Race Track and he was unconditionally accepted and considered a member of that family. So there he remained, performing all the charges given him by Kay Spence before he headed up East to race. When Spence and Harry returned that October in time for the Fall Meeting of the Latonia Jockey Club,

Tommy's new life began and he was prepared to give it his all, just as he promised Margaret on her death bed.

After the 1917 Fall Meeting had ended, Mr. Spence was off to Havana, Cuba for the 100-day long winter racing meet there. Lunsford would go along with the trainer and a couple of his most trusted senior grooms. There would be plenty of itinerant hot walkers and rubbers to be found down there upon their arrival. Tommy would have to sit the winter out, get back to school, and prepare for the spring meets.

"I'd sure like to go, Mr. Spence, to help out."

"Maybe next year, son," replied the trainer. "I gotta concentrate on Harry this meeting and get him up to speed for this next racing season. Your time will come. I can guarantee it, so long as you keep learning all the basics and fundamentals of the horse business."

"I won't let you down, sir," Tommy assured him.

By the spring of 1918, Mr. Spence and his stable were back racing in the states. A number of trainers shipped their horses up East to Maryland for a couple of short meetings in that part of the country. However, Kay Spence, along with many other trainers leaving the Winter Meeting in Havana, headed directly to Douglass Park in Louisville. This is where he would set up his command for the Spring Meetings in the Kentucky horse country of Louisville and Lexington, even though the first meeting would be the Lexington track's Spring Meeting of fifteen racing days. Other trainers from Hot Springs were also overloading the cars headed for Louisville for the ever more popular and competitive offerings in the Commonwealth of Kentucky. Stable space was becoming a highly sought-after commodity. Matt Winn had had a master plan in mind, and it was obviously getting national attention and building up steam.

"During the two decades prior to World War I, Latonia was acclaimed nationwide as a leader in the introduction of modern ideas and praised as one of America's most beautiful courses, which, at times, offered purses second to none. However, Latonia ultimately made its greatest contribution to the evolution and modernization of race track wagering in the standardization of the $2 bet." (Claypool, 1998). This change from a two-dollar minimum from five dollars made pari-mutuel betting more affordable to the less wealthy patrons while keeping the bookmakers at bay on track grounds. Overall, it had a positive effect on the general public's view of horse racing and race tracks in general and eased the pressure from the anti-racing, anti-track factions. This new wagering format soon spread to all the major tracks nationwide and became the industry standard.

The April 23, 1918 *Daily Racing Form* reported: "Lexington, Kentucky, April 22---Racing on the '3-L' circuit for this year will be inaugurated tomorrow, when the Kentucky Association track will begin its meeting of fifteen days, the longest period of racing there at any one time since the racing commission has had supervision over the date allotments to Kentucky courses." The article went on to mention that another factor contributing to the excess amount of stables and horses present was the recent complete closure of racing at the Canadian tracks, which had always been a natural stepping stone for the Eastern U.S. Maryland and New York stables to follow after their meetings concluded.

The May 10, 1918 *Daily Racing Form* listed the standings of the top U.S. riders during the time span of January 1, 1917 through May 10, 1918 inclusive. Harry Lunsford, who had had no wins after 13 attempts when they left for Cuba, now was in seventh place in the list of leading U.S. jockeys with a win percentage of 0.18, having 67 first place finishes, 63 seconds, and 48 third-place finishes out of a total of 370 mounts. That was quite an accomplishment over the winter racing period in Havana and quite a feather in both Harry's and Kay Spence's hats. There was another apprentice jockey from the Eastern circuits by the name of Earl Sande who placed ahead of Harry in the jockey standings with a win percentage of 0.19, but this was calculated on just 46 wins on a total of 240 mounts. Overall, Harry actually had 21 more winners, but on 130 more mounts. Like all record keeping systems, this one was flawed in that it didn't tell the whole comprehensive story. Conceivably, a jockey who had one winning finish out of a total of just three mounts would have a win percentage of 0.33 but that is how it was set up.

By mid-June and early July, Tommy had anticipated their arrival back at Latonia for the Spring Meeting. He was there to greet them, complete with Margaret's coverlet and a couple of changes of clothes. He planned on staying forever this time. He was a dedicated worker for Mr. Spence and he was an eager learner for Lunsford, who had Tommy actually exercising some of Spence's three-year-old colts as soon as they established their headquarters at Latonia. Tommy and Harry seemed to work fairly well together and the horses seemed to listen and respond to Tommy. The mutual respect that was developing and maturing was indeed palpable and Kay Spence noticed it very early on. After all, not only was he an excellent conditioner of competitive Thoroughbred racing horses, but he was also considered by his peers as one of the best conditioners of competitive young jockeys in the business.

Postcard of Latonia Racetrack

CHAPTER TWO
Latonia, Fall Meeting, 1918

Opening day finally arrived at Latonia for the Fall Meeting on Wednesday, November 13, 1918. It was officially designated the Latonia Jockey Club Autumn Meeting of 14 Days. The day was perfect. The weather was clear with a temperature of 65 degrees. The track was fast. The racing would commence at 1:45 p.m. As the field of 12 went to the post for the first race of the meet, Mr. Spence called Tommy over to him where he was seated in front of his stalls.

"Murray, that's what people will be calling you now, I entered High Gear into the second race and I want you aboard. Let's see what you got."

Lunsford walked out of the stall with the silks and a pair of brand new shiny riding boots.

"C'mon kid, let's get on over to the jockey house and get you ready for your big day."

The bell sounded and the horses were called to post. The first race was underway.

At 2:15, Tommy took High Gear to the starting barrier for the start of the second race. At 2:18, Tom Murray's professional jockey career began with a good but slow start. The field of 12 broke away slow but finished driving. High Gear and Kinney forced the early running but both tired in the stretch, with High Gear finishing fourth and out of the money but oh what a joyous fourth place it was for Tommy and his stable associates! It was his very first professional race and he took fourth place out of a field of 12. The kid caught the eyes and attention of many an owner and trainer that day, known only as "that new kid of Spence's." Soon, they would soon learn his real name.

Tommy and Harry talked all the way back from the paddock to the barn. Tommy had a hard time containing his exhilaration and excitement, but he listened intently to what his instructor had to offer about the handling of High Gear. After all, up until today, Lunsford was the only jockey to have ever taken him to the post. He knew the horse well and Tommy wanted to know all he knew. Back at the barn, Tommy led High Gear around the shed row to make sure he was completely cooled down before rubbing him down and grooming him as his regular groom watched on with a critical eye. All the while, Tommy was whispering to the horse, rubbing behind his ears and staring him in the eyes and the horse seemed to respond to the attention, every once in a while nudging Tommy backward and clear off his feet.

"Where's the kid?" Mr. Spence announced as he returned from his spot along the rail, where he preferred to watch every race as opposed to watching from the owners' boxes. He liked to be where he could see what horses were completely spent and which ones still had something left in their tank. He liked to hear the sound and quality of their breathing. He kept mental notes of which horses were sweaty or lathered, which horse had their heads down, and which ones had their tails up – telltale signs of fatigue, or even worse, total exhaustion.

"In there with Gear, they must be bonding," answered Lunsford from another stall as he was making his mount ready for the next race.

"Tommy, you handled him pretty good out there. Fourth place ain't bad for a first try! I want you to keep getting up on these nags and working them out every morning and evening, till you feel natural up there on their backs. It's got to be second nature to you before you can really become competitive, because you won't have time to think about staying on the horse. You'll be concentrating on thinking, adjusting, planning, and reacting to the things you can't even plan on."

"Oh, I'll do it, Mr. Spence. I'll do just as you say. I won't let you down, sir. I swear on St. Patty's grave!"

"Lunsford, get Murray ready again. I'm going to put him up on Clairvoyant for the sixth race."

"But, Mr. Spence, he's been awful heady lately. You think the boy can handle him?"

"That's just what I'm about to find out, Harry. Between you and me, I think he can. Let's just see."

So for the second time that day, Tommy and his veteran jockey instructor headed to the jockey room and made ready for the next race. This time, the other jockeys acknowledged Tommy's presence. Some of them even introduced themselves. One of them, named Gruber, welcomed Tommy to the jockey room and shook his hand, wishing him luck.

They went to the post at 4:13 p.m., all 12 of them, a pretty good field for this claiming race for three-year-olds. Two minutes later, it was a good, but slow start. Redmon set the early pace, but tired quickly allowing Clairvoyant to overtake. Then they both fell to the outside as Diversion raced into a good lead at the half and won unextended after Mountain Rose challenged when an eighth out, and tired, taking second place. Tommy finished ninth, but handled himself and his mount very well for a good showing. It was that same J. J. Gruber that introduced himself to Tommy before the race that rode Diversion to a first-place finish. Tommy made sure to extend his congratulations to him back in the jockey room.

On the second day of the meeting, Spence didn't have any horses running. He spent the morning milling about the stables, talking to other owners, trainers, and horsemen, catching up on the latest around the industry. He was approached at lunch time by another owner, J. J. Troxler, who asked him to join him in the clubhouse for something to eat. As they dined and conversed with each other and other owners and horsemen, Troxler mentioned that he was looking for a rider for one of his three-year-olds later in the fifth race. He said he knew Spence wasn't running and wanted to borrow one of his jockeys.

"I got this kid, he's still green, but he sticks to the horse like stink on shit. He's going to be a good one after he gets some mounts and more experience. You interested?"

"If he's the kid you put on High Gear yesterday, I am. I got one runs just like him and I'd like to see what he can do with him."

"Yep, that's him. Name's Murray. I'll have him over your place soon as things get started."

Tommy was thrilled, but a little confused.

"How come you want me to ride another stable's horse, Mr. Spence?"

"It's not that I want you working for a competitor, Tommy, but I'm not running any horses today and the experience will do you good. Besides, jockeys at these meetings can all work as freelance jockeys. Whoever has your contract has the first call on you, but any other owner or trainer can hire you to ride for him if it's approved by your contract holder, which is me. If you're good and in high demand, then you will get your pick of the best contenders, and the more you win or place, the more money you earn and the better mounts you will wind up getting. It's all about winning and being the best and if an owner and trainer think they got the best horse, then they're going to look around and go for the best jockey. That's how this business operates. Now you better get on over to Troxler's."

So Tommy ran into the tack room and gathered up his gear and was heading out when suddenly Mr. Spence hollered, "Hold on now Tommy, back up a second. There ain't no need for you to be taking your silks over there. Today, you'll be wearing Troxler's colors!"

"Sorry Mr. Spence, guess I wasn't thinkin'!"

"That's quite okay, son. Just be thinkin' and on your toes when you're maneuvering that horse flesh around that track! Ride safe, but be aggressive. Remember, nobody ever won a race by pullin' back on the reins."

"Not unless he's rating his horse or conserving him for his next go round. Ain't that right, Mr. Spence?" Tommy chimed in, winking his eye at Harry.

"Alright you two smart alecks. You got me there! Glad to know you're payin' attention to what we're teaching you. Now, on your way!"

At 3:38 p.m., the field of nine went to the post. The track was fast and the horses fidgety. It took five full minutes to get them situated and off. It was a good, but slow start. Grundy, ridden by future Hall-of-Famer Mack Garner, was the winner. He took the lead at once and set the pace all the way, but was ridden out at the end. War Machine managed to close a gap and finished second with a threatening rush. Sands of Pleasure ran third being crowded when going to the first turn, but recovering to run a good race and finish fast. Fern Handley, Murray up, stayed with the pack and raced forwardly, but tired at the finish and ran a good fourth. It was a new track record for the mile. This was Tommy's third professional race, with two of them being fourth-place finishes.

The next day, Friday, November 15, 1918, was the third day of the meeting. It was a cloudy day and a very warm 65 degrees considering it was the middle of November. The track again was fast. Latonia was known for its hard track, which made it fast. Mack Garner was explaining this to Tommy the day before, right after he set a new track record on Grundy. "The harder the track, the faster the horse can run, and records can be broke. But ya gotta be careful, 'cause a hard track can also break down a horse real fast, and a lot of owners won't hire you again if they think you're too hard on their horse flesh. They just want you to win. They don't care if you set a new track record or not. Of course if ya do it while neck an' neck down the stretch an' win by a nose at the line, then they're happy to have the new track record. An' when they're up to the jockey room a lookin' fer a rider, they always know which jocks has set track records an' they go fer them first."

As Tommy was hanging on the paddock fence, surveying the horses in the day's first race, Kay called him over to the stables.

"Tommy, I want to give Lucky Pearl a go at it today in the second race. It's a claimer for two-year-old fillies. Think you can handle her?"

"I sure can, Mr. Spence. I've exercised her a hundred times!"

"Well," Spence followed after a hearty laugh, "if you exercised her a hundred time, then ninety of them musta been in your dreams, son!"

"I know her good enough, sir. I know she likes to chase whatever's in front of her and the more she's chasin', the happier she is."

"That's a very astute observation Tommy, but I don't want you to force her."

"Oh, I know, Mr. Spence, that track out there is really hard and I don't want her to injure her feet. I'll just let her follow the lead and chase and see where we are down the stretch. I ain't gonna push her more than she can tolerate, sir."

"Tommy, very good strategy! When did you become so race horse savvy?"

"I'm a good listener in the jockey room, sir. You can learn quite a bit in there, just actin' like you ain't even listening."

At 2:09 p.m., the field of 12 went to the post. After two minutes, it was a good but slow start. Legotal quickly sprinted for an unopposed lead and held it the entire time. The second and third place finishers followed in quick pursuit, fighting it out in the end for their final positions. Close behind the pack and running well was Murray and Lucky Pearl, running an uncontested fifth after gaining that from the ninth spot at the ½ pole.

"Good run! You handled her well," Spence yelled from his spot on the fence at the finish line as Tommy was cooling her down.

"Seems you got a promising prospect there Kay," a voice from behind announced. Spence turned around to see the source of that comment and quickly answered, "Well, Rome, that's my hope and wish, but she's still just a follower. Still needs a lot of work."

"I'm talking about your kid, Kay, not the filly!"

"Oh, yes sir, you mean Murray. Good kid! Lots of determination and plenty of unpolished talent! He'll be one to watch in the future."

"I agree, Kay! I'd like to give him a try sometime this meet."

Jerome Bristow Respess was a well-respected and very successful breeder of Thoroughbred race horses in the Northern Kentucky region. He was renowned all throughout the Commonwealth of Kentucky and across all the racing lines in the entire U.S. He was born in November 12, 1863 on his grandfather Bristow's farm, between Florence and

Independence, Kentucky. His father then purchased and moved to a farm in the Union, Kentucky area while Jerome was just an infant. They remained there until 'Rome' (his nickname for the rest of his life) was sixteen years old, when his father bought another farm near Florence, Kentucky and moved the family there. Rome had a very early interest in horses. By 1883, he was regularly making the fair circuits showing saddle horses competitively, which eventually led him into the breeding, raising, and training of Thoroughbreds. Probably the most famous Thoroughbred he ever produced was Dick Welles, who was always considered the very best Thoroughbred in history until Man O' War. Dick Welles was foaled in 1900 and died in 1923 and is buried along the Dixie Highway opposite the home of Mr. Respess. A son of this famous horse by the name of Wintergreen, won the 1903 Kentucky Derby for Mr. Respess. To his credit, Rome Respess also bred and raised Billy Kelly, which he sold as a yearling for $1500.00. Billy Kelley turned out to be the very best two-year-old for the year 1917, and subsequently sold for $40,000.00. Rome continued his reputation as a nationally acclaimed breeder of excellent Thoroughbred stock for many years to come on his famous 555-acre horse farm near Florence, Kentucky, called Highland Stock Farm (Boone County Recorder, Historical Edition, 1930). Tommy and Rome were long-time friends and cohorts all throughout Tommy's long racing career.

For the next week, Tommy took every opportunity to hone his riding skills by exercising and breezing Mr. Spence's string as well as freelancing for other owners and trainers. He was easily putting in 14 to 16 hours a day, constantly watching, asking, learning, assimilating, testing, and practicing his riding techniques. Sleeping on his mother's coverlet every night in the stalls with the stock, he would be out on the track every morning at 4:30 a.m. exercising the horses. Then, after wiping them down and giving them their daily morning ration, he would hit the track himself to keep his weight and strength at its prime.

On Friday, November 22, 1918, which was the ninth day of the Latonia Autumn Meeting, both Lunsford and Tommy managed to pick up rides at the jockey room. They both would run the fourth race for different owners and trainers. The outcome of the race of a field of six proved polar opposites for the two apprentice jockeys. Lunsford sprinted from third place in the stretch to overcome the first-place and second-place leaders, to win. Tommy fell to sixth and last place at the ¾ pole and remained there. The track was heavy. Lunsford also got a mount for the fifth and sixth race, while Murray sat on the sidelines and observed, watching his stable partner take another first place in the fifth and a second place in the sixth. *"Some days you're the hammer, and some days you're the nail,"* Tommy thought to himself.

The next day, Saturday, things were basically unchanged. Lunsford and Tommy both were picked up by different owners and trainers. Since Kay Spence did not have either of his apprentices scheduled to ride one of his horses, he was more than willing to let them ride for another trainer. In fact, he encouraged it. He felt it was a good learning experience for his boys to ride different horses and to take riding orders from different trainers. It would improve their learning experiences and prepare them for the future when they would become journeyman jockeys.

In the first race, on a cloudy day of 55 degrees, Lunsford took second place on Dixie Carroll for J.O. Whitlow, running right behind the winner from the very start. Tommy once again pulled up the rear, riding Georgiana for A.G. Elliston. That was two last place finishes in his last two starts. Lunsford had a mount in almost every race that day, with two first places, one second, and one third.

"Some days you're the pigeon, and some days you're the statue," Tommy said to himself.

Of special note that day, was the fifth race, the running of the Latonia Cup. There to run it was the 1918 Kentucky Derby winner, Exterminator, ridden by future Hall-of-Famer, Johnny Loftus. Purchased by Willis Sharpe Kilmer earlier in 1918, he promptly ran him in the Kentucky Derby on May 18 and won the 2 ¼ mile classic. He then came to Latonia on June 22 for the 1 ½ mile Latonia Derby, where he lost by two full lengths to H.P. Whitney's Johren. This day's classic was a full 2 ¼ mile run for a purse of almost $8,000. Exterminator won by a nose. Exterminator proved to be a stayer, a sprinter, and could run and win at any distance. He was to be America's top money winner for four consecutive years, from 1919-1922. At the end of the day, Tommy was just as excited as Lunsford about Harry's showings of the day and Mr. Spence celebrated right along with his two rookie jockeys.

Tuesday, November 26, 1918, the twelfth day of the Latonia Autumn Meeting, would prove to be Tommy's epiphany day. A clear day of 55 degrees and a good track, combined to make it a day he would never forget. Lunsford had managed a number of mounts that day, several from the owner, W.F. Knebelkamp. In the first and second race, Lunsford took third place. He improved to second place in race number three. He repeated a second place in the seventh and final race of the day, a claiming race for three-year-olds, in which he forced the early pace. He fell back in the stretch when he and the leader were overtaken by a rush by High Gear, trained by Kay Spence, Tom Murray up, when an eighth out and winning going away, paying $41.10 to win, $11.00 to place, and $5.20 to show. Lunsford took second behind his stable partner who just won his first professional race. At first, all Tommy could do was clutch his crucifix and St. Patrick's medal pinned to the inside of his undershirt. He lamented the fact that Martin nor Margaret were there to see it, but he felt certain that they had both witnessed his very first win, sitting right there at the right side of God himself, who Tommy knew for a fact was a Thoroughbred racing fan. Otherwise, why would He have created such wonderful and majestic creatures! Of course, everyone from his neighborhood would hear all about it that evening after work down at the corner saloon, cattycorner from St. Patrick's Church, where several of them had already stopped to light votive candles to give thanks for young Tommy's milestone accomplishment.

"You will never forget that race or this day for the rest of your life, Tommy," Spence told the boy that night back at the barn. "Now, if you can only do it thirty-nine more times, you can lose your bug!" (According to the latest Jockey Club rules in 1918, an apprentice jockey had to win 40 sanctioned races in order to go from apprentice to journeyman status. This applied to all the Eastern tracks. However, in Kentucky, an apprentice was not able to advance to journeyman status until the one-year anniversary of his first win, even if he had the 40 required wins before that. When he gained his journeyman status, he also lost his five pound weight allowance. This weight allowance is the reason a very accomplished apprentice could pick up some very promising mounts in the good races).

Day 13 saw Lunsford picking up several rides, claiming a third, fourth and a first in the first three races, all for other owners and stables. Tommy rode for Mr. Spence in the third race on Lucky Pearl. The track was good that day, but this particular race was held up a full 10 minutes when the starter's barrier broke down just as the horses were lining up. It was speculated that this long delay at the post affected the concentration and intensity of both the jockeys and the horses. In the long run, it bode well for Lunsford, who finished first on Carrie Moore, for C.T. Worthington but it didn't turn out so well for Tommy, who finished tenth in the field of 12. Back at the barn, Harry shared another very valuable lesson with Tommy.

"While we were being held up at the barrier, did you happen to notice what I was doing?" Harry asked Tommy.

"No, not really. I was concentrating on getting my horse lined up and acting civil, like the starter was callin' for. So, what were you doing?"

Harry explained, "Since me and my horse were situated right next to the rail, I was keeping my left foot up on the rail the whole time. This kept all my own weight off of my horse, and was saving a lot of his strength and energy by not having to support his weight plus mine. All the milling about and commotion was just tiring the other horses out before the race began. So, I really had the only fresh horse up there and I was able to get him to the wire first."

On Day 14, the final day of the Latonia Autumn Meeting, Lunsford again managed to get rides for nearly every race. His only race for Mr. Spence was a claiming race for three-year-olds and up, the sixth race of the day. He finished dead last after being pinched back while in close quarters, after which Lunsford chose not to persevere, probably for safety's sake on a muddy track. The feature of the day was the running of the Latonia Thanksgiving Handicap in the fifth race. Exterminator was the favorite in the field of eight horses. He won handily by 2 ½ lengths as "Exterminator clearly demonstrated his superiority by going to the front when called on and winning as his rider pleased."(*Daily Racing Forum*, 1919). Johnny Loftus, his rider, would finish the year 1918 as the leading jockey based on percentage wins, at 30%, which was 37 wins for 120 mounts. More impressive numbers, however, were L. Lyke's 178 wins for 756 mounts and Earl Sande's 158 wins for 707 mounts. H. Lunsford, who was riding War Machine for F.D. Weir "hung on with rare gameness" and took third place. The final race of that day and of that Autumn Meeting found Tommy freelancing for S.K. Nickols on Redmon. He took third place while running in close pursuit throughout the entire race, besting Lunsford who finished fifth in the field of eight.

The Latonia Autumn Meeting was over. Tommy was pleased with his third place in the very last race of the meeting. It felt good to him this time - not the outcome, but the physical race itself. For the first time, he felt relaxed and at ease and in concert with his horse. He felt every muscle of his mount respond to the ever changing challenges and obstacles before him. For the very first time, Tommy experienced the race from his mount's point of view. He wasn't consumed with what he should and shouldn't plan and implement if this or that occurred or factored into his horse's style of racing. He became a part of the horse in this last race, and something clicked. He figured out that regardless of what the experts told him, he had to pay attention to the desires of the horse he was on, and if that horse was lazy or tired or hurt or doped-up or nervous it was up to him to give the horse confidence, direction, incentive, free-rein, or pain and punishment, whatever the horse needed at any particular point in time to perform just a bit over his max and maybe just a little longer than he can or wants to. Tommy made it back to the stalls of Mr. Spence's operation with a totally different outlook and understanding. It wasn't something he could put into words, but it was something he could demonstrate in vivo.

"Mr. Spence, when ya pack up for Cuba and the winter meets this year, I'm goin' with ya. I got what it takes to be a winning jockey. All I need now is the chance to run in races and meetings, as many as I can. I want to go with you to Oriental Park for the winter meeting this year. I'm ready! I want to ride every day till I'm good enough to win the Kentucky Derby."

"Tommy, do you even know where Cuba is?"

"Well, sir, I know it's down below Florida somewhere, and ya have to get there on a train, and it stays warm all winter. That's what I know!"

Spence let out a hearty gut laugh, not so much at what Tommy just said, but at how he said it. Tommy's pure determination and heart pleased him very much and his laugh was one of happiness. Tommy just showed him the very thing he looks for in every horse.

"Yep, I think you should go, Tommy, but you sure can't get all the way to Havana on a train. How 'bout we just take one to New Orleans and then get on a ship?"

"Horses and all, Mr. Spence?"

"Yep, horses and all!"

1901 Latonia Track

Airplanes at Latonia Track*

*When racetracks across the country were dark (not running), alternative sporting events and attractions often were held to generate revenue.

Automobile Race at Latonia Track

Grand Stand at Latonia Track

Bird's Eye View of Latonia Track

Clubhouse at Latonia

25

Clubhouse Turn at Latonia Track

Finish Line at Latonia

General View of Latonia Track

Grand Stand at Latonia

27

Harper's Weekly at Latonia Airplanes

Motorcycle Races at Latonia

Judges' Stand at Latonia Track

"In the Stretch" at Latonia

29

Judges' Stand at Latonia Track

Clubhouse & Grandstand at Latonia, 1914

L&N Railroad behind the Latonia Grand Stand

Grand Stand, Derby Day, Latonia Race Track, Covington, Ky.

Derby Day at Latonia

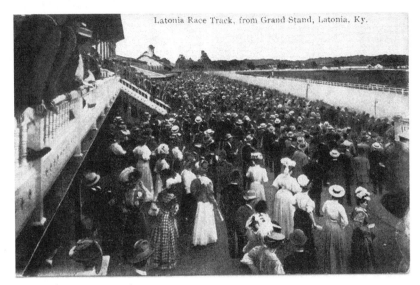

View from the Grandstand at Latonia, 1914

Lake at Old Latonia

Postcard of Latonia Track

LATONIA RACE TRACK, LATONIA, KY.   F-189

Latonia Race Track

Racing Fans at Latonia

Latonia.

Latonia Depot

"In the Stretch" at Latonia Race Track

Running at Latonia

The Start at Latonia

Crowd Gathers at Latonia

Latonia Race Track

Aerial View of Latonia

37

New Latonia/Turfway Park

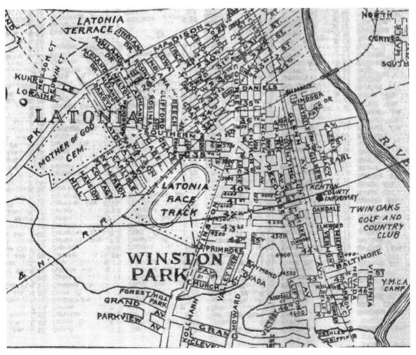

Latonia Track on Map

Racing Scene at Latonia Race Track

CHAPTER THREE
"Horses and All"

Kay Spence set about making the arrangements to move his troupe. They would load up and board the train right there in Latonia, Kentucky, at the loading station which was right behind the track. "Set picturesquely with the Kenton hills as its backdrop, the track was near the intersection that joined the Louisville Shortline with the Kentucky Central Railroad..." (Claypool. 1998). They would take the train all the way to New Orleans, and even a bit further, to Chalmette, Louisiana. There they boarded the S.S. Chalmette, the steam ship which would take them to Havana, Cuba - horses and all.

The experience of traveling by rail and by ship was new and exciting for Tommy. He took it all in and thoroughly enjoyed every new site, sound and situation but nothing was even close to the exhilaration he experienced every time he rode in a race, and that was all he thought about and talked about. He picked Mr. Spence's brain until there was nothing left and he learned much more than he realized at the time.

Winter horseracing in Cuba served many purposes and filled many voids. From a horseman's point of view, it allowed year round work for trainers, jockeys, grooms and stable laborers. This was essential for the racing industry to remain viable because most every one involved depended upon the business for their livelihood. Only the millionaire horse farm owners and breeders would have been able to survive just warm weather seasonal race meetings and that is exactly what the reformers who were opposed to gambling, wagering, betting, bookies, and so on at the tracks were counting on. States all over the U.S. were outlawing all forms of betting. This was especially so in the warm weather states where the winter campaigning usually occurred every year. Eventually the reformers put an end to horse tracks and racing in every state except Kentucky, Maryland, and New York.

"And had it not been for our own Colonel Matt Winn, they woulda had their way in those three states too," explained Mr. Spence in answering Tommy's question as to why they had to travel out of the country to race every winter. "Used to be we'd go across the border from El Paso, Texas into Mexico for the winter race meetings. Mr. Winn built a track in Juarez, and then later one in Mexico City, but he locked that one up after one meeting because of the warring rebels. We went over the border for about seven or eight seasons in a row but, I'm tellin' ya, it just got to be downright dangerous and nerve racking down there."

"Why's that, Mr. Spence? Cause of all them mean bulls runnin' around loose in the streets trying to gouge up a matador," Tommy chimed in with a giggle.

"Not quite, Tommy, but not too far off. Those outlaw Mexican bandito leaders and rebel armies were forever fighting each other for control of the city and government. Why it seemed like a different group held control of the city every day; wasn't much law and order down there. That's why the bookies liked it so much - anything goes. They could bet as much and whatever way they wanted. There were no rules whatsoever. It was nothin' to be ridin' in a race and have bullets flyin' over your head from all the fighting going on in the streets right outside the track," Spence added.

"Didn't it spook the horses none?" Tommy asked.

"I'm here to tell you, Tommy, it spooked all of us but we were very safe inside the track. You see, Poncho Villa, the famous Mexican rebel took a real likin' to Mr. Winn and he made sure that the Colonel and all his patrons and track workers and horse people were out of harm's way at all times. Why he'd often ride into the track with a couple of his ruffians just to have lunch with Mr. Winn, or to watch a race or two. When the Colonel mentioned to Villa once that hay was being stolen from his barns, he posted signs all over Juarez stating (in Spanish): 'Anyone who molests El Colonel Winn or any of the property of the Juarez race track will be shot - Villa.'

Spence continued, "One of the Colonel's favorite stories involves Poncho Villa there at the track. He was watching a few races in the Colonel's private box and told the colonel he was going to bet on a certain horse because it looked like the best one in the field and he felt it would win. Mr. Villa, being quite an expert handler of horses in his occupation, felt he was the best judge of horse flesh in the compound that day and he proceeded to place a fifty-dollar bet on that particular horse. He then assumed that the Colonel would follow suit and confidently bet on the same horse. Mr. Winn then informed Mr. Villa that ever since he assumed the role of a track owner, or partner, or racing official or served in any other official capacity in the business, it was his personal policy to never bet on a horse or a race but, he added, that if he did, his money would have been placed on a different horse, and he named the horse and pointed him out to Villa."

"They relaxed and watched the race, and Villa's horse was a good four lengths ahead of the second horse, and 12 ahead of the rest of the field, coming into the home stretch. He sat contentedly, chewing on the butt of a soggy foul smelling remnant of a cigar, all smiling and proud like, waiting for the finish. He looked over to the Colonel who was also looking quite content and composed, and nodded his head to him as if accepting the colonel's concession on the apparent outcome of the race."

"In anticipation of a payoff, Poncho briefly took his eyes off the contest to look over his comrades for their approval just as the Colonel's horse, a good 12 lengths back, began his bid along the inside rail and like Moses parting the sea, was soon gaining on the Mexican's choice. The two crossed the finish line in what appeared to be a dead heat. It would have to be settled by the judges, all three of them strategically stationed in the judges' stand at the finish line. By this time, the bandits were all standing, guns drawn, and sure their leader's pick would be declared the winner but their celebration was soon snuffed when the judges' decision was posted. All eyes were on Villa! His men were all grumbling and fidgety, waving their guns through the air, just waiting for Villa to give the word. His personal bodyguard and gunman was screaming in Spanish, 'Your horse won! Your horse won! They lie!' Villa slowly stood, looked over to Mr. Winn, and then to his men. After several seconds which seemed more like the amount of time the race itself had just taken, Villa announced 'The Colonel's horse won,' and he and his contingent calmly walked down to their horses, mounted, and quietly left the track."

"Sweet Paddy's pig! I'll bet Mr. Winn was scared fer his life, wasn't he?" inquired Tommy.

"Actually, Tommy, besides being an excellent judge of good horse flesh, he is also a very good judge of character in men. He wasn't threatened or worried at all. Villa took the loss just as he expected he would, in stride! Anyway, the major breeders and owners liked the winter meetings in Mexico because it allowed them a chance to test their latest promising potential champions against those of the other major farms and breeders. The lower level trainers and owners liked these winter meetings for the fact that they could replenish and improve their strings simply by putting in a claim on the horses they thought showed more potential than their current trainers gave them credit for, and thus win them away from the current owners. Conversely, they were also able to cull out their stable by losing the horses they considered 'used up' to a claim put in by another trainer or owner. Any horseman who was registered at any particular track meeting was eligible to put in a claim and claiming races made up the largest majority of races at any of the major and minor tracks. Live racing competition against other green contenders and some seasoned veterans of the track showed what a horse was truly made of, compared to running alone against the clock. It also provided trainers and owners the opportunity to give their rookie jockeys some live track experience, running against other horses and jockeys, again something they could not get while breezing and clocking their mounts in the morning sessions at the tracks. There was nothing that could substitute for on-the-track experience for both the animal and the boy."

"From a horseplayer's point of view, winter racing in Mexico also filled a great void. Gamblers thrived on horse racing. It fed and nurtured their pastimes and addictions. It provided year-round gambling entertainment instead of only the seasonal kind available in the United States, and most of that was localized in the eastern, midwestern, and northern states. On- and off-track betting followed very different and lax rules than it did in the U.S. Also, there were even enforceable laws and rules at all. Wealthy American tourists who enjoyed the winter meetings across the border eventually realized that the reason they were leaving their money there and not taking any back home was due to the crooked gambling practices of the bookies that went unchallenged as much as it was due to their poor handicapping skills."

"Sometime in March of 1916, Mexican rebel forces crossed the border into Texas and had killed some U.S. citizens. By the time the scheduled 1916-1917 winter meeting was about to begin, there were already U.S. Army troops, under the command of General John J. Pershing, in Mexico searching for Poncho Villa who was blamed for the attack. By February of 1917, El Paso was garrisoned with U.S. Army troops and the atmosphere in Juarez was becoming volatile and unsafe. The Army strongly suggested that the current meeting be terminated, and all Americans and their property return to the safety of the United States. Colonel Winn would not close the meeting without first discussing the prospect with all parties involved. It was a unanimous democratic decision to quit Mexico post haste. In fact, some of the major stables were already packing up and leaving, not so much because they feared injury or violence, as they feared theft of their horses for the personal use of the ever increasing numbers of Mexican rebels and bandits. So, on March 1, 1917, Matt Winn closed the meeting and the track and turned the property over to the Mexican government."

"I was there, right with the rest of them," Spence added to Tommy, "when the Colonel turned over the keys. El Paso and Juarez were surely fun and exciting back in those days. Nobody had a care in the world but when that crazy fighting got so bad, no thanks!"

Lexington Association Track, circa 1910

CHAPTER FOUR
Circling the Drain

Eventually, during the first two decades of the 1900s, the reformers convinced public officials of the evils of horse racing and wagering, which only resulted in a breeding ground for organized crime and this blemish would open up and fester with payoffs to fix races, use of ringers, hopping (drugging) of horses, bribing of officials and track stewards and anyone else who could artificially influence the outcome of a race and that included the trainers, the jockeys, the grooms, the rubbers and the transient stable help.

Shortly after the post-World War recession of 1920-1921, the elements of organized crime, like maggots drawn to the rotting flesh of this gaping wound, caused mainly by the influx of the men returning from war to a paucity of employment opportunities and a stagnant economy, established a hold on the horse racing industry and the running of horses became akin to the running of booze and the running of drugs. Crime-ridden Havana was no longer the minor league training facility for U.S. horse racing. Instead, it had become the Caribbean haven of organized crime. The need for winter racing in a warm climate with some semblance of honest gaming and honest sport would not be answered until 1925, when the Miami Jockey Club formed and established a race track in Dade County, Florida at the Hialeah Park grounds, a recreational park established in 1921 to serve the residents of a newly residential suburb of Miami of the same name.

In the meantime, an older, almost forgotten form of horse race wagering, developed in France way back in 1867 known as pari-mutuel betting, was actually a legal form of wagering in the United States. It was not banned by any of the current laws because the pool of money wagered, minus a five-percent commission to the track, was the amount of money paid out to the winners of winning tickets. This method was not considered gambling or book making, and therefore, perfectly legal. It was Colonel Matt Winn who revived and initiated this system of horse track wagering in the tracks he managed. Eventually, other tracks around the country began to re-appear and adopted this form of wagering which was legal in every state. According to James C. Claypool, "Latonia, along with Churchill Downs, became one of the earliest major tracks to use pari-mutuels exclusively. Latonia took it a step further, and in so doing made a lasting mark on the history of American horse racing." (Claypool, 1998).

"If it wasn't for Matt Winn, Tommy my boy, you or I wouldn't be here right now having this conversation, and we for sure wouldn't be running these horses like we are. We are truly fortunate to say we know Matt Winn," claimed Spence.

"But I don't know Mr. Winn," Tommy retorted almost apologetically.

"Maybe not, Tommy, but I guarantee you that he knows you! He knows everything about horse racing and horse racing people and he knows you, believe me!"

Claypool also explains, "Latonia Race Track was sold in 1919 to the Kentucky Jockey Club, the most powerful racing syndicate ever formed in Kentucky. They purchased Churchill Downs, the Association Track at Lexington, Douglas Park [in Louisville] and Latonia for $1,650,000. Matt Winn was offered $650,000 for Churchill Downs but he refused. Instead, he joined the new organization as a partner. Douglas Park was turned into a training facility, and in 1933, the Association Track at Lexington failed and permanently closed." (1998).

Two years later, in 1935, Keeneland was founded just west of Lexington and has conducted horse racing meetings every April and October since 1936.

*   *   *   *   *   *

The first quarter of the twentieth century heard on several occasions horse racing's death knell. Miraculously, it dodged that fatal bullet and emerged just a little stronger each time. Anti-gambling laws in 1908, criminal involvement and influence in the early 1920s, and the 1929 crash of America's economy all threatened to bring about racing's demise.

Thanks to just a handful of the industry's greatest giants, whose courage, determination and financial backing saved the sport as it was circling the drain, it recovered and prospered.

Tommy broke into the business right in the middle of racing's darkest days. He witnessed the crime and corruption, the tricks of the trade of trainers and jockeys to influence the outcome of a race or a horse's performance, the bribes and the counter-bribes, knowing when a race is being thrown or throwing it oneself, cheating the weight requirements, hopping a horse, or starving and thirsting a horse for a day and then feeding and watering him right before the race to slow him down or make him quit. These are the things he either observed or heard about and learned from talking to his fellow jockeys, grooms and trainers around the track during his first 100 day Winter Meeting in Havana.

"Mr. Spence, do you ever hop your horses?" asked Tommy during one early morning workout.

"Now, Tommy, where in thunder's name did you learn about hopping horses?"

"I been learning all kinds of things down here, Mr. Spence...from everybody."

Spence looked up from his stop watch and commenced telling Tommy a story. "About eight years ago, back at Latonia, I was running this chestnut gelding named Charley Hill. It was in the last race of the day and he was leading the entire field in the final stretch and he was makin' his run. I mean he was drivin'! Then all of a sudden, right through the inside fence he goes. He just took a spill for no apparent reason. It broke him up real bad. We had to shoot him on the spot, soon as the grandstands emptied and all the trackers left." Spence paused for a moment to wipe his nose. "The track veterinary told the track officials that the horse had been given a stimulant, and that's what made him fall down. It was a common practice to dope horses. Everybody did it and everybody knew it was being done. For years and years it was done."

"Did ya give Charley Hill something, Mr. Spence?" Tommy asked.

"Yeah Tommy, I'd been working with him for about a week, and noticed he would always flatten out right as he entered the home stretch. So we decided to dose him with a little cocaine right before that race, just to help give him that little edge he needed. Well, all of a sudden this was a national news story and within twenty-four hours, I was ruled off the track. I lost my license and privileges for doing something that every trainer did whenever it was necessary. Sometimes those horses wore out during these long meets, an' they didn't eat right or sleep right and just lost their drive and determination. Hopping them gave them their edge back. It didn't hurt them none, it just stimulated them. So here I am with one dead horse and thrown off to boot! Now how bad was that?"

"Pretty bad, I guess," answered Tommy, encouraging Spence to go on with his story. "What did you do next?"

"Well, Tommy, I was desperate. I went to every track official, judge, racing steward, every owner and trainer to plead my case and gain support for me. I was just doing my best to win and I couldn't see no crime in that. I wasn't the only one taken by surprise by Latonia's decision to ban giving stimulants to horses. One day nobody cared and then the next day it was illegal. Just didn't figure! About three days later, another incident occurred. The veterinary pulled a horse from a race because of his wild behavior in the paddock before the race, and determined that the horse was drugged. The officials called for the trainer and it was Harry Guy ('Hard Guy') Bedwell, the most successful trainer on the grounds. Since Latonia officials raised such a stink about doping horses, they had to give Bedwell the same treatment they gave me. They threw him off but went on further and banned him and his whole stable and string of over twenty Thoroughbreds from racing. They figured that every one of his horses was tainted some way or other by dope, and they banned the whole operation."

"Wow, then what?" prodded Tommy.

"Well, about five or six days later, because of some breech of procedure on the veterinary's part, they re-instated me and I was back to racing but it wasn't so simple for Bedwell. He fought and fought for months, but the racing commission just wouldn't budge. He even got August Belmont, the chairman of the Jockey Club from up in New York, to be on his side. Still didn't help. Sometime in the fall, that veterinary suddenly died and couldn't plead his case against Hard Guy, who kept up the fight. By early 1911, he was fully reinstated and went on that year to become the winningest trainer in number of wins in the country."

Tommy knew that Kay Spence wasn't crooked. He truly believed that Spence saw no harm in doping a horse if it seemed like it was necessary, especially back then when it wasn't even illegal or controlled. "Sure seems odd that veterinary fella just up and died, though," pondered Tommy.

"Yep, sure does!" whispered Spence.

Postcard of Oriental Park, Havana, Cuba

CHAPTER FIVE
Havana, Cuba

It was on the 11th of December, 1918 when they arrived at Oriental Park in Havana, Cuba. The place was bustling with activity. The weather was clear, sunny and warm. The daily temperature stayed around 75 degrees. It was a perfect racing atmosphere. Tommy was surprised by the number of Americans there, and they were all speaking English. Somehow he pictured something very different. He was expecting to see only Cubans hanging around - even though he didn't know what a Cuban really looked like - speaking some language he wouldn't be able to understand.

"Why this place looks just like it could be Latonia, if I didn't know better," he excitedly announced to Spence. "I sure didn't expect this!"

"Well, just what were you expecting, Tommy?"

"I don't know. I guess a bunch of natives holding spears and dancing around and speaking a foreign language and shrunken heads hanging all around."

With a hearty belly laugh, Spence assured Tommy that every thing here would be just about the same as it was 80 miles away in the United States. "But I must warn you son, the rules are a lot different here than they are back home. They're not as strict here and the horseplayers and gamblers are always lookin' to fix a race one way or another down here so they can win big. You gotta watch out for their tricks and the things they tell you 'cause they're not always on the up-and-up. So watch yourself and don't get bamboozled by their slick tongues. Just keep to the jockey house and whoever picks you up to ride their horse, listen to what the trainer tells you and then just do the best you can following those instructions and you'll do just fine. You're going to get a lot of valuable experience down here, so keep your eyes and ears open and do your best. Understand?"

"Got it, Mr. Spence, sure do!"

"Okay then, let's get to our barn and get settled in. What do you say?"

"I'm all for that, sir. I want to get rested up and ready for tomorrow's program," Tommy answered excitedly.

*   *   *   *   *   *

Oriental Park was indeed 'just like Latonia', as Tommy commented to Kay Spence. In fact, it was probably a lot fancier and drew a lot more of the higher social class patrons and vacationers from the United States. It was located about nine miles from Havana in the township of Marianao in the province of Havana. It was built by H.D. "Curly" Brown and opened on January 14, 1915. Brown was a very colorful fellow, a businessman in the construction profession, and a horse farm owner in California. He was also involved in the construction of other race tracks, including Laurel Park (1911) in Maryland and Arlington Park (1927) in Chicago. It was a very popular spot for winter racing, gambling, and entertainment long before the horses became popular in South Florida.

The track itself was a one mile oval dirt (clayey loam) track. There were two chutes, one entering the backstretch for ¾-mile races and one entering the main track for races of 1 ¼ miles. The length of the stretch from the last turn to the judges' stand was 440 yards. From the judges stand to the first turn was 110 yards. The backstretch was 70 feet wide, while the main stretch was 80 feet wide. The seating capacity of 5,000 included 3,000 in the main grandstand area, 1,200 in the boxes, and 800 in the field stand. The entire compound was beautifully landscaped with palm trees and flower gardens everywhere. The infield was adorned by the name of the park spelled out in flowers. The clubhouse was top-of-the-line luxury and splendor. The winter meetings attracted many Americans who would fly to Cuba for a weekend of drink, gambling, dancing, and parties. It was a popular hang-out for celebrities and professional ballplayers since prohibition had changed the complexion of night life in the U.S.

The next day was Day 4 of the Winter Meeting of 100 days or more. Tommy was up early and on the track exercising the horses, then completed the rest of his morning chores. When Mr. Spence returned from taking care of all his duties, he announced, "Tommy, I entered you in the last race today on Jack Snipe. It's a mile and a sixteenth for three-year-olds and up. I figured that would be a good horse and a good distance for your maiden this winter."

"Ready as I'll ever be, Mr. Spence. I'll do a good job for you, sir."

It took forever for that last race to be called. They went to post at 4:54 p.m., and they were at the post for another 12 minutes. It was a very nervous wait for Tommy. The start was good and slow. The same could be said of Tommy's ride, good and slow. He ran a brief fourth behind the three leaders, but quickly was outpaced and dropped to last place. He held up the rear until he managed to just get ahead of the sixth place horse. After getting back to the stables, Tommy told Mr. Spence, "I'm glad that's behind me. I was really nervous out there, a strange new track and all."

"A good lesson, my boy. You can't start controlling a horse's nervous feelings until you can control your own! It wasn't any different than it was at Latonia, was it son?"

"Nope, not one bit now that I look back on it, Mr. Spence."

"Okay then, now you're ready to race."

Tommy hung out the next day at the jockey house. Spence wasn't running any of his horses today, so he thought he'd familiarize himself with the other jockeys and what ever trainers or owners he might meet. The next day, he was approached by C.T. Worthington to ride one of his horses in the fourth race.

"Sure would, sir. I'll give you my best ride."

It was a claiming race for three-year-olds and upwards. The trainer, W.N. Potts, motioned Tommy over to him.

"Follow me, son, and I'll show you The Duke."

"Wow, he looks like a duke!" Tommy muttered when they got to the stall.

"Now son, listen up. He likes the sport of chasing and overcoming another horse so let him do that at the start, but after he gets the lead for a while, sometimes he gets bored and quits. So you got to push him when he gets to that point."

"Got it Mr. Potts. I'll do just as you say."

They went to post at 3:47 p.m. At 3:48, they were off. It was a good but slow start. The horse in the fifth post position got a good jump and served as The Duke's chasee. As he took the lead, he set the pace of the race in a gamely fashion. Just as Mr. Potts told Tommy, The Duke started to quit at the eighth pole and the second place horse was making a run. Tommy showed his horse the whip, but he had already heard his challenger gaining and he left him in the dust, crossing the finish in a canter. Tommy recorded his very first Cuban win. It felt good, especially with having been picked up out of the jockey house.

"This will surely lead to more mounts," he thought.

And it did. The next day, he rode in two races, one for Kay Spence finishing fourth and one for P. Moran, holding third place until the final stretch when the horse just quit.

The following day, Tommy got rides in five out of the six races of the day. These included horses of three different and new owners. He finished in the money one time that day. The next day, he secured two rides, finishing once in the money. The first race of the following day was a claiming race for horses of all ages. The field of eight went to post at 2:34 p.m. and was off after one minute. Tommy's horse started in the seventh post position and was on the extreme outside on the stretch turn, where she then dashed across to the inside, and taking the lead, won under restraint. Tommy had three more races that day, but failed to finish in the money.

Tommy continued in this same manner throughout the month of December, riding for Kay Spence mainly, and picking up rides from other trainers the rest of the time. He was holding his own, considering he was a 16 year-old rookie. He finished in the money enough to keep busy and to make his name familiar to the owners and trainers.

RACE TRACK, HAVANA, CUBA

Race Track Havana, Cuba

CHAPTER SIX
The Greatest Birthday Present

Wednesday, January 1, 1919 was Day 21 of the Havana Winter Meeting. *"New Year's Day,"* Tommy thought to himself. *"Mother always said that whatever you did on New Year's Day, you would be doing every day the whole rest of the year."* It was an old Irish belief and tradition that she would talk about while they all would be enjoying their traditional New Year's Day meal of corned beef, cabbage, and potatoes, boiled all night long in the same pot. It was the good luck meal and Tommy's parents were both very superstitious, just as his grandparents and great-grand parents on both sides had been. *"I'm gonna finish first place on the first race I run today! I'm gonna win the first race of the year down here and I'm doing it for mother, 'cause I miss her and I love her and I want her to look down on me and be proud."*

It just so happened that Tommy got approached early that morning while he was breezing Mr. Spence's horses, by Kay Spence himself.

"You're out early today, Tommy. What's up?"

"Ah, I just wanted to give 'em all a good work out, bein's as this is this very first day of the New Year. I think it'll bring us good luck."

"That so, Tommy? Where'd that notion come about?"

"From my mother. It's an Irish thing you wouldn't understand."

Spence gave a hearty gut laugh. "You'd be surprised at the things I can understand, son. Now see if you can understand what I'm gonna say. You know, I been training a couple of horses for W.W. Darden while

I been here. He's got this one, by the name of Corson. It was bred by Ed Gardner out of Ivan the Terrible. He's a real handful. He's lazy at the get-go, but loves to sprint at the end, and the more horses he can overcome, the better. He's a real gamer. Darden wants to run him in the first race today; it's a claiming race for three-year-olds. He asked me if I knew any jockeys that could handle him. Get on over there and get a look at him 'cause you're riding him in the first race!"

"Yes sir, Mr. Spence! Can I fool with him some first?"

"Let's see, what time is it? Almost eight, that leaves us about six and a half hours to post. Yeah, Tommy, go ahead and exercise him some. But I want you to lead him around first, let him smell you; and talk to him...a lot. He likes to be talked to. Then take him out and walk him, and keep talking to him. Then, if he gets prancy, ask him to show you what he's got, but no more than two furlongs at breezing speed, and don't push him. I don't want no lather. Got it? Be sure to cool him down real good and then rest him. Good luck, kid!"

Tommy turned and made a bee line to the Darden stables. There stood Corson, his head out over the stall door bobbing up and down almost like he was expecting Tommy.

"Wow, boy, you're a beaut!"

Corson blew out in response and then bobbed his head up and down some more. "Wanna take a walk around the track, boy?" Again, the big three-year-old let out a positive whinny. It sure sounded like a 'yes' to Tommy.

It was a perfectly clear day and a very pleasant 75 degrees when the horses and riders went to post for the first race of the first day of the New Year. A lot of the riders and trainers had just started showing their faces not long before. There must have been some serious celebrating going on the night before, because hardly anyone was out early working horses. That didn't bother Tommy one bit. He used the opportunity to get real acquainted with Corson and vice versa.

They went to post at 2:32 p.m. and Tommy lined up first. All the while he kept whispering in Corson's ear. "I want to win this race, ol' buddy, 'cause my mother always told me that whatever I was doin' on New Year's Day I would be doin' the whole rest of the year. Besides, there's another reason and I'll tell you that at the finish line."

And they were off, not even a full minute at the post. Corson found himself and Tommy quickly running fifth in the field of seven. It was a slow start for them, but Tommy kept talking to Corson the whole time and Corson looked like he was listening and paying attention. After rounding the far turn, he began moving up steadily, gaining on the front runners and overtaking them one by one and then taking the lead, he drew away in the stretch drive.

Tommy was ecstatic! He did it! Once past the finish line, he just kept talking to Corson and patting him on the neck. "You did it, boy, you did it!" He just couldn't seem to contain himself. "Now I'll tell you the other reason. Today is my birthday! January 1st and it's my birthday. My seventeenth birthday and the first day and first race of the New Year, and we won it, boy, we won it! Better still, my mother always said that whatever you do on New Year's Day you will do all year long. Winning horse races all year long is what I'm going to do. Just wait and see!"

"Good race, son," Mr. Darden shouted as Tommy and Corson entered the winner's circle. Then he joined Spence and put his arm around him and was saying something in his ear, talking for a good two minutes or so. Tommy was on cloud nine and just thoroughly enjoying the moment. Even Corson looked to be entertained by the flurry of activity all around. Tommy reached inside his silks and clasped the St. Patrick medal that was pinned to the inside of his shirt, right over his heart. It was the one his mother used to wear around her neck. She gave it to him for good luck and protection right before she died. As he fingered the charm, he said a prayer of thanks to God, St. Patrick and his mother, his Irish triumvirate of horse racing.

Tommy walked Corson until he was completely cooled down. The groom took him to the stable and washed him down as Tommy watched, still talking to the horse. Tommy massaged Corson's feet to make perfectly sure all the heat had dissipated. He then headed back to the jockey house, just to see if anybody was looking for one to ride for them.

"Hey Murray," one of the veteran jockeys hollered across the room, "What'd you hop that horse with?"

"That horse wasn't doped with nothin'," he fired back. "And if you say it again you'll be spitting out teeth!"

"Whoa boy, slow down now. Sure looked like something kicked that horse in the final stretch and with Spence being the trainer, it sure wouldn't be a long shot." That pretty much dampened Tommy's euphoria. He left the jockey house and headed straight for their digs at Spence's stables.

"Hey, that was some fine riding out their, my boy. You and that horse looked like you been doing that forever. Congratulations!"

"Thanks, Mr. Spence," Tommy whispered.

"What's up, son? Something's weighing on your mind. What is it?"

"Over in the jockey room they were saying that the way Corson ran so good, he musta been hopped up and you were known for doing that but I took up for you, sir! I know you wouldn't dope a horse, not anymore. Right, Mr. Spence?"

"That's right, Tommy, not anymore. Just like you and me talked about, not anymore. That horse was running on pure heart and your encouragement, and don't ever think otherwise. Those guys were just trying to rattle you, trying to take something away from you, Tommy. That's part of the game, the psychological mind games."

Tommy's spirit returned, even more uplifted than before. "Thanks, Mr. Spence, for giving me that chance this afternoon. That was just the best birthday present ever!"

"Why I didn't know this was your birthday, Tommy. New Year's Day is your birthday? Well, I'll be…" Spence then added, "My mother used to always tell me that whatever I was doing on New Year's Day, I would do the whole rest of the year."

"Well, I'll be…" chuckled Tommy.

"Okay, birthday boy, you got about forty-five minutes till your next race. Let's get you dressed into my colors and ready to weigh out."

"I don't get it," Tommy muttered. "How come before the race you weigh out, and then after the race is over you have to weigh in? Shouldn't it be the other way around, Mr. Spence?"

"Tommy, the more you hang around horse racing, the more things you'll find just don't make any sense at all. It's like the Derby and the Oaks, the two biggest races we got here in Kentucky. How do you reckon they got those names?"

Tommy pondered, "Well, I ain't never really thought about how they got their name, but I sure have thought a lot about me riding in them and winning them both! I thought a derby was a hat. What's a hat got to do with a horse race? Is it 'cause of the brim looking like a track running around the crown which looks like the infield?"

"Nope, not even close, Tommy. But your explanation makes more sense than the real reason. You see, in England, where Thoroughbred horse racing began, long before there even was a United States of America, the most important horse race in the country was named for this rich and powerful feller who started it, the Earl of Derby. So the race became the Derby and the name of this fella's estate was the Oaks. So they named the big race for the fillies, the Oaks. So when we came over here to our country, we wanted to keep the same kind of tradition so they used the same names because of the national importance and prominence these races held."

"Did they call us jockeys monkeys over there too, Mr. Spence?"

Spence nearly spun himself clear around on his right foot, powered by a big belly laugh. "I call you a monkey because you are one," Spence roared, still laughing and shaking his head.

The field of seven went to the post at 3:45 p.m. for the fourth race of the day, a claiming race for four-year-olds. The track was still heavy, having been muddy all day the day before. Tommy had the third post position, which he thought suited Beauty Shop very well. They were at the post for less than a minute and off to a slow but good start. The leader set the pace and was driving hard the whole race, closely challenged by the second and third place horse. The winner, Blanchita, a local favorite, tired at the end and would have been overtaken by the second place horse in just another stride. The winning jockey, W. Gargan was also the owner. Tommy finished a disappointing sixth.

The fifth race of the day was the Peace Handicap for a purse of $800, followed by the feature race, the Second Running of the New Year's Handicap worth $1,200 to the winner. Spence had a different horse entered in each race, a field of just four horses each time. Jockey R. Wingfield, one of the more popularly recognized journeyman jockeys of the day, was aboard in each race as Tommy watched from the rail. He finished in third place in race five and fourth in race six. Tommy didn't feel so bad now.

CHAPTER SEVEN
Give That Man a Vuelta Abajo

The next day, Thursday, January 2nd was clear and a pleasant 75 degrees. It was Day 22 of the 100 days or more Winter Meeting. The first race was for three-year-olds, maidens, fillies and special weights for a purse of $500. The field of 11 went to post at 2:31 p.m. and in two minutes was off to a good but slow start. Tommy started from the fifth position on Terrible Miss. In a hard driving competition, first place Surplice set the pace and, after being passed, came through on the inside and got up to the win in the final strides. Terrible Miss was a forward contender to the last eighth.

"I really thought I had a good shot, but she gave it up when Surplice kept coming up the inside. That horse had some magic, I'll tell ya," Tommy reported to Spence.

"You bet she had some magic," replied the owner. "It's called Aug Belmont."

"You mean the big guy up to New York?"

"One in the same, my boy. The most influential and famous horseman in the business. He was Surplice's breeder."

"Praise the Lord and Saint Paddy," Tommy whispered as he squeezed his St. Patrick medal. "I been beat by the very best there is."

Kay Spence had no other horses running until the sixth and final race so Tommy accepted a mount in the fourth race for owner H.E. Leigh. It was the Vuelta Abajo Handicap for three-year-olds. Tommy could hardly pronounce the name of the race, much less know what it meant, but at post time, he found himself in the second post position and at the start, he came out a miserable fifth. In spite of running fairly well, he finished only fourth and out of the money. When Tommy got back to his stable, Kay handed him a fancy wrapped Cuban cigar.

"What's this?" Tommy inquired as he wrinkled up his nose.

"It's your very own Vuelta Abajo. Give that man a cigar!" laughing that deep roaring gut laugh of his.

"What?"

"You ran that race for a cigar!" Spence explained. "You see, Vuelta Abajo is a brand of Cuban cigar. The tobacco is grown down in the Vuelta Abajo region of southern Cuba and it's supposed to be the very best tobacco in all of Cuba."

"I'll just keep this in my trunk for good luck, the very first trophy I ever won."

Spence had one other horse entered that day. It was the last race on the card, a claiming race for three-year-olds and up. Tommy was aboard Hemlock and drew the fourth post position in the field of eight.

They were at the post two full minutes, then a good slow start. Tommy jumped out in front at the start and led to the quarter pole when he was overtaken by Driffield, who then set the pace to the homestretch and, after being headed, finished resolutely on the inside and outstayed El Pladit. Hemlock quit badly after his first challenge and drew up the rear.

"What happened Tommy? Did he get a hold of your cigar before the race?"

"I don't know, Mr. Spence, something got to him. He just up and quit as soon as we were passed on the quarter. I thought hemlock was a poison. Maybe you should change his name," chuckled Tommy.

"Now you being a superstitious shanty boat Irishman, of all people, should know it's bad luck to ever change a horse's name!"

"Yeah, I know that but what's worse than last place?"

"Now think about it Tommy," Spence interjected. "How about broke down? Now after he's cooled down and rubbed, let's give his legs a real good inspection and some therapy, just to make sure he isn't sore or inflamed."

This made Tommy think. As a matter of fact, he worried all night long. He thought to himself and made a mental list of all the things that could be worse than running in last place. He came up with such a long list it made him feel guilty for even complaining. At least the horse didn't sustain some kind of irreparable injury and have to be destroyed. At least he just quit running because he became tired and not because he lost his mount. *"That's a good way of killing yourself,"* shuttered Tommy in deep thought, *"or hurting yourself real bad so you could never ride again."* He dwelt so much on all the negative things that could happen he couldn't sleep. At some point though, his worries and bad thoughts left him. Unfortunately, they turned into bad dreams.

The next day was a Saturday, January 4th, another pleasant and warm day with plenty of sunshine. This was the 24th day of the 100 day or more winter meeting at Oriental Park. Tommy found himself in the first race of the day aboard Kay Spence's four-year-old Sasenta, in a claiming race. They had post position number one. At the start, they were seventh and remained seventh the entire race.

"He didn't quit, Mr. Spence. He never started," Tommy lamented as he moped his way back to the stall.

"Tommy, you're in some kind of funk, ain't you, boy?"

"Don't know what's wrong. Don't even know what a funk is," Tommy blurted.

"It means you ain't even fit to be around because you're so melancholy. You're feeling sorry for yourself, when there ain't even any need to. You need the day off boy. Walk around, blow the stink off! Maybe you'll meet a pretty girl or something."

"Ah no, Mr. Spence, I got me a girl back home in Latonia. Her name is Virginia, but everybody calls her Sis. I'm gonna marry her someday but she don't know it quite yet."

"Well, maybe you ought to go over and get on your hay pile and write her a letter so she knows your plans, and she don't go finding herself another beau while you ain't even around."

Tommy came back to life. "You're right, Mr. Spence. You're right as you could be!"

That night Tommy finally had a good night's sleep and he awoke in great spirits. "I'm thinking I want to go to church today, Mr. Spence, this being Sunday and all."

"Well, seems to me like every person in this country is Catholic, so I don't imagine you'll have any trouble finding a church. I reckon you gotta go pray she'll say yes, huh?"

"What?"

"Nothin' Tommy, nothin'. Just be sure you're back here by race time. I don't want you to miss your golden chance."

"What's my golden chance, Mr. Spence?"

"You'll see Tommy. Just make sure you're back in time."
An hour and a half later, Tommy was walking back across the infield with a group of jockeys, trainers, grooms and other track workers.

"They had a Mass over in the clubhouse for folks here at the meeting to attend, Mr. Spence. You're right. Everybody around here must be Catholic. Good thing the Mass was in Latin, 'cause I could follow it but when they read the Gospel and gave the sermon, they completely lost me. It was all in Spanish. Now, what's this golden opportunity all about?"

"I said Golden Chance, Tommy and I got you a ride on him in the second race for Mr. Diaz. He approached me last night asking about you and I told him you were one of my apprentice jockeys down here with me this meeting. He was impressed with your style and wondered if you were interested in picking up a few extra mounts while you were here so I took the liberty to speak in your behalf and accept the opportunity. You'll be starting in the third post position and post time is 2:55 so you better get on over there and learn what you can from Mr. Diaz and his trainer about that horse."

"Yes sir! On my way." His level of enthusiasm and excitement was back to normal and Spence was glad about that.

They were at the post for one minute and the start was good. None of the horses got an early jump. They started slow and even. Tommy rode hard and coaxed Golden Chance from fifth place into third at the three quarter mark. Into the stretch, however, Golden Chance was being challenged on the outside by the rapidly gaining Ague and simply quit running, settling for fourth place. Spence was waiting for Tommy back at the paddock.

"That was a really exciting race overall," Spence told Tommy. "A bunch of four-year-olds with mostly apprentice jockeys up. Should'a named it the Bug Boy Stakes. You guys took second, third, fourth and fifth over the veterans in a very close race."

Tommy smiled because he too thought it was an exciting race. "I was having a good run till Ague came up on me on the outside and I couldn't find a spot to get over. Then my horse just quit."

"Hurry on over to the jockey house and get changed into my colors. I want you to ride Lady Order in this next race."

"Why?" Tommy asked, puzzled.

"I don't know," Spence fired back. "Just something I saw and I wanted to check it out."

So Tommy hurried back and dressed for the next race. It was a claiming race for three-year-old maidens. He drew post position number nine for a field of 10 horses, none of whom had ever won a race. At the post for one minute, they were lined up and a good start ensued. Tommy left the barrier in first place with his mount and maintained it until the half mile pole when he slipped to third, behind Fustian. At the three-quarter, Tommy again regained the lead, with Fustian a close second. Into the stretch, the two were head to head, and Fustian was going away at the end after Lady Order tired badly.

"Two more apprentice jockeys finishing first and second," Spence was saying to himself as he made his way to the outer fence of the winner's circle. Tommy's second place finish paid very well: $25.10 to place and $10.40 to show on a $2.00 mutuel.

"Tommy, I got you down for one more race today, the seventh. It's another claiming race for four-year-olds and up and it will pit you against four more apprentices and two veterans. One of the veterans is riding the favorite. I want you to get exposure to the different styles and tactics a veteran will use to get the position he wants compared to the young kids who don't make any aggressive moves until they see what the rest of the field is doing. If you want to become a winning jockey, then you've got to know the make-up and temperament of the horse you're riding and you got to be aggressive from the start. You need to set the table instead of someone else doing it and seating you where they want you to sit. Take the lead; don't react to someone else's lead. Get the jump at the start. Anticipate the starter's signal. You gotta take note of how the other nags are behaving at the line and how much they are paying attention to their jock. They are easily distracted by things you don't even see. They hear noises, they smell smells, they sense if you are nervous or calm. If they feel your confidence and authority and control, then they become just an extension of your body and they pick up the messages your brain is sending out, just the same as if you yourself were running a foot race."

"Now Unar likes to run but more than that, he likes to chase something, catch it, and then dominate it. Now you'll be starting from the outside position so you'll have some distance to make up at the get-go. The favorite is posted in the fourth position, the dead middle, just where he likes it and he likes to get the lead right off and head to the inside. What I want you to do is anticipate the starter, get an early jump, even if it results in a bad start and they have to call you back. It will upset Maxim's Choice's composure and routine. On the restart, get the anticipated jump again. The confusion will reduce any mental advantages the horses or jockeys may have or think they have."

"Is that cheating, Mr. Spence?" Tommy asked timidly as if he didn't really want to hear the answer.

"I don't know, Tommy," Spence responded, as his shoulders shrugged, his palms opened and turned upwards following his eyebrows. "That's up to you to decide. There are no written rules that say it is cheating but it's all up to the starter's discretion. If you cause enough bad starts and he thinks you are doing it on purpose, he can scratch you right then and there. If it seems like you just have a nervous horse, and it's the horse's doing, then he is more tolerant, but just a little more tolerant. You have to make up your own mind about that, Tommy. When do you plan your strategy for a race? None of them will be the same. They're all different. When do you figure out how you will get that slight edge over your competition? When the starting rope goes up? When you're led out on to the track? When you weigh out? That morning? The night before? How you lay things out and mentally prepare is all up to you and there are all sorts of ways to improve your advantages for each individual race."

"You can study and observe the different running and riding characteristics and styles of the horses you race and the jockeys you run against. You can study the records and charts of previous races and outings and learn their particular running preferences and habits. You can watch the horse and jockeys work out. You can listen to what the jockeys, trainers and owners talk about. You can bond with your mount and win his trust and affection or maybe you choose other methods to win races. Maybe you realize there's more money made in losing. Maybe a bookie gives you four or five times more money to fix or throw a race than you could make by winning it, maybe he gives you extra money to hop a long shot on cocaine or heroin, or stop a favorite with a chlorine capsule, or put a buzzer under the saddle, or maybe he convinces your stable to paint up and substitute a ringer for the real entry."

"There are as many ways to throw a race as there are people in the horseracing business. I've seen 'em withhold a horse's water and food for a day or two and then over feed and overwater him right before he runs. I've seen 'em alter the shoes to add drag and impede their gate and throw off their stride. I've see 'em stuff cotton plugs up one nostril to cut off their wind. Money'll make some people do anything to a horse and those are all strategies, too. You just have to decide how and what you are willing to do in order to be a successful winning jockey. You have to decide what's right and what's wrong, what's legal and what ain't. Can I win on my own talent and my horse's talent or do I have to cheat to win and take bribes to get wins? Better start thinking about all of this now while you're down here in Cuba this winter because when you get back to the States and into the eastern and northern racing circuits, you'll be riding against all those jockeys who have already figured that all out and the ones who haven't figured it out ain't even riding. They do the grooming and exercising. Then, if you ever make it to the eastern circuit, Hail Mary and God help you if your head ain't true and plumb. Those New York tracks and owners and breeders are part of a whole different world - the world of high finance, stocks and bonds, power, society, money, importance, and competition. Your reputation has to precede you there if you ever hope to find work with them, and it better be a damned good reputation."

Tommy was expressionless. He never heard so much wisdom and advice ever come out of one person's mouth in his entire life and it wasn't just track or bar talk. This was like something a father would share with his own son. Tommy's own father, or his parish priest, or any of his teachers in school had never even come close to a talk like this. Very few lectures he ever got at home rivaled the intensity of this spontaneous interaction. Tommy was pensive. He was weighing and pondering that freight train of information that just steamed through his head.

"Boy, that was faster than any horse I have ever been on," he mused to himself.

He looked up with the same slight smile that would cover his face whenever he had completed a good ride, not one of personal pride or pleasure, but one of enlightenment and discovery. No other words were exchanged. Spence put his hand out for Tommy's left foot and up he went onto Unar's back, and a halo of confidence was the spirit of the moment.

Tommy and Unar were led to their post position without incident. There was a ruckus occurring at the third and fourth spots, which required some re-alignment maneuvers. The starter surveyed the scene, and as his gaze moved ever so slightly, Unar jumped the start. They were called back, and an apologetic Tommy blushed and nodded a slight mea culpa to the group. Unar's ears were perked up and honing in on every direction, as if listening to the comments of the officials and other horses and jockeys. Actually, Tommy was whispering in his ear soothing praises and pleasantries. Unar responded in stillness and focused anticipation. The start was signaled again and Unar got off a solid stride ahead of the others, but it was a good start. Tommy held back on his mount as the favorite bolted to set the leading pace, just as Spence instructed but Tommy wasn't consciously replaying Spence's instructions. He was navigating by his own senses and feeling and the animal's instinct and strength. By the time they reached the first turn, Unar saw that he had something to chase and he was in full pursuit. At the quarter pole, he was clearly in the lead and easily gained the inside rail. By this time, St. Jude, with another apprentice up, was in close pursuit of Unar, but Tommy gave him his head and he galloped easily in front to the stretch, then drew away and finished in a canter. Austral's veteran jockey closed a gap and, finishing fast, caught St. Jude in the final strides, to place.

Tommy was leaning over the neck of Unar for the longest time as he was cooling down. It looked like he was clutching his chest, but he was just reverently fondling his mother's St. Patrick medal and giving a prayer of thanks in the horse's ear:

"You are God's most perfect creation and I am blessed that I am one of the few He shares you with."

Spence was silently pleased with the outcome of his experiment.

CHAPTER NINE
Don't Call Me Sir!

For the next few days that second week of January, Kay Spence was going to lay off entering any races in order to rest his stable and to work out some of his less motivated runners. He also wanted to secretly work on Tommy's inherent, but undeveloped, horse-jockey relationship. He had been watching Tommy's unconscious interactions with his mounts, and their response to him. Tommy seemed to always make time to visit each horse in its stall several times a day and talk or whisper to them, touch and rub their chest and belly, feel their lower legs, check their feet, scratch behind their ears and upper lip, and just continuously fuss over them and pamper them almost like they were family. Maybe they really were substitute family members for a homesick 17 year-old orphan. Whatever the case, there was a palpable horse-human bond growing between this boy and his adopted charges and Kay Spence could see it.

"Tommy, how 'bout you breezing these fellas for me this week and I'll clock 'em and see what I see when they run, and you see what you see and feel what you feel from their backside, and then we compare notes and try to figger what's there and what ain't? You up fer that?"

"Sure am, Mr. Spence!"

"Tommy, I wish you'd quit calling me 'Mr. Spence'. It makes me feel old."

"Well you are old, Mr. Spence. I mean, older than me, and my mother and father taught me early on to respect my elders and say 'yes, sir' and 'yes, ma'am' and to know my place."

"Tommy, I know that you know your place and that you respect your elders, so you don't have to call me Mister Spence anymore."

"But all the other stablehands call you that."

"I know that and they're supposed to. That's just how it is."

"I don't get it Mr. Spence. I work for you too and besides, how come you call Mr. Winn, 'Mr. Winn', up there at Latonia? How come you don't call him Matt or Matthew or something like that?"

"Okay, Tommy, I just can't explain why, but if you and me are going to be working very closely together with these horses, then we don't really need all that formality. You're kinda gonna be like my assistant."

"Wow, an assistant? To you, Mr. Spence? Saint Paddy's pig! You mean it?"

"Yeah, Tommy, you'll be my assistant. Just remember, I'm still the boss."

"Yes sir, Boss!" Tommy responded enthusiastically with a brisk military salute.

"That's it," Spence beamed as the light bulb went on. "Just call me 'Boss' from now on. I like that a lot better than 'Mister Spence'."

"Yes sir, Boss," as Tommy saluted again.

They both laughed and Spence patted him on the back as they walked toward their stables. "Now, let's get to work, son."

They worked long and hard that week, up every morning at 4:30 a.m., with Tommy up and Kay and his chronometer leaning on the rail. Spence already knew what adjustments each horse had to improve upon and he would relay solutions and suggestions to Tommy, inviting his input as well. Without Tommy knowing it, Spence was actually working on Tommy's basic fundamentals and techniques and his critical thinking and problem solving. Spence would point out a deficiency in the horse's performance, and then give Tommy the opportunity to improve on or fix the discrepancy. For the afternoon races, Spence encouraged Tommy to take other trainers' mounts for a chance to earn extra income ($10.00 to $15.00 for a win, and proportionately less to place or show), but really to develop Tommy's experience and ability to listen, take instructions from an unfamiliar trainer, and guide and orchestrate a good competitive run on an unfamiliar horse. Then the two of them would critique and evaluate the entire experience, from pre-race mental preparation, equipment, tack, parade to the post, the quality and technique of the start itself, and then almost every stride and movement of the entire length of the race, revisiting good maneuvers and missed opportunities. Then they would analyze from the finish line back to the barn. How did you feel mentally and physically? Did you have good balance and center of gravity? Did the horse respond to your subtle movements and signals? Did he fight your commands? Was he having any physical manifestations at the end of the race? Trouble breathing? Coughing? Wheezing? Pink foaming from nostrils? Limping? Favoring a foot or leg? Heat or swelling in the fore leg? Nervousness? Lethargy? Any subtle little change?

"All these are very important to look for and to report back to the trainers and owners. You are the eyes and the ears of the owners and trainers when you are entrusted with their horse. They depend on you alone to assume responsibility for the welfare, health and safety of their animal while under your stewardship, knowing that you will urge and demand the best performance possible out of the beast at the same time. There's a very thin line there, Tommy, and it holds all the power that can make or break a jockey. There are thousands of kids out there every year who say they are going to be a professional jockey but just how many of them really make it? Just look through my racing magazines back at the stables. Look how many new two-year-olds are entering the racing scene every year and then how many of last year's two-year-olds become this year's three-year-olds and run that circuit and class. Same for the three-year-olds, and the four-year-olds and over. Then think how many aspiring jockeys there are all vying to be the ones chosen to be good enough to direct all this horse flesh in the right direction down the track and fast enough to beat their competitors for a piece of the money pie at the finish line. The odds are staggering, Tommy. There ain't a bookie alive that would give decent odds on you or any other monkey around here or anywhere just on the mere mention that you're a professional jockey. 'Show me!' That's what they say! Show me by your example, and your talent, and your determination, and sacrifice, and your twenty hour days, and your compassion for the beasts, and your love of the sport, and your desire for competition. By your honesty, and integrity, and dedication. Show me all that and then I might consider you to ride my champion horse. Maybe. It's just like baseball, Tommy. Remember how many of your buddies would play baseball every day back home, thinking that someday they would be playing for the Cincinnati Redlegs? How many of them really make it? None, right? Well, just like all them big strappin' strong bulky bullies think they will become professional baseball players some day, all you little skinny, lightweight fellas think you'll be jockeys some day. It ain't so. It's just like being a doctor, or a priest, or a railroad executive. You gotta work harder than the other guys, you gotta study everything there is about your profession, you gotta sacrifice a lot of things before you get there, and you have to put yourself last. Even then, still there ain't a guarantee! That's where just plain luck and the good Lord's providence come in to play."

CHAPTER TEN
Irish Superstition

Thursday, January 9, 1919 was a showery day and 75 degrees. It was the 26th day of the Winter Meeting of 100 days or more. Tommy picked up rides for the fourth, fifth, and sixth races, each one for a different trainer and owner. They were all three claiming races - two of them for three-year-olds and up, and the other for four-year-olds and up. In the fourth race, he finished fifth. In the fifth, he finished sixth. In the sixth race, he finished fourth.

"Wow, Tommy," Spence laughed. "It looks like four, five, and six are your lucky numbers!"

"Yeah, and I'm gonna write each one on a piece of paper, sprinkle them with holy water, and then light a votive candle down at the church tonight with each one of them and that will take care of that!"

Spence had a bewildered look about him now. He knew Tommy was a superstitious Irishman and Catholic, but this sounded more like voodoo than religious faith. "You sure that'll help, Tommy?"

"Keep the faith, Boss. There is no doubt in my mind," as he made the sign of the cross and looked in his trunk for paper and a pencil.

The next day, it was cloudy but dry. Tommy managed to get mounts for four races, all for owners and trainers different from the ones the day before and all different from each other this day. One of them was Kay Spence himself. The outcome for this day was a bit different for Tommy. In the four races he rode, he came back with a first place, a second, a third, and a fourth place. That amounted to a total of $500.00 in winnings for the day for the respective owners.

"Not a bad day's work for a bug boy!" Spence said proudly as he slapped Tommy on the back.

"Thanks, Boss, but it wasn't all me, you know?"

"Yeah, I know, Tommy." Spence found Tommy's faith and superstitions amusing but at the same time he was becoming concerned. He was by nature, more of a pragmatist and didn't have much room for hokey-pokey and witchery.

Tommy managed three more starts the next day. In the first and third races of the day, he wound up in the rear aboard his also-rans but the fourth race was impressive. Tommy drew the sixth post position out of eight aboard Twenty Seven, got off dead last but moved up fast on the outside chasing Lady James who was setting the pace up until the three quarter pole when Twenty Seven raced into an easy lead and won in a canter. Lady James quit after setting the early pace. A $2.00 mutuel bet paid $44.10 to win, $19.30 to place, and $6.70 to show.

"Good show, son," as Spence greeted Tommy in the winners' circle.

"Thanks, Boss. That one felt good from the start. Me plus Twenty Seven makes a first place on the twenty-eighth day of the meeting, get it? One plus twenty-seven makes twenty-eight!"

"Ah, Tommy, you're an incurable Irishman, double kissed by the Blarney Stone," Spence laughed and just shook his head. "Let's get back and talk about tomorrow. What do you say?"

The next day, Sunday, was the day decided on by Spence to resume racing of his stable. It had been a very productive, but tiring, week for him and Tommy, working with the whole lot of Spence's horses and their weaknesses and idiosyncrasies. Working on their starts seemed to be the order of the week, and that was very tedious work and something the horses themselves were not very fond of. When they saw the track, they just wanted to run. They had no interest in just jumping the starting rope.

Spence had a horse entered in four races that day. Three were claiming races and one, the sixth race on the ticket, was a stakes race with $1,200.00 added for three-year-olds and up. It was the Second Running of the Antilles Stakes, with net value to the winner amounting to $1,410.00. The first and fourth races had disappointing outcomes for the Spence Stables but the sixth race, the feature stakes race, was much more exciting for Tommy and his boss.

The six horses went to post at 4:10 p.m. The day was clear and the track heavy. They were at the post for a full five minutes before they were lined up for a good start. It was a slow start and Tommy got Rafferty off from his second position poorly and was quickly chasing two front runners before overtaking them and the lead at the half pole, then setting a very fast pace for the remainder of the race, it looked like he would take his challenger, Fort Bliss, who was still running under restraint. Into the stretch, Rafferty was tiring and Fort Bliss was given his head and took the lead, crossing the finish line in a canter. Spence was decidedly disappointed with the outcome. Tommy could see it on his face and in his mannerisms all the way out from the middle of the track but he focused his attention on Rafferty and his physical condition, cooling him slowly and bent over talking into his ear and patting the left side of his sweaty neck. The horse responded with a sneeze and a shake of the head. He had mud and dirt crusted around his eyes and nostrils and seemed very annoyed with the sensation it caused, almost appealing to Tommy to remedy the problem.

"Boy, he don't like dirt in his face," Tommy said as he and Spence encountered each other at the paddock.

"What happened out there? I thought you had it all the way," Spence countered. "Why didn't you use your whip at the end?"

"Boss, the whip wouldn't a made any difference. I was just outta horse. Nothin' left in him. When Fort Bliss caught him, he knew it was over. He was just plain run out, and he told me so. No need for the whip."

"Did he act sore or hurt?"

"Nope, just run out. Maybe he didn't sleep well last night," Tommy offered.

"Yeah, maybe," Spence mumbled as he gave the groom strict post-race care instructions for the sporting four-year-old. "Now where's Tommy?" Spence hollered, "We got one more race to go!"

"I'm over here with Unar," he answered. Spence mellowed as he watched Tommy and the horse interacting with each other. Tommy was talking and whispering to Unar, and the horse was bobbing his head up and down on Tommy's right shoulder and pulling at his cap. Neither one of them appeared nervous. They looked like two mischievous kids deciding what game to play next. At 5:05 p.m., Tommy and Unar left Spence from the paddock area to make their way to the starting line.

"See you at the finish line, Boss. Neither one of us will have mud or dirt on our face!"

And they didn't! Unar made a good start and took the lead quickly and drew far away on the backstretch to win easing up. He paid $8.20, $4.50, and $3.40. The victory gave the owner, Kay Spence, the $400.00 prize money and just an all-around good feeling about things in general.

CHAPTER ELEVEN
Keeping Weight

Oriental Park had no racing on Mondays. The track was closed but there was still plenty of activity and plenty of work to do. Jockeys, grooms, valets, owners, trainers and even the track officials were all still around even after the morning chores, workouts, exercising and stable duties were attended to. Tommy would spend an extra few hours on off days running around the track dressed in long johns and layers of woolen shirts or sweaters, all covered over by his rubber suit. This is one of the methods jockeys used to keep their riding weight down. It was the number one concern of jockeys. The lighter they kept their weight, the more mounts they would get, along with the better horses. The most common weight goal was 110 pounds for Tommy. He managed to maintain it without killing himself. There were other jockeys who wound up doing just that, killing themselves by malnutrition and dehydration.

The many methods they resorted to would lead to a compromised immunosuppressed state, caused renal and hepatic damage and failure, kept the body in a state of ketoacidosis, and would burn out the pancreas leading to diabetes. A lot of jockeys resorted to drug abuse and alcohol dependence, choosing a half shot of whisky over food as a source of energy. If they didn't kill themselves by these methods directly, they killed themselves indirectly by ruining their body's metabolism and creating a state of generalized weakness, muscle atrophy, hypoactive reflexes, pneumonia, bone density loss, poor critical decision making and responses, mental and emotional changes, depressive disorders, anxiety, agitation, chronic diarrhea, upper GI bleeding, esophageal tears and bleeding, overdoses and suicide. Not to mention the critical riding errors which resulted in catastrophic falls, killing or maiming either themselves or their fellow jockeys.

Others resorted to steam rooms and sweatboxes, putting their finger down their throats after eating a meal in order to regurgitate every thing they had just taken in by mouth (known as "flipping" in jockey jargon), and even regularly abusing laxatives and diuretics. Jalapa or Jalap was quite popular around the tracks and jockey houses. Derived from a plant found in Mexico and other southern hemisphere locations, it is a well known and commonly used cathartic from very early civilizations and cultures. Its quick acting and powerful results cause complete evacuation of the stomach and bowels by inducing explosive diarrhea and fluid loss as well as vomiting. In many cases, its use proved fatal

The jockey profession can easily lay claim to originating job related anorexia and bulimia and its resultant untoward sequellae. It's just not natural for a grown man to maintain a consistent body weight of 100-

110 pounds. Even if he does, how can he have enough strength and stamina to control a 1,200 pound Thoroughbred? Tommy heard all the stories and the tricks of the trade in the jockey house on these off days.

"Not me," he'd say to himself. "I'm never going to do that. I can keep my weight by running and exercising, just like the horses do."

Some of his fellow jockeys at the Havana winter meeting even resorted to "The Pill". It was actually a capsule containing a live tape worm which would attach to the intestinal mucosa and actually ingest all the nutrients taken in the body before they could be processed and used by the body as an immediate energy source or stored as fat for future use. The jockey's body then resorted to breaking down its existing fat stores to turn into needed energy, thus maintaining a desirable riding weight without going through all the extreme torture and self-inflicted punishment regimes. When he lost too much weight or was in a state of chronic illness, he would simply resort to the Jalap remedy which would also kill and expel the tape worm. When the weight went back on and approached his desired limit, then it was time for another capsule. It was pretty simple.

"Boss, what becomes of jockeys that get too heavy?"

Spence belted out a hearty gut laugh, "They become trainers, my boy, just like me, and they make even less money in the racing game!"

"Naw, really! What do you do?"

"Well, you hope you're a good enough rider and well known enough as a good rider to get a contract with an owner who runs the higher weight horses, like up east to Belmont and Saratoga and in Canada and the like. Even the Kentucky Derby allows 126 pounds. If you're one of the best monkeys around, you could hook up with the stable of the number one horse in the nation because it will always be assigned the highest weight ever for each of his races. Look at the horse Billy Kelly. He's getting assigned 127-129 pounds for certain races. That's a lot of weight! A trainer and owner a lot of times would rather have 127 pounds of live weight than 110 pounds live and 17 pounds of lead but, son, chances like that are few and far between. Only once in a blue moon will that opportunity come around. Just try to imagine how many senior jockeys plus all the new apprentices we got right here in these United States this year. Just how many of them will make it in this game?"

"Well I don't have no idea, Boss. All I know is that I'm gonna be one of 'em."

"Tommy, just remember. If you intend on being one of 'em, then this is the time to establish your methods of keeping your riding weight and you have to keep strong and healthy at the same time. You need to be making these things your highest priorities while you're down here in Havana and while you're still an apprentice. You have to look good and perform well in front of all these trainers and owners down here, so when you're looking for work in the racing season on the different circuits, they will recognize your name or remember your riding ability. I would say that this winter meeting will be the most important time for establishing and laying out your racing career."

Spence was really talking to Tommy now like a father speaks to a son and Tommy recognized that fact and took heed, because Martin Murray died early in Tommy's life and he didn't get the chance to have heart to heart, man to man talks with his father, or for that matter, with any male adults. Of course, there was always the good Father down at St. Patrick's but you couldn't talk boy stuff or man stuff with a priest. They just didn't understand that kind of stuff. Spence knew that Tommy had potential and the right stuff to make a leading jockey but he also knew how most young 17 year-old boys viewed life - live it now and live it to the fullest. He'd seen it a hundred times already with young apprentices, especially here in Cuba where booze and drugs were readily available to anyone and where the young boys can carouse around all night long whoring and mixing with the ever present criminal element. He wanted to make sure he gave Tommy every opportunity he could in order to avoid those temptations and vicious traps.

CHAPTER TWELVE
Keeping Current

Since more and more people from the U.S. were making their way down to enjoy the Cuban racing, wagering, and the alcohol for consumption, which was not available in the states due to prohibition, attendance at Oriental Park was at an all-time record high. It was mostly the rich and well-to-do businessmen and their families who made a vacation out of the trip. There was plenty of nightly entertainment available to top off a day at the track. With this influx of tourists, it was fairly easy to obtain copies of the *New York Times* and the *Daily Racing Form* around the track. This is how Kay Spence kept up with the current events around the world and around the country. It was how Tommy learned every thing he could about other jockeys, trainers, horses, owners, tracks and anything related to horse racing. He kept a racing scrap book of sorts, in which he filed away torn out newspaper articles, wrote down names and places and records and winnings and anything he found to be interesting and important. He even reserved a section to keep newspaper articles about himself. It was empty at this time, but wouldn't be for long. He had no doubt about that.

In the evenings at the stables when Tommy kept up his book, Kay Spence would pass the time reading the paper and keeping up with the world news. He would read aloud as if reading to Tommy, interjecting his own editorial comments along the way. Spence always liked to read about the post-war goings-on. He was always talking about the world war, especially now that it was over. Armistice Day was just two months ago, November, 11, 1918, putting an end to the hostilities along the western front between Germany and the Allies. However, there still remained fighting in other locations around the world and Spence liked to keep abreast of it. The whole idea of war scared Tommy and he didn't like talking about it because it reminded him of all the effects it had on his hometown and neighborhood back home. He had uncles and cousins and friends and neighbors who went over to fight and some of them did not come home and it reminded him of the turmoil and the hatred it caused in his neighborhood in Covington. He was the son of Irish immigrants and lived in the parish of St. Patrick's Catholic Church and just a very few blocks away was the parish of Mutter Gottes Kirche. It was the German neighborhood where the German immigrants all lived. They even preached the sermon in German in their church and a lot of times Tommy and his friends would attend just to experience the difference, and grew able to follow along just as if it were being said in English. Because they were all still Catholics, no matter what language they spoke or where their ancestors were from, the main parts of the Mass were said in Latin and they could still follow along.

The war ruined their neighborhood. The kids who were all playing together one day were fist-fighting each other the next. The parents would talk at supper about families they knew of for years and years, and say mean and derogatory things about them, and forbid the children to play with them. It was a horrible time for Tommy to live through (it was one reason he had wanted to go to Cuba with Mr. Spence the year before but couldn't). Those people didn't do anything to him or his family or their country. Why, they even changed the name of the church to Mother of God and began preaching the sermon in English. A lot of the families changed their names to something less German sounding. They quit publishing their newspaper in the German language. They did everything they could do to distance themselves from the real Nazi enemy. Eventually, things calmed down and everyone's loyalties were clear and needed not to be questioned.

Then there was the horrible influenza pandemic that scoured major cities across the country in 1918, killing hundreds of thousands of people. It was another strain of the same influenza that took Tommy's mother's life the year before. Again, Tommy and his family lost loved ones and neighbors all over the two states of Kentucky and Ohio. Mr. Spence was reading aloud from the paper that predictions had been made that the return of the Asian flu pandemic would strike this coming winter all over again and possibly it would be more potent and deadly than the one the year before. Tommy clutched his medal and thanked God that he was here in Havana and prayed that God protect his family and friends back home from any form of the illness, including death. He crossed himself and buried his face in his racing book, occasionally acknowledging that he had heard what Mr. Spence just read aloud.

"Tommy, I don't have you on any horses entered tomorrow but you've got a couple of mounts scheduled, right?"

"That's right, Boss. Let me check in my book here. I'm riding Rob. L. Owen in the first for the O'Meara brothers and Conscription in the second for Mr. Dortch and Mabel Trask in the sixth for Mr. Baxter."

"I'd like to work with Beauty Shop some and have you exercise him real good and maybe work on his starts. I'm gonna run him on Wednesday in that first claiming race for four-year-olds and up."

"Sure Boss," Tommy responded. "I'll have him out on the track about 4:30, ready to work."

"Good enough, my boy. I'm turnin' in. You want the rest of this paper?"

"Wouldn't mind it a bit, thank you, sir."

Tommy paged through the paper, ignoring most of the headlines, unsuccessfully searching for horse racing related news. As he folded the paper up, his eyes caught the word 'Cuba' on one of the pages. Thinking it was about the winter meeting there in Havana, he began reading "All Cuba in Mourning." The article, dated January 6, 1919, went on to say: *"Cuba's flag will fly at half-staff over all forts, naval vessels, public buildings and military posts on the island until after the funeral of Theodore Roosevelt, in accordance with a decree issued by President Menocal tonight. The decree, in part, follows: 'Ex-President of the United States Roosevelt is dead. His irreparable loss is not a motive of deep mourning for his own country alone, but also, in the highest degree, for Cuba, for whose liberty he fought so bravely on the fields of battle, and whose national independence he, as President, proclaimed and instituted. His name will remain, by virtue of these unforgettable deeds, which are engraved in the hearts of our people, perpetually united to the history of the foundation and consolidation of our national existence'."* (NYT, 1/8/19).

Tommy was taken aback. He had no idea that Teddy Roosevelt had died. Roosevelt had always been a childhood hero for Tommy, not so much because he was a President of the United States, but more for his excellent horsemanship and cowboy image. He read stories about Roosevelt and his Rough Riders as a child, and now it came back to him why Cuba would be mourning his loss. He played a major role in the Spanish-American War, which freed the island of Cuba from the defeated Spanish Empire. As he put the paper down and closed his eyes, he thought to himself,

"If it hadn't been for T.R., I might not even have been here racing right now."

Tommy was up and at it on the track early next morning, exercising Beauty Shop like he said he would.

"You are a beauty, old boy," he kept telling the four-year-old who was gentle and relaxed as he scratched behind his right ear, while he was trying to steady him with his left hand in front of that intimidating starting net. Waiting for that thing to spring up into the air signaling him to run made him really nervous. It always startled him and forced him back, eyes closed.

"It won't hurt you boy. It's your freedom. It's your chance to run. Here, let's get near it and smell it. Now put it in your mouth. See? It's just plain ol' hemp rope. Smells just like hay, don't it? See it won't hurt you, boy. Now, watch it jump up and down. See? No big deal, is it?"

Tommy would lead the horse up to the rope, and Spence would spring it at different times during the ritual, trying to catch Tommy off guard as he was trying to get Beauty Shop to anticipate the release.

"Hey Boss! You tryin' to train me or him?"

"Both of you, my boy," he laughed. "Both of you! Repetitio est mater studiorum."

"What'd you say?"

"What's the matter Latin boy? Can't you understand your own Catholic language?"

"Well, sure I can - if I'm in church! But this ain't church. It's a race track."

"I said 'repetition is the mother of study'. You know, 'practice makes perfect'." Spence replied.

"Did ya hear that, Beauty? He wants us to do it some more. C'mon!"

After the morning chores and workouts, Tommy donned his wool clothes and rubber suit and jogged around the track in the bright, warm Cuban sun. It was a clear day and already 75 degrees. It didn't take long to work up a drenching sweat under that outfit. After his vigorous workout, a plunge into the infield lake with a cake of lye soap felt pretty good and relaxing. He was ready to race.

At 2:39 p.m., they went to post. Tommy was in position number three in a field of 11 on the O'Meara Brothers four-year-old Rob. L. Owen, carrying 103 pounds. He wound up fifth at the start and was outpaced by the leaders, but he came up fast and driving hard in the stretch to overcome two contenders to finish a very fast third.

"Good ride, my boy," Tommy heard from behind him. "That's a lot of horse to handle, I'd say."

"Oh, yes sir, he sure is but he's a player. He likes to run and likes to chase, and he likes openings that pop up. I believe that if we'd had another pole to go, he'd a won it. First time ever I rode him. Hope it ain't the last," Tommy confided to the stranger.

"Name's Dortch. I was watching you in particular in that last race because I had my man to hire you to ride my entry in the next race, Conscription's his name."

"Oh yes sir, Mr. Dortch. I was just gettin' ready to head over to your stables and dress for the second race in your colors."

"Let's walk over together," replied the commonly dressed rotund man chewing on what appeared to be last night's cigar stub.

Dortch explained to Tommy that his horse, too, was a player; a three-year-old in a four or five-year-old's body was how he put it to Tommy.

"I take it you mean he's not as nervous and excitable as other three-year-olds, but more reserved and focused," Tommy offered.

"Well, yeah, that, and he's kinda set in his ways. He likes the race to go his way and he gets discouraged, even insulted, when another horse gets in his way or cuts him off. Every monkey I've put up on his back seems to want to hold him back at first to see what the field is doin' and that's okay, until he gets trapped. Then he becomes panicky and loses his focus. This is when the rider needs to re-direct his efforts. It's like he pouts or gets insulted or something when he gets in a trap. This is the point when he needs to be ridden and encouraged but he won't respond to the stick, makes him cower even more."

"So how do I get him to respond, Mr. Dortch?"

"Come over here a minute, boy, and I'll tell ya. He likes to be sung to, in his ear, and he likes to be sung Camptown Races!"

"You mean that 'do-dah, do-dah' song?" Tommy inquired.

"That's the one, my boy, that old Stephen Foster song. You see, Conscription had the same old black groom tend to him most all of his life. His name was Winston and he adored this horse. He sang to him every day of his life them old Negro folk songs and such. Conscription's favorite was De Camptown Races. It made him spark! His eyes would come full open and sparkle and he'd snort an' prance and parade around like a peacock wooing a hen. When Winston told the trainer and breezer about how the horse responded to the song, they tried singing it to him as he worked out. They absolutely could not rein him in. He ran like a lightning bolt shooting across the universe. Do you know the song?"

"Why, sure I do," responded Tommy with genuine enthusiasm. "I know a lot of Stephen Foster's songs. He used to live in Cincinnati, across the Ohio River from Covington, Kentucky, where I was born and raised. Sure, I know that song!"

"Well, when you need the opportunity to inspire the ol' boy, try singing in his ear. See if you get the response you are looking for."

"I'll surely do it, Mr. Dortch. I love singing!"

They went to post at 2:55 p.m. and one minute later a good start followed. Tommy was in the first post position, but was out jumped by Weymouth Girl at the start and quickly found himself in third place all the way to the half pole. Then, Conscription seemed to perk up a bit as the challenging Little Mistress decided to make the bid for third.

"What the hell is your bug-monkey doing out there Dortch?" asked the owner's companion there at the rail, a local Oriental Park tout posing as a reporter for some small town newspaper sports page. "What's he doing a climbin' up that animal's neck for?"

"Dammit, man! He ain't climbin' up his neck! He's singing to him, in his ear, jus' like I told him to. Scrip likes to be sung to. Makes him more competitive. Look how he's challenging that Linkstrap right now in the stretch. Look at him, would ya? He's going for place money. Go Scrip! Pour it on, honey! You can do it!"

"Looks like that monkey is singing flat now, Dortch. Look how them two just crowded your horse back and shook him off in that stretch drive. Tough break, my friend. Fourth place and a third rate singer!" chuckled the tout as he penciled in the results on his race program. "Maybe that boy should learn how to sing "I'm Always Chasing Rainbows". Ha! Ha!"

"Just go on with you boy. You don't know nothin' about makin' horses run!" Dortch shouted back as he turned to make his way back to his stable.

"Did you see that, sir? Did you see how them two crowded me back at the end of our stretch drive? My horse was driving and still gainin' when I felt somebody's bat across my left thigh. Conscription musta felt it too, 'cause he had a slight hesitation and couldn't get it back. It was just so slick and quick, the stewards couldn't have even noticed it."

Dortch knew what Tommy was talking about and he felt Tommy's frustrations.

"It's just part of the game, son. No, it ain't fair, and it ain't sportsman-like, but it's there. It's part of it. Thank God it ain't like it used to be years ago. Why, you couldn't run a fair race anywhere in the U.S. fifteen or twenty years ago. The high-rollin' gamblers saw to that. There wasn't an honest track official, jockey, owner, trainer, groom, bookie, tout or any person had anything to do with racing to be found hardly anywhere. The horses were drugged, the races were fixed, the officials were bribed, the general public was cheated, and the whole damned horse industry was about ruined. All the goody-goody reformers got laws against betting the horses and gambling of any kind. Then they concentrated on booze and beer and got them made illegal and the only thing all this done was to make crime worse and the thugs richer and more powerful. It damn near put an end to the breeding and continuation of the Thoroughbred lines all together."

Tommy was all ears as Dortch continued on his soap-box. He could tell that the old timer was indeed passionate about honest, above-the-board horseracing and the proper propagation of the sport and the bloodlines.

"I'll tell ya, boy. If it wasn't for such fine men as Aug Belmont, and Colonel Ross, or Mr. Matt Winn and the rest of that bunch, why horseracing in this country would be nothin' more than ya see at them camel circuits and county fairs out West now-a-days. Why we'd all be runnin' quarter horses and saddle breds who couldn't even beat a camel or a big dog. Thanks to these men who saw the real need for outstanding horse flesh with strength, endurance, stamina, spirit, spunk and intelligence for use in cavalry units in our military, we still have the pure bred Thoroughbred lines that we almost lost forever because of those crooked, greedy, money hungry low-lifes. Just look at the difference our horses have made to help us win in this stupid World War that we just went through. It's the difference between winnin' and losin', plain as that!"

"You mean that Mr. Belmont breeds horses just so our soldiers have the very best mounts in the war?"

"Yes, son. That's precisely what I mean. Mr. Belmont is a true patriot of our country. Why he even sold all of his racing stable so he could enlist in the Army and serve over in France with the cavalry there. Sold some of the greatest Thoroughbred stock in the world so's he could join up and fight for his country. Now that's a hero in my book!"

"Wow!" Tommy marveled. "I wonder if any jockeys ran out and joined the Army, too. I'll bet they could use a bunch of them for all those horses!"

Dortch just laughed, "Son, they don't want no ninety-eight pound boy with a little whip to ride them horses. They want them big college football-lookin' brutes who can carry a couple of rifles and bayonets while they're riding at full speed."

"Well, someday, you'll see! I'll join the Army and defend my country too, just like Mr. Belmont."

"I'm glad to hear that, my boy, glad to hear that!"

CHAPTER THIRTEEN
Black Jockeys Were Always the Best

Tommy was tending to his tackle and brushing down Scrip, still humming his do-dah, do-dah song, but he was also wearing a really blank stare which gave away the fact that he was daydreaming. Suddenly, as if no time at all had passed, he said, "Mr. Dortch, who was the very best jockey you ever saw or knew?"

"Oh boy, son! Now that's a toughie. I'll ponder that one just a bit, but I'll tell ya right now, the answer ain't gonna be no white boy!"

"What?" questioned Tommy, obviously startled by Dortch's response.

"Yes, that's right son. It sure ain't gonna be no white boy!"

"Then, who sir? A Cuban? A Canadian? A Frenchie?"

"Now, boy, what'd I say? I said it ain't no white boy and last time I looked, all them you named is white, ain't they?"

"You mean a Negro was the best jockey you ever saw? But there ain't even any colored jockeys around, least as far as I know."

"That's right Tommy. There ain't none around these parts but there sure used to be and they was the best riders you could ever want. They stuck to them horses like they just growed out of their withers somewhere, and they bounced and flew in the wind like they was a piece of the mane. They made the horse respond and perform like they was its brain but to answer your question, I've got it down to two boys. It's between Isaac Murphy and Jimmy Winkfield. Knew 'em both and loved to watch 'em ride. They was the best, no question!"

"Tell me about them. What was so good about them?"

"Well, I'd love to tell you about them, but don't you have another race to get ready for now?"

"Nope. I don't have another ride until the sixth, the last race."

"Well, in that case, flop down on that trunk and I'll tell you a thing er two about these fellas."

"Isaac Murphy is probably the winningest jockey ever. Out of over 1,400 hundred starts in his career, he won over 600 races. The handicappers say that that amounts to winning 44% of his races, which is something they figure will never be able to be equaled now-a-days, considering how many horses and jockeys and races there are. He was born down near Frankfort, Kentucky right about when the Civil War was starting and his daddy was actually in the war and died in a northern prisoner-of-war camp. After the war, the boy lived with his grandfather in Lexington and was around horses a lot and became a good rider. He wasn't but fourteen years-old when he rode his first race. He wound up being the first jockey to win the Derby and the Oaks and the Clark all in the same year. He won the Latonia Derby from up where you come, five different times."

"Wow," chimed in Tommy. "That's what I want to do. I want to win the Latonia Derby. I want everybody I know to watch me win the Latonia Derby and I want Virginia waiting for me in the Winner's Circle. She's my girl!"

Mr. Dorch continued, "Isaac Murphy rode in the Kentucky Derby 11 different times and he won it three times, the first and only person to ever do that. I watched him race many times back in '94 and '95. He died of pneumonia in 1896 when he was only thirty-five years-old. It was a great loss to horseracing when Murphy died."

"Do you think he was Irish, Mr Dortch?"

"Why no, Tommy. What makes you think he was Irish?"

"Well, I know a bunch of Murphy's and they're all Irish. That's a real Irish name!"

"Yes it is," replied Dortch. "But Isaac was black and I don't think his ancestors were from Ireland. They were probably the slaves of a family named Murphy somewhere down the line and just eventually wound up with that sir name. It is quite common that that happens."

He continued, "Now Jimmy Winkfield was also another excellent black jockey, but he didn't have the same opportunities open to him as Isaac had. Wink was born a lot later than Murphy, probably twenty years later. He too was born in Kentucky, down around Lexington. His father had a tenant farm and Jimmy worked hard on the farm from a very early age. There were a lot of Thoroughbred horses bred and raised around Jimmy's farm and he had the opportunity to find extra work at these farms and learned how to handle and ride these magnificent creatures. His whole life would be devoted to Thoroughbreds and he loved nothing more than horses. When Wink entered his very first race at the age of sixteen, it was close to the turn of the century and racial prejudice was already making life ugly for black people, especially black people who were better at their professions than their white counterparts. Wink was constantly being harassed on and off the track. He would be intentionally interfered with in races, run into the outside rail, run through the inside rail, often sustaining injuries to himself or to his horse or both. He would still get plenty of mounts because he was the best jockey around, but his competition would sabotage his efforts. He persevered and in 1901 at the age of nineteen, he won his first Kentucky Derby. Then, in 1902, he proceeded to win his second Kentucky Derby. He was just a nose short from winning his third consecutive Kentucky Derby win in 1903."

"Racial issues were infecting the track and Jimmy was getting fewer and fewer mounts each race meeting. The white horse owners and trainers were beginning to employ white jockeys exclusively, not so much for their talents and natural abilities, but because there was such racial tension and violence directed toward the black people in general so it also affected the black jockeys. It came from everywhere, even the Clan. At most of the southern tracks, they were all run out. Blacks were beginning to pack up and move to northern states. Wink, who did a lot of racing at Latonia in the early years, eventually couldn't even get a ride there so he picked up rides at the lesser ranked tracks around. He circuited all the leaky roof tracks, making pennies instead of the dollars he could be making if he was white. Finally, despite the love he had for American horseracing, he decided to try racing in Europe and he became very rich and very famous and above all, very respected. He was close to being treated the same as royalty."

Dortch continued, "Why the first thing he done in Europe was to become the winner of the All-Russian Derby and the Czar's Prize, followed by many more famous stakes races throughout Europe. He truly became royalty. He had him a Russian heiress for a wife and money and land and a large estate and he rode all the best horses of the Russian king in all the prestigious Russian races. He was a very famous person. He won the Russian riding championship three times in a row. Then, just two years ago, the Russian Revolution changed all that for the poor lad. It was driving all the aristocratic Russian community, who were the major horse people, out of Moscow and south to Odessa on the Black Sea. He lost every thing - his land, his money, his stables and his horses."

"Then just last year, as that same revolutionary army was making its way into Odessa, burning everything in its path, including racetracks and stables, Jimmy banded together with other jockeys, trainers, owners and horse people to save over two hundred Thoroughbreds by driving them over a thousand miles over treacherous terrain and freezing conditions across the Transylvanian Alps into Poland and safety. It was a deadly ordeal. They lost many men and horses to the cause. Wink survived by eating the very horseflesh he was trying to save. He eventually made it safely into Poland with a considerable number of the Thoroughbreds, just assuring the propagation of the blood lines and the sport. From Poland, he eventually made his way to Paris, France, where he is attempting to resurrect his innate talents and to re-establish his legendary abilities in riding and breeding and I have no doubt that he will do it. This stupid racial strife in our country has cost us one of the all time finest jockeys in our history. When is this country going to let that war between our states go? If a man can handle a race horse, then let him ride. It don't make no difference what color his skin is."

Tommy laughed to himself. "Good thing horses don't think that-a-way, or we'd have to have stakes and claimin' races for bays, and chestnuts, and grays, and reds just like we do for two-year-olds, and three-year-olds, and fours and over. That would be a mess, Mr. Dortch, wouldn't it?"

"You ain't wrong, my boy. You ain't wrong at all."

After several minutes of deep contemplation, Tommy asked, "Mr. Dortch, could it be that God sees racing as a sin and an evil and is trying to wipe it out?"

"Now what in heaven's name makes you think that, my boy? Do you really think that God thinks racing is one of the cardinal or venial sins or something?"

"Well," Tommy pondered, "Look at everything that is going on all of a sudden. There's the world war that just been fought, killing millions of people all over the world; then there's those two years of the influenza epidemic that has killed millions of people all over the world; then there's the prohibitionists and the antigambling people; and then there's crime and cheating in horseracing; and then all this hatred and killing of black people and running them out; and hopping horses and other cruel things being done to them just to fix a race. Seems like God is saying to clean up our act or he'll just get rid of the whole human race and start over."

"No, no, no. Not at all, my boy. To the contrary! God has made us a special gift of Thoroughbreds and Thoroughbred racing. He wouldn't punish us and take them away. He loves us. He wants us to be happy. He wants us to race these incredible animals that he has blessed us with. He isn't at all trying to punish us with all these things you said."

"Then why is all this bad stuff going on at the same time?" Tommy asked.

"I just don't know," answered Dortch. "But I do know that God brought us all to Havana so we could improve our training and riding and performance over the winter months so we can go back to the U.S. of A. this spring and put on the very best season of horseracing ever seen in the history of man and horse. Now you better get back to your chores and start getting ready for your next race. They're already at the post for the fifth."

Tommy finished up with Conscription, and hightailed it to the jockey house just in time to meet with Mr. Baxter, the owner of his next mount, Mabel Trask. He dressed into Baxter's colors and walked with him and his trainer to the saddling area, listening with his undivided attention to everything the owner was saying about his horse. The race was a claiming race for four-year-olds and over and Mabel Trask was a veteran at these kinds of competitions. However, when Tommy made it to the paddock with her, the trainer would give him a different set of instructions. The track was slow today, and Tommy was in the number eight post position, with the favorite in the fifth.

"Son, with a slow track as it is, I want you to get a fast jump and get to the inside rail right off the rope and let her drive all the way. She don't like the bat. Just give her head if she gets the jump."

Then the trainer helped Tommy to get a leg up and on they went to the post parade. They were only at the post for one minute and the start was good and slow. Tommy immediately jumped out in first and was heading for the inside rail when Dimitri, the favorite, started challenging and overtook first place at the half pole. Dimitri set a fast pace for the going and held on resolutely in the final drive. Mabel Trask was in close pursuit all the way and was gaining at the end, but there wasn't enough track left for her to win. When Tommy hit the scales to weigh in, he was two pounds over.

"Ate a lot o' mud that go-round, did ya, boy?" laughed the steward as he wrote on his official report. "Second place jockey picked up two pounds of mud. Leave your tackle right here and go clean that stuff off your silks and face and weigh in again, so we can make this thing official."

Tommy swallowed his disappointment and appreciated the humor of the moment. He truly looked like a tar baby and that wasn't what he had envisioned at the start of the race because he planned on being the mud slinger, not the hapless recipient.

CHAPTER FOURTEEN
The Golden Age of Racing

That night, sitting on his cot in the stall next to the tack room, Tommy was cutting out newspaper stories and reports about horse racing from all the remnants of papers and magazines found lying around the club house and grandstand from the past day of competition. He was pasting them in his scrap book after reading each one. This way, he stayed current on what was happening around the country in anticipation of the upcoming 1919 meetings all around the U.S.

Little did he realize that he would be beginning his professional racing career in probably one of the most significant years ever in the history of American racing. If *The Golden Years of Racing* (a variable mix and multitude of years and eras have been called this, depending on the time frame any particular author is writing about) needs to have a starting point, then let it be 1919. Maybe resurgence or rededication or restructuring would describe the times better or maybe renaissance describes it better. Whatever its most accurate descriptive moniker, 1919 was a banner year. Horse racing survived the antigambling demons thanks to the ingenuity and dedication of Matt Winn, who among many other significant accomplishments in horseracing, resurrected the pari-mutuel form of betting on horses as a totally legal dance around the wildfire storm that was closing tracks in every state of the Union. Bookmaking and bookies at the tracks brought shame, dishonesty, and crime to one of the oldest competitive sports associated with our relatively young country. We may have rebelled against our mother country and her form of government and religious institutions and fought with our lives for our freedom from the anarchy and despotism of kings, but we dearly clung on to the sport of these same kings. To legitimize our passion for the age-old past-time, we merely changed the direction in which they ran. Racing counter-clockwise showed our complete disregard for the British bastards, but preserved a very human instinct - the need for competitive speed, strength, and stamina to prove that you or yours is the very best.

Before the United States got tangled up in this current World War in 1918, the racing community was already in the process of recovering from a major war against itself which began seven or eight years prior. The war against horse racing essentially put an end to horse racing in New York. It was also crippling the industry in other eastern states. The only states that had legalized gambling were Kentucky and Maryland. The reformers finally got their way and the death knell was tolling for American horseracing, but the public began to fight back and gain some ground just as the fighting in Europe began to escalate around

1916. By the time the U.S. entered the war in 1917, the total days of racing had been reduced to a paltry all time low, but racing enthusiasts and those stalwarts of the industry persevered and racing slowly regained it position of prominence in the eyes of the public.

Racing also was poised to survive the Prohibition movement and laws. The 18th Amendment, which was first proposed in 1917, was ratified on January 16, 1919, and took effect beginning January 16, 1920. The religious zealots and do-gooders associated gambling to liquor to crime to impurity to hell-fire and damnation to horseracing so by lobbying the very politicians who conveniently overlooked these social vices to pass laws against these same vices, the public outcry almost succeeded in the extirpation of probably the most popular and prestigious American sport and industry in our history. However, bigotry begat bootlegging, which begat bookmaking, which begat bribery, which begat blackmail, which begat banishment, which begat betterment, which begat believability and bounty.

The First World War just ended. A peace treaty was signed and made it official. The country rejoiced and celebrated. It also mourned. For the estimated number of lives lost in fighting at over nine million persons and an additional six million civilian casualties, this mother of all war - a *world war* - was hard to fathom. The entire world involved in a war, to the death. Those poor young men who gave their very lives for our continued freedom. *"Please, God; please never allow another war like this to ever occur again."* That was the prayer on everyone's lips.

But wait! Just think of all the innocent people, men and women, young and old who tragically lost their lives this past year to that horrible pandemic, the Asian flu. More Americans died from that than were killed in the war. How could that be? Pray God that it will not return this winter.

All American families had definitely been touched and negatively impacted in one way or another over the past couple years, either by illness, loss of life, loss of work, financial failure, crime, alcoholism, gambling, hunger, depression, or other maladies of the decade. They sought diversion from their worries and woes. There were a number of choices available. There was the entertainment offered by theater, musical concerts, dances, socials. There was family entertainment in the form of parlor games, sing-a-longs, picnics and hikes in the out-of-doors of the natural environment. The new popularity and availability of the automobile offered families expanded choices of adventure and travel.

Such activities and diversions served to soothe the melancholies of the second decade of the new century but nothing seemed to take off in the way the *Golden Age of Racing* did. It was just the potion for what ailed a listless and emotionally defeated population. The continued breeding of Thoroughbred horses for the use of American Cavalry in all theaters of the war effort provided a plethora of exceptional animals with strength, determination, energy and heart, all biting at the bit to compete and show their stuff and the track patrons were also there in numbers to support the rebirth of professional American Thoroughbred horse racing at its finest hour. Men such as August Belmont, Matt Winn, and all the other stalwart owners, track superintendants, officials of the several Jockey Clubs in existence, all made sure that American racing would aspire to the highest level of professionalism, integrity, and quality of honesty and fairness imaginable. Strict rules and regulations were created and adopted by various professional Jockey Club organizations across the U.S.

Tommy Murray didn't realize it at the time, but he was right there when the real golden era of racing popped its fragile chute through the ground and took nourishment through its established roots and grew strong and straight and true. Into the late 1920s, it continued to flourish and support itself. Its past experience would prepare it for the hard times of the future 1929 financial failure and stock market crisis and once again it would survive hard times and come out of it even stronger, but Tommy had no way of knowing what the future had in store.

"Look at this Boss," Tommy shouted from his cot as he was cutting clippings out of an old edition of *The New York Times* newspaper that he found in the stands last week.

"Theodore Roosevelt has died. He died at his home in Oyster Bay, New York. It says that his last words were 'put out the lights'. What'd you suppose he meant by that, boss?"

"He meant that its getting late and you should turn in because you're riding in the first race tomorrow. That's what he meant. Good night, son."

Oriental Race Track, Havana, Cuba

CHAPTER FIFTEEN
The Rough Riders

The next morning after exercising the horses, Tommy was examining the right front leg of Beauty Shop in his stall when Kay Spence walked in. "What's ailing him, boy?"

"Don't know boss. He seemed a little unsure of himself after we finished the run and I thought he was favoring his right front. I thought maybe he struck himself when we were running, but I don't feel or see nothin'. I feared he might have bowed a tendon or something."

"I don't feel nothin' either boy. He ain't tender but I might be feeling a little heat. Why don't you whack off a chunk of ice out'n our ice box and put it in a pail of water and keep cold wet rags around that lower leg. Keep him quiet and don't feed him none. I'll re-check him in a couple hours. He's a player. He'll let us know if he can run or not. Ol' Lunsford won many a race with that ol' boy, I'll tell you."

"Ah, I miss Harry, Boss" sighed Tommy. You know, he's a cousin to my gal Ginny back home. That's how I met him and how I started hanging round Latonia, when he was apprenticing with you."

"I am well aware of that, son. You and Harry both have made certain that I shall never forget your relationship."

"When is he supposed to get back from his visit up to Covington?"

Spence explained to Tommy that Harry will return later in the meeting, when trainers and owners begin culling out their poorest performers, both the equine and the human variety.

After the prescribed treatment time, Spence checked Beauty Shop's leg for swelling or heat for any evidence of a bowed tendon. "Don't feel anything out the ordinary. He ain't tender and his ears are perked and he's excited in the eyes. I'd say he's ready to run. How about you, boy?"

"Yes sir, Boss! Looks like he does any other time he's anxious to run. We're ready to win!"

"Tommy, at the start, just let him decide how he wants to run. There's going to be quite a big crowd at the first turn fightin' for the rail. Don't get him in to a big pile where he could get hurt if he ain't up to it. If he prefers the outside, then let him have it. It'll be less stress on that tendon."

"Got it, Boss! I'll be singing in his ear as we pass the field on the outside."

The 11 horses went to post at 2:30 p.m. and in less than a minute the barrier sprang up and the start was good. Tommy was the only apprentice jockey in the race. Just as Spence predicted, there was a mad dash for the inside rail position right at the first turn. Bright Sand, one of the favorites, started in the eleventh position and quickly set the pace of the race as the first front runner, crossing over to the inside almost immediately. Beauty Shop in the ninth post position had a good jump and a good start but quickly was cut off by the leader as he made his bid for the inside rail. This caused Beauty Shop to hesitate ever so slightly, but not enough to interrupt his stride. Tommy felt the irregularity and feared the worse, the tendon bowing, and he didn't ask him for anything. As the pack cleared, there was a lot of bumping and crowding going on at the inside. Beauty Shop continued his run on the outside, staying ahead of number 10 and 11 for the rest of the race. He was running well with no hint of favoring the right front, which eased Tommy's mind considerably.

"Well, boy," he said as they crossed the line. "We started ninth and we finished ninth. We should'a just stayed back at the barn and read a book."

Back at the paddock, Spence's mind also seemed at ease after Tommy told him how he ran.

"I didn't push him at all, boss. He ran like he wanted."

"Well, he'll never make horse of the year with that kind of race strategy. He might as well have been out pickin' daisies but I'm glad there's no tendon issues."

"Tommy, did those other monkeys bump you at all? It appeared to me from back at the rail that a lot of contact was taking place up in that first pile. I don't like to see that and neither do the stewards and believe me, they're looking out for them kinds of shenanigans this year. The Jockey Club ain't gonna tolerate any king of interference between the monkeys or the horses this year and they'll sit you down if they take a notion to. The organizations want clean, professional racing from here on out, so's as to keep our reputation good and honorable. None of that Jungle Circuit crap anymore. Believe me, there'll be plenty of good horses and trainers and riders around this season, now that the war's over and the boys are coming home. The big guys know it and they sent the word out that they expect the strictest discipline and professional behavior. You tell them other monkeys that and you tell the judges and me if you get fouled or interfered with. They can't see every move from every horse and every jockey at every minute from where they sit in the judges' stand. You know, that's just exactly what got Patrick O'Neill killed last May up at Pimlico, and I don't want to see anybody else get killed or hurt this season so tell them monkeys fair warning; Kay Spence will be watching for foul play and he will take the culprit to task."

Tommy did get bumped at the start and he felt it was intentional but after hearing Spence's tirade just now, he sure wasn't going to say anything. Walking from the paddock area, Tommy's deep contemplation was interrupted by a voice shouting, "Murray! Over here! We need to talk to you."

It came from the judges' stand.

"Yes sir, be right there." For some reason, his adrenalin was pumping into his blood stream faster than it had ever done during any race he could remember. He could hear every beat of his heart swishing loudly in each ear and the beats were getting faster and louder as time went on.

"Murray, we want to know if you got interfered with by anyone in that race, and if so, who it was and we want to know if you saw any other kind of illegal contact taking place between the jockeys and the horses. We have been hearing reports of some jockeys trying to intimidate other jockeys, especially you apprentices. We ain't gonna have none of that down here this year. Trying to throw a race or intimidate another jockey to hold back or lose ain't gonna be tolerated. You were the only bug in that race, and we want to know if you were threatened or interfered with."

There was no way Tommy was going to squeal but he sure was going to have a talk with Nolan as soon as these judges had their say with him.

"No sir. I don't recall any interference. I mean my horse hesitated just a second when we got cut off, but we weren't bumped or hit or nothing like that, not as I can recall."

"Well, Murray, let me recall for you. Nolan, on Bright Sand, bumped your horse just before the first turn, as he was seeking the inside rail. That's called interference and we ain't having it here this year, no way, and they ain't having it anywhere in the major tracks and meetings neither. Now we already talked to Nolan. Once more and he's sat down the rest of this meeting. Anymore after that, and he's banned for life and that goes for each and every one of you monkeys. Now we expect that you and Nolan get out and spread that word around a few times to your other cronies and if it keeps happening, we just might forego the warning the first time and commence to setting the culprit down then and there. The same goes for hopping horses, or interfering in any way with a horse or the tack or other equipment. Anything done to fix a race or change the outcome of a race will be dealt with severely, probably for life! Any questions?"

"No sir. I understand completely and I ain't never done anything to any horse or person to fix a race ever in my life. I swear it on this Saint Patty medal around my neck."

"That's fine, son. That's what we want to hear. Now run along and be sure to spread the word around."

As Tommy was taking the steps to the judges' stand down two at a time, he thought to himself, *"If something out there happens and it's an accident or even a stupid mistake, then I can accept that but if it's something done on purpose to hurt me or my horse just for the purpose of cheating, then I'm taking care of it right then and there. To hell with running to the judges and squealing, just so they can give out another warning. I ain't interested in being called a tattle-tale snitch. I'll just fix it right then and there, and if the judges missed it the first time, they sure won't miss it the second time."*

They were already at the post for the second race when Tommy left the judges' booth. He knew that Nolan had another mount in this race, so he decided to watch very closely this time. The start was good and Nolan drew The Blue Duke away into a long lead after rounding the far turn and hung on gamely in the final drive. Dainty Lady finished second driving, but tired after making a threatening challenge in the home-stretch. Everything appeared to Tommy to be above board with nothing out of the ordinary. Roundel got crowded into the rail at the half mile post and pulled up, but he was in ninth place in the field of nine, far behind the contenders. It looked like a normal horse race, nothing more and nothing less. Tommy had cooled down now and felt better. He just dismissed the earlier incident as accidental happenstance and not to malicious premeditated cheating but he was going to make a conscious effort to keep his eyes and ears open none-the-less and his observations would wind up duly recorded in his scrap book.

The third race on the card for the day was a claiming race for three-year-olds and up. Tommy landed a mount on Roscoe Goose and to look at the boy's face and glow of excitement, one would think he was riding Exterminator in the previous year's Kentucky Derby. His excitement wasn't because of this particular horse. As a matter of fact, he had never even heard of the horse until two days ago when he was approached by the trainer to ride him. He was excited because the horse was the namesake of one of Tommy's earliest heroes, Roscoe Goose, the jockey, who was actually born and raised in Louisville, and spent a lot of time at Latonia where Tommy got to know him well. Roscoe Goose won the 1913 Kentucky Derby on a 91-to-1 long shot named Donerail, and it was truly his ability as a number one jockey that won the race. Tommy was only 11 years-old at the time, but he remembered his uncles and older brothers talking about the race and how a two-dollar bet won close to $200.00 (actually $184.90 at the local bookmakers). Roscoe Goose was the talk of Covington and Latonia for several years to come after that famous Kentucky Derby long shot ride.

Tommy left the paddock for the post parade with a grin of pride and satisfaction on his face. He was going to honor one of the great all time jockeys in the history of Thoroughbred racing by giving him the best run for the money he could muster in this insignificant claiming race for three-year-olds and up. Chances were, not a handful of people in the grandstands that day even ever heard of Roscoe Goose but nobody could have convinced Tommy of that fact. He was chosen especially for this mission of honor today by Pegasus himself. Why? He didn't have a clue. He just knew that he was chosen and that he wasn't going to let anybody down.

Tommy drew the third post position in the field of 10 claimers. They were at the post less than one full minute and the start was good. Tommy jumped the barrier as the second horse out and quickly set the pace and took the lead at the eighth pole and through the half into the stretch. He was challenged by Ed Garrison down through the stretch running a close second behind Roscoe Goose. Just before the finish, Roscoe Goose had run out badly. Ed Garrison had to be ridden out to maintain the final advantage over the second and third place finishers who were driving hard at the end and both of whom had been caught up in pockets at different times during the race. There was a lot of horse to horse contact in this race at the outset, which quickly changed into jockey to horse contact and jockey to jockey contact at the end. It was a very aggressively run race. Every jockey carried a stick and most of the horses were wearing blinkers. It was suggested that the officials were wearing blinkers as well, as no jockey was called in and spoken to and nobody was set down.

Even though Tommy had his heart set on winning in the name of one of his heroes, it turned out that maybe this hero instead had been giving Tommy an invaluable lesson in aggressive horse riding and the proper use of his bat, both on his own mount and his opponent's mount, and then, if necessary, on his opponent.

"Hurry up, Murray! You gotta dress for this next event. Quit lollygagging."

"I'm not lollygagging," Mr. Spence. "I'm just real sore in my left leg and shoulder."

"Well, sure you are! You let them damned fools Dominick and Doyle beat the shit out of you with their whips. What'd you expect to feel like? Why didn't you call a foul? They were flailing you!"

"I ain't callin' no foul, Boss. If a foul needs callin', then the officials should call it. If they don't see nothin', then nothin' happened and that's fine with me. I been here a month or better now, and I'm learning that there's other factors involved in race ridin' that don't have nothin' to do with the strength and speed and stamina of the horse, or the talent and skill of the jockey. There's other things that weigh heavy in the outcome of a match, and most times it ain't even visible to the stewards and officials, much less the spectators and players."

"Say no more, Tommy. You just graduated from elementary horse race school, right before my very eyes and I didn't even realize you were that far along! Welcome to the real world of Thoroughbred competition."

CHAPTER SIXTEEN
The Birds and the Bees

Tommy readied himself for the next race on the day's schedule, a cheap claiming race for four-year-olds and up. He was riding Sasenta for Kay Spence and finished seventh out of a field of eight. Tommy was over weight by two pounds as Sasenta was assigned the lowest weight of 97 pounds. At 99 pounds, at least Tommy was keeping competitive.

The fifth race of the day was the Key West Handicap. Tommy was aboard Cleek for Mr. M. Lowenstein, who had two entries from his stable in the seven horse handicap. Cleek was assigned 101 pounds, which was exactly what Tommy weighed out. It took three full minutes to line them all up, but they broke into a good start. Cleek, in the seventh post position, broke in fifth place and set a fast pace from the start and drew away into a long lead on the backstretch. As Sasin gained steadily from a slow beginning and finished fast and just barely failed to get up, taking the second place money as Cleek was tiring and just lasted long enough to win. The other Lowenstein entry, Barney Shannon, despite being four pounds overweight, ran well enough to take the place money and outstayed the other contestants easily.

Tommy had a mount in the sixth race also, for owner T. Cheek. Tiger Jim drew the eighth post position in the field of eight. As Tommy loaded and got into position, the barrier sprung and Tiger Jim wheeled and was left at the post. The rest of the field ran themselves a race as Tiger Jim stood there dumbfounded and just watched.

That night back in the tack room, Kay Spence pulled the door shut and seriously commenced with Tommy Murray's secondary education in the subject of American Thoroughbred racing. He realized that Tommy was beginning to get street-wise and peer-educated, so to speak so now it was time to teach him to separate the chaff from the wheat and to distinguish the shit from the Shinola.

"Son, it's time for you to learn about the birds and the bees," said Spence as he broke the pea-soup silence in the inner sanctum of Spence Stables, Inc.

"Mr. Spence, I already had that talk years ago from the priest at St. Patrick's and he swore me to never tell my mama, or anyone else for that matter. He already warned me about the nasty ship wenches who take your money and leave you runny and causes pain where you should feel pleasure. Besides, Ginny's my girl back home and she's the only one I care to indulge," confided the young athlete.

"I ain't even talkin' about those birds and bees, dammit!" screamed Spence. "I'm talking about the birds and bees of professional jockeying. You're far enough along in this profession to have an idea of which path you're gonna be following. Are you gonna be one of the birds or one of the bees?"

"I don't know what you mean by that, Boss. What's a bird, and what is a bee? I can tell right now that it ain't what it usually is."

"Tommy, in the profession and sport of Thoroughbred horse racing, there are the good guys and the bad guys and a lot of times it gets confusing for a fella to tell the difference between the two. Horseracing has too many variables in its make-up to be called just a game of chance. It ain't like flippin' a coin or rollin' the dice. The different variables are what make it thrilling and exciting because the outcome ain't always predictable. There are always people who think they know something about a horse or a trainer or jockey or how a horse is feeling or if he's rested, or if he's a gamer, or nervous, or lame, or if the track is too muddy, or the distance too short or too long, or if he's out of so-and-so line or family, or a thousand different things. That's what makes people want to bet their money on the outcome of the race, especially if they think they know more than the other guy so they bet their money, hoping to make more money off of it, and this makes the horse race much more exciting for the fan because now he actually has a stake in the race, the same as you do, or I do, or the breeder does and on and on. This is what keeps horse racing going and keeps every one of us employed, right down to the farmer that grows the hay or the boy who mucks the stalls."

Spence continued, "Now, Tommy, because all this money is involved, there's people out there who want to control how the races will turn out, and they'll do anything to get it their way. They might pay off a jockey to hold back his horse so another one with better odds will win and they will make a lot more money, and the jockey will get paid a lot more money behind the scenes than he could have made winning the race or they might get to a trainer, or the jockey, or a groom or valet to dope the horse or sponge him, or over feed and water him before the race. Maybe they get to a track official to declare a foul and disqualify a winner, or set down a jockey who wins consistently on the odds-on favorite before a big stakes race."

He added, "With all these possible variables being part of the equation, there are countless ways to cheat and throw a race and for years and years, this was the case and it almost ruined horseracing. Nowadays, the track officials and stewards and the Jockey Club are all keeping a closer eye on what is going on out there on the track and behind the scenes. There are a lot more rules, regulations, and laws governing all aspects of racing and the sport is starting to gain back its respectability again now. It's been a long, hard climb up a very rocky and steep course. I'm tellin' you this because horse racing can make a fella a living again and support a family. It can even make the good race riders rich and famous but you got to respect the business and the rules. You gotta treat everybody right, and play straight and you got to keep away from the track vermin - the touts, and the crooks, and the bookies and bootleggers. It ain't hard to tempt a kid like you with the promise of money or popularity or a roll in the hay with some common backstretch whore and trick you into pullin' a horse, or interfering with another rider, or hop a horse, 'just this once'. Then it's 'throw this race or that race', or 'run this horse into the rail', or 'get your groom to conceal the saddle weight after you weigh out and replace it before you weigh in when the race is over', or else one of our other boys will file an objection against you and we'll see that you're set down and thrown off the track forever, along with your boss and his string."

"I'm telling you, Tommy. The Jockey Club and the track officials and owners are determined to clean up racing and they're starting right here in Cuba. The stewards are watching every move of every player here, and that includes owners, trainers, grooms, valets, bookies, gangsters, everybody. They're also keeping notes of who is associating with whom. That's what all these pinks are here for. They're watchin' and takin' names and when the season starts in the states, they'll be kicking ass! You just hide and watch, my boy!"

"Wow, boss! How did you know all this was going on? I ain't seen a single thing of the sort."

"You just ain't looking in the same places I look, Tommy. You gotta remember, I been at this game a long, long time, and I know a lot of people and many of the people I know are the ones trying to turn things around, like Matt Winn back at Latonia. He and I go way back and he told me what was up and so I'm telling you just enough for you to know to keep your nose clean, and maybe become a successful jockey. I'd like to see you make it, son. I really would."

"Wow, Mr. Spence! That's the best thing I had said to me since my mama hung this here St. Patty's medal around my neck and told me to make her proud. Now my eyes are a running from this dusty hay."

"If it's that dusty, Tommy, then maybe you ought to get to mucking these stalls out, so your eyes don't get any worse."

Tommy knew that Spence knew he was crying and he knew that blaming the dust from the hay was a pretty lame thing to say. Maybe cleaning out the stalls would cause him to remember to think first next time instead of saying something stupid and bogus. Tommy finished his chores and got his cot ready, then sat down and opened his scrapbook. Right below the pictures of his mother and dad on the very first page was a vacant space. He was thinking to himself that he would save that space for a picture of Kay Spence, if he could ever be able to acquire one. The rest of the evening was spent going through a pile of old outdated newspapers and race forms that he collected off the floor of the clubhouse grandstands, among the two resident stoopers looking for accidentally discarded wining pari-mutuel tickets. He faded off to sleep while mentally tracing how a *New York Times* sports page could make it all the way to Havana, Cuba. Then at one point during the night, he abruptly awoke, eyes popping wide open, pondering for a moment the fact that he still didn't know the difference between a bird and a bee.

CHAPTER SEVENTEEN
The Tout

The next morning, Tommy beat the railbirds and clockers to the turf. By 4:30 a.m., he had already blown out Rafferty, whom he would be piloting in this afternoon's Atlantic Handicap for Spence Stables. Tommy meticulously placed Rafferty's cooler over him and was leading him around to cool him out, when he heard a voice trying to get his attention. It was coming from behind the stable area, across the backstretch fence.

"Hey, I clocked him at fifty-one seconds for two furlongs. Think he's got any more steam for today's race?"

"Who are you, anyway?" retorted Tommy.

"Who, me? Ah, just a player trying to get ahead of the other touts."

"You're a tout?" Tommy asked, almost like he just ran across a mythical character in some enchanted forest.

"Well, yeah. I am. That's my calling and I'm blessed to be one of the best around. Matter of fact, I managed to score a sawbuck yesterday in the fifth on you and Cleek. Thought I'd check out your mounts for today's program and see what they got you in the morning line. So, is this here Rafferty just another morning glory, or does he have a little staying power?"

"Well, why don't you just stop by the winners circle today around five minutes to four and let me know how many saws you won on me and him!"

"Ha, this ain't my first day on the job. I know a plater when I see one and your Rafferty ain't nothin' more than a common turkey. He'll for sure be looking for a hole in the fence soon as he clears the stretch turn."

Tommy was visibly taken aback by this strange little creature that seemed to appear from out of nowhere.

"Now don't go taking any offense to my God given expertise on the quality of horse flesh. It's not under my control. It's a gift and I'm simply sharing my gift with those unfortunates who were overlooked."

Again with a very puzzled look on his face, Tommy responded. "You share this gift with others? Why how Christ-like of you; a true Christian in our presence, I say! It certainly doesn't surprise me in the least that Jesus would enjoy a good, honest horse race and marvel at the sheer grace and beauty of this majestic creature but bestowing the gift of prediction of the outcome of horse races on just a very select few of the population seems just a bit skewed or unfair. How is it that you were chosen for this rare and most coveted, and I assume, divine power?"

The tout returned his stopwatch to his vest pocket as he stood and addressed Tommy. "Your references to Jesus Christ lead me to believe that you are at least familiar with the scriptures and I assume you are aware of the four horsemen of the Apocalypse? Well, I happen to be the divinely appointed stable manager of the Apocalypse Stable. As such, I know in advance the outcome of any race involving the horseflesh of the Creator. Your Rafferty is merely a cow pony in the great scheme of things."

"This guy is serious," Tommy realized, snickering to himself. "Or else I'm still sleepin' and having a very bad dream." About the same time he was contemplating this strange encounter, Rafferty nipped his shoulder as if to say, *"C'mon, let's get going. You're late with my breakfast."*

"So, if you know the outcome of every race, then why are you here so early clockin' my horse?"

"Listen, kid. In my business I just can't give out the winner to every Joe that seeks my services. I wouldn't be able to survive in my profession if I did. I have loyal customers that depend on me for their betting action but I just can't give every one of them the winner every race. If I did that, then the odds would drop faster than a horse-apple at a full gallop. So I have to study the also-rans too, so my Joes think that some outside unavoidable and unpredictable element got in the mix somehow and dropped the monkey wrench into the machinery. Now sometimes it's different too if my client happens to be the bookmaker himself. In that case, I just try to sway the heavy betting onto the inferior nags, so as not to overburden my bookie with a lot of unnecessary payoffs, so to speak."

"Sounds like cheating to me," chimed Tommy in a disgusted tone of voice. This is just the very thing he and Spence were talking about the night before and he found it surprising and hard to believe then that there were people at the tracks who made their living in such a way. Now he's face-to-face with one, with only a board fence between them.

"I don't consider playing both sides against the middle as being very honest," Tommy added. "It's plain old cheating and you're the reason horseracing got into the state it's in."

"You ain't in no state, you stupid kid. You're in Cuba and anything goes!" he laughed. "I thought you were a jockey, not an altar boy."

"And I thought you were the track guardian angel, appointed by God himself," Tommy retorted.

"That I am, little man. Pock's the name, short for Apocalypse, and I taught the four horsemen everything they knew. Ha, ha, ha!"

Tommy walked Rafferty back to the stable and handed him over to a groom, after fussing over him and whispering something in his ear. He then proceeded to get Unar, who was impatiently bobbing his head up and down over the stall door as he watched Tommy approach. Unar knew it was race day for him. He was uncanny about being able to anticipate when it was his turn for all the pre-race paddock fooferah and the glorious post parade where he could majestically strut his muscular four-year-old stuff and hear the chatter and thrills of his loyal subjects as he made ready for the easy task of being the first one back to the wire and the only one to unsaddle in the winners circle.

Tommy had him under wraps today for his exercise run, so as not to expend all his energy in keeping warm. As they were headed to the track, Kay Spence called out, "How's my boy, this morning?"

"Just fine. Thanks, Boss. How are you?"

"Not you, Tommy! I'm talking to Unar."

"Oh, my bad, sir."

Spence let out one of those hearty gut laughs that a person would never expect could come out of a man of his size. It would nearly blow off his moustache and cause him to make wind. "Just kidding, Tommy, I was talking to you." His facial expression confirmed the fact that he was never a very good liar.

"How did Rafferty breeze this morning? Did he feel confident?"

"Oh yeah, ready to go. I didn't let him all out, but you could tell he wanted his head. I really had to pull him up."

"What's bothering you, boy? You look like somebody put a cat turd in as a ringer for your Tootsie Roll."

"Naw. Remember what you and me were talking about last night, about cleanin' up horseracing, and people like Mr. Winn doing everything to make it respectable again, and all the crooks and cheating and gambling?"

"Yeah, Tommy, what about it?"

"Well, early this morning, I met this tout named Pock. He was watching me and Rafferty work out and he was clocking us and somehow I got this feeling that he figured that I had Rafferty goin' full out and driving, 'cause he was implying that it wasn't enough to win this afternoon, but it was convincing enough for him to sell his name to his birds as the predicted winner and convince them to bet a lot of money on him. Now, if he thinks Rafferty ain't good enough to win, but he's getting paid to give his clients tips on the best horses, and who's going to win, then he's just flat cheating, ain't he, Mr. Spence?"

"Yep. It sounds to me like he's working for a bookmaker on the side. He's like one of them double agents from in the war just passed who showed loyalty to the Germans, but spied and passed on information for our guys. Ain't no other word for it except cheating! What'd you tell him?"

"Nothing. If he was so convinced that Rafferty was showing his best, then who was I to argue with an expert? So, I'm guessing this Pock fella is one of the 'birds' you was talking about last night. Am I right, Boss?"

"Right as rain, son," Spence gleamed. "There's rail birds, and jail birds. Sometimes the one is also the other, but it ain't an easy task tellin' the two apart. They look and dress the same. They're quiet and secretive and suspicious acting, always glancing over their shoulders to see if somebody is looking at their race form trying to get some useful information. The only real difference is that the one is willing to part with some of his money for this useful information and the other is more than willing to supply it, even if he has to make it up! Around the track, if a person or a horse is referred to as a bird, it's usually not a compliment or a positive inference, just like rail bird, or jail bird, or crazy old bird, or bird brain. You know what I'm talking about?"

"Sure do, Boss! I know exactly what you're talking about. So I suppose, that means we are the 'bees', right?"

"That's the ticket, Tommy, one to keep in your boot. The bees are the workers, the ones that keep Thoroughbred racing alive here in the states, or I should say, back in the States. The bees are the breeders of the horses, making sure that the bloodlines remain the very best, and the get is of the very best combination of qualities of both the sire and the dam. The bees are us trainers, who work day in and day out developing these babies to their full potential, and are ready to compete in strong and healthy condition. The bees are you young apprentice jockeys who listen and learn from the veteran jockeys and the trainers so you can navigate these beasts safely yet competitively to be the first to the wire. Just like the worker bees found in nature's hives, the ones who work the most and the hardest, get the most honey. Simple as that!"

Tommy nodded in the affirmative and without another word got back to his intended duties. It was now looking more like his Tootsie Roll had turned back into chocolate. "Just wait till the fourth race is over and see who has the mud on his face," he hollered over his shoulder to Spence, as Unar nodded in complete agreement.

CHAPTER EIGHTEEN
The Hat Trick

After his lunch, consisting of a few grapes and half an apple, Tommy made his way to the jockey room. He wasn't running in the first race today, but he just wanted to be in the company of the other jockeys just to hear what they were talking about. He seldom paid much attention to what was being talked about, from time to time, in the isolated little groups of jockeys because he was always concentrating on the upcoming race, and reading the form and charts. He always figured they were just bragging about their success in the crap games, or card games, or drinking and whoring around from the night before, or lamenting the outcomes of the same. Tommy hadn't quite made it to this point of the added amenities and pleasures of professional race riding. His only adventures away from the track and out of the Spence stables were to attend the Catholic mass from time to time. He felt the only way he was able to help his family and friends back home remain safe from the ravaging influenza and his friends who had been fighting the World War in foreign countries, was to pray for their protection and light his customary votive candles to insure his prayers made it all the way to God's ears.

The opening race today was a maiden race for three-year-olds. Kay Spence had an entry in this contest, with one of his other contract jockeys aboard. Tommy was familiar with all the faces in the room; after all, this was the thirty-second day of this meeting. He milled around, trying to listen in. Nothing out of the ordinary struck him from the chatter about the room. No conspiracies or plans of cheating or fixing a race emerged. Of course, this was a race for only horses that have never won a race before so who would even care?

As it turned out, the first race was cleanly run, with no calls of interference, no objections, no bumping, and no injuries. The front runner went wire to wire. It was a model race. Tommy wasn't able to see the race from the jockey house, but the valets' reports were as good as seeing it. He continued dressing and tacking up for the next race, thinking, *"Either I'm dimwitted or Matt Winn and the Jockey Club have really succeeded in getting racing back to a respectable sporting contest. I just don't see any cheating going on but there's something about that Pock that I don't like and don't trust. I'm going to keep an eye out on him. He's got them weasel eyes and whiskers for some reason."*

The second race on the day's card was a claimer for four-year-olds and up. Of the nine going to the post, three horses were being ridden by apprentice jockeys. Spence had farmed out Tommy to another owner in order to get Tommy as much riding time and experience as he could. He wanted Tommy to develop his skills of listening to another owner and trainer in order to get their perspectives and strategies of race riding, and to ride mounts he was not familiar with, much less slept with every night. Spence's entire stable knew Tommy's scent and they were used to it. Tommy needed to win mounts that couldn't tell his scent from that of a train car, and mostly all of them hated train cars. Kay Spence was not only the leading winning trainer in the racing business for 1918, but he was also known for developing the finest jockeys around. He was committed not only to fielding the strongest and fastest runners that he could, but also to mentoring and producing precision horsemanship and racing talent. When Kay Spence took a rider under his wing, it meant that a potential professional jockey would be the resultant fledgling emerging from his nest.

Tommy had no idea that his boss was held in such high esteem by the industry. Spence's reputation completely escaped Tommy's knowledge because he was the first and only trainer that Tommy had ever come in contact with. When he hung out at Latonia, he hung out at the Spence stable because that is where Harry Lunsford apprenticed. Tommy knew Harry from living in Covington. They grew up together. Tommy's sweetheart back home was Harry's cousin. Her name was Virginia Conley. Her mother and Harry's mother were sisters. Virginia considered Harry her favorite cousin because he rode the horses at Latonia and she was fascinated by horses. It was only natural that she would show an interest in Harry's friend as well. Tommy would regale Virginia with stories of when he would become a famous race rider and he and she would marry and travel all over the country, and even to Cuba and Mexico and Canada. Spence started taking an interest in Tommy because he was always around the stables and always willing to help out and his eagerness to learn was almost irritating. Just to get him out of his hair one day, Spence assigned Tommy the job of gathering up all the horse apples in a particular horse's stall, count them, weigh them, and then break each one of them apart to see if the horse was completely chewing up his grain and getting the proper nutrition it required. Tommy completed the task without even questioning the necessity of doing it. If Spence wanted it done, then he would do it.

The third race on the card was a claiming race for three-year-olds and up. Tommy had secured a ride on one of the Baxter Stable fillies, Mabel Trask, trained by E. Glass, one of Spence's associates. Tommy drew the eighth post position out of nine. The field lined up in an orderly fashion at the barrier and after one minute, the barrier sprung up and Tommy jumped into a fifth position as Miss Gove set the early pace with a good show of speed which she maintained through the half mile and three quarter mile mark, closely pursued by Nib. As the two front runners were battling it out in the stretch, Miss Gove was still in front at the last eighth, but gave up the lead to the advancing Nib on her outside, who was fully extended heading toward the wire, but feeling pressure from behind. This is when Tommy called on Mabel Trask and gave her her head and in the last few strides she took the win driving. After disposing of Miss Gove, Nib was simply spent and Tommy still had some horse left.

Advancing toward the winners circle, Tommy nodded to the judges and they returned the nod indicating that the results were final and he could dismount and weigh in. With the remnants of the heavy track concealing his facial expression, Tommy was wearing a smirk as he spotted Pock at the rail getting an ear-full from an apparently irate customer. He wondered to himself, *"What's more irritating? Getting peppered with dirt and sand or being beat in the face with a rolled-up racing form?"* He handed Mabel over to her groom and headed for the jockey house to get ready for the next race.

Race number four that day was the running of the Atlantic Handicap. This was the race Tommy was looking forward to since his early morning exercise run of his scheduled mount, Kay Spence's Rafferty, a three-year-old showing a lot of promise at this Cuba meeting. Tommy had a very good rapport with Rafferty and Spence acknowledged the fact by giving Tommy pretty much full control of how he planned to run him against his current competition. It was all part of Spence's technique in developing a professional jockey, without the jockey knowing it. Spence would observe the interactions and the reactions that one of his jockeys would have with one of his horses, and similarly the reactions of the horse to the boy. When he spotted a compatible mix, he would allow it to nurture and gel and he did it in a way that was not even apparent to others. That was his gift and his talent as a trainer. Yet he never revealed this part of his technique.

In the paddock area, Tommy scanned the crowd. He caught a glimpse of Pock holding court with a couple of his patsies over by Tippler's saddling area. Tommy knew what the tout was selling was pure bologna - expensive bologna at that! Pock would refer to his note book and his stop watch and would point to this horse or that, and point to the track in a trailing motion, indicating his expertise in the running abilities and strategies of the various horses and their jockeys. Tommy just snickered to himself, *"That fool doesn't even know what end of the horse burps and what end farts."* Tommy knew that if Rafferty could make the half mile mark in 51 seconds like he did this morning under wraps, then there would be no contest today.

They went to post at 3:48 p.m. and a good start followed after only a minute in front of the barrier. Tippler, in the first post position, showed the most speed and took the lead at the start on the inside rail and maintained it at the quarter and at the half. Skiles Knob, piloted by one of Tommy's buddies, Willie Kelsay, claimed second behind the leader and was maintaining that position until he stumbled and went to his knees upon entering the final stretch. Tommy was in third place at the time and his heart skipped a beat when he saw the spill, but he did not falter or get out of his rhythm and Rafferty did not break stride. Tommy was perfectly balanced forward and whispering in Rafferty's ear, hand riding him and never showing the whip. He shifted to the outside and took over second place. Faux-Col then started closing up a big gap, gaining third place in a rush. In the final drive, Tippler was beginning to tire and he flattened out, as Rafferty moved up and finished gamely to win going away.

Kay Spence arranged for Tommy to be aboard the entry of another trainer for the fifth race. This was to be a claimer for four year-olds and older. It would be good experience for the boy, Spence thought, because all these horses were veteran racers over long distances. It would be a good scramble for positioning early on. The horse, Harry Gardner, drew the fourth position out of six. Tommy was the only apprentice riding this time, but by no means looked or felt a rookie. The betting favorite, Ballad, had the first post position, led the start, and ran wire to wire on the inside rail and won in a canter. On the outside it was the completely opposite scenario. Tommy started last and remained in the rear spot till clearing the quarter marker, when he pulled up Harry Gardner lame and quickly dismounted. A bowed tendon in the right front lower leg was apparent to his naked eye immediately. Tommy tended to the horse and eased him off the track where he compressed the swelling with his jacket tightly wrapped around the leg. There was no suffering involved but it depressed Tommy just the same.

"Shake it off, son." greeted Spence back at the paddock. "Ain't nothin' you done."

"Oh, I know that," Tommy said. "It still makes me feel like tossing. I wish horses had stouter lower legs."

"Then they couldn't run so fast," chuckled Spence. "Maybe you should start racing elephants; a'course you could only run one or two races a day, and think what it would be like mucking out their stalls! Now, come along. Somebody's having a common fit waiting for you."

When they arrived at Unar's stable, he was bouncing his head up and down in vigorous impatience and anticipation of getting to the business at hand, which was to out run anything game enough to try. It was a mile and sixteenth claiming race for four-year-olds and upwards, and with Tommy's apprentice weight allowance at 98 pounds, Unar probably wouldn't even realize that Tommy was along for the ride, except for the serenading that would tickle his ears and help him concentrate.

Spence always said it helped because the horse was trying to outrun that awful noise but Tommy knew better.

The groom and Spence started for the paddock and saddling ritual as Tommy made his way to the jockey house where his valet had his favorite silks laid out and ready, grabbed his tackle and headed to the official scales, where the clerk weighed him out for the upcoming contest. After saddling and a leg up from Spence, Unar was ready to take over and lead Tommy in the post parade to the barrier.

"I got you one in the boot," he heard Spence whisper, as he patted Tommy's right calf.

"See you back in the circle," and he winked back.

Tommy's buddy Kelsay drew the first spot on top of Waterford. Tommy got the fourth position. When the barrier lifted, Kelsay had Waterford out front but not for long. By the quarter pole, Unar took the lead and never looked back. This horse absolutely loved to race and wanted to do it as long as and fast as he could. After rounding the first turn, he drew away into a long lead and Tommy still had him under restraint. He finished in a canter. Woodford and Egmont, the initial close contenders, both tired and Woodford flat out quit. John W. Klein managed to close a big gap in the last half and was able to overtake Maxim's Choice for a second place finish. Paying $5.90 on a $2.00 wager, the ticket in Tommy's boot was worth $44.25 when cashed in.

"Not bad for a couple of minutes' work, eh, son?" Spence grinned. Tommy really knew that Spence was well aware of all the work and effort involved in bringing in a winner, but it was fun acting like it was so easy.

That night, back in the Spence stables while Tommy was finishing up his evening chores and preparing his cot in the tack room, Kay stuck his head in the partly opened door and announced, "Well son, how's it feel to have pulled off your first hat trick?"

Tommy looked up from his scrap book and newspapers inquisitively and responded, "Pretty good I guess, but I'm not sure what hat I tricked you out of!"

"C'mon, Tommy," Spence fired back. "You know what I'm talking about! Takin' three first places on one day's card. That's called a hat trick. If Harry Gardner hadn't a come up lame, you would have done four outta six. That would have put you in next year's *Racing Report*. Not many jockeys accomplish that feat very regularly, especially apprentice jockeys. Congratulations, boy! You're definitely gaining people's attention. If you can keep your nose clean, you may have a promising future in this business. If you don't, and become an also-ran, then that'll be your doin', not mine. Keep focused, Tommy, and you will never regret a thing. A good start deserves a good follow-up. Just remember that."

With that, Spence's face disappeared from the crack in the door and Tommy pondered what the hell just took place.

CHAPTER NINETEEN
Sunday Morning with a Tout

The next day saw Tommy in the money twice, but nothing of any significance took place. Saturday, things were about the same, the highlight being the fifth race in which Tommy took first and his buddy, Willie Kelsay, took second. They were number two and three until the final stretch when Tommy's horse went to the front with a rush and won going away, while Kelsay's horse tired after forcing a very fast pace for the first half. It made for good talk in the jockey house afterwards, but it was clear to all that the horse with the most heart and the jockey with the most perseverance came out on top. Tommy was soon gaining a reputation against which other jockeys were comparing their own and others' performances.

That night, even though a Saturday night in the backstretch community, Tommy opted to stay put at the stable and catch up on a pile of newspapers he gathered from the grandstand and around the track. He had a *New York Times*, dated January 16, 1919, just two days ago. It was in this paper that he read that on this day, Nevada became the 36th state to ratify the 18th Amendment to the U.S. Constitution, thereby establishing prohibition and making the consummation and sale of alcohol illegal in all the states of the United States of America. *"Now what good is that gonna do?"* he thought to himself. *"If people don't want to drink beer or whisky, then they don't have to go into saloons. They sure didn't consult with the Irish or German folks back in Covington, that's for sure!"*

Tommy was always particularly pleased when he was able to recover entire discarded newspapers every evening when he searched the grandstand and clubhouse. Not only did he cut out and save the horseracing stories and articles that he fancied for his scrapbook, but he also searched every copy for Seckatary Hawkins stories. These were weekly stories that Tommy used to enjoy every Sunday from his own hometown newspaper *The Cincinnati Enquirer* written by one of the staff newspapermen named Robert F. Schulkers. The series had recently been syndicated and now appeared daily in many other newspapers across the country. These stories really provided solace to a homesick boy like Tommy.

Seckatary Hawkins stories consisted of simulated real-life situations and events involving a group of pre-teen and early teenage boys who were dues-paying members of the Fair and Square Club. They had a rather formidable clubhouse on the banks of the Licking River in Covington, Kentucky. Directly across the river was a rival boys' club who were their designated 'enemies'. They were called the Pelham's. Pelham was the name that Schulkers assigned to Newport, Kentucky. They also had a rival club across the Ohio River in Cincinnati (which was named Watertown in the series).

Tommy easily related to the adventures of these kids, not only because he was in the same age bracket, but also because he recognized and was familiar with all the places referred to in the stories back home in Covington, even though they were identified by different names. He, too, played and had adventures on the banks of both the Licking and the Ohio Rivers. He also wandered Banklick Creek and the huge dairy farm there surrounding Latonia Springs. He literally grew up just 11 or 12 blocks from where the author of these stories was born and raised. Schulkers also worked as press agent for Latonia Race Track in 1918, and later on took a job at Oriental Park in Havana, Cuba in that same capacity. Chances are extremely good that their paths crossed many a time without even knowing it.

Tommy was out early the next morning. He had on his rubber suit and was running the mile long oval in the pre-dawn darkness. He was concerned about the two extra pounds he had been tipping the scales with on his last few outings. He added extra time to each morning routine and began carrying two pound weights while running. He hadn't been eating any more than usual and he convinced himself that the two pounds were nothing to worry about. *"If it's nothing, then why is it on my mind all the time?"* he thought to himself.

"Psst, hey kid! C'mere"

Tommy looked up from his preoccupying cooling out walk and turned his head toward the sound. It was Pock and his little rodent-looking eyes were pealed right on Tommy.

"Hey, kid. C'mere!" Tommy walked over toward the fence reluctantly.

"What can I do for you, there, pal?" Tommy asked politely.

"Ah, nothin' much. I just saw you out there running. Puttin' on a few pounds there, are you?" he inquired laughingly.

"No, why?" Tommy snapped. "Do I look like I have or something?"

"Hey, I didn't mean nothing by it. Just small talk, that's all," Pock returned. "Hey, anyway, how's it lookin' for Rafferty and Unar today? I see you got 'em both on today's card. Think they got the stuff?"

"I ain't got any reason to think they don't, just the same as any time I get up on 'em, or any other horse for that matter. I don't do this just to come in second or third."

"Well, I figgered that but there's other variables involved that you ain't got no control over, like the horse is not rested, or ornery, or sore, or limp, and so on. Just wondering if any of that is going on today, that's all?"

"Well, if it was, you'll know when Spence pulls them from the race or when the veterinarian or judges scratches them! That'll be your best clue. Right now, I'm planning on bringing both of them to the wire and back to the stable first. Does that help you any?"

"Not really," Pock answered. "I got business to conduct and in order to give my customers what they want, I need some inside information. That's what I need from you, some inside information. You got my ticket, boy?"

"Oh, yeah," Tommy assured. "I sure do and here's my inside information for you. Don't drink the water from the inside of the flipping pot."

"How come you don't like me, kid? I ain't never done anything to you. You seem like a nice smart kid and I'm just trying to be your friend."

Tommy countered, "Listen, my mama drowned all the dumb kids. You're just a tout, and a crooked thief preying on innocent, vulnerable desperate people who trust your lies and smooth talk. Then you steal their money. Besides, you even look like a rat. Where'd you come from, anyway? An abandoned corn crib?"

"Look, kid, I don't force nobody to use my services. They come to me on their own free will and offer remuneration for my expertise and advice. Simple as that. Just as legit as a New York stockbroker. If you're headed up to Mass at the church, I'll tag along if you don't mind."

"You gotta be kidding! You're Catholic?" choked Tommy. "I cannot believe it. You are Catholic and a tout? Why you'll be in confession so long, you'll miss the entire mass."

"Oh contraire," Pock assured. "The good father there doesn't understand English. My penance is always just three Hail Marys and three Our Fathers, easy enough to understand in Spanish. Then I'm good to go for another week."

Tommy could just not believe this guy. In an odd way, he was almost likable. "Sure, come along," Tommy relinquished, "but you better sit in a different pew. I got races to ride in today and I don't need to be getting hit by no lightning bolt!"

The tout merely sighed and off they went.

Later that day, Tommy was scheduled to ride in five of the seven races on the card. The feature of the day was the sixth race, the second running of the Oriental Park Handicap for three-year-olds and older. The distance was one and one-sixteenth miles. Tommy would be aboard Hocnir for Kay Spence. Kelsay contracted for a mount on an also-ran for another owner. All the way back from Mass, Pock tried to pry valuable bits of information from Tommy about his competition and his own chances in the feature race. Tommy merely toyed with him though.

"I can guarantee you this," Tommy confided. Pock was all ears and his eyes bugged out like the headlamps on a Model T. "The winner will have four legs and will be the first to cross the wire!"

And that was all he had to say. Tommy headed back to the stable and his cot in the tackle room to look over the program for the day's races. It was a big card today, he thought, actually two handicaps. The fourth race was the Hippodrome Handicap for three-year-olds and up. He would be aboard Rafferty for this one. Rafferty had been training and running very well lately for Spence, but Tommy was worried if he had enough rest between races. After all, he had just run and won three days ago in that five and one half furlong race beating out Tippler, the favorite. Today's three quarter of a mile affair was just another sixteenth farther, but still, he would need to be driving to win. Tommy noticed that the other entries and several jockeys were not new to the game. He saw that Willie Knapp was here to ride one of Mr. Diaz's horses and Diaz was the leading horse owner and breeder in all of Cuba. His buddy Kelsay also had a mount in the race as well as a couple of other veteran jockeys. Tommy welcomed the challenges that proven horses and jockeys brought to the game. He was here to learn and train and what better way to gain experience than to face new challenges?

The first race featured a field of eleven horses. It was Sunday and the grandstands were full. The day was clear and 75 degrees and the track was fast. It was just a perfect day all around for Thoroughbred racing. The colorful jockeys maneuvered their steeds into place like clock work and after one minute at the post, they were off. Sister Susie, with eight to five odds, in the fifth post position got the jump on Tommy and Shandon who started in the sixth spot. By the half, Sister Susie had set the fast pace and led second place Shandon who raced in closest pursuit and finished gamely.

Tommy rode a 50-to-1 entry of Kay Spence's in the next race which was also a claimer for three-year-olds and up and sported a field of 11. He finished far out of the money in sixth place while Kelsay took the winner Sarasota into the lead position out of the far turn and kept it to the end, crossing the wire in a canter.

"It's about time you were in there," Tommy hollered to Kelsay in the winner's circle as he was headed back to the barn.

"It's kinda nice in here, Murray! Think I'll come back to visit more often."

Little did William Kelsay know at the time, but he would end up the year 1919 frequenting the winner's circle a total of 58 times. Not to mention 55 second place finishes and 49 thirds to make him number 18 in the standings for the winningest jockeys for the year, earning a total of $69,089 in prize money (*American Racing Manual*, 1920). That was quite a bit of money, considering the average yearly income for a wage earner in the United States that year was $1,125.00, and the average prices for a house and an automobile were $5,626.00 and $826.00 respectively. Gasoline was twenty-five cents a gallon due to a newly imposed gasoline tax.

A lot of Tommy's friends would do well as jockeys that year. Harry Lunsford, Tommy's old hometown inspiration, would wind up being the fourth place winning jockey in the nation with 100 first place finishes, 84 seconds, and 80 thirds accounting for $96,384.00 in total prize earnings. Laverne Fator, Clarence Kummer, Max Garner, Eddie Ambrose were all in the top twenty riders. There would be just under 120 jockeys listed in the leading jockey section of the 1920 edition of the *American Racing Manual*. That was fierce competition for any apprentice to face.

Of course, Tommy would have no idea at this time how he would turn out in the mix since it was still January but he approached his calling with confidence and determination and he worked under one of the best jockey producers in the business. Kay Spence would also emerge as a noted leader in his field by the time 1919 Thoroughbred racing came to a close. He would be recognized as the leading trainer of the year in the United States "in the number of winning horses sent to the post under his superintendence"(*American Racing Manual*, 1920). He had 96 winners, totaling $67,352.00 in earnings. Quite ironic is the fact that the second place leading trainer with 63 wins was H. G. Bedwell, while his total winnings amounted to $208,728.00, which placed him first in money won. Sam Hildreath, trainer of Purchase (who started 11 races and won nine and second place in the other two) and Mad Hatter, finished fourth in the standings with 60 first place wins and second in money won with $123,986.00.

Tommy was idle for the third race on the card and watched from the rail as Kelsay could only come up with a fourth place, though his horse raced well but was outpaced. They both sat out the fifth. Tommy came back with his own fourth place finish in the next race while Kelsay could only manage sixth out of an eight horse field.

"We haven't even earned our supper for tonight, have we ol' buddy," Kelsay said to Tommy on their parade back to the paddock.

"Naw, it ain't looking good, and I'm sure tired of oats," laughed Tommy.

CHAPTER TWENTY
A Lesson in Doctoring

As he headed back to the stables, Tommy was still having reservations about racing a horse on only three days rest. He felt that had something to do with the earlier result of second place instead of first on Rafferty in the fourth race. He confided his concerns to Spence as the groom was preparing to saddle Unar for the last race of the day.

"No, son, I don't think there's any problem with three days off so long as their feet and legs ain't showing any stress. These two ain't babies any more; they're four-year-olds. They're peaked at their strongest and all they want to do is compete. Head, heart, and hoof, my boy. It's all there. Not to fret."

"Okay then, Unar. You ready to get out there and show 'em some head, heart, and hoof?"

As if he completely understood every word, Unar bobbed his head up and down, stuck out his chest, and proudly paraded himself from the paddock area, hardly able to contain his excitement. He knew exactly what all this pageantry, and bright colors, and nosey, noisy people staring at each horse and rider as they passed into the tunnel leading to the starting barrier and he seemed up for the task at hand. Unar would start in the sixth position out of eight and he lined up in a well mannered fashion. When the barrier lifted, there was a rush for the lead and the rail position. Tommy held back till all the dust and confusion cleared and dealt with fifth place for only a very short period of time. By the quarter mark, he was setting the pace and clearly out in front to the far turn, but quit badly. John W. Klein who squandered the first post position very early on and a distant follower in the early running, slipped through next to the rail on the stretch turn and got up to win in the final strides. Tommy had no idea why Unar quit so badly, but he pulled him up to finish dead last, praying out loud that it wasn't a bowed tendon that made him quit.

Back in his stall, Unar stood almost perfectly still as Spence and Tommy inspected his feet and lower legs. The horse even wore an expression of worry and concern, if that is even possible. At least, that is how he appeared to Tommy. He wouldn't even make eye contact.

"What's the matter, boy," Tommy whispered in Unar's ear as he stroked his neck. "You didn't do anything wrong."

"Tommy, when you get him over his pout and guilty spell, fetch me some bandages so I can wrap this back leg."

"It ain't bowed is it, Mr. Spence?" Tommy stammered.

"It don't appear to be ruptured, at least not clear through, but there's definitely heat in it so it's at least strained and inflamed. See if you can fetch some cold water so we can soak this leg a bit. After that we'll put some liniment on it and rewrap it."

"Then what, Mr. Spence? Will it be alright?"

"Son, we'll just have to hide and watch. Hide and watch."

Tommy ran over to the tackle room, a few stalls down and slid the stable chest out away from the wall and opened the lid and propped it against the wall. In the very front was the medicine cabinet, a removable tray containing all the various veterinary supplies, lotions, rubs, liniments, leg paint, elixirs, pills, tablets, capsules, soaps, pastes, and dressings. He found *Harlton's Speed Tablets—Two Great Tablets for Race Day*. The writing on the box unequivocally claimed "No Dope-No After Effects. Harlton's Speed Tablets will hold up your horse and enable him to perform prolonged and extreme exertion without tiring." It further went on to explain, "WHY ? Powerful heart stimulant, nerve tonic, stimulates respiration, acts on the blood circulation and kidneys, contains no narcotics, non-injurious, no bad after effects, feed and water as usual, horse will come out of his race fresh. Easy to carry and use. Absolutely safe to give to all horses as directed. Per tube of 25 tablets, $2 postpaid."

Next to that he found *Harlton's Anti-Nervous Tablets - For Every Horse on Race Day* - "Prevents THUMPS, NERVOUSNESS and FEVER. Horse will blow out better, race gamer and come out of his race fresher. Recommended for every horse on race day. WHY? Acts on the respiratory tract, stimulates the heart, expels gas from the stomach, tones the nerves, acts on the blood circulation and kidneys, reduces fever, strengthens the muscles, non-injurious, feed and water as usual, not a dope. Will positively help every horse on race day. Per tube of 25 tablets, $2 postpaid."

"Holy Mackerel! What is all this crap in here?" Tommy hollered down the barn promenade.

"Just find the bottle of *20th Century Equine Liniment* and the *Harlton's Leg Wash Tablets* and bring them here. And hurry up about it!" Spence called back. "Oh, and find that leg paint, *Bell's Leg Paint*. There's a bottle of it on the shelf overhead with the brushes and bandages."

Tommy gathered up all the items requested and hurried back down to Unar's stall. When the horse saw Tommy enter, he began to whinny and bob his head up and down, as if he realized that all was forgiven and it was time to race again.

"Naw, ol' boy. We ain't gonna race anymore today. We ain't even gonna exercise. We gotta tend to your leg."

With that, Tommy stroked the horse's nose and rubbed his neck and Unar resumed his position of stillness and cooperation while they treated his malady.

114

"Boss," Tommy quietly began. "What's all them pills in that medicine cabinet? I thought you said you quit hoppin' horses."

"I did, Tommy. I don't hop them any more. I bought that horseman's trunk last get-away day at Latonia, from some jungle circuit owner and trainer who decided to try his luck running his nags up a class and lost about everything he had. He couldn't even give his stable away in a hundred dollar claiming race. They were that run out. He was looking to borrow some money to get back home, wherever that was, and I told him I couldn't give him any, but I might be interested in some of his gear. So I bought the trunk and contents and some of his better tack. I haven't even gone through everything in that medicine box yet but to answer your question, no, I don't use them pills on my animals. I imagine he did and that's why he ain't racing no more."

"Whew! I'm sure glad to hear that, Mr. Spence. I sure wouldn't want you to get in any trouble with the track stewards or commissioners."

"Well, that would surely be a good and quick way to do it, my boy," Spence laughed. "Don't you worry none. This business is getting back on the good track and regaining the trust and respect of the people again, and I sure wouldn't want to do any thing to spoil that and I hope that I have at least taught you that same principle, if you learned anything from me at all."

"Well, then, how come you didn't just throw all that stuff away when you saw it?"

Spence pondered that question a few seconds before answering, debating if Tommy was matured and ready enough to hear his answer. "Tommy, sometimes a trainer has to keep certain secrets of his to himself and keep the others guessing and wondering. If you tell all your techniques and strategies to every one, then they will know what to expect out of you and your horse every time you run him so you gotta keep things to yourself and let the others find out from other sources about what you're up to or what your secrets are. So they speculate on things they think or heard that you do and by the time they are repeated a couple of times and make the rounds, then it's just taken as Gospel fact. Do you understand what I'm getting at, Tommy?"

"Not exactly, Mr. Spence."

"Okay, Tommy. It's like that time that you caught that fella Pock clocking you and Rafferty at fifty-one seconds for the quarter, and he assumed that you had him wide open. Now instead of telling him different, that you had him under wraps, you just let it be and let him believe what he wanted to, right?"

"Right, Boss."

"Okay, so the tout goes and spreads this information around to his customers, for a price, planning to see a few dead presidents come his way after you lose to a horse he clocked going faster. Now you knew what Rafferty could do and you had no concern that he wouldn't be able to win, did you? But there ain't nothing to say that you have to tell that to the tout, now is there?"

"That's right, Boss"

"Okay, so if some backstretch snoop or stoolie decides to go snooping around my gear and tack when I ain't around, and sees them pills in my trunk and decides to sell that information to your tout, so he can spread rumors around about my horses and how they might run one day compared to another, then he's just making the odds better for me for when my horse actually does win, and he loses money when my "hopped up" horse loses. So, as long as I know I don't use the pills, and I ain't ever going to use the pills, then there isn't really reason to remove them from the trunk, because they serve as ballast, so to speak."

Tommy was completely amazed and mesmerized. Mr. Spence had as brilliant an understanding of human nature as he did equine. "In other words, boss, just let the cheaters and swindlers set their own traps, and they'll eventually cook their own goose."

"Couldn't have said it any better, my boy. Now, can we finally get to work on this leg?"

Tommy paid very close attention as Kay Spence doctored Unar's sprain. Spence explained every step and the principles behind every action he performed. An added bonus by way of a detailed lesson in equine anatomy accompanied the rubbing, cleansing, wrapping, massaging, kneading and the various applications of liniment, ointments and compression bandages.

"Tommy, if you're really interested in veterinary, by all means look through the medicine chest and read the labels on that stuff so you can get acquainted with what it is and what it's for. There's also a *Tuttle and Clark Manufacturers* catalog in there. They make all kinds of turf goods, tack, and veterinary. Since you enjoy reading so much, you might really like this catalog. You could learn some handy information from it."

When they completed Unar's treatment, Tommy cleaned every thing up and returned all the supplies to the tack room and medicine chest. He took some time to read the information on some of the other products' boxes and containers. Some proved to be very amusing and he would even laugh out loud at some of the words and some of the claims. He picked up a can of *Newton's Heave, Cough, Distemper and Indigestion Compound- A Veterinary Medicine for Wind, Throat and Stomach Troubles.* The label on the side of the can claimed, in no uncertain terms: "This preparation is the best known to the Veterinary profession for what it is recommended to do. In the treatment of heaves, it relieves the trouble by correcting the cause which is chronic indigestion. Indigestion also causes

116

colic, scouring, staggers etc. It is effective in coughs, colds, distemper, influenza, indigestion, skin eruptions, (or blood purifier), and valuable for expelling worms, and a grand conditioner. As our testimonials show, many horses that were useless to their owners have been fully restored. We recommend this very strongly for horses used for hard and fast work, as it acts directly upon the digestive and respiratory organs, and tends to keep them in good condition. This preparation is the most economical to use as the dose is small. Equally effective for cattle and hogs. The Newton Horse Remedy Co., Toledo, Ohio."

Tommy read to himself, "It says here that 'It Tends to Keep Them in Racing Condition'. I guess that poor schmo that sold this stuff to Mr. Spence just didn't buy enough for his stable of nags or they'd still be racing." He laughed out loud.

That night, after several treatments to the affected leg, Tommy dragged his cot from the tackle room and moved it to just outside Unar's stall door.

"What's this, a camp-out or something?" Spence asked half seriously.

"I'm just going to sleep out here so I can keep an eye on him tonight, that's all," explained Tommy.

"Well, I'm not so sure who is going to keep an eye on who. Maybe it'll keep him from pouting all night," assured Spence. "Since you enjoy reading about racing news so much, I'm going to let you read my new *American Racing Manual* for 1918. It was just recently published and I had it shipped down to me here in Cuba. I think you'll enjoy it."

"Gee, Boss, that would be terrific! I've heard all about the *American Racing Manual*, but I ain't never seen one. They say it's the racers' Bible."

"Well. I don't know that it's the Bible, but it's at least the racers' New Testament," Spence laughed. "Enjoy your reading. Tomorrow's Monday and there's no racing so you can read all night long."

Tommy started paging through the book and soon realized that several hours had passed. Toward the end were listed the leading owners, trainers, horses, jockeys along with statistics of number of races won and amounts of money won and almost every category of things that pertained to Thoroughbred racing. Tommy came to a section titled *Standing of the Jockeys of 1918*. It listed the names of jockeys, the number of mounts they had in 1918, the number of firsts, seconds, thirds, unplaced; their winning percentages; and the dollar amount of their winnings. It was fascinating to Tommy to read all about the jockeys he knew and worked with, the ones he didn't know but had heard of, ones he never heard of, and ones who would never be heard of. He was plainly flabbergasted by the shear number of jockeys racing in the United States and this list didn't even include the jockeys who hadn't had over ten wins over the course of the year. The number was staggering.

"Just what are the chances," he thought, *"of becoming one of the leading jockeys in the country?"*

It was almost dream shattering. He read on, and found the names of the leading jockeys in the U.S. in order of most wins. Why, he knew the first five leaders and he knew 10 or 12 of the first 20. Harry Lunsford was listed as the fourth over-all win leader and Frank Robinson was the very first, having 864 mounts with 185 firsts, 140 seconds and 108 thirds, winning a total of $186,595.00 for the year.

"This is unbelievable!" he said out loud. "How do you go about getting that many mounts in just one year?" As he fell off to sleep, he noticed his buddy W. Kelsay listed as number twenty with 44 wins for his 369 mounts in 1918.

The next morning, Tommy was up very early checking on Unar's leg. He didn't seem to be favoring it at all. When he unwrapped the bandages, it didn't feel near as warm as it did the evening before. He began messaging it, just as he watched Spence do many times on his horses. Unar didn't seem to mind the attention much. He could hardly keep his eyes open.

"How's the patient today, Doctor?" he heard from the barn promenade outside the stall door.

"Oh, good morning Boss. His leg don't feel as warm today and I can't feel no bow, so I guess that's good news, eh?"

"Eh? What the hell? You practicing to go ride for Commander Ross's stables up there in Canada or something?"

"Why no, Boss. How come you asked me that?"

"Oh, it's nothin' son. Them Canadians are just always ending their questions and sentences with 'Eh?' So, is he favoring that leg at all?"

"Not as I can tell in here, Boss."

"Well, let's walk him a bit and see what's what. Remember, Tommy, the circulation in a horse's foot is very delicate. Anytime you take a horse out of his stall, it is very important to walk him first in order to stimulate the circulation in the legs and feet. When you take a horse out and immediately work or run him, the small capillaries in the lower leg and foot can collapse and become permanently damaged, and the horse will never recover. Just remember this saying, 'Walk the first mile out, and the last mile in'. This will help to keep a horse's feet and legs healthy and the delicate tissues adequately nourished and oxygenated. If you ever had a charley horse before, you'll know you'll never want another one. Same goes for a horse."

"He seems to be walking fine on it today. Let me feel his leg."

Unar followed Tommy's instructions and cooperated with the exam perfectly.

"You're right, Tommy. Still a little heat in there, but I don't feel an unusual amount of swelling and he sure doesn't flinch like its tender when I poke on it. He may have just picked up something in his sole or frog that irritated things a bit. Did you notice a stone or anything in his foot?"

"Nothin' like that at all, sir," he responded. "I looked several different times."

"Good, Tommy. That's good. Rub his leg down real good with rubbing alcohol and then cover it with white liniment and re-bandage the leg. We'll continue that treatment for two days, while walking him a mile at a time three or four times a day. He should probably get just a little more water each time you water him, till the heat's all gone."

"Mr. Spence, did you know that Harry was the fourth winningest jockey in the whole country last year?"

"Well, Tommy, I didn't realize he was number four, but I figured he was up there on the list. That's a pretty good feat for a young man like him to accomplish, wouldn't you say Tommy?"

"I sure would, sir! I just couldn't believe it myself when I read it in your book last night. I mean, here is plain old Harry Lunsford, from Covington, Kentucky, my chum and schoolmate, and he's the cousin to my best girl at home, and he brought me out to Latonia to hang out at your stable 'cause I wanted to be a jockey, and now he's the fourth ranked jockey in the country. It's just like a story, ain't it Boss?"

Spence didn't even bother to answer that last question. He knew it was rhetorical.

CHAPTER TWENTY-ONE
Number One Trainer

After Tommy attended to his doctoring duties, he took Unar out for his first mile-long walk, ever attentive to his gait, looking for the slightest sign of favoring, limping, or discomfort. Back at the stall and satisfied that his charge had been well attended to, Tommy got comfortable on some hay bales and went back to reading Mr. Spence's *American Racing Manual.* Just as there was a leading jockey section, there was also a leading trainer section, owner section, steeplechase jockey section, gentleman rider section and other equally pertinent categories to peruse. As he scanned the trainer list, he exclaimed, "Oh, my God! I can't believe it! Mr. Spence was the number one trainer in 1918. I had no idea!" Unar must have thought he was talking to him because he immediately answered with a snort as he poked his head over the stall door.

"Gee whiz! I'm apprenticing with the number one trainer in the country! Holy mackerel! No wonder Harry was the number four jockey. He's being trained by the number one trainer."

Tommy was unquestionably beside himself after reading that bit of information. He started getting butterflies in his stomach just thinking about his close association with Spence. His emotions just wouldn't lighten up. They vacillated from excitement to intimidation to joy and laughter to worry and fear to feelings of inferiority and unworthiness. He read on and the words seemed to jump off the page. The article said:

"The year 1918 witnessed the deposition of H.G.Bedwell from his long held monopoly of the position of leading trainer in the matter of races won. His place was taken by Kay Spence, with a record of fifty-eight races won by the horses under his care. But Bedwell finished second with fifty-five races and was first in the important matter of money won, a natural consequence of his having a charge of the leading money-winning stable of the year."

"He won more races than Bedwell?" Tommy marveled to himself.

Bedwell, of course, had been the leading trainer for the past six consecutive seasons, and seven out of the past nine. Besides being the leading trainer for 1916, he was also the leading owner as well. It was after this that he sold out his stable and took the position of private trainer for the impressively growing Thoroughbred operation of Commander J.K.L. Ross, the wealthy Canadian heir to the Canadian Pacific Railway fortune and successful businessman and war hero.

Tommy heard plenty of stories about Bedwell and his equally colorful employer. Ross was the leading winning owner for 1918. The *American Racing Manual* for 1919 said this:

"First place was won by the formidable aggregation of horses gathered by Commander J.K.L. Ross, regardless of cost, it being the first time a Canadian owner has occupied that exalted position in North American racing. The acquisition of Cudgel in 1917 from John W. Schorr was the master stroke that brought about the stable's success, that excellent race horse winning more than a third of its total of $99,179."

Tommy was still reading with such focused intensity that he didn't even realize that Spence had returned to the barn.

"You must have come up on something really interesting in that book, my boy. Why you ain't moved a muscle since I left here an hour and a half ago. They're about to call for the horses in the first race to head for the paddock."

Tommy quickly grabbed his tack and headed over to the jockey's house to get prepared for the second race. There he saw Kelsay, all dressed and ready for the walk over to the saddling area for the first contest of the day.

"Billy, did you know that Mr. Spence was the number one trainer of 1918 and he even saddled more winners than Hard Guy? Did you know that?"

"Well, yeah, I knew he was way up there in the standings, but I didn't know the final count. So he finished first, even out of all those Easterners, huh?"

"Yeah, and he doesn't even let on that he was the number one trainer. He ain't at all snobbish or stuck-up or acting like he's better than any one else. He's just as regular as he always is."

Tommy was duly impressed with his master and mentor. He felt warmth in his throat and chest that he knew was pride and admiration, because he felt it plenty of times before whenever he was recognized and praised as Martin's boy, back home in Covington. His father had always been well respected and a leader of sorts around the neighborhood and Saint Patrick's parish.

Tommy drew the second post position for the second race of the day. It was a claiming race for three-year-old maidens. Kay Spence felt that Miss Ivan had a fairly good chance of winning her first race and the odds being given supported his feelings. Spence had instructed Tommy to get the jump at the start and let her set the pace and she should persevere. They were at the post less than one minute when the barrier flew up and Tommy and Miss Ivan got the jump but just as quickly found herself in fourth by the half pole. Billy Kelsay was running second behind the long shot leader, Mike Dixon, but not for long. Mike Dixon was setting a fast pace from his first move on Miss Ivan. Coming up on the stretch turn, Tommy showed his whip and Miss Ivan was running well and wearing the leader down when she jumped on his heels at the half mile post. Mike Dixon hung on resolutely to win by a nose, paying $108.30 to win; $56.60 to place; and $19.40 to show. Miss Ivan finished eight lengths ahead of third place Stone Daisy, who raced gamely and paid $29.30 to show. Miss Ivan paid a modest $4.20 to place and $3.30 to show.

Back at the paddock, Tommy handed Miss Ivan off to the groom and supervised her cooling as Spence walked up and put his hand on Tommy's shoulder.

"What's up, son? Why so pensive?"

"Oh nothing. I was just going over that race in my mind again and I can't figure out what I could have done different."

"Way I watched it, there weren't nothing you could'a done, son - at least nothin' legal. That long shot just plain got his nose over the wire while yours was still up in the air."

"That ain't what I mean, Mr. Spence. I'm pretty sure I spotted that Pock clocking me this morning."

"So, what are you getting at?"

"Well, suppose he convinced his clients, that what he calls them, clients; just suppose he convinced them that Miss Ivan was the one to bet? And maybe that's why her odds were so low. And maybe he got his bets down on the long shot because he got to some one in Mr. Graham's stable. Or maybe he got that jockey to wear a buzzer or something?"

Spence understood Tommy's suspicions and added, "Well, I'm not saying that none of that didn't happen Tommy, but there weren't any complaints raised and apparently the judges or stewards didn't see anything out of the ordinary. But that don't mean that you're not right in being suspicious. It shows me that you're maturing and observant and paying attention to what I tell you. Now you just keep your eyes and ears open and don't worry about the things that you can't control yourself. If there's any cheating going on, remember, sooner or later it'll come out. All we can hope is that nobody gets hurt or killed in the process and that the Pinks and track officials are on top of things. Now hurry on, boy, you gotta change out of my colors and put Griffin's on and get to the paddock."

They were at the post for two full minutes for the start of the day's third contest. This was a 12 horse claiming race for three-year-olds and up and some of them were hard to line up. Tommy was riding George Duncan and was starting from the second post position, while Kelsay drew the first spot. When the barrier flew, it was a real scramble for positions and Tommy found himself in eighth place at the start, which he maintained up to the three quarter pole. There he found a slot in the middle of the bunch and eased up into the fourth place spot which he kept through the turn and into the straightaway. At this point, he challenged Kelsay for second place and took it as he was closing on the frontrunner, J.B. Harrell. The top three contenders were driving hard and there was less than a horse's length between them combined. It was hard to hear, but the fifth place Phil Unger was on the outside driving harder and harder, finishing with a rush and getting up to win in the last few strides and won by half a length in front of Tommy's George Duncan, who took second by only a neck over Colors, who was a game and close up contender throughout.

The fourth race of the day was a disaster for Tommy, coming in at eleventh out of 12 horses. The winner was a nine-year-old and even an 11-year-old placed ahead of him. He didn't get a mount for the fifth race so Tommy retired to the jockey house and rested this one out. It turned out that Billy Kelsay took first place in this race on High Tide, by working his way up the outside and making a fast finish in the final drive and winning going away.

"Good job, Billy," Tommy shouted over to the winners circle. "Maybe I'll try that in this race."

Tommy scurried on over to mount Austral in the paddock and saddling area, in preparation for the sixth race. After a briefing from W.E. Scott, Austral's owner, Tommy made his way to post position number eight. He was in the very last spot at the barrier. He got a bit of a jump at the start, but fell back quickly to last place and remained there the entire race. Then Austral closed a big gap with a rush after coming on the outside when entering the homestretch and won drawing clear. Sure enough, he won that race just about the same way Billy Kelsay won the prior race, in a classic Garrison fashion. Back at the jockey house, the two of them had a good gut-wrenching laugh over that riding strategy.

CHAPTER TWENTY-TWO
The Boxer's Fracture

Tommy and Billy changed out of their silks and left the jockey house together. They were headed on down to the backstretch community kitchen to see about some supper.

"How many rides you got tomorrow, Billy?" Tommy asked.

"Four, I think. How 'bout you?"

"Five," responded Tommy. "But they're all claimers. I didn't get a mount for the Haiti Handicap."

"Well, not to worry, my friend. It don't even matter if you didn't get a ride, 'cause I'm winning that race. I already know that," Billy said with a twinge of cockiness.

"Now how can you say that with such confidence, Billy?" Tommy asked, almost hoping he would not get an answer.

"Because I just know, that's how!" Billy laughed. This really worried Tommy. Billy must have been influenced with idle promises from the evil elements that were infiltrating horse racing.

"I just can't believe they got to him already." Tommy thought to himself. They continued walking, but Tommy wasn't talking anymore. He was in deep thought and not even aware that they had been joined by another.

"Gentlemen, you look hungry! May I accompany you to the kitchen and join you in a fabulous equine repast? I understand the cook was awarded the remains of yesterday's cripple that ran the fence in the fourth race and has prepared an exquisite pot roast with all the fixin's."

"Well, well, if it ain't ol' Pock the Clock," chimed Tommy, when he realized that the space between him and Billy had been invaded. "How about I just stuff a few physic balls down your throat and keep you busy all night?" Tommy added.

"D'you know Harold, Tommy?" Billy asked.

"Harold?" Tommy recanted. "You mean his name is Harold?"

"Yeah. Harold Rosenthal. He's one of the track's major book makers and handicappers." Billy assured.

"Oh my God!" Tommy choked out. "You tryin' to make me flip before I even eat anything? Why he's just a low level tout who would pimp his own mother if he thought he could get her to run. Rosenthal? If your name is Rosenthal, then what were you doin' going to Mass with me the other day? Why, you even went to confession, didn't you?"

"You bet I did, you naïve prude. The good padre' is one of my best clients, and I confess to him purt near every day. But he don't give me Hail Marys and Our Fathers like he does you. He gives me Lincolns

124

and Jeffersons and sometimes Jacksons and Franklins and I give him divine providence, in the form of winning horses," laughed Pock.

"Why you blasphemous bastard," Tommy offered as he crossed himself. "Billy, are you supplying this piece of shit inside information about your mounts?"

Billy was caught off guard with this confrontation because he thought the tout was really a legit track businessman, making book and handicapping for the bettors who asked (and paid) for advice.

"Harold ain't never done me any wrong. We just sit and visit and shoot the breeze about the races and such at night. He brings whisky over and we just sit and talk. You oughta come over one evening and join us. It's a good time spent in fellowship and conversation. He's a good man, really."

"Yeah, by all means, Murray," the tout added. "You should join us each night and shoot the breeze. You must be getting bored spending the time by yourself just reading and writing and such. Come join our circle. We even give special toasts to the winners of the day."

The irregular and contradictory combination of the tout and the parish priest laying down wagers in the confessional presented a mental image that absolutely flabbergasted Tommy. He was no prude, to be sure. And he had reason to visit the confessional quite regularly himself; that is, for its intended purpose. He even subconsciously stepped to the side of Harold as they were walking, to put some space between them two for when the lightning bolt would find its mark on Harold's balding crown which no doubt looked like a perfect bulls eye as viewed from the seat of God in heaven above. He crossed himself again.

"What's the matter, Murray?" the tout chided. "You don't believe your man of God plays the nags? Whudda ya think that collection plate is for that they pass around each mass?"

Harold elbowed Billy and they both chuckled. They were really getting Tommy's Irish up.

"Playin' the ponies ain't even the half of it. When he ain't betting away the Pope's bread and butter, he's face down into the altar wine and grabbin' at the little altar boys. Now that ain't no lie."

With this Tommy popped the tout squarely in the face, his fist fitting comfortably in the concavity of the boy's upper cheek, bony orbit and lateral nose. It was a lightning fast jab one would expect only from Jack Dempsey himself. The tout fell back with a thud like the bar across a stall door.

"We were always taught that the Jews were responsible for the death of Jesus Christ and were not even sorry about it. Now I know why Catholics hate them so much," Tommy said to Billy as he massaged the back part of his hand.

"Billy, tell me the truth. You ain't really giving tips out to that guy for money, are you? Tell me the truth."

"No, Tommy. Honest! He just comes by at night and we sit around and talk."

"Talk about what?" Tommy asked.

"Nothin' particular, you know, baseball, boxing, girls, racing, stuff like that. Just regular talk."

"Did he ever pay you money for what you talked about?"

"Course not," Billy assured. "Why would he?"

"Cause he's a tout, Billy. You know what a tout is, don't you?"

"Well, yeah, I guess. He's like a bookie, ain't he?"

"No, Billy, he ain't no bookie. He's just a common lying cheat who sold his soul to the devil before you ever even sold your first newspaper back at home. He tries to get inside information from backstretch workers about the horses and all the goings-on between the breeders and owners and trainers and the conditions of the horses and strategies for the races so he can go out and sell it to his suckers as hot tips and sure things. He's just the low life you find underneath the horse shit when you're mucking out stalls. He's one of the reasons horse racing was almost banned for good in every state in the United States, and why people like Matt Winn and Mr. Belmont and the Jockey Club and all the other big wigs are trying to get rid of the crime and the cheating at the racetracks."

"Naw, he ain't never gave me one cent, I can assure you of that," Billy returned in a proud and confident tone.

"But you said he comes around at night with whisky and just sits around and talks?"

"Oh, yeah, that he does. And we sit around and some of the boys join in and pass the bottle back and forth and have a good time."

"When the bottle comes his way, does he pull on it too?" Tommy asked.

"You know, come to think about it, I'm usually sittin' right next to him and he just nods the bottle on by cause he's got his note book in one hand and a writin' with his pencil with the other."

Tommy sighed, "That's just what I'm talking about Billy. That tout is getting you boys drunk and talking outta school and getting pointers and information and tips from you and you all don't even realize what's going on. He's pimping you, plain and simple. Don't ya see?"

After they finished their supper, Tommy and Billy were making their way back to the stables. Along the way they spied Pock sitting under a big sycamore tree holding court with his followers and holding a slab of raw meat on his eye.

That night while Tommy was doing some reading of weeks old newspapers and months old racing magazines of Mr. Spence's, and writing down notes in his book, he noticed that it was getting more and more painful to hold and write with his pencil. The back of his hand at the base of his little and ring fingers was starting to get stiff and tight. It hurt to move it certain ways. The back of his right hand was bigger than the back of his left. He sought out the medicine chest in the big horsemen's trunk in the tack room to see if there was something in it that would help his injury. He read all the labels, but just couldn't come up with what he seemed to need. Finally, he found a bottle of *Dr. Rolling's Blue Grass Absorbent.* It said right on the bottle that it: "Removes all external defects of horses and other animals. It cures bowed, strained and filled tendons, curbs, capped hock, bog and bone spavin, weak joints and enlargements of any kind.". Tommy felt pretty confident that this would fix what ailed him, so he rubbed in the magic potion and wrapped up his hand with some linen bandages.

Tommy went back to his cot and lay down and continued reading. He had dozed off at some point and awoke when Mr. Spence came in checking on things.

"My lands, boy, what's wrong with your hand?" Spence asked in a worried tone of voice.

"Aw nothin' much," Tommy shared. "I hurt the back of my hand earlier today. I doctored it with some of that *Dr. Rolling's Blue Grass Absorbent*, and now it hurts and burns both."

"Tommy, that stuff's made for tough-hided hairy beasts. Why that'll burn your skin off, son. Come on, now. Let's get that crap off and get your hand soaking in some cold water."

Spence led Tommy outside to the rain barrel and thrust his right forearm down into the cold water. "Now swirl your hand around in there to neutralize it."

Spence let Tommy soak a good full five minutes and then pulled his arm out so he could inspect it. The back of the hand was a tender rosy pink color, but not blistered yet. Underneath the pink hue, Spence noticed the tell-tale ecchymotic color and swelling at the base of the last two fingers on the back of his hand.

"Well, I'll be damned," he said. "Who the hell did you punch?"

"Nobody, I didn't punch nobody," Tommy pleaded.

"C'mon now, boy. This ain't my first day on the job. That's a classic boxer's fracture if I ever did see one. Now who'd you punch?"

"Pock," Tommy whispered, visibly ashamed of what he had done, along with being caught in a stupid attempt to lie to Spence.

"You punched a tout?" Spence laughed out loud. "Now what made you think that would get his attention?" still laughing.

"He was saying some very terrible things about the good padre down to Saint Ignatius, the Cathedral of Havana," Tommy explained.

Spence paused a moment, then responded, "You mean things like he's a compulsive player of the horses and allegations that he uses collection plate money to do so?"

"You mean that's all true, Mr. Spence?" Tommy asked, hoping for the negative.

"'Fraid so, Tommy. Been going on for years and when they opened up Oriental Park here in Havana in 1915, it just got worse and worse. Once they find a sucker like that, the touts just won't let off so long as there's still some meat attached to the bone, just like the true carrion scavengers they imitate."

Tommy was silent, pensive. Spence could read his face, so there was no need for him to speak. He felt duped and betrayed by his spiritual steward. He felt anger with himself for the way he reacted to the tout. He felt guilty because he knew his actions were not Christ-like. He felt stupid, inferior, foolish, and ashamed. Plus, his right hand hurt like hell.

Spence finally broke the silence, "We need to get that hand packed in some ice. I'm going to walk down to the kitchen and get some out of the meat locker or one of the ice boxes. Just sit here and keep your hand up in the air. We don't need to be fightin' gravity, too!"

Spence made it back with the ice in a short time.

"Boy, you're the talk of the whole backstretch community, my boy. It's all a buzz out there. From what I'm hearing, most folks are happy about what you done. That fella must have aggravated and irritated every body he met. Let's keep this ice on and off all night and get that swelling down some. Then we need to work on coming up with something to help you be able to grip the reigns so you can ride tomorrow. I want you to swallow these two aspirin tablets to help take some of that heat and pain out of your hand.

"I'm sorry, Mr. Spence. I'm sorry for causing you this here trouble," Tommy apologized.

"Not to worry son. Quod nos non necat nos fortiores facit," Spence laughed. "What does not kill us, only makes us stronger."

Tommy thought on that a while. Then he looked at Spence and with renewed hope and confidence, said, "I like that saying, Boss. It's like 'learn from your mistakes', isn't it?"

"Yes, Tommy. Now you're back on the right horse on the right track."

CHAPTER TWENTY-THREE
Together Again

The next day was Wednesday, January 22, 1919. It was the thirty-seventh day of the Winter Meeting at Oriental Park, in sunny Havana, Cuba. The day was clear and the temperature a lovely 75 degrees. The six race program for the day included five claiming races and one handicap stakes race. Tommy was scheduled to ride in each of the claimers.

"How's that hand today, son?" Spence inquired as Tommy handed off another horse to the groom after an early morning breezing.

"It's sore, to be sure, sir, but I've managed to pull them all up just fine so far this morning. Now maybe I can appreciate what it's like to be made to run with a sore foot or leg," Tommy answered.

"Well, we could bandage it up for today. It would make it feel better, but you'll run the chance of being stopped and questioned by the stewards, and if they don't like the looks of your hand, they could sit you down for a day or two," Spence suggested.

"No thanks, Boss. I'm here to ride horses and win races and today there's five different trainers and five different horses counting on me to do just that."

With that, Tommy donned his layers of sweaters and his rubber suit and took to the far outside rail to run a few miles before breakfast.

"Massa Spence? That boy goin' 'mount to sumthin, I'm tellin' ya. He jes' puts me in mine of yoself, when you was a youngun like him, yesss suh, he shore do."

"Yes, Cupe, he's got a good future ahead of him if we can just keep him focused when we get back to the states and the big apple. Now let's get to them chores."

Cupe was probably Kay Spence's most trusted and loyal employee over the many years they were together. He was the indispensible groom, stable boy, and right hand man of the entire operation. They had been together back since Spence himself was a jockey. Thomas Miles was his given name and he had been around horses from the time he began crawling. His daddy was the lead stable boy back at a central Kentucky Thoroughbred horse farm ever since he gained his freedom from the same farm owner after the War Between the States. Cupid worked side by side with his daddy all throughout his youth and young adulthood. When Spence had come to that farm as a young teenaged exercise rider from Oklahoma, they both took a mutual liking to each other and they remained together ever since. It was Spence who gave him his nickname. Seems Cupe would freely offer his opinion as to what mare would be most appropriate for any given stud to breed so as to produce the very best offspring as far as a superior Thoroughbred race horse was concerned so Spence started calling him Cupid, after the mythological Roman God of compatible love matches. The name progressively shortened to just Cupe.

It was coming up on 2:00 p.m. and Tommy was making his way to the jockey house, carrying his saddle and tackle in his left hand, while swinging and twirling his whip in his right, just to make sure he had full control and dexterity of the hand.

"No gains, without pains. No gains, without pains," Tommy kept repeating to himself.

This was one of his favorite quotations by Benjamin Franklin. He really admired Franklin because he wrote things about farting and about beer, things that really mattered to a young Irish urchin growing up in Covington, Kentucky. Besides that, Franklin wrote about being poor and unprivileged and still being able to realize dreams and aspirations with lots of hard work and perseverance. Franklin wrote about using common sense and dreamed about doing anything he set his mind to doing. Tommy loved to read and repeat the wise sayings and quotes of Benjamin Franklin, and the proverbs and maxims and words of wisdom from the old *Poor Richard's Almanacks*.

Harry Lunsford was there, dressing for the first race. He was riding one of Mr. Baxter's five-year-olds named Starlike.

"Harry! Oh my God! I haven't seen you for so long. How have you been?"

They embraced and danced around hugging each other, laughing and crying and really whooping and hollering. Harry had spent the first part of the Havana meeting in Saratoga, racing in the stable of a friend of Kay Spence who was also a good conditioner of young jockeys. He wanted Harry to be able to get a good taste in his mouth for what race riding was all about up there on the Eastern circuits. He always preached, "It's a whole different ball game up there in the Apple." Plus, he wanted more time to spend on developing Tommy down there in Cuba where the winter racing was a bit more subdued. After his accelerated training was completed up East, Harry got to go home to Covington for a short stay to visit his family and friends. He had just arrived in Cuba to finish the Havana Meeting with Spence to condition him for the upcoming racing season in the states.

The call for the jockeys finally interrupted their joyous reunion and they scurried to the paddock, still donning their colors and grabbing their tackle.

"See you at the finish line," Lunsford hollered as the two old friends headed in their separate directions toward the pre-assigned saddling areas for their respective steeds.

"Okay, Harry, but only one of us can fit in the winner's circle!" Tommy returned.

Harry drew post position number two, while Tommy was assigned the sixth spot. It took two minutes to line them up and the start was good and slow. Harry's horse hesitated ever so slightly at the start and came out fourth, but quickly battled for first place and gained it by the half pole, while Tommy was alone in sixth place, with second, third and fourth all bunched up with not a quarter of a length separating the three of them. Number five was a length behind them, with Tommy a head behind that. Harry had raced Starlike into a quick lead and drew away in the first eighth, but was ridden out hard at the end. Robert L. Owen raced in closest pursuit and just lasted long enough to outstay Pontefract. The latter made up ground and finished fast and gamely. Harry's horse paid 16.5 to 1 to win. Tommy's show paid $3.30. Heading into the winner's circle, Harry saluted the judges first, and Tommy second, who tipped his cap and whip back with his right hand as a show of respect and congratulations to his old buddy.

That was the last time Tommy saw Harry that racing day. He worked one race, won it, and that was it. Tommy still had several more rides that day. He was clear out of the money in the next two contests, but came back in the fourth race with a convincing ride and a win. He was aboard The Blue Duke, riding for J.J. Timmerman. After racing close up from the start, The Blue Duke responded resolutely when Tommy called upon him in the stretch and he was going away in the last few strides to win by a length.

The next match of the day was the Haiti Handicap for three-year-olds and upwards. It was a mile and 50 yards. With the $800 added, the race was worth $640 to the winner, $125 to second place and $75 for third. Billy had a ride for this one, but Tommy sat it out. Daddy's Choice was a six-year-old J. Marrone horse that was even money at the start, and Billy would be aboard. The only three-year-old in the race was Sunningdale, and he ran poorly and finished last. Daddy's Choice was in post position number one and at the start was beat out for the jump by second starter Sir Wellons, who kept the lead into the last eighth. Daddy's Choice followed Sir Wellons in closest pursuit to the last eighth then raced into the lead and was under restraint at the end. Sir Wellons set a good pace and stayed longer than usual.

The sixth and final race on the day's card found Tommy in another claiming race for four-year-olds and up. He accepted the mount and agreed to give it his all, but he just wasn't convinced that it was the right thing to do. The horse, Austral, was the very same horse he won on in the sixth race the day before and now, one day later, he was expected to perform again in a winning effort. Tommy just wasn't sure this was the right thing to do to a horse. For sure, Austral showed no signs of wearing out the day before, no signs of tenderness or overexertion after the race, and no signs of being any worse for the wear. However, Tommy did not agree with Mr. Scott's decision to run him again today with only less than a day's rest. He thought it too much to ask of a horse like Austral, and he decided that he would let the horse dictate the amount of effort he felt he could expend in this race and not try to whip him into another gear that he might be lacking. Of course, he didn't tell Mr. Scott this. Tommy even thought it was pushing it to race a horse again after one week's rest, but Mr. Spence did it often, with no ill effects or untoward sequellae that Tommy was ever aware of.

Austral came off at 6-to-5. He was four years-old and the youngest horse going to post in the mile and sixteenth claiming contest. They were at the starting barrier two minutes to get lined up and Chilton King, at 5-to-1, got the initial jump and led all the way to the stretch turn where Burlingame took a small lead and kept it. Austral raced sluggishly in the early running but came fast through the home stretch and almost got up to win, taking second by three full lengths over the 30-to-1 third place finisher, Get Up. The early race leader, Chilton King, finished fourth and out of the money. Back at the paddock, Mr. Scott was there with his stable crew and groom.

"Thought you had it there at the end, son." Scott hollered over Tommy.

"Tell you the truth, sir, if we hadn't run out of race track when we did, we would have had it. He's a real competitor, this horse is. It was like he felt the others tiring and he just poured it on. Don't know where he got it after running so hard yesterday."

As soon as he said that, Tommy started wondering to himself that maybe the horse had been hopped. It seemed odd that the owner and all the stable crew and the groom met him at the paddock area. Was something going on, or was Tommy just getting too suspicious of every thing and every body? After dismounting and weighing in, Tommy made his way over to the jockey house to change and clean up some. Billy and Harry were both there shooting the breeze with the other jockeys.

"Hurry on there boy, we're hungry," Harry shouted to Tommy. "I'm just dying for some of that backstretch burgoo and barbecued brisket."

That night, as Tommy was reading his dated newspapers and magazines, Mr. Spence walked in and sat down next to him.

"Tommy, I wanted to talk to you about Harry."

"Sure, Mr. Spence, go ahead but I know what you're gonna say."

"Oh, you do, do you?" Spence laughed.

"Sure. You're gonna say that since Harry is back down here, you're gonna give him some of your horses to ride and that's okay by me. Harry is my old friend and buddy from back home and I want him to get plenty of work down here so he can help out his folks back home."

"Well, Tommy, I knew you would understand, but I didn't think it would be that easy. No sir I didn't!"

Tommy replied, "Boss, we all gotta look out for one another in these times and I feel pretty confident that if you're a good conditioner like you are, or a good race rider like Harry and Billy and me, then you're going to find plenty of work around the tracks. There's a whole lot of new owners and new horses coming out every day, and every one of them will be needin' a trainer and a rider. Ain't that right, Boss?"

"Couldn't have said it any better myself son," Spence responded. "I think that's exactly what I told you myself, not too long ago, if I ain't mistaken."

Tommy laughed, "Just shows that I'm listening, don't it, Boss? Now, can I ask you something? It's serious, Boss."

"By all means, Tommy. Shoot!"

"Well," Tommy started. "It's about that last race today. Did you happen to see it?"

Spence replied, "I can't honestly say I was paying any attention to it, Tommy, considering I didn't have a horse in that race. You got a beef about it?" Spence asked.

"Well, no, I guess not, really. It's just...," his voice trailing off.

"Spit it out, boy! You got a beef? Let me know about it."

"Okay, Boss. First off, I wanna know why Scott was so set on running Austral again today in that claimer. I mean, he just run him yesterday and we won. Why would he want to risk injury to a good stayer like that, by not resting him sufficient? Day after seems a bit too much to me for a horse to compete at the level he competed yesterday. Just seems fishy, that's all."

Getting that off his chest and out on the surface like that reset Tommy's suspicion-meter, so to speak. "I just got a bad feeling, Boss, and I can't tell you why, 'cause I can't prove nothin'. All I got to go on is what I seen. I seen Pock hanging out with Wilkin's trainer and stable boys last night, and he had plenty of his corn libation passin' round that circle. Then he got the fellas to arguing amongst themselves about Scott's horse Austral, who I rode to a win earlier yesterday, saying their Get Up could'a give him a good run for the money, and if Get Up would'a been in the race, then I would have been forced to a third place finish at best. Well, this got Austral's trainer all turkey-puffed-up and hollered that Pock needs to run his money as fast as he runs his shriveled mouth, cause he's gonna enter Austral in the sixth race today and show them all that their nine year-old nag needs to get a good jump start to the glue factory before he keels over with a heart seizure. Now this got them all a hollerin' and cussin' and trading licks and punches and next thing I know, I'm called down to the backstretch meeting and told I need to repeat what I done on Austral that day on the next coming day, because they got themselves a little grudge match goin' on. I told him right then and there that it's too soon to run Austral again like that and I said that Kay Spence would never a run a horse like that again without proper rest. Then, that stutterin' slop-mouth trainer said, 'Well Kay Spence ain't in charge, I am! He ain't nothin' but an undercover Pink anyway!'"

Spence was interested in hearing more, but he didn't want to let Tommy know he even cared. "So, how'd it turn out, boy? Did you accept the gauntlet?"

"What?" Tommy inquired.

"Did you accept the challenge? Did they threaten your manhood and principles enough to make you accept the challenge?"

Tommy jumped up and faced Spence square in the face. "Damn right, I took the challenge."

Things were silent for a very long couple of minutes.

"I took it, sir, because I don't want that horse to suffer any unnecessary injury from being raced again too soon. I took it because I know that horse, and how he thinks and acts. If he feels competitive and spunky enough to race, then that's up to him. I decided right there and then to guide him around that course like I was in command, but full aware that it would be up to him how and when he would run. It was going to be his call from start to finish. If I didn't accept the challenge, they would find somebody willing to grind him down into the dirt and cripple him for good. He don't deserve that, sir."

Spence stared Tommy squarely in both eyes but didn't mutter a sound. His lower lip quivered just a slight bit and his eyes started to glisten ever so slightly but that was it. Warm satisfaction and pride ran down his body as fast as gravity would allow it.

"So, tell me, son. How did things play out?"

"Well, their horse went to the post at 30-to-1, and I was 6-to-5, because of the performance the day before. I swear, their horse was a bad actor at the starter barrier, down at the seventh spot, very nervous and fidgety. Had to be hopped up on something. Meanwhile, Austral stood motionless the whole time at his fourth position, except for his head bobbing and regular snorting with every breath, like something was bothering him. He kept blowing and shaking his head to the right. I leaned over his right ear and started singing and rubbing the right side of his face. Then I saw it! Somebody had sponged his right nostril and he almost had it blown out. I took a swipe at it as the barrier was about to lift and I kept it in my hand for the entire race. Had a better grip on it than I did the whip. I swore right then and there that this sponge was going up somebody's nose tonight at the whisky circle, and I had a feeling it would be the tout's. Now, I can't prove that Get Up was hopped up, but I can damn sure prove that Austral was sponged and it wasn't by me and I don't think it was his trainer either. Somebody who had a lot running on that 30-to-1 bird fossil done it. It's got to be the tout and he must be getting the grooms or stable boys to do all the cheat-fixing."

By this time Spence was all ears and could hardly contain his interest, but he didn't show it at all to Tommy. "Now son, how do you reckon a stable hand or a groom could afford or even obtain the cocaine or heroin or whatever drug they got to hop that horse?"

"Why, the very same way I could do it to one of your horses without you knowin' about it - just going through the medicine chest in your horseman's trunk and getting it. I know that dope is still in there from times past and I know you ain't been using it at all. The same is probably true of Mr. Wilkins's trunk, too. Only in that case, somebody might be helping himself to it and using it to fire that old boy up. I can't prove any of it. It just seemed awful odd how it all played out. I think they just put Austral down so much in front of Mr. Scott that he accepted the challenge on the basis of pure pride and faith in his horse, and when he took the bait, the backstretch boys took it from there."

Mr. Spence fully accepted Tommy's theory. It wasn't like he had never seen it before, and he was fairly certain that Tommy was correct in his suspicions and the way it went down, but he purposely didn't let on that he agreed that Tommy was right. He simply dismissed it as something that could indeed have happened, but where was the proof?

"You can't just go to the track stewards and tell them you think this happened. You have to have rock solid proof before you levy a complaint as serious as this," Spence said with a degree of pressure in his speech. "If nothing gets proved and they get away with it, then you will be a marked man in their circle. You might as well change the design on the back of your silks to a bullseye, 'cause they'll be aiming for you every chance they get."

"Oh, I'm not gonna do anything of the kind, Mr. Spence. I ain't mentioning this to anyone but you. I'm just gonna hide and watch and sooner or later I might be able to doctor their plans enough for them to get caught red-handed. Pock is the mastermind, and the others are all simple enough to swallow his backstretch wisdom, so long as it's chased with a mouthful of that ever clear corn."

CHAPTER TWENTY-FOUR
Family Reunion

The next day, the three comrades started a very enjoyable day with each other with the early morning breezings and workouts. In each of the six races of the day's schedule, at least one of them had a mount and in four out of the six, two of them competed against each other. After all the morning chores and duties, they spent the rest of the day in the jockey house in pleasant fellowship and philosophical conversation between their various matches. The competition amongst themselves added a much higher level of fun and enjoyment in each race that day. Already, after only 38 days in the 100 day Winter Meeting, a few of the owners and trainers had pulled out due to poor performance and lack of income. Naturally, the jockey population was also reduced for the same reasons.

At the same time, some of the winning stables were importing more experienced jockeys, or at least drawing them to the meeting with hopes of securing work, as the spring meetings in the States were just around the corner. The potential horse riders for the 1919 season were looking for winter work, workouts to get into shape and shed the winter pounds, and audition themselves to the trainers and owners looking for riders for the upcoming season. This was the case for Harry Lunsford. It was also the case for Laverne Fator, who was discovered in Idaho running the half-mile tracks by a horseman who brought him to Cuba to train. As fate would have it, by the end of the 1919 season, Fator would find himself under contract to none other than Sam Hildreth - Racing Hall of Fame trainer, three-time leading owner, nine-time leading trainer - who purchased his contract for the paltry sum of $15,000 after seeing him ride only one time. Laverne was very successful that first season and won most of the big money races for Hildreth in 1919 but he never led the jockey list of the most total wins in a year. Perhaps Tommy or Harry would get a shot at that distinction.

The fun continued for the boys again the next day, Friday, January 24th, 1919. At least one of them had a mount in each race, two of the three were in two races, and the three of them ran against each other in another two races. Tommy got the call in the second race aboard High Gear for Kay Spence. It was a claiming race for four-year-olds and upward with a purse of $500. Willie and Harry entertained Tommy in the jockey house as the valet was assisting him with his colors and tackle.

"Tommy," Harry confided, as he squeezed the nape of Tommy's neck. "High Gear was the very first horse I ever won a race on. That was three years ago when Kay first allowed me to show him that I thought I had the grit and spunk it took to be a race rider. Because of High Gear, I got my chance to apprentice with the very best."

Tommy assured Harry, "Why don't you meet me in the winner's circle and we can have us a family reunion! See ya there."

Tommy took his five-year-old to the seventh post position and awaited instructions from Jimmy Milton, the starter. Jimmy didn't like any fooling around at the barrier and he had them off in a clean getaway in less than a minute, with High Gear leading the pack. Scotch Kiss then set a fast pace and showed much speed for five-eighths, but gave way in the final drive as Tommy brought High Gear around the leaders when entering the homestretch and, coming fast, got up to win in the final strides and finished gamely by a neck over King Tuscan who tired right at the end, and five lengths over Scotch Kiss. It was an exciting finish and made for a fine family reunion back at the winner's spot.

"All right you guys," Spence ordered. "Back to work! Harry needs to get to the jockey house fast and dress for this next race."

"Don't fret, boss," laughed Harry. "I'm getting on Dixie Highway and headin' for home."

That claim, however, just wasn't to be. Harry found his 30-to-1 plater ending up eighth in a nine horse field.

"Maybe Mr. Spence should have named him 3L Highway instead of Dixie Highway," Harry whispered to Tommy back at the paddock. "That way he'd have been more familiar with what goes on at racetracks."

They both laughed, but not before looking around to see if Mr. Spence heard them.

The fourth race of the day found all three boys engaged. Billy Kelsay was in the first slot on Sarasota; Tommy was stationed in the second post position aboard Mr. Dortch's Conscription; and Harry started in the third spot on Kay Spence's Corson. This line-up had all the makings of a potential Keystone Cops silent film, only on horseback. It was the first time all three of them raced together in the same race, and to add a little more powder to the charge, they were lined up, one, two, three, right next to each other. The official report went like this: *"At post one minute. Start good and slow. Won easily; second and third driving. Major Domo forced a fast early pace and raced into a clear lead the last fifty yards. Lucky Lady set a fast pace and finished gamely, but tiring. Comfort ran well and just lasted long enough to outstay Sarasota. The latter was ridden poorly and finished fast. Corson was messed about."* There's not even mention of Tommy's horse, Conscription, except for the fact that he was two pounds overweight.

Back at the paddock area, the grooms took over as the boys weighed out. Mr. Dortch and Spence were in a deep conversation. While in line at the scales, Harry nudged Tommy.

"What'd ya reckon that's all about, them two over there. They sure seem to be chewing some serious fat."

"No idea, Harry but I'm bettin' we'll soon find out," Tommy returned.

On their way back to the jockey house, they were walking through the paddock and passed Spence and Dortch, still in serious conversation.

"What the hell was all them shenanigans about out there? Did ya think that was a race to see who could come in last?" Spence fired.

"What'd ya mean by that, Boss?" Tommy respectfully answered inquisitively.

"I saw Harry batting you on the ass around the clubhouse turn. What was that all about? I sure hope the judges didn't catch that!"

"Sir, let me explain all that," Harry volunteered. "As we was positioning out of the turn, I seen Tommy come up way forward over his horse's neck, almost up to his ears. I thought he was losin' his balance or bearing or something. Looked like he was going over top. Thought for sure he was out of his wits and was going to tumble. His head was way down into his horse's upper neck and his ass was apointin' straight up. So I commenced to whipping it, hoping to get him back to his senses 'fore he took a bad spill."

"What? What the hell? Is that true Tommy? Were you dazed or something? Weak? Faint? Confused? Did you get hit in the head with a dirt clod or something? Do you remember any thing, boy?"

Tommy's eyes looked like somebody was checking his temperature with a horse thermometer and his mouth dropped wide open. As he took a deep breath, biding for the time to come up with an adequate answer to Spence's question, he happened to glance over toward Mr. Dortch, who was suppressing an ear-to-ear grin and fighting back a full blown belly laugh.

"He was singing," Dortch offered. "Scrip likes to be sung to. It calms him down and makes him want to run. Tommy was following instructions. He's rode Scrip before and knows what the old fella likes."

Then came the belly laugh and it spread throughout the circle like a grandstand cheer.

"All right boys, back to work. There's two more races today. Let's go out and see if we can ride horses and win races. Leave the singing to Vaudeville."

Harry couldn't hold back another belly laugh with that statement, because that is exactly where Kay Spence first discovered him back in 1916 when he first gave Harry and his older brother, Guy, their very first jobs at the tracks back at Latonia.

"Okay, smarty," Spence countered at the laughing clown. "You couldn't sing then, and you can't sing now and don't give Tommy any encouragement to start either, because I've heard him try it before. He got every cur dog in the stables to howling and escaping over the fence. Remember, I'm the one who rescued you from the stage and brought you to the backstretch where you can finally earn your keep. Now get over there and help Cupe get Sasenta saddled and ready. You're starting in the ninth spot and Billy's right next to you in eight. No shenanigans!"

They were at the post for three full minutes as Jimmy Milton got the 11 horses lined up to his liking. The start was good, as the horses scrambled for their positions. After a little bumping and crowding, the 20-to-1 Will Soon found the lead and set the pace all the way to the far turn and then just quit, turning over the lead spot to Guide Post. Harry kept a tight hold on Sasenta throughout the entire race, picking off the competition one at a time. Sasenta gained steadily and, finishing fast and gamely, passed Guide Post in the final drive and won going away. Billy stalwartly held eleventh place throughout the entire race on Almino until he could make his move at the end of the final stretch and finish tenth by a length. Sasenta paid $9.80 to win. Unbeknownst to Harry, he had one in the boot that Spence slipped in as he was getting a leg up in the paddock.

"Maybe that's why I was a pound and a half over," Harry laughed when he discovered the surprise.

At 4:36 p.m., the horses went to post for the final race of the day. All three of the boys had a mount for the final contest, contracted individually by different stables. Spence didn't even have a dog in this fight, so he played the role of spectator and horse player as he visited several of the pari-mutuel machines. He usually didn't wager on the races, especially not on other owners' or trainers' horses, but he thought he'd help the boys out a little if they performed like they could and should. He was also subconsciously wagering on his own ability to fashion and develop jockeys, even though he was full aware of the cardinal rule to never bet on the jockey.

The bell sounded and the machines were closed. Spence wandered over to the rail and took an inconspicuous position right at the finish line, pulling the brim of his hat down over his forehead for the dual purpose of shading his eyes from the descending sun and of augmenting his inconspicuousness. The 11 horse field was at the post only one minute before Jimmy had them off to a good start. Harry started in the first position on Annie Edgar, a 12-to-1 shot; Tommy drew the seven spot on Mary's Beau, at 2-to-1; and Billy Kelsay was aboard the 10 year-old Pontefract, who placed third in his previous race, starting in the tenth position, going off at 8-to-1.

"At least those hoodlums are well separated from each other this time," thought Spence to himself. "Maybe they'll concentrate more on racing than on singing and showing off."

A warm smile came to his face as he remembered just how boring a 100 day meeting could be for a teenage boy away from home and how exciting it was to finally be reunited with a best pal and buddy. He was recalling his own experience as a young jockey when the barrier went up and his attention switched back to the moment.

Harry got a good jump with Annie Edgar at the start and set the pace for most of the race, holding first place into the far turn, showing the most speed, when Mary's Beau, after racing in close pursuit early in the race, took an easy lead in the homestretch and won easily by a full length. Harry finished gamely on Annie Edgar, five lengths ahead of the third place Ballad. Billy worked his way up from tenth place at the start to finish eighth.

"I had to stop and let the old boy take a piss at the three-quarter pole," he hollered at Tommy as he passed the winner's circle back to the paddock and scales.

As the boys left the jockey house after weighing in and changing clothes, Kay Spence caught up with them walking back to the stables. He put his arms around Harry's and Tommy's shoulders, complimenting them on their finishes.

"Good job out there, boys. That was a finely run race if ever I seen one. You boys made the right moves at exactly the right times, especially you, Tommy, when you were all bunched up in the middle of that sea of horse flesh. Bet your arms are sore from holding back and Billy, I hear you were two and a half pounds over weight. No wonder you pulled up eighth. Do we need to get you a dose or two of the worm?"

"Ah, Mr. Spence," Billy responded. "I'm just glad it wasn't longer than a mile race. Otherwise I'd a' had to stop and let the old boy piss again, and I'd still be coming down the stretch."

"Let's hit the kitchen and get us some supper. Maybe we'll be lucky and they'll be serving something other than horse meat with oats and bran," Spence suggested.

"It's fish fer me, sir, being's as it's Friday and all." Tommy interjected.

"So it is, Tommy, my boy. Maybe I'll join you in some fried fish and tomato and onion slices."

As they were finishing up their supper under one of the big shade trees outside the backstretch kitchen, Kay presented each boy a folded large-sized twenty dollar bill.

"I took the liberty today to place some wagers on that last race you boys were in, and due to your expert riding and horsemanship, we all are twenty dollars richer."

"Wow," said Tommy. "It's one of those new double sawbucks. Look, there's Grover Cleveland's picture on the front, and a steam locomotive and a steamship on the back. They just came out last year, but I ain't never seen one. I just read about them in *The New York Times*. Wow, that is fancy looking money. Thank you, Boss. What a nice thing you done for us."

"That's okay, boys. You been good students and hard workers and you deserve a cut of the pie as much as any body."

"So, who is Grover Cleveland anyway?" asked Billy as he visually explored the strange piece of currency he held in his hand.

"He was our president," Tommy responded. "Two separate times but he's dead now."

"Now that's one dead president I'd like to have a whole bunch more of," Billy laughed.

They all four agreed with that statement and laughed some more.

CHAPTER TWENTY-FIVE
A Tout in Training

The next day, 5:00 a.m., found Tommy out on the track exercising Miss Ivan. The first race on the day's card was a claiming race for three-year-old maidens and Tommy wanted to make sure she was relaxed and up to the challenge. Just four days earlier she was in a similar competition with 10 other maidens and lost to a 20-to-1 long shot that broke away at the start and retained first place all the way to the finish. Miss Ivan chased him gamely and was on his heels at the half mile marker. She was gradually wearing the leader down, but ran out of race track. Mike Dixon was carrying 110.5 pounds compared to Miss Ivan's 96.

"He flat out ran like a bat outta hell" he remembered telling Mr. Spence after the race. "He didn't seem natural." Nothing else was said about his performance.

Tommy concentrated a while on Miss Ivan's getaways at the barrier, and then got her up to speed a couple of times and folded his energy and motion into hers to create an overall unit of strength and speed with grace and form. They were one animal, one person. As he breezed along the backstretch, the background incandescent glow of the barns and stabling area cast the shadow of a figure leaning over the outside rail fence, with head cast groundward. Tommy made out that it was Pock. He was looking down at his chronometer.

"Now what the hell is he out this early for, clocking me and my horse?" Tommy thought to himself.

He went on with his pre-race routine, hand riding and whispering into Miss Ivan's right ear. He wanted her to feel perfectly at ease with him aboard, and it appeared that she was.

When Tommy returned to the barn, he dismounted and checked each leg for heat or tenderness. He lifted each leg and inspected the underside of each foot and hoof for redness, inflammation, and foreign body and dirt. Then he handed Miss Ivan over to Cupe, the groom, for hot walking and he applied a light weight blanket over her back and flanks.

"How was the workout?" he heard coming from around the corner of the barn.

Tommy looked up and saw that it was Pock asking the question. Tommy's face got red and he slowly stood erect.

"Whoa, whoa, hold on, hold on," sputtered Pock with both hands held forward, palms out. "Don't get your Irish up! I'm here to help and I don't want to get popped in the eye again."

"Now just what in God's good name could you help me with?" Tommy brashly inquired, as he deflated just a bit.

"Well, I overheard some talk last night down at the backstretch amongst some of the stable hands and muckers. Whisky and dice make for braggarts and vice."

"Yeah, go on," Tommy urged.

"Seems like seven out of the twelve starters in the first race today are long shots, each one looking to improve its class to get into bigger money and there's already a lot of heavy money being wagered off track already, so's as not to upset the pool betting here. Word is they're worried about Miss Ivan and Stone Daisy running like they did four days ago in that other maiden race. Just wanted to let you know to keep your eyes open and be on the lookout for the sponge."

With that, Pock disappeared around the corner of the barn before Tommy had the chance to interrogate.

"I don't know if that weasel was on the up-and-up or just setting me up for some trap," he thought to himself. *"Trying to get me to blow the whistle to the officials and come off as the paranoid fool to discredit me in their eyes. All I know is that that Mike Dixon ran off like a bat outta hell the other day against Miss Ivan and I don't have one doubt that he wasn't hopped for that race but why would Pock want to forewarn me of more possible shenanigans today?"*

While Tommy was playing the various scenarios over and over in his mind, Spence appeared and asked Tommy how Miss Ivan looked today. Tommy immediately unloaded all that had taken place between himself and Pock asking Spence for his thoughts and interpretation of the encounter.

"Tommy, I can't rightly say. If there is some kind of plot going on with the backstretch workers, then it means that somebody is paying to see that their horse wins this maiden race over Miss Ivan and Stone Daisy so a sponge sure ain't out of the question. I'll be posting a continuous guard on Miss Ivan's stall immediately, and I'm also going to give the Pinks a heads-up to be extra vigilant while rounding in the barns today. If somebody's going to hop a horse today, it'll be awful hard to catch him unless the horse is a bad actor at the starting line and causes suspicion with the judges. No good whatever can come out of us alerting the officials that something might be afoul, because that just puts the suspicion on us. If something is going on, then the Pinks or the stewards and judges need to be the ones uncovering it. All we can do is protect our interests, and right now, that is Miss Ivan.

"Cupe!" Spence called out to his longtime groom. "I want you to stick to that horse like stink on shit, all day long. Not out of your sight or immediate touch for even a blink. Got it?"

"Shore does, Massa Spence. Yo' shore can count on ol' Cupe fo' dat. Dis hoss is become a bump on ol' Cupe's sore an' sorrowful ol' body."

"Good Cupe. I know I can count on you. I don't want any human being around that horse except for you, me and Tommy. Got that?"

"Ain't nobody get a tween ol' Cupe an' dis hoss, suh! No suh!"

Tommy spent the day lounging across a couple bales of hay propped up against Miss Ivan's stall door, while Cupe remained inside with the horse, rubbing her down and brushing her according to Kay Spence's tried and true routines and procedures. It's what Cupe would have been doing that morning and early afternoon anyway, except for the heightened vigilance and security measures which were purposely kept at a covert level. After Spence had finished his rounds, putting the Pinks on alert for any unusual activity, he packed in some fresh fruit and cold water and joined Tommy under the shed row in front of his stabling area and Miss Ivan's stall in particular for some lunch and conversation.

"Boss?" Tommy asked. "Am I drawing too much pus out of this sore?"

"What do you mean, Tommy?" Spence replied.

"Am I letting this tout and his way of life get my goat? Am I just imagining that he or his cronies are some how affecting the outcomes of some of these races by resorting to illegal means or do you think his kind can really have an effect?"

"Well, by all means, son, those folks can do a lot to change the outcomes of races. I've seen that happen all my life but it is most prevalent and successful in the big circuits where the high stakes races take place. I've seen the big-time gamblers and bookies and crime damn near put our sport out of existence and six feet under, thanks to corrupt politicians and city leaders on the take. Why, not a handful of years ago horse racing was legal in only two or three states. They managed to make it illegal just like they did to beer and liquor a few months back. You see, if something is enjoyed and popular with the masses, and viewed to be evil by the religious do-gooders, then the politicians jump on board to make it illegal, so the gangsters and criminals can take it over and make lots more money selling it back to the masses who enjoyed it in the first place when it was legal and more affordable. Sorry to say, but that's just the American way of life."

Tommy pondered Spence's explanation and asked, "So those types just might be training their apprentices down here just like you are training claimers for the stakes races and apprentice jockeys to ride 'em. Right, Boss?"

"You know, Tommy, you just might be right indeed! I never thought of it like that before. A tout in training!"

At 2:31 p.m., the 12 entries for the three-quarter mile claiming race for three-year-old maidens went to post. After one minute, they were lined up satisfactorily and the barrier went up and the start was good. Tommy and Miss Ivan in the eleventh position got away fast and grabbed second place, with Stiletto in front by a neck. By the half pole, Miss Ivan trailed by only a head. Stiletto set a fast pace to the stretch and tired, but finished gamely. Miss Ivan forced a fast early pace and easily raced into a long lead in the last eighth. Stone Daisy ran well and outgamed Bagdadine in the final drive to place third. As Tommy entered the winner's circle and saluted the judges' stand, he caught a glimpse of Pock leaning on the rail and writing in his book. He was there alone.

Harry Lunsford and Billy Kelsay would also enjoy the winner's circle one time each that day as well. Harry piloted Walter Mack to victory for Kay Spence in the fifth race by drawing away into a long lead in the first eighth, set a fast pace, and was pulling up at the end. In the final race of the day, Billy Kelsay won a claiming race for four-year-olds and upwards with nine year-old Gordon Russell, owned by H. W. Plant. Harry was aboard Woodthrush in this race, but finished close up in fifth place. Back at the jockey house, not a word of race fixing or tampering was even mentioned by any one at all. There were no complaints or objections filed and no penalties or fines levied. There were no claims of foul or interference and no fights or arguments. Tommy concluded that most of his suspicions were just that, suspicions with no foundations.

At the Track – Havana, Cuba

Crowd at Havana

Race Track at Havana

Oriental Park Clubhouse Entrance

Guest Room at Havana Jockey Club

The Oriental Park Clubhouse featured very high style architecture and trappings

Clubhouse Dining Room

Men's Lounge at Havana Jockey Club

Women's Lounge at Havana Jockey Club

Dining Room at Havana Jockey Club

Game Room at Havana Jockey Club

Advertisement for Havana Jockey Club

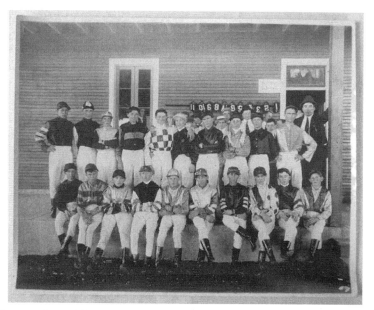

A group photo of the participating jockeys at a meeting is a tradition at all tracks.

Race Track – Havana, Cuba

Porch at Havana Jockey Club

Judges' Stand at Oriental Park in Havana, Cuba

CHAPTER TWENTY-SIX
A Lesson in 'Real' Race Riding

The next day, Sunday, found Tommy up and out on the track early exercising the Spence stable's entries for the coming race day. Then he breezed High Gear, Beauty Shop and Walter Mack as Mr. Spence recorded their times with his chronometer. They would all be running later in the week. Harry was also out doing the same with Rafferty and Hocnir and others. Spence would have the boys breeze certain ones together so they would have something to pace and chase. Spence lined up Walter Mack (Murray up), who had just won the fifth race on the day before, and Sasenta (Lunsford up), who was running in today's seventh race, at the barrier and gave the signal "come on". Sasenta grabbed the rail and set a quick pace, running the first furlong in 12 seconds. After the third furlong in 36 seconds, Tommy had High Gear within a head of Sasenta and gaining on Harry's horse. As High Gear nudged a nose in front, Tommy suddenly felt a strange pressure on his left leg. Glancing down he saw his buddy Harry's right leg wrapped around his foot and stirrup and in-between him and his horse. It appeared that Harry was using that momentum to push off ahead of Tommy and at the same time holding Tommy back, which momentarily threw Walter Mack a bit off his stride. Neither horse nor jockey could recover from that instantaneous interruption of concentration and performance and Harry pulled away on Sasenta to finish a length and a half in front.

"What the hell were you trying to do to me, Harry? Kill me or somethin'? Tommy screamed over to Harry as he pulled up to his side again.

Harry could see that he was mad as a hornet. His face was all red and his eyes were bugged out and he was talking louder than Harry had ever heard him talk.

"Easy now, easy. Just rein that Irish temper of yours in a minute and I'll tell ya what the hell I was trying to do," Harry recanted.

They slowed their mounts down to a walk and conversed as they cooled the horses down back and forth on the backstretch, out of sight and hearing of Spence.

"Tommy, you been race riding long enough now to have your fundamentals and basics down pretty good. You're a good listener and a quick learner and you're learning from the very best, Kay Spence. Besides being a famous conditioner of race horses, he is also one of the very best trainers of jockeys in the whole business and when he trains you, he trains you to respect the sport and the profession and the whole racing business because he lived through racing's hard times and its near demise. He trains jockeys to be fair and honest and play by the rules and he'll teach you a few things that might be questionable but if they ain't exactly against the rules, then they're Kosher. He ain't no prude and he's been around the track a few times, but he's honest and he don't like cheaters."

"I know all that, Harry," said Tommy. "Me and him talk about that stuff all the time. We even talk about the times he used to hop his horses. He done it to make his horses run better with less pain and complications. There weren't no rules then about how you could doctor your horse but what's all that got to do with what you just done to me out there. You damn near could'a killed me or worse!"

With that last statement, they both broke down into a fit of laughter.

Back on a serious note, Harry continued, "Tommy, when you get back to the States this spring, and even in the later parts of this meeting, you're going to find that the competition will get much stiffer as owners and trainers are bearing down for the more lucrative stakes and higher caliber races back home. This means they will be looking for the more experienced and proven jockeys who have shown they know how to guide the horse into the money. They ain't gonna be looking for jockeys who are honest and follow all the rules and consistently place out of the money. They are going to go after the ones who are aggressive and take risks, as long as that risk doesn't harm their horse. What I done to you out there is one of the most common moves a jockey will pull on you every chance he gets if the two of you are running a close contest and he will usually pull it on you in the backstretch where no one will be able to notice it - not the spectators, not the owners or trainers, and especially not the judges or stewards. He'll get away with it because you or any other jockey won't report it for fear of later retaliation and that's what'll get you killed, the retaliation on a squealer. Nope, it don't seem fair but that's just how it is. That's real life at the races and that's why I done that to you out there, so you will know what really goes on and what to expect. You gotta be aware and prepared for it and believe me, that ain't all the tricks you gotta watch out for. There's plenty more."

The look on Tommy's face spoke volumes. It wasn't that he was so naive as to think that stuff like this didn't occur on the track. It was more a look of disappointment and exasperation to have one more level of training to have to go through, one that was probably the most significant for his survival as a jockey, yet one that had to remain covert and completely out of the eye of the public and the knowledge of the racing officials.

"Oh Lord," he thought out loud. "A whole other bunch of variables that can affect the outcome of a race? No wonder it's so hard to pick a winner for a race! There's just so many different variables in play with each race and each horse and each jockey."

"Exactly," chimed in Harry. "It ain't like a baseball game where there's one team against the other, and each team has nine guys all playing the other team's nine guys, and if one of the guys just ain't up for his game, then somebody else steps up to make up for his lack. And it ain't like a boxing match where there is just one guy against another guy, and one wins and one loses. Horse racing is each horse pitted against the other eight or ten or whatever number of horses there is in the race. Plus, its each jockey pitted against the other jockeys so the outcome depends on a horse giving its very best effort underneath a jockey who also gives his very best effort. They both have to perform at their highest level together. A good horse with a bad jockey or a bad horse with a good jockey don't win very many races. Do you understand what I'm tellin' you?"

"Why sure I do, Harry. I knew that all along. I just didn't know that you had to know how to cheat and not get caught in order to be one of the good jockeys!"

"Damn it, Tommy. I didn't say you had to cheat to be a winning jockey. All I'm saying is that it's the survival of the fittest out there and if you want to survive the major circuits, then you need to get your head out of your ass and learn the reality of it."

With that, Harry spun Sasenta around and headed back toward the stables. Walter Mack snorted and bobbed his head up and down insomuch as saying he completely agreed with Harry and now let's get back to the barn for breakfast.

"Three in thirty-six," Spence hollered to the boys as they left the track headed to the barn. "We'll put them together in two days again and shoot for the three furlongs in thirty-three seconds. Then we'll just walk'em a day and they should be ready again for race day. What the hell was so urgent out there that the two of you had to talk about for so long before getting back to the barns?"

"Shop talk, Boss," Tommy answered. "Harry was just giving me some pointers he thought would help me, that's all."

"Well, Harry's a good boy and a good teacher. He wouldn't ever steer you wrong. Now turn them over to the grooms and let's breeze the others. Cupe, just a little hay for Sasenta today after you cool him down real good. He's running in the seventh today."

"Yes suh, Massa Spence. Ol' Cupe'll have that hoss all shiny and primed. I'll give the ol' fella a good baff and den rub him down real good and doctah his feet. You can count on dat, suh."

"You're a good man, Cupe. You get him ready and I'll put his bandages on."

Kay Spence had only two horses entered on the day's race card, and they were in the third and the seventh with Harry up both times.

They both felt good after Sasenta's workout this morning because he was in very good form. After the chores were all completed, the boys headed on over to the jockey house where they met up with Billy. They all three had procured rides during the day for other owners and trainers and they wanted the opportunity to talk amongst each other to compare notes and information about the horses they would be riding. Harry had five different mounts, three of which ran out of different stables and were new to him. Billy had three for the day, and Tommy two.

"Willie Knapp is here," Billy announced with unadulterated excitement, as he saw Harry and Tommy come up the steps. "He's here to ride for Diaz in the Morro" (Willie Knapp had been around for several years and had become somewhat of a role model for the younger boys. He was a successful stayer in the jockey business, despite all the criticism he had endured during his career for being a left-handed jockey, which meant that his whip was always used in his left hand and never in his right like most every other rider). The Morro Castle Handicap was the fourth race on the card for the day. Morro Castle was the ancient (1589) military fortress which guarded Havana Bay. It was only 11 years before that loyalist Spaniards in Cuba took action against a U.S. naval fleet by firing on the Flagship New York in April, 1889. The ship was five miles out at the time and in no imminent danger when the 10 big guns fired, but it represented a step closer to all out war between the U.S. and Spain. Later that month, Spain declared war on the U.S.

The feature race was a $1,200 added handicap for three-year-olds and up. This was the second year for its running. A. H. Diaz was the Cuban sportsman and leading Cuban owner of Thoroughbred horses. His stable traveled the New York and Eastern U.S. racing circuits. Obviously, winning the race meant a lot to Diaz by the fact that he imported the jockey of Exterminator, the 1918 Kentucky Derby winner, to ride his Orestes. Perhaps some national pride played into it, or perhaps Diaz had a statement to make about his stable and his intentions to dominate the Cuban racing. At any rate, it was a real jockey-house treat to have Willie Knapp around (Later that same year, Willie Knapp would be responsible for handing Man o' War his only stakes race defeat in the 1919 Sanford Stakes. A controversial denial of license renewal in 1920 found Willie Knapp finished with riding, but becoming the new trainer of Exterminator).

At 3:47 p.m., they were at the post for the second running of the Morro Castle Handicap. The track was fast and a good crowd turned out on this pleasant clear 75 degree Sunday to watch the feature race. Out of the seven horses entered, only Billy Kelsay's horse was a three-year-old. After two minutes at the post, a good start was orchestrated by Jimmy Milton and Diaz's horse in the first post position hit the track dead last and was outpaced while the others fought for position. By the three-quarter mark, Billy took the lead on Tippler by a head and increased it to half a length coming into the stretch. Suddenly, coming on the outside, Willie Knapp was making his move with Orestes, closing in from sixth place and gaining ground. Billy could hear the hooves resounding off the compacted surface of the track and out of the corner of his right eye caught a glimpse of Knapp making his bid with Orestes, while on his left, Wise Man was doing the same from the fourth spot back. Billy let Tippler out one more notch and that was all he had. Orestes finished with a rush to win going away as Wise Man was closing a gap and finishing fast to claim second place by a length and a half over Tippler who beat out the remaining four horses by half a length while they filed under the wire with not a neck separating them from each other. The crowd sensed a new track record and remained on its feet until the official time was posted. It was 1:11 3/8. Orestes was victorious, equaling the track record, while giving 12 pounds to Tippler. Second place Wise Man, a six-year-old, carried 17 more pounds than Tippler, and five more the Orestes. His effort paid $250, while Billy Kelsay was happy with his third place winnings of $150, but more thrilled to have been racing against the proven Willie Knapp.

The next two contests of the day found the boys all out of the money. The last race on the card was a mile and 50 yards claiming race for four-year-olds and upward with a total purse of $600. Kay and Harry were conversing in the paddock area as the saddling ritual was being completed. They were talking about Willie Knapp's ride earlier and how he seemed to be struggling to keep weight off.

"I'm glad to see he has turned out to be a top-notch rider, Harry," Spence confided. "Now he can get mounts on the highly weighted three and four-year-old best contenders in the handicapped stakes races up East and continue his success another year or so before he has to give it up. He's a bit older than you and Tommy and it's a lot harder to lose the pounds as you age. I can tell you that from my own experience. You gotta keep fit and exercise. All this pill and booze and dehydration crap will only make you weak and unfit. You gotta keep strong. You'll find out what I'm talking about in just a few minutes when you'll be holding Sasenta back for most of that mile. You'll need all the arm strength you can imagine, and then some. That fella is just plum set to tear loose. You can see it in his eyes. Just remember, hold him back as long as you can into the very last quarter. He'll have plenty left at that point to finish the job. The others are going to try and set a fast pace to lure him out and wear him down. He'd love to take that challenge. Just don't let him out till it's time."

With that, Spence gave Harry a foot up and Sasenta was finding it difficult to contain his excitement. He knew full well what this paddock ritual and post parade was leading up to, as he almost pranced all the way to the starting barrier.

Sasenta and Harry drew the fifth post position in a field of 11 starters. It took a full three minutes to get all eleven to line up for a good start. As the field vied for positions, Harry held his horse back for fractions of 24 3/5, 48 3/5 and held him under restraint for the first three quarters. After the stretch turn, he let him out a notch and Sasenta was going full force with plenty of reserve and still under restraint. In the meantime, Mud Sill, an 11-year-old veteran was quickly closing a gap, getting from eighth place to fourth place entering the stretch and gaining on the leader. Harry let his horse out another notch and Sasenta pulled away, winning by two lengths, still under wraps. Mud Sill continued his campaign to take second by a neck from four-year-old pace setter View, who simply wore down at the end of the stretch.

Sasenta knew he had done well as he led himself to the winner's circle, still full of steam and confidence. Harry dismounted after saluting the judges and weighed in, while Spence and old Cupe tended to Sasenta who was still basking in the glory of the moment, eyeing the crowd and bobbing his head to a select few.

"You know," said Harry when he got back to the near side of the horse where Spence was standing, "you're absolutely right about that strength and fitness lecture you gave me. If I had not been running every day and lifting those weights to build up my arms, I don't think I coulda held him back one more second. He has the strength of a locomotive. It took every thing I had to hold him and maintain good balance. I don't think he even knew I was on his back till he realized something was holding the reins back. Good thing I didn't need my bat. I wouldn't have been able to use it with the hold I had to keep."

"Lecture, huh?" Spence interjected. "I didn't realize I was giving lectures. You know, this ain't my first day on the job so when I tell ya something that I think will benefit you, or the way the horse will run, or the outcome of a race, it ain't a lecture. It's a fact of race riding and it would do you good to remember it, embrace it, and store it away somewhere under that helmet, 'cause you will need it again someday. No question about it," Spence laughed but he meant every word of it. Harry laughed, too. He realized that Spence was absolutely correct.

Back at the barn, Spence oversaw Sasenta's cooling out and bath. Then he checked his feet and legs as Cupe assisted and Tommy and Harry watched and listened.

"Boys, just remember this little ditty and repeat it every time you finish a race:

Though the beast is fit,
And the rider strong,
Still more is needed,
To hear the winner's song.
It's the gift of God,
To get the nod.

CHAPTER TWENTY-SEVEN
The Art of Bandaging

On Monday, there was no racing. However, it was still to be a complete day of hard work around the Spence stables and then some. Tommy was up and on the track at 4:30 a.m., breezing High Gear, whom he would be riding in the next day's third race. Harry joined Tommy about an hour later on Rafferty, whom he would pilot in the Jamaica Handicap in the fourth race on Tuesday. Both boys had ridden both horses in numerous contests in the past for Kay Spence and they both exercised and galloped them every morning of this campaign, so all four of them were very comfortable with each other and with the morning's routine.

As dawn was clearing the darkness away from the track, the boys decided to take their charges around the mile long oval at a brisk gallop. As they came out of the first turn and approached the backstretch, they were side by side and not at all at full steam. Harry was on the inside next to the rail and Tommy had High Gear about two lanes over on his outside. Suddenly, with no apparent reason known to Tommy, High Gear abruptly turned inside, almost forcing Harry and Rafferty through the inside rail. Tommy's face was buried in his horse's neck, but he quickly corrected his balance and was able to straighten High Gear out before he bumped into Rafferty. Harry was not as lucky though as he lost his seat and slipped off the saddle on the horse's near side and landed between the galloping mass and the rail on his back and immediately rolling under the fence. Tommy quickly gathered the run-away Rafferty with his horse, neither of which even broke their strides, and hurried back to check on Harry.

"Damn you, Murray!" Harry shouted, halfway laughing. "Where'd you pick that trick up at? Running me through the rail and not even bumping my horse? That's a better trick than locking legs or grabbing saddle blankets will ever be!"

"I didn't do that on purpose! Are you all right, Harry?" Tommy quickly asked.

"Yeah, yeah, I'm fine. Just a little befuddled. I didn't even know what hit me!"

"Nothin' hit you, Harry. My horse spooked at something and bolted over which spooked Rafferty and he started to bolt but thought better of it and you wound up on the ground. I didn't run you through. Honest!" Tommy pleaded.

"Well, it's a hell of a good move if I do say so myself," Harry sneered. "I'm putting that one in my own bag of tricks for sure."

After the two boys made sure each of them and both the horses were uninjured and unharmed, they looked down the track to survey the situation and maybe make some sense of what had just transpired. There in the middle of the race track they could see a gaggle of fryers who apparently escaped the chicken coop outside the backstretch track kitchen. There they were as if nothing even happened, feasting on and picking through a pile of still steaming manure which had attracted them to that spot just before the boys came barreling through.

"Good thing those weren't elephants feasting on peanuts or we both would be dead!" laughed Harry as Tommy gave him a leg up. Then Tommy mounted off the rail and they both walked their steeds back to the stables.

"How'd they do this morning, boys?" inquired Spence as they removed their tack and began to wipe the horses down.

"Oh they did fine, Boss, up until they decided to play a little game of chicken," Harry announced.

They gave Spence the whole story as he thoroughly inspected the two horses' legs and feet. It wasn't until Spence turned the horses over to the rubber and groom to finish their care and morning treatment, that Harry asked, "Were you wondering if me and Tommy was all right too, Boss?"

"Well, of course, Harry. I was just going to check out your boys' feet and legs too before I chased you 'round this barn with your own whips! Now get back to your chores. We got a lot to do today and I don't want anybody getting hurt – especially my stock!"

After Spence's string was all exercised, bathed, fed, watered and tended to, and their stalls all mucked out, cleaned, and refreshed with new straw, Mr. Spence called for Tommy to come help him.

"Tommy, I want you to learn how to apply standing bandages on a horse's legs, and I want you to learn it the correct way while at the same time you learn the principles behind using them in the first place."

"Ain't it about the same as taping the handle of a ball bat, Boss?"

"Any fool can tape up the handle of a baseball bat, Tommy and no, it ain't the same. Matter o' fact, it ain't even close. You tape up the ball bat in order to be able to grip it better. Ain't nobody I know of is planning on gripping the legs of a Thoroughbred going thirty some odd miles an hour! Now look here and pay close attention, 'cause I'm going to teach you something that even not many trainers can do right. A horse's legs are the most delicate, yet the most important, features of a Thoroughbred. They must be durable and strong enough to withstand tremendous stress and pressure from the thousand or twelve hundred pound animal they are holding up, while this mass of weight is being projected forward at speeds hard to fathom. Now if the track is fast, that's good for the track owners and the bettors because that means the weather is dry and not raining and more people come to watch and bet and the horses will be running faster in the races. Track records are always set on fast tracks but a fast track means a hard track and a hard track is tough on a horse's feet and legs. All the impact is absorbed by the horse's bones and joints because the track surface has no give to it. A good dose of this kind of punishment will make the feet and legs very sore and the horse can come up lame before you know it. That's why most trainers tell you not to use up all of the horse if you can keep from it. They could give a rat's ass about a new track record. They just want to finish in the money with the least wear and tear on their horseflesh. Now some of the owner's might see it differently. They may want to be associated with the horse that owns the track record, just to see their own name immortalized in print. We call those guys 'star trainers' but a class trainer could care less."

Tommy nodded his understanding and agreement as he paid very close attention to what Kay Spence was showing him.

"Now, Tommy, there are many reasons why we apply bandages to a horse's legs and each one is for the horse's own good. Now in this fella's case, I noticed that after his winning effort in the last race, his ankles looked a little beefy to me but they aren't holding any heat and they aren't tender, and he ain't favorin' any leg so I'm going to put on standing bandages over night and during his gallop in the morning just to get the beefy condition out. No doubt it's only mild swelling from his run on that fast track and it would go away on its own in a day or two but with him standing in his stall all night, the force of gravity will keep him puffy longer. These bandages will add some compression and help his body move that fluid out. I also noticed a little nick in the skin of his right front foreleg. Could'a been he took a hit from some other horse's back foot or got something kicked up from the track so we'll clean it out real good again and paint it. Then the bandage will keep it from getting dirty so it can heal up properly. You cannot be too careful when dealing with feet and legs. If you only remember just one thing I teach you, remember that!"

"Oh, I remember everything you teach me, Boss and I write it down in my book too, so if I forget I can go re-learn it."

"Okay, son. Now pay very close attention and then write it in your book later, not now. When you make cloth bandages, you cut up a bolt of it into four or five equal widths after you cut away the edging on the cloth. If you leave the edging in place in order to get another width, you may just be causing injury to your horse without knowing it. That edging on the cloth has no give to it, and if you wrap it around your horse's leg it can act as a ligature and do irreversible damage to a tendon and other parts. The edge is made to keep the cloth from unraveling. It won't contract or expand like the rest of the cloth so cut it off! Next, cut or tear the strips of cloth into nine-foot lengths and then roll them up tight into rolls."

"Now it's time to get the canton cotton. Always pre-wrap the leg with cotton before ever applying the cloth. Start at the foot along the coronet and then wrap it down to anchor it to the ankle. Then proceed up the leg making sure to keep it smooth and wrinkle free. A single wrinkle can cause a pressure spot that could cause a sore on the skin. After this is done, wrap another thickness of cotton the same way. Now if you're applying the bandage to create warmth and heat for a joint or tendon, then go ahead and roll one more layer of the canton cotton on before wrapping the leg with the cloth bandage."

"Now watch very carefully how I finish this. When you get to the top of the lower leg, be sure you are not interfering with the action of the knee and the bending of the leg in any way. Be sure you finish the wrap well below the knee, but high enough to cover the leg as completely as possible. As the bandage comes around the last time, take the two outside edges and fold them over slightly and then double under the end a bit and pin with two steel safety pins, but make sure they are pinned along the side of the leg and not in the back of the leg where they could injure a tendon. When you are finished you should be able to slip two fingers between the horse's leg and the cotton. The only place the bandage should be snug is around the ankle where it cannot do any damage to the tendons. A properly applied bandage will do no damage to the legs of the horse and will be perfectly smooth and very neat."

"When you are applying galloping bandages, either to keep dirt from a blister, cut, or abrasion or if you are putting it on to keep the horse from injuring himself with his own hooves while working out, this same bandage can be used but I never put any more than one or two layers of cotton underneath the bandage. Be sure the bandage is very securely anchored around the ankle so it will not loosen and slip down which could cause injury to a tendon. There is nothing in this world worse than a bowed tendon. The use of bandages helps to treat and even prevent bowed tendons but if not properly applied, they can cause tendon injuries. Never, ever, partake of alcohol or any other spirit or patent medicine while applying bandages to a horse. Just the smallest mistake could ruin a horse forever. As a matter of fact, never, ever even get around a racehorse when drinking or drunk. If ever I find one of my workers in this shed row under the spell of that intoxicant, they will be fired on the spot and will never set foot in my stable again. No exceptions!"

Tommy had seldom ever seen the stern side of Kay Spence, but there was no doubt in his mind right now that there was indeed one.

"Gee, Boss, I didn't realize you were a prohibitionist" Tommy softly responded, mainly to hear more of his mentor's philosophy.

"I ain't no damned prohibitionist, Tommy. Unlike our equestrian charges right here, I prefer my corn in clear liquid form and my wheat and grain with a foamy head on them but there are appropriate times and places for these libations and it damn sure ain't in a stable or shed row in the vicinity of a racehorse. I've seen drunk grooms, trainers, rubbers, exercisers do things to a horse that would make Satan himself blush with shame. The drunk recovers from his hangover, but the horse is injured for the rest of his life. The horse is God's most perfect creature. He blessed him with the grace and beauty of the clouds, the promise of a sunrise, the speed and power of lightning, the strength and endurance of the trade winds, the will of gravity itself, and a heart the size of a universe. The horse is the very reason that man did not perish throughout the history of the world. Just look at the importance the horse has played in this past war, the bitterest of all times. In my barn, the horse is king and he will be treated as such by his subjects. Any cruel treatment of a horse around here and it's off with your head! I will not even tolerate the thought of it" (Collins, 1959).

"Wow, Boss," Tommy forcefully sighed. "You made that clear as new goggles. You don't ever have to worry about me ever treating a horse mean 'cause I feel the same way as you. Next to you, these horses are the closest family I got and I would never raise a hand against them."

Not that Spence needed convincing other than Tommy's word, but the welling up in Tommy's eyes as he said that only reinforced Spence's admiration for the little Irish lightweight that he treasured as an own son.

"I know that, Tommy. I know that. I just want you to remember that booze and horses is a dangerous combination, and it's always the horse that winds up suffering. Now go fetch me that Mason jar of sour kraut from the tack room. It's up on the shelf above the medicine trunk and there's a jar of confectioners sugar right next to it. Bring that, too. I want to treat this proud flesh on Gear's knee joint while I'm bandaging him."

"Is that what that stuff is?" Tommy inquired in a voice an octave higher and his face all contorted. "It really stinks, you know."

"Well of course I know," snapped Spence back. "What'd you expect?"

"Well, I dunno. I never even knew what that stuff was. All I knowed was that it stunk."

"And how'd you know it stunk?" interrogated Spence.

"Because I opened it one day to see what it was."

"Yes, an what'd you figger it was?"

"Well, tell the truth, I figgered it was just Harry's flippin' jar that he forgot to empty. Ain't never touched that nasty beast since."

Spence could hardly contain himself and his signature gut-laugh rang out through the barn and probably invaded the adjacent ones. "Does Harry have his own flipping jar, Tommy?"

"Well, I don't know that for sure, sir but he'll flip anytime he takes a notion to and it don't matter where he is or what it is he's flippin' into so, I just figgered that was his."

"And what'd you figger the sugar was for, my boy?"

"Well, I, I just…uh…I figgered…"

"Quit stammering, boy. Go on with your story."

Tommy was all red in the face by now and it was plain to see he was too embarrassed to continue.

"I just figgered it was the powder Harry uses for when he gets galled. He says sometimes his balls get all sweaty before a race and when he's gripping the horse firmly between his legs, the saddle rubs him raw so he powders his balls."

Still laughing to the point that he couldn't stand up straight, Spence commented between gasps of air, "Powders his balls?! What is he, a muzzleloader or a jockey? That's the funniest thing I've heard this whole meeting."

"Please, Mr. Spence, please don't tell Harry I told you that. I don't want him sore at me."

Still laughing, Spence assured Tommy that he would try his best to keep it to himself. "I haven't thought of 'sweet nuts' since I was a foal. My mama would make them for us every Christmas. Now every time I see Harry I will have visions of sugar plums dancing through my head." Spence could still be heard laughing as he walked down the entire length of the shed row.

Tommy went back to his cot and got out his rubber suit and his scrapbook out of his trunk. He jotted a few things down in the book and then donned several layers of clothes and the rubber suit and headed for the track, whistling "Joy to the World" out loud. He remembered reading that the old time turf legend Sam Hildreth would always whistle happy tunes because whistling and smiling always brought along good things and it was happy thoughts going through his head right now thinking about Christmas, and his family and friends back in Covington, Kentucky, and Harry's sweet nuts.

After his workout and a refreshing bath and swim in the infield lake, Tommy met Harry and Billy down on the backside near the track kitchen. They were talking about the horseshit eating chickens that almost killed Harry that morning.

"I don't see them nasty critters around now," commented Harry.

"That's 'cause everybody's inside eating them for supper," laughed Billy.

As they walked in, sure enough, everyone in the place was munching down on some piece of chicken anatomy. Tommy spied Pock sitting at a table with a group of his cronies, his greasy lips sparkling as his mouth was running the mile at record speed and waving that drumstick like a jockey would his bat.

"Wonder what crooked set up that chicken shit-eating weasel is cookin up with those riders? No doubt he's trying to fix a race or two on tomorrow's program. Bet it's the Jamaica Handicap, Harry. That's the one you're up on Rafferty for, the fourth race and that's Dominick there sitting next to the tout. I think he's got a mount in that race, too. Better watch him, Harry."

"He ain't nothing to worry about, Tommy. If he gets in my way I'll just run him through the rail like you done me this morning, without ever touching his horse. I'm just dying to try that trick out on some one. He might as well be the one."

"Harry, quit joking around. That tout is up to no good. Every time I see him, he's up to no good. You just watch the backside tonight. He'll be holding court somewhere, passing around the whisky bottle and the cigars and convincing some poor stiff to hop a horse, or to hold one back, or to some how sabotage some component or other in order to fix the outcome his way and he don't care if it even hurts a horse or a rider. Just so long as he comes out a winner. I've been watching him closely and I know how he operates. When he wins big, it means he's pissed off a lot of people along the way and then he just disappears for a while to let things cool off. Then he'll pop up on the backside again and start all over. Just remember what I'm tellin' you, Harry. Be careful!"

"I'm on him like sweat on balls, Tommy," Harry assured.

Tommy quickly jerked his gaze up into Harry's eyes. *"Oh my God! Does he know something about my conversation with the Boss today?"* Tommy fretted to himself.

But Harry showed no other indication of knowing. He was just trying to be funny and his choice of simile was merely coincidental.

CHAPTER TWENTY-EIGHT
Sponged

The next day was a busy day for the boys. They all had several mounts. Tommy won the third race, a claimer for four-year-olds and up, on High Gear who came off at 3-to-2. They were at the post for four full minutes trying to get lined up after one of the horses unseated his rider and ran off alone back to the barn.

Tommy remained calm and laughed to himself as he whispered into Gear's ear, "That fella must have smelt your leg as he was lining up to us. It ran him all the way back to the barn. Glad he ran that way, 'cause if he'd a run with us, he'd a won by twenty lengths."

Gear just nodded in agreement as if to say, "Let's get going."

They were in the seventh post position and High Gear got a good jump at the start and grabbed second place right away, just behind Sparkler, the favorite in the rail post position. Tommy did a good job of rating his horse as High Gear raced into the lead while rounding the turn into the homestretch and drew away to win in a canter. As Tommy got the nod from the judges, he dismounted and weighed in, just as Billy was walking his horse back to the saddling paddock.

"Where were you, Billy? I was looking for you," Tommy shouted. Tommy knew he got left at the post, but he just couldn't resist.

It was the next race that was really on Tommy's mind all morning. It was the Jamaica Handicap for three-year-olds and up. There were six horses entered and Harry and Billy each had a mount. Harry was on Kay Spence's Rafferty and the morning line on him was 2-to-1, making him one of the favorites. Billy's horse didn't get any better than 25-to-1 and he was the long shot at post time, but had the first post position. In the second spot was the horse Dominick was riding. He was the jockey that Tommy saw with Pock the tout the night before in the track kitchen. As Billy and Harry were getting saddled up in the paddock, Tommy made sure to warn them both to keep an eye out for Skiles Knob and Dominick. He was going off at 13-to-1 odds. Meanwhile, the tout was working the apron vigorously and Tommy watched as Pock set up his unsuspecting victims with inaccurate information and "hot tips". He would then take the money from his clients to make their bets for them with his good bookie friends, while in reality; he placed bets for himself, with their money, on Skiles Knob.

When "Come On" was vocalized by Jimmy Milton, the starter, Skiles Knob immediately jumped out in front and set a very fast pace. Harry settled in at fourth place and rated Rafferty in order to save some horse for the end. At the three-quarter mark he then let Rafferty out a notch and went around the crowd and challenged the three front runners, finally gaining second place coming out of the homestretch turn by a head. Down the home stretch, on the outside, Barney Shannon came from the rear and overcame Rafferty to challenge the two frontrunners. Rafferty just up and quit, finishing the race dead last. Dominick had to ride his mount hard at the finish to hold off the second place finisher who was responding in gamely fashion just before the wire. There was no sign of the tout now out on the apron as he was poised to collect $28.40 on each two dollar bet.

Back at the paddock, Harry called Tommy over as they unsaddled Rafferty. "You were right, Tommy. There was something strange going on with them horses all right. You should'a seen the crazed look in the eyes of that Skiles horse and he was frothin' at the mouth something awful. He reminded me of a dog with distemper, just real detached and spooky-like. That horse was hopped up on something, but he damn near stopped dead in his tracks at the wire. Why he only won by a neck after having a two length lead there at the end. And Rafferty here. Why, after we got passed on the far side by Barney Shannon, it was like Rafferty was shot through the heart with a lead slug. All his life and energy was just snuffed out, just like some common stiff in a Chicago alley."

As they walked back to the barn area, they kept their eyes on the winner. He was absolutely spent. His head hung down to the ground so far it looked like he would step on his lower lip with every tenuous step. Rafferty, on the other hand, raised his head upward and frequently shook it back and forth, as if he was trying to get Harry's and Tommy's attention to tell them something.

"What's the matter old friend, Harry whispered to Rafferty as he rubbed his nose and upper lip. What's bothering you?"

It was then that the sponge dislodged from the right nostril into Harry's hand.

CHAPTER TWENTY-NINE
Why My Horses?

"Hurry on up over here, Murray," shouted Kay Spence from the saddling area in the paddock. "Let Harry fester by his self in his self pity. You're riding in this next race, in case you forgot or something."

Tommy hightailed it into the jockeys' house and quickly slipped into his silks and grabbed his saddle and tack from the valet. Out in the paddock he assisted Spence with the process of saddling Beauty Shop.

"Boss, what's your take on that last race?" Tommy asked meekly.

"You mean other than a poorly run race? Why it was a give-away. Harry and Rafferty looked like it was the first time either one of them ever seen a race, much less run in one. Don't know what to make of it, but I plan on finding out. Now don't you go and pull the same stunts Harry did. There ain't no reason that the Shop should finish out of the money with these underclassers."

"Boss, before you go jumping on Harry, I need to tell ya something. Somebody sponged Rafferty in that last race. He blew it out into Harry's hand back at the barn."

"What? What in the Sam Hill did you just say, boy? A sponge? In another one of my horses?"

"Yessir, Mr. Spence. It come out into Harry's hand when he was rubbin' Rafferty's upper lip."

"Who all knows about this, boy?" Spence demanded.

"Why, just us three, Mr. Spence: You, me, and Harry."

"Okay, son. Make sure it don't go no farther than us three. I'll get to the bottom of this one way or 'nother. Just keep your eyes peeled for any shenanigans in the race. There's four long-shots in this race and I'm curious just how they're all going to finish. Something tells me it ain't gonna be the way the morning line had 'em. Keep your eyes and ears open."

Tommy circled around Beauty Shop and made a complete visual inspection of both beast and equipment. He gently felt each leg and ankle for any tell-tale signs of warmth, swelling, tenderness, or anything unusual. Next, he double checked the straps, stirrups, saddle, and rest of the tack for strength and signs of tampering. Satisfied that everything was in good order, he then took a leg up from Spence and lined up in the post parade. Beauty Shop seemed alert and attentive. His ears were perked and tuning in to all the various sounds. He didn't seem overly nervous or excitable and there was a prance or bounce in his stride that let Tommy know he was ready to run and compete.

"All good signs," Tommy thought to himself but why was he feeling this paranoia, like someone had tampered with his horse, or

something was about to happen? He was not one to worry about things that could possibly happen. He had no time for that but, there was this strange gut feeling there.

As the parade entered the track headed for the starting barrier, Tommy glanced along the rail in front of the grandstand apron, something he always did just to get a feel for the number of patrons present to watch the races and participate in the betting and excitement. He enjoyed feeling the reaction of the crowd there before a race, it was all anticipation and excitement and real positive energy. It was a lot different than the reactions you would experience on the way back to the paddock after the completion of the race, especially if you were one of the losing jockeys. The crowd's reaction was a lot harsher at this point. That initial excitement and positive energy was now all up by the winner's circle. Out of the corner of his eye, Tommy caught a glimpse of Pock along the rail, apparently conducting some kind of business as he was surrounded by a fairly large group of men waving programs, all obviously vying for his attention. Either the tout pulled something to make them all angry or he somehow convinced them that he had information that no one else could supply. Either way, it didn't matter to Tommy. It only strengthened his convictions that Pock's apparent popularity and the sponge in Rafferty's nose just might have a lot in common.

Tommy's senses were fine tuned by the time they were all lined up at the starting barrier. Not only did he have the task at hand that would require his total concentration and attention, but also the task of being on the alert for any unusual occurrences relating to the other horses or jockeys or their performances and behavior as they relate to the final outcome of the race. In other words, he was going to be the self-appointed racing steward during this fifth race of the day, besides being a participant in the event.

Nothing occurred. No fouls or interferences, no rough riding, no contact between horse and rider or rider and rider, no interference of any kind that Tommy could see. In spite of the fact that the second place horse was at 12-to-1 odds and the fourth place horse was at 25-to-1, finishing ahead of Tommy and Beauty Shop who went off at four-to-one nothing unusual happened, as far as Tommy could tell.

"What happened out there?" Spence greeted Tommy back in the paddock. His last two workouts were better than that. Is he favoring something?"

"Not as I could tell, Boss. He had a good, even stride and seemed to have plenty of heart, but it just wasn't there under me. He wasn't all there. When I let him out down the stretch when we took on Darkey for fifth place at the finish, he had some left, but he just wasn't the same today. Maybe he's coming down with something."

"Now what's that suppose to mean, Tommy?"

"I don't know, boss. Just something my mother would always say when one of us was not our self but there wasn't any kind of interference or traps out there on the track. I can tell you that."

"I'm glad to hear that from you Tommy. This sponge thing has got me upset and a little bit on edge. Not that I don't know it happens but why to one of my horses?"

The next day was the forty-third day of the Cuba meeting. Tommy was homesick, for sure, but the clear sunny day and the 75 degree temperature worked wonders for his melancholy. Tommy was out on the track early, walking and exercising Kay Spence's string, and breezing Walter Mack for two furlongs on the inside track. That was to be Tommy's mount in the afternoon's fourth race and the horse was just full of himself. He knew he was going to run today and he was anxious and excited to get on with it. It took all Tommy had to hold him back in the two furlong work. He looked and felt good and fit. Tommy was encouraged because he knew he would only be there for the ride. Walter Mack already indicated his intentions to go wire to wire.

However, deep in the back of Tommy's mind was that ever present knowledge that someone had tampered with one of Spence's horses. Tommy felt for sure it was directed at him and not at Spence at all. He suspected that Pock was still at his little games of touting his "sure bets" to unsuspecting horse players and then bribing backside workers to provide certain little fixes that would interfere with the outcomes of certain races. Just a few days earlier a stirrup strap failed at the end of a stretch run and dumped the jockey of the leading horse, which had also been the favorite, allowing a 15-to-1 shot to cross the wire just a head in front of the second and third place contender. Somebody cashed in some big tickets, but at the expense of the health and welfare of an unsuspecting horse and human. The strap had been cut, so it wasn't an accident. That really got Tommy's Irish up, but he was resolved not to be vocal about it. Instead, he decided to "hide-and-watch" and keep a low profile. He did, however, go back to his trunk and dig out his Saint Christopher medal and pinned it to his shirt along with his mother's crucifix and St. Patrick's medal. He realized that there was no patron saint of horse racing, but since St. Christopher was the patron saint of travelers, his image would serve the purpose of guaranteeing a safe trip from the barrier to the wire. Now he had no worries and no fears and could concentrate on good rides.

After Tommy finished his morning chores and duties, he donned his layered flannel and wool garments and put on his rubber suit for laps around the track. Making weight this way was very exhausting, but it helped with his own conformation and muscle strength, and this was something Mr. Spence had always harped on.

He would say, "If you're not fit and strong, then I don't want you on my horses. They are too valuable to trust to a rag-doll and if you have to take pills and powders, or worms and whisky to make weight, then you are nothing more than a rag-doll, weak and flimsy. I don't want you in my barn or near my horses. It takes a team to win races, a good horse and a good jockey and I condition both!"

Tommy took much pride in meeting Kay Spence's standards, as did Harry and Billy. When they put on the Spence colors, they knew they represented the best in the business and they knew people were watching them. That is why they were sought after by other owners and trainers to ride their mounts and if Kay Spence didn't already have his boys entered in a race on one of his string, then he was more than happy to loan his boys out. Spence always watched each of his boys' races, regardless of for whom they were riding and at some point after the race, he would then discuss the race individually at an informal debriefing.

Tommy was anxious for the fourth race to take place. Harry was equally anxious for the fifth. They had a friendly bet with each other that they would win their respective races that afternoon, even predicting their strategies and guesses how the races would pan out. Spence quietly enjoyed overhearing the boys exude their confidence in themselves and their mounts, but didn't let on he was paying any attention. He even secretly sent one of his grooms over to place a five dollar win bet on each of the boys' races for him to put in their boot when he gave them the leg up in the paddock.

Tommy drew the second post position on Walter Mack. To his left in the first position was a five-year-old filly named Mae Murray. Tommy looked over at her and whispered, "Girl, I hope you're faster than the rest of us Murrays. You sure are prettier!"

With that, Jimmy Milton hollered "Come on!" and they were off. Just as Tommy had predicted to Harry, Walter Mack ran his own race, setting a very fast pace and leading all the way. When second place Miss Wright challenged him in the stretch, Walter Mack found another gear and easily disposed of her in a timely fashion. Back at the winner's circle, Tommy got the nod from the judges' stand and dismounted, gathering up his tack and weighing in.

"Be sure to check your boot when you change in there," Spence told him as he patted him on the back and sent him on to the jockeys' room.

Spence then headed over to where Harry was standing to weigh-out for the next race.

This fifth race on the day's card was the Overseas Handicap for three-year-olds an upward, with a prize of $800, worth $650 to the winner. Spence had two entries in this handicap. Harry was aboard eight-year-old Hocnir starting from the fourth position and Tommy was on four-year-old Woodthrush who drew the first post position. Billy Kelsay also had a mount for the Handicap, five-year-old Deckmate, owned by G.W. Loft. Also in this race was Willie Knapp riding the six-year-old Wise Man for Armonia Stable.

The field of six was at the post for two minutes before a slow and good start. Belle Roberts set a fast pace and tired after racing Wise Man into defeat. Deckmate was in close quarters while rounding the far turn and came fast when clear. Wise Man tired after racing in the lead on the last turn. Hocnir settled in fourth place until the stretch run where he came around the leaders and finished fast to win going away. Woodthrush on the rail quickly fell into last place after the start and Tommy couldn't get him to recover and finished ten lengths behind fifth place Daddy's Choice but at the end of the day, that line-up was just a testament to Kay Spence's ability as a jockey conditioner. Out of six jockeys, three were Spence's boys and one was the proven veteran Willie Knapp.

"I knew the old boy had it in him," Harry told Spence back at the winner's circle. He's just like my ol'beagle dog back home. Give him something to chase and he'll run all day long till he catches it and puts it away."

Spence replied, "Harry that's because you played him real smart and kept him under wraps until the end of the stretch. When you let him go, he still had some race left in him. A smart jockey on a proven veteran will work magic every time. Good job, son. Oh, and be sure to check your boot when you change colors."

Both Tommy and Harry each had a mount for the final race of the day for other trainers, and even though Spence had nothing entered, there he was at the rail keeping an eye on his boys.

That evening back at the barn, Tommy recalled the events of the past day and could not come up with any kinds of unusual occurrences with the races or the horses. His last race of the day for Spence aboard Woodthrush was indeed a poor showing, but there were no indications of tampering or race fixing. He thumbed through the outdated newspapers and racing reports he collected and cut out the ones that interested him to put into his scrapbook. In anticipation of getting back to racing in the states, particularly Latonia, he kept track of all the warm weather winter meetings, and who were the big winning horses, trainers, and jockeys. He recorded their names in a special section of his book because he was going to beat them all this coming spring. Every night he dreamed of going home and racing at Latonia, where he could once again be with his family and friends, and especially with his best girl, Virginia, who he was going to marry as soon as he could get back home. Only she didn't know it. Which he did (this was the signature last line to many of the Seckatary Hawkins stories, which Tommy so admired).

CHAPTER THIRTY
"That's Racing"

The remainder of January at Oriental Park was basically a continuation of what had been. The Spence boys were developing into some fine horse riders and were getting plenty of mounts in the Cuba meeting. Kay Spence was making a very good showing with his stable, even picking up a potentially good claimer here and there. Besides training and conditioning his own string, he was also adding other owners' horses to his stable to train. His barn was filling and his workers had plenty to keep them busy and employed.

It was just about the halfway point of the winter meeting and the time of the year in which everyone was beginning to anticipate getting back to racing in the states, and every body had their own dreams and goals to pursue. Tommy's was to become one of the leading riders in the country as soon as possible and that goal was reflected in his determination and work ethic there in Cuba. He would have ridden six or seven races a day if he had had the opportunity to do so. Spence gave him as many mounts as he could justify. There were just some horses better suited for one of the other jockeys. A lot of times there is certain chemistry between horse and rider that doesn't materialize when another jockey gets the call. Spence was an exceptional horseman and trainer and he picked up on these little subtleties and used them to his advantage. After all, the bottom line was to get to the wire first and safely. Second choice was to be in the money but Tommy got his chances on these other horses in the early mornings, because Spence knew how important it was for a young rider to experience every possible difference in the make-up of horses' personalities, running styles, behaviors, attitudes, strengths and weaknesses, quirks, and idiosyncrasies.

So all through the month of February, Tommy petitioned for all the rides he could get. When Kay Spence didn't have a spot for him in a particular race, he would help Tommy find rides with other owners and trainers, much like a personal jockey agent would do. When Tommy would get back to the States and work as a journeyman jockey, he would have to hire a personal jockey agent to find him mounts when his contract holder couldn't use him but Spence held Tommy's contract and thereby was Tommy's first obligation. However, he encouraged Tommy to get out and meet all the other owners and trainers and offer his services to them. That way, he would become familiar to them and they would recognize his name and his face and would subconsciously stay in the back of their minds and if he was polite and convincing and walked the walk and talked the talk, then they would someday call on him.

"Just remember, Tommy," Spence would say. "When you're out there working and riding, I'm not the only one watching and paying attention to you. There are a whole lot of eyes out there sizing you up and how you conduct yourself right now down here in Cuba will play a big part in determining how well you will do when we get back to the States. You are in the public's eye, and it's an eye that sees it all."

Tommy continued to work hard and tirelessly. Every night before falling asleep, he would write in his book about the events of the day, the races he ran, what he learned, the mistakes he made, the people he interacted with, information about the horses he rode and how he handled them, anything he could think of that had any bearing on his goals and ambitions. On Saturday, February 8th, he wrote, "MY SECOND HAT TRICK" in big letters across the page. Under that, he had pasted the page from the racing form that showed the charts of the day's races (Since his first hat trick never made it to newsprint, he was particularly proud to have one to paste in his book). Tommy finished first in the first three races on the card for that day, and each race was for a different owner and trainer. He even managed a third place in the sixth race as well. He was entered in four of the six races of the day and finished in the money in all four of them. As he clutched his two medals and gave thanks, he thought of Virginia and his brothers and sisters back home in Covington and how much he missed them, wishing they had been present to witness his accomplishments.

For the next week, Tommy continued in this same vein. He was getting mounts in a majority of races each day and coming through with some winners and places. Harry and Billy were also getting their fair share of rides and successes, but they just weren't as hot as Tommy was at the time.

"That's racing," Spence would tell them.

"That's his answer for everything," Harry lamented. "Like everything happens the way it does because that's how it's supposed to happen. What about skill and strategy and smarts and stuff like that? Don't that have nothin' to do with it?"

"Sure it does, Harry," Tommy chimed in. "He's just saying that racing is so unpredictable because there are so many variables involved that nobody can control so it's important to control the ones you can so maybe you can get the better of the ones you can't! Ya see? Racin' with skill and smarts and strategy gives you the edge over the guy who doesn't have them and that gives you the advantage over him when it comes to dealing with those variables that nobody can control."

"In other words," Harry retorted, "it's just plain ol' luck."

"No, it ain't just luck at all," Tommy insisted. "Don't you think being a fit and strong athlete has something to do with it? Or having a good trainer who really cares for the health and well being of his horses? Or knowing how to deal with a bowed tendon? Or what kind of shoes to run on the horse? These are all advantages over the ones that don't have these things, and that's what makes the difference."

"Well, if luck ain't got nothin' to do with it," Harry chided, "then how come you're all the time crossin' yourself and wearin' medals of saints and steppin' over cracks and runnin' away from cats and stuff like that? Now answer me that!"

"Harry, now dammit," Tommy retorted. "I ain't saying that luck don't play a part in race ridin'. Sure as life, it does! I'm just trying to avoid the kinda luck that *you* wind up with all the time!"

With that, Tommy smacked Harry on the back and let out a hearty gut laugh as Harry took off chasing him through the stable and outside around the barns.

"Hey you two! Knock it off! I got enough doctoring to do around here without having to worry 'bout my monkeys getting hurt too," Spence shouted as Harry tackled Tommy at the edge of the muck pile where they rolled and wrestled around until they were exhausted from all the laughing.

As they were beginning to make their way back to the stable, their arms draped over each other's shoulder and still laughing, Spence hollered, "Stop right where you are. Don't dare step foot in this barn! You think I want all them flies to get on my horses?" He tossed a big rectangular bar of yellow lye laundry soap at them and pointed at the big lake at the other end of the backside. "Don't come back until you're soaking wet and white again!"

In other words, Spence was telling the boys that he would finish up the barn chores while they took a little time off for some fun and recreation and maybe work in a bath on the side.

The boys were starting to get restless and giddy in anticipation of the impending spring season approaching. Already there was talk and plans for getaway day being discussed everywhere on the backside, and it wasn't even March yet but Lent was quickly approaching and that always made for thoughts of spring, which meant getting back to the states and seeing family and friends and beginning a brand new racing season. For the backstretch community, getaway day meant different things to different people depending on what track and for what race meeting they were headed. For Tommy and Harry though, it meant Latonia, not the race track, but the city. Home sweet home!

CHAPTER THIRTY-ONE
Labor Strike

Tuesday, March 4, 1919 was Day 75 of the Cuba-American Jockey Club meeting at Oriental Park. The completion of the sixth race on that day's ticket marked the beginning of an eight-day layoff holiday at the track in honor of the beginning of Lent. At least that was Tommy's interpretation for the interruption of daily racing.

"What you gonna give up for Lent this year, Tommy?" inquired Harry.

"I don't know, Harry. Mother always told us to give up something that we enjoyed every day, so's it was a real sacrifice."

"Then I guess you should give up finishing out of the money in every race you ride," chided Harry obviously more impressed with his own wit than he was by the hard bristle grooming brush fired his way by Tommy and finding its mark just above his right eye.

"Damn, Tommy, I'm bleeding."

"Then maybe you should give up pissing off an Irishman for Lent," retorted Tommy.

"What the hell is going on, you two?" screamed Spence from down the shed row. "That ain't the kind of horsin' around we do here. Yeah, it's funny till one of you puts a damn eye out. Now get outta here. I don't want my horses smellin' fresh blood. It'll get 'em upset. Harry, you're ridin' in this first race, so get that cut doctored up and get ready. Tommy, you take him into the tack room and get some of that wound liniment and salve on his forehead and be quick about it!"

In the paddock, Spence gave Harry a leg up while giving instructions. "I think Plain Bill has a good chance to break his maiden in this race but you're gonna have to rate him good. That horse of Diaz's is a Madden-bred colt, and Billy's up. You gottta save some horse for the stretch run. That's what it's going to come down to. How's your head feeling?"

"Oh, I'm fine, boss. Just where am I?"

"Away with you, clown," Spence grumbled as Harry lined up in the post parade.

They were three minutes at the starting barrier before Jim Milton could get them away cleanly. Plain Bill took off from the get go and was the front runner for the first quarter, even under Harry's restraint but in the homestretch, Billy Kelsay was driving Sea Bat hard and he was in close pursuit by Grey Rump, who bettered Harry's horse by a neck at the wire.

Spence didn't have much to say back at the paddock. He watched the race and saw that Plain Bill didn't have anything left at the end. At least the thirty-dollar third-place winnings would help pay the hay bill. Harry hurried back to the jockey house to change into another stable's colors for the second race. Billy was also there changing.

"Ain't you feelin' good, Harry?" Billy asked.

"Why you ask?" a startled Harry answered.

"Oh, I dunno. Seemed like you could've took second if you'd a gone to the whip."

"Who knows?" Harry replied. "Guess I could have driven him harder at the end, but I had him under wraps so long, I didn't wanna confuse him by punishing him at the end. I think he's got the heart, he just needs to learn to conserve a little energy for the end."

"Well, looked to me like he wore you out, Harry," Billy whispered.

Truth be known, Harry wasn't up for his game. He was feeling lightheaded and generally weak, almost loopy. He wasn't sure what was going on, but he didn't feel normal at all. He kept wondering if this was how it felt to be drunk, because he had never been intoxicated. He just felt detached and he had a headache and just wanted to lie down in his cot and take a nap.

At the paddock, Spence and Harry discussed their strategies for this next race as they usually did. It was a claiming race for three-year-old maidens and Spence had good feelings about this Blondel's racing ability. He was just hoping that other owners or trainers didn't have the same premonitions about this horse's future, because he surely didn't want to lose him to a claim. He just didn't have the right conformation for a superior runner, but he sure had the drive and determination and he loved competition. His ears were perfectly perked and his eyes piercing as his anticipation mounted. As Harry mounted, he felt Spence slip something into his boot. He winked and Harry winked back.

"Let's meet up in the winner's circle in a couple!" shouted Harry as he joined the post parade headed for the ninth post position.

Blondel was extremely calm at the starting barrier; his ears still perked straight up and his piercing eyes straight forward for the full two minute interval before Jimmy Milton had them off. Harry sat perfectly motionless and limp, which had an obvious calming effect on the horse. The horse broke well and patiently allowed the crowd to settle into their lanes before he took over. By the half mile pole, he had moved from eighth place to third by a length and he was still coming, going out in front on the last turn and keeping it, winning easily. The second and third place finishers were neck and neck down the stretch and finished driving in a gamely fashion. The win paid $11.20 straight and Harry was thankful for the one in his boot. The net value to the winner was $400. So far it was a good day for Kay Spence Stables.

Harry got the nod when he pulled up to the winner's circle and Spence helped him unsaddle and make it over to the scales after the winner's presentation. By this time, Harry was feeling rough. He had a very bad headache and felt like he was going to regurgitate, which he indeed did when he walked into the jockeys' room. Tommy soon entered the room to dress for the next race. He had picked up a mount on another trainer's English bred five-year-old for the next race, a claimer for four-year-olds and up.

As Tommy was being assisted by the valet, he looked around and asked, "Where's Harry? I just saw him walk in here ahead of me."

"He's in there, flippin," another jockey answered, pointing to the flipping sink in the corner of the room.

"But Harry don't need to flip. His weight is just fine."

As Tommy was headed out to the paddock for the next race, he asked his valet to check in on Harry. "He must be sick," he said as he was walking through the door.

"Lord, if I was to go in there now while he's a flippin like that, I be gittin' sick too! No sir! Long as he's makin that noise, I knows he's still 'live," said the valet out loud to himself.

The race was underway in just under a minute at the barrier. Tommy was in the fifth post position in the field of seven. First Ballot, next to him in the sixth spot, jumped to take the lead quickly and set a good pace. At the head of the stretch, it was First Ballot in the lead by two lengths over Kingfisher. Tommy was in fifth place, but his horse had found another gear and was coming along in a rush. He finished driving and won drawing clear, a half length ahead of First Ballot who also was driving but gave way at the wire. Tommy felt good. It was his only race of the day, but he was the only apprentice in the race and he had won it.

Tommy was in a hurry to get back to the jockey room to check on Harry. He knew that Harry had a mount on one of Spence's horses in each of the last two races of the day. When he arrived, he found Harry sound asleep and snoring on a bench, still in his silks from the third race. Tommy tried to wake Harry up time and again, but he wouldn't open his eyes.

"C'mon Harry. Wake up. You got two more races to ride. Get up!"

He smacked his cheeks, poured water in his face, and shook him continuously. One of the valets came over to assist and handed Tommy a small green bottle with a black stopper for a lid.

"Here, try this," he said.

Tommy pulled off the stopper, took a whiff, and commenced to jumping up and down shaking his head back and forth. "Damn! What the hell is that stuff?"

182

"It's smelling salts," said the valet in a very low tone. "It's for women. When they faint," he went on. "It was my mother's. She gave it to me to carry when I go to church because women are always fainting in church because their corsets are usually cutting off their blood supply to their head."

"You think Harry's blood supply got cut off?" asked Tommy.

"I ain't no doctor nor veterinary," said the valet, "but it's sure worth a try, ain't it? Seein' as how you're trying to wake him up quick like."

"Yep, let's try it," Tommy agreed. "We gotta do something, and in a hurry, too. Mr. Spence will be having a cow shortly if Harry ain't over in the paddock soon."

They placed the bottle right under Harry's nostrils and then pinched his lips shut so he wouldn't mouth breathe. It wasn't but a few seconds and up off that bench came Harry, flailing his arms back and forth and jumping around in circles, screaming and hollering like somebody had put a battery under his saddle cloth and turned it all the way up.

"Whoa, whoa, Harry! Now calm down. It's me, Tommy! You was plumb out of it and we been trying to get you to come to for a long time. C'mon now. You're riding in this next race. Let's get out there," Tommy pleaded.

They led Harry through the jockey room door and across a small lane to the paddock area, where Spence was waiting with Anlace and a groom. As Spence gave Harry a leg up, he patted him on the thigh and whispered, "Now don't forget our strategy, son," and off he went to the post.

Harry couldn't have been in a thicker fog if he had found himself at a 4:30 a.m. workout on a track right next to the Ohio River on a humid night. He knew there was a purpose for which he was perched up on the back of a 1,200 pound animal and being led to a spot where other similarly huge animals were lined up, but he just couldn't quite seem to find that missing piece to the puzzle. Soon, that cacophony of discordant and incoherent sounds, mixed with the familiar smells of freshly oiled leather, camphor and sulfur-based liniments, and equine sweat and musk, manure and dirt suddenly started making sense. Harry abruptly realized what was going on as Jimmy uttered "C'mon" the signal to commence racing.

Harry was in the seventh post position out of nine as the horses broke cleanly. His head was pounding and his vision was cloudy. He actually felt to see if he had goggles on. By now, he was fully aware of his surroundings and what he was doing but he couldn't for the life of him recall what Spence had meant when he told him to not forget their strategy. Harry couldn't even remember ever talking to Spence, much less what their plan of strategy was. As he and Anlace were steadily overcoming the others, coming out of the last turn and into the final stretch, they were just a neck behind the leader Kimpalong who just had found another gear to put away the challenging and briefly leading Cabello just before entering the final turn. As they were both still driving at the line, it was the nose of Kimpalong that broke the plane. Anlace and Harry had to settle for the one hundred dollar second place payoff.

Tommy met Harry back at the saddling paddock, anxiously concerned about his friend's condition but consciously avoiding seeming alarmed.

"You okay, Harry?" he asked.

"Well, yeah, I guess. Who are you?"

"C'mon, Harry. I'm serious. How do you feel? I think you are suffering a concussion from when I hit you with that grooming brush," Tommy said apologetically. "I was reading up about it in the veterinary book."

"Well, what is it?" inquired Harry.

Tommy explained, "It's when your brain inside gets whacked against the inside of your skull when you hit it hard enough. It can actually bruise your brain and make it swell if you get hit hard enough. It'll make you forget stuff and act goofy and confused, like you was earlier. If the brain swells or bleeds too much, then you just up and die, like when you leave a mason jar full of water outside in the winter and it freezes and it busts the jar in pieces. Harry, I didn't mean to kill ya! I swear," Tommy sobbed to his best friend and partner. "The book says that if the swelling gets too much, you should drill a hole in the skull to let off pressure. That's when it happens to a horse or cow. It don't tell you what to do for a person. Harry, I don't want to drill a hole in yer head, less you tell me to go ahead an' do it. Don't die on me, Harry!" he sobbed even more.

At this point, Kay walked up to the boys with Sasenta on a lead. She walked right up to Harry and nudged his back, almost as if she were saying *"Hey, pay attention to me and let's get going."* She knew she was about to run a race and she couldn't contain herself. This was not the time to be wasting her time on Tommy.

Harry looked back at the four-year-old filly and greeted her with a loving rub down her forehead and nose. Then he looked over at Kay Spence who calmly, but sternly, said, "C'mon Harry. Look alive. Get mounted and get out there. The old girl can't stand it any longer. She wants to run now. This is the last race before the break. You two can lollygag for a whole week after this and what the hell is Tommy crying for?"

He helped Harry with a leg up and slipped something in his boot. Just like that, Harry was back to earth. As he and Sasenta joined the post parade, Harry answered Spence's question, "Ah, he thinks he's gonna have to drill a hole in my head."

Spence just nodded in agreement and headed over towards the finish line, taking a quick visual inspection of the winner's circle, where he planned on beginning his week off.

"I think I'm the one with the hole in the head," he murmured to himself.

CHAPTER THIRTY-TWO
Closed For Lent

Sasenta automatically headed for the winner's circle. It wasn't her first day on the job. Harry just shook his head back and forth, grinning all the while.

"I started my week off up there at the starting barrier," he hollered Spence's way as he waited for the nod from the judge. "I didn't have to do anything in that race, but just sit still. She done it all! She rated her own self and then switched to that next gear all by herself when Gordon Russell challenged her at the end. What a filly!" he said as he made his way to the scales.

When they all got back to the barn, Kay Spence was in a pretty good mood. He just won another $450 and he rewarded the boys with the two tickets he slipped into Harry's boot just before the race.

"Kids, I ain't gonna work you to death on this break. You been working very hard this whole meeting and we've made a pretty good show of it so far. Now we got plenty of daily chores and doctoring to attend to, along with exercising, walking, breezing, and works and of course, there's plenty of housekeeping, cleaning, tack repairs and conditioning. Other than that, I want you two to enjoy the week.

At that, Tommy and Harry commenced to split a gut. *"He's got to be kidding,"* they both thought to themselves but dared not say it.

"What's so funny, you two?" Spence grinned. "You want me to find you some more things to do? I can do it, you know!"

When the horses were fed and attended to and the rest of the chores were completed, the boys headed to the infield lake with their cake of lye soap. They took their time today and enjoyed the water swimming and bathing.

"Harry," Tommy said solemnly, "I sure would 'a missed you a lot if I really had 'a killed you. I'm glad you're okay."

"Me too," answered Harry. "It would be awful hard to stay on a horse if you was dead and that's all I want to do is race ride."

"Harry, when we get back to Kentucky, we gotta stick together and watch out for each other, okay? So we don't get hurt, or injured, or swindled, or tempted to take bribes or fix races, or any of that stuff that goes on in the big circuits. Okay?"

"That's a deal, buddy," said Harry as they shook hands.

"And another thing," Tommy added. "I'm gonna marry Virginia as soon as we get back."

"What?!" shouted Harry. "Why you can't do that, she's my own cousin!"

"Why not?" asked Tommy indignantly. "What's wrong with that?"

"Cause if I'm your best friend, then that means I get to kiss on your wife any time I want to and I sure don't want to be kissin' my own cousin, now, do I?"

Tommy cocked back the bar of soap as he took keen aim on Harry's head. Then he caught himself and remembered all that had transpired over the past day.

The next morning, Tommy made his way over to the clubhouse where Ash Wednesday services were being held. There he joined many others from the track in the celebration of a High Mass to officially kick off the Lenten season of the Roman Catholic Church, probably the most significant religious event and celebration of Christianity in general and Catholicism in particular. For several days prior, the locals were celebrating what they called Carnivale. It was essentially the same thing as Mardi Gras, which Tommy had heard so much about from the veteran jockeys who rode the New Orleans circuit. Literally translated into the regional dialect, carnivale meant "goodbye to meat." The partying and festival atmosphere leading up to Ash Wednesday was a chance to indulge, or more accurately, over-indulge in the things that were to be voluntarily given up for the next 40 days as penitence for sinning, culminating in the crucifixion and death of the son of God for the forgiveness of all mankind's sins and then his resurrection from death to join his father in the Kingdom of Heaven. Meat was the mandated, or implied and expected article of abstinence.

Why the racing was suddenly going to cease starting today, Ash Wednesday, Tommy did not really understand. All that Spence told the boys was that the track was closing down for a while. He didn't explain why, and they didn't ask. Tommy just assumed that it was in respect for the beginning of Lent, but Tommy wasn't convinced that that was the real reason. He figured it was just a good time for the track to close and give all involved a much-needed break, since patronage would naturally be at a low because of people abstaining from their favorite vices, all of which were featured and plentiful at Oriental Park. It just made good business sense and after several days of penitence and abstinence, most people by then will have broken their Lenten vows and things would be back to normal. Tommy always was convinced that humans were much more creatures of habit than horses were and therefore, easier to figure out. After this sabbatical ran its course, attendance at the track would be better than it had been for the entire meeting so far.

The real reason for the track's unplanned and unannounced closing was due to a general labor and transportation strike called by Cuban labor leaders. Oriental Park was located on the outskirts of

Havana, in the town and municipality of Marianao. It was about six miles southwest of Havana and was connected by a rail line, which was the major transportation resource between the two. With the strike going on, attendance would be sparse at best, so the track owners decided to curb their losses and suspend racing. Havana, at this time, had basically two social classes, the very rich and the very poor native peasants. The rich class was comprised of the high society celebrity vacationers from America who came there because alcohol and gambling were not controlled or banned as was the case in the United States. There were also the major Cuban and American business and industry magnates who monopolized the various local industries at the expense of the poor laborer and worker, like the sugar industry. Other major agricultural exported products such as tobacco and fruits and vegetables for American winter consumption kept the labor force busy. Some Cuban ranchers did very well in cattle ranching and export. Along about 1911, the Cuban government sent representatives to the U.S. to purchase Thoroughbred stock to begin experimentation for the establishment of Thoroughbred horse breeding. By 1919, there were approximately three quarters of a million Thoroughbreds in Cuba. Deep down, Tommy figured the track didn't close in honor of the beginning of the Lenten season.

"I thought you were going to church, son," commented Spence as Tommy made his way into the tack room.

"That's where I been, Boss."

"Well what the hell is that black shit all over your face, boy?"

"Huh?"

"You got black shit on your forehead, boy. What you been into?"

"Them's ashes, sir. For Ash Wednesday. The priest burns up all the Palm leaves from last week's Palm Sunday and then uses all the ashes from that to put on our foreheads today."

"Just more of your Irish hokie- pokey superstitions, eh?"

"No, Mr. Spence. It's part of Lent. It's a reminder to all of us that Jesus died on the cross to absolve all of our sins so we can have eternal salvation in our next life. The ashes are a sign that we are mortal beings and when we die we turn back into ashes and dust so we put the ashes on our foreheads to show our penance for our sins. It's like the sackcloth and ashes from the bible, sir. You know."

They both could hear Harry chuckling in the background.

"What you laughing at, Harry?" demanded Tommy.

"Nothin," Harry answered. "It's just that it seems so complicated trying to be a Catholic. Do you ever get to lose your bug and become a journeyman Catholic like the ones that hang out here and drink hooch and play the horses?"

"Enough of you, Harry!" Tommy shot back with a half way smirk on his face. "What you know about Catholics wouldn't fill a dog tick!"

"Oh yeah? Well I know this much. I know my uncle won't never allow my cousin to marry a Catholic! How 'bout that for knowing something?"

That really struck a nerve with Tommy because it was already weighing heavily on his mind and he knew Harry was right. Warren Conley didn't have much use for Catholics or Catholicism. He thought they were too uppity and self righteous for their own good. His long established Anglican upbringing assured him that certain teachings of the Catholic Church were blatantly false and did not reflect the biblical infallacy of King James. He would never allow such a union.

Tommy was quiet the rest of the day. He completed all his chores and then helped Kay Spence thoroughly inspect each one of his horses and treat their individual needs and concerns accordingly, from firing an ankle to applying bandages to just quality time rubbing and massaging certain good horses.

"Wish I could spend this kind of time with each one of them," Tommy told Spence. "I think they all need special personal attention."

"Yeah, prob'ly so, son but then there wouldn't be enough time to train or run them, would there?"

"Guess not, sir but we got time now and I plan on spending time with each one of these fellers."

"Well, that's fine, Tommy. Just don't you go getting out of shape or gettin' heavy. We gotta be on the top of things as soon as this strike is over and as much as this place caters to the rich and famous from the U.S., it sure ain't gonna last too long. I guarantee that!"

That night, Tommy had trouble getting to sleep. He was suffering from a touch of melancholy and he knew it was from his worrying about how he was going to be able to marry his girl, Virginia. If only he could just snatch her up and run off somewhere to get married. It just wasn't fair that he couldn't marry a non-Catholic. It wasn't fair of her father and it wasn't fair of the church. He may have cried a little that night but by next morning he couldn't remember for sure if he did or not.

CHAPTER THIRTY-THREE
Race Day, Again

One afternoon, about a week later, Tommy spotted Pock snooping around the stabling area and the barns. He was dressed like he was rich and important, just like the vacationers who party all night at the Hotel Inglaterra in Havana and then catch the special train and spend all day at the track in Marianao. He looked rather hideous, Tommy thought, wearing a lightweight white cotton suit and a straw hat banded with a black silk ribbon around the crown. He would constantly be writing down things in his little spiral notebook as he infiltrated the grooms and rubbers and hotwalkers. Seldom would he be seen talking to a trainer, and that was probably due to his repulsive demeanor and personality. He tried so hard to come off as genuine and informed, but in reality, there was no mistake that he was just that last pinch of manure as the sphincter closed and the tail went down.

"Harry!" Tommy called to his buddy. "Look at what I see over there."

Harry snickered, "Well, I'll be. That means the strike is over and we'll be race riding tomorrow. Yee haw!"

That indeed was the fact. There could be no other explanation for the return of Pock and the fact that he was there at Oriental Park could only mean the trains were running and the transportation and labor strike was over. He was trolling for tips and the latest gossip and news around the backside. It didn't matter how insignificant or general it was. He would take common knowledge and alter it and spin it into something he would offer as privileged, inside information to those people who were eager to part with their cash in exchange.

Spence walked into the shed row announcing, "Have ya heard, boys?"

Tommy called out from the tack room, "We ain't heard nothin', boss but we just figured out that we'll be race riding tomorrow!"

"Now how'd you find that out?" Spence asked.

"Oh, you might say a little rat told us, right Harry?"

"That's right, sir. The vermin don't show up until things are ripe and that was our sign that things were ripe!"

Spence had a very puzzled look on his face compared to the smirks on the faces of his two boys.

"You two are just daft! You just ain't quite right!" Spence continued, "I just came from the chief steward's office. They called all us trainers and owners in for a special meeting. The strike is over for now and they will be resuming racing tomorrow afternoon. They're going to start right where the strike had stopped us eight days ago so that means you two will be back in the saddle and will hopefully boot a couple home so we can pay some feed bills around here."

The boys hadn't slacked up any during this unexpected break in the routine. They both kept in shape and maintained their riding weight and they kept the horses in good health and good form. Everyday had been treated as any other normal day at a meeting as far as works and breezes and gallops and walks were concerned. The horses were more contented when their routines were not changed or interrupted. Afternoons even included some intramural events for the stable, allowing different horses each day to participate in practice contests with each other and with other stables. It was fun for the jockeys and good for the horses.

Spence would say, "If it's good enough for the professional baseball teams to practice on off days, then it's good enough for us, too!"

The next day came and went just as if nothing had ever happened. Tommy and Harry each had a winning ride for the Spence Stable, and even his newest apprentice, L Woods, all 84 pounds of him, took a first place win. The boys also managed two third-place finishes that day.

"Now that'll cover some feed for a while, won't it, Harry?" Tommy said as he rode into the winner's circle where Kay Spence could only just shake his head and grin.

He was proud of his boys and he was pleased when they showed pride in themselves. Besides being one of the country's most consistently successfully horse trainers, Spence had a reputation of conditioning excellent jockeys that succeeded in the racing profession long after leaving his nest. As a matter of fact, unbeknownst to Harry, Spence recognized that it was Harry's time to get out on his own and try his luck on the higher class circuits and tracks as a journeyman jockey. As he watched Woods win his first today, he realized it was time to condition a new boy and give Harry his much deserved wings.

"Harry, my boy! Come in, come in," Spence said as he laid aside his copy of the *Daily Racing Form*.

"Tommy said you wanted to see me, sir, in private. Something wrong, Mr. Spence?"

"No, Harry, no. Ain't nothin' wrong. You can relax. Here, sit down on this hay bale. I need to talk with you," Spence returned, clearing off a spot for Harry to sit.

"How long you been with me Harry?"

"Since the fall meeting up there at Latonia, sir, nineteen and sixteen. Remember? I tol' you I was gonna be a jockey, only I didn't have no horses to ride and you said I looked more like a choir boy who got lost on his way to church. Remember that, sir?"

"Ah, indeed I do, Harry. Indeed, I do. As I recall, you were dressed up in an ivory corduroy suit with a frilly, lacy shirt, and a matching corduroy cap. All clean and proper like."

"Yep, that was me. I was on my way down to the old theater on Ritte's Corner where I sang in a vaudeville show with my older brother, Walter. Mama always slicked me down and made me wear them suits. I felt like a little girl or something, all dressed up like that. I wanted to be a race rider, and live at the track, and work hard, and get dirty and sweaty, and become a famous jockey like Roscoe Goose and win the Kentucky Derby at 100-to-1 odds."

"Yes, I remember that" said Spence reminiscing. "That's when I told you that I was there at Latonia in 1915, when Roscoe's younger brother, Carl, was killed in a racing accident."

"Yes sir, I remember that real good. You told me that race riding was very demanding and dangerous and it wasn't all fun and glory. You told me to stick with singing and performing Vaudeville because it held a better future for a little fella like me."

"Ha, ha, yes, and you told me that 'this little fella wasn't gonna ride no stage. He was gonna ride the horse!"

"Well, Harry, you accomplished what you told me you were going to do. You've developed into one of the best horse riders in these circuits. Always been on the top ten list of apprentices according to the *Form*. It's time now you struck out on your own. You've completed your apprenticeship and it's time now to lose you bug."

"Wow, Mr. Spence," Harry choked out in a broken voice. "You mean it? You really mean it? I'm good enough to be out on my own?"

"Well, Harry, that's up to you to determine. I think you're good enough. That's why I recommended you to my friend John Schorr and he wants you to meet up with him at Churchill in April. You're going to be one of his contract riders. That is, if you want it. He's been begging me to cut you loose so he could get you into his stable."

"Holy Mackerel!" Harry shouted. "You mean John F. Schorr? The trainer for Mr. McLean, the big newspaper publisher?"

"That's right, Harry, Edward Beal McClean, the Cincinnati and Washington newspaper publisher. He's got himself quite a string of horseflesh in his barn, and one hell of a trainer."

"I, I can't believe it, sir. He wants me to be one of his riders? Why, he's even got a horse he's entering in the Kentucky Derby this year!"

"That's right, Harry. And if you play your cards right and keep working real hard and steer clear of the dope and the crooks and the scum, you might find yourself a mount for that race this year."

"Yee haw!" Harry screamed as he jumped up from the hay bale and flung his cap in the air.

A couple of the horses answered with a snort to this outburst, the others just watched but obviously entertained by Harry's shenanigans.

"What's all the commotion about?" asked Tommy, bolting through the tack room door. "I heard the screaming all the way down to the kitchen. What's up?"

"Oh, nothin' much, Tommy," Spence answered. "Come the first of the week, Harry is headed home to Covington."

"Yep," smiled Spence. "Figgered he might's well spend a couple weeks visiting with the kin folks and friends up home, a'fore he went on to Louisville. It'll do him good to have some time to blow out some of them cobwebs in his head. He's gotta get mentally prepared for his next adventure. I got his ticket right here," holding up an envelope and waving it above his head. "Yep, a train ticket back to Havana. Then boat passage back to Miami and another train ticket to Covington Depot."

"I can't believe you're doing all this for me, Mr. Spence," Harry half whispered and half choked out.

"Ain't no sense in training horses if I can't see how they do in the races and it ain't no sense in training good jockeys if I can't watch them boot home the winners," Spence replied.

"Well, how can you afford it to send me all the way home and then back to Churchill?" inquired Harry, apologetically.

"Now, boys, come on. You know I got my ways to manage things like this. Why, I merely had ol' Cupe place a bet here and there for me, when I saw the odds were right and I knew one of you would bring home a winner. Stuck the winnings in a sock just for occasions like this."

Harry started fighting back tears, but his sobs ratted him out. Tommy laughed out loud, as tears clouded his vision. The two boys embraced and then began jumping around in unison, laughing and crying at the same time. The horses continued to watch the show and occasionally let a whinny to voice their approval. Harry was officially a professional journeyman jockey, with a Kay Spence recommendation that was as good as gold in any top notch racing circuit around.

THE KEN
CHURCH
Photograph by Royal Photo Co, and Sutcliffe Co.

DERBY
OWNS

—Tinsley-Clingman Co., Engravers

CHAPTER THIRTY-FOUR
Waitin' On a Train

Monday morning dawned another clear and beautiful day. The temperature was a very comfortable 75 degrees and it was a perfect day for racing. Tommy woke up extra early and was in an unusually cheerful mood. He made his way on foot, wrapped in his rubber suit and running the 15 miles into Marianao to the local Catholic Church for a special Saint Patrick's Day mass and devotion. It was March 17th and very likely Tommy's most favorite holiday, even more than Christmas. Back home on Second Street in Covington, in the neighborhood of all Irish-Catholics who worshipped in the parish of Saint Patrick's Church, Tommy sprouted and nurtured his love and respect for his ethnic background and roots. He was Irish and Catholic through and through and, by God, he was going to pull out all the stops to see that this particular St. Patrick's Day would be one of his most memorable. Later this morning, Harry would be leaving Oriental Park and the Spence Stables forever.

Tommy lit a candle and prayed, *"Dear God when the train from Havana arrives to let off all track patrons for today's races, and Harry gets on to go back home, please watch over him during his trip and let him make it home safe and sound so he can tell my girl Virginia that I love her. I pray this in the name of Saint Patrick and of Jesus, your son. Amen."*

On his way back to the track, Tommy thought of this addendum to his prayer, *"Oh, and God, please let Harry succeed and keep him free from injuries in his next step as a professional jockey. Any successes I may have on today's race card, I humbly dedicate to you, dear Lord, for all the blessings you have granted me and for those I have asked for."*

As he was walking back to Oriental Park, he was thumbing through a copy of the *Daily Racing Form* that he picked up in the town after church. He read aloud as he walked:

"HAVANA, Cuba, March 16---Today was a gala occasion at Oriental Park. The program was made up of nine races, with the Havana Handicap as the outstanding feature. Additional attractions were a novelty handicap, in which foot runners, horses, automobiles and motorcycles participated, and a race for mules in which there were eight starters."

"The novelty race was won by one of the foot runners, A. Rodriguez, winning easily. He ran the 480 yards in fifty-six seconds, a creditable performance considering the footing. One of the motorcycles was second, and one of the horses, Major Domo, was third. The queen of the Mardi Gras carnival, attended by her ladies in waiting, drove to the course in state and occupied boxes in the middle of the grandstand adjoining the president's box. An immense gathering was present, society turning out in force."

"The Havana Handicap, worth $1,960 to the winner was won by Wise Man, which beat Hocnir and Sasin in a whirlwind finish. They passed the judges' stand so close together that it took an official placing to decide which was first, second and third."

"At the conclusion of the races at Oriental Park course on Saturday the following horses were disposed of at auction..."

Tommy didn't even read this portion of the article. He already knew who bought what and why. It was getting close to getaway day and the owners and trainers were beginning to have their fire sales in preparation of their next season of racing.

When he read about the Havana Handicap, he smiled and garnered a warm feeling inside, because it was the Darden/Spence team entry and the Murray/Lunsford combination of strategic horsemanship that almost netted Spence Stables the $1,960 instead of the $300 second place prize money. Tommy, at 98 pounds, on Darden's Corson, trained by Spence, was to leave his post position number one and be the rabbit on the inside rail, setting the pace for the other contenders. At the half mile pole, he fell back to second as Harry took the lead with Hocnir and kept it all the way down the stretch, only to be nosed out at the wire by Wise Man who was seemingly designated the third place runner till the very end.

Tommy thought to himself, *"Harry had that race for sure, even if it was by a whisker but the judges saw things differently, and that was that! In my and Harry's book, he's leaving Cuba a real winner!"*

Harry was all packed and waiting and ready to go by the time the train arrived at the track. Spence accompanied him to the train and gave him his last riding instructions and tucked one last ticket into his boot.

"Cash this ticket in at one of those betting parlors in Miami when you get back to the States. It's $50.00 on Tommy to win in today's second race. Ain't a horse entered that stands a chance. It will make up for the winning jockey portion they hornswaggled you out of yesterday in the handicap! That should keep you in good shape till you get to Churchill. Now off with you, boy. This is your big opportunity!"

There just may have been a couple of tears in Spence's eyes, but he turned away so quickly, no one would ever have even noticed. Not so with Harry. He was sobbing all the way to his seat.

Tommy was already at the post for the first race of the day as the train was pulling away with an emotionally wrecked Harry Lunsford; soon to transform into a very excited and ecstatic traveler.

"This is for Harry," Tommy whispered into Zoie's ear while at the barrier.

He knew his 20-to-1 mount didn't have much chance in this claiming race for three-year-olds, but he was going to do everything in his power to make the other horses earn their oats.

"Wish this was yesterday and we was racin' agin' them mules and motorcycles, old girl. We'd show 'em what good racin' was all about, wouldn't we?"

"Come on!" shouted Jimmy Milton.

The start was good and slow. As expected, the odds-on favorite, Lucky Lady, took the lead immediately from the break and set the pace for the others. Tommy lay back patiently in seventh place out of the eight horse field and waited. It was all his 98 pounds could do to keep her under wraps, keeping the reins tightly wound twice around his wrists. She was in good stride and showing no signs of tiring out. Coming out of the stretch, Lucky Lady quit her fast pace and allowed the 4-to-1 Wise Joan to overcome her. At this point, Tommy loosened one wrap of the reins and Zoie responded immediately and closed a very big gap, coming from fourth into second place approaching the finish. Tommy let out another notch as he clucked to her several times, but they just ran out of racetrack. Still, she finished a very impressive second, paying $20 to place.

As Cupe assisted Tommy with his tack and led Zoie away, Tommy asked him,

"Cupe, d'ja git them place-show tickets like I asked?"

"Shore did, Massa Tommy, shore did. An' I dun laid dem on de Boss's trunk 'neath his bible like yo' tole me."

198

"Good job, Cupe. Thank you. Mr. Spence can use them winnings for the feed man, since he spent so much money on Harry's passage back home."

"Ah yessir, Massa Tommy. He shore'll be tickled to fine dem tickets an' dem winnin's a layin' dere, 'specially wit git-a-way-day a comin' up, yessiree, he will!"

"Cupe?"

"Yes, Massa Tommy," as Cupe turned back to Tommy's call. "An, quit callin' me 'Massa Tommy,' would ya please? I ain't your master. That stuff all ended over ffity years ago, remember?"

"Ole Cupe shore do 'member that, massa, he shore do! Was ten 'er 'leven years ole' back then but my daddy was allowed to stay and keep us all on at that ole hoss farm down dere in the bluegrass, so's we could keep workin' as free people an' still do the work we was good at. Yessir, we was all free men, a'doin' what we loved, and fo' the mostest massa in de bluegrasses. I loved that ole massa, jist as I loves massa Spence an' you, Massa Tommy! Dat de onliest name I kin call you, yessir."

"Okay, Cupe, okay. I git it. I sure ain't gonna change no stripe on this ol' polecat, I can see that so I guess I'll jist start callin' you Massa Cupe. Now we're both equal and happy. Now git along. I got another race comin' up here and I'm in a big hurry to get home first, if ya know what I mean."

"I shore does, Massa Tommy, I shore does," chuckled Cupe all the way back to the barn.

Cupe quickly returned to the saddling area, leading Phoneta for Tommy's next race, another claiming race for three-year-olds and upward. He was trailed by the two Oots brothers, the horse's owners and breeder, and by Mr. Lowenstein, who was Phoneta's trainer. After a short conference, the trainer gave Tommy a leg up and continued his pre-race instructions.

"As long as nobody interferes with you or traps you into a pocket, this race should easily be yours. The only horse I am concerned about is the horse in the number two spot, Syrian. He is an experienced seven year-old and a very fast sprinter. He likes to set a fast pace. Just keep Phoneta under restraint and then let him out after the last sixteenth. That's when that old pace setter will tire out and won't have anything left when you challenge him. Phonetta should have a gear or two left and will leave Syrian sitting in his tracks. Oh, and here's one in your boot, son. See you in the winner's circle."

The race went, just as it was scripted. Besides the Oots's and Mr. Lowenstein waiting in the enclosure reserved for the winner and his people, Kay Spence was also standing there with the happy horsemen, engaged in pleasant conversation.

"Fine boy you got there, Kay," said Lowenstein. "A very smart, patient rider and a magical technician with horseflesh, I might add."

"Yes he is," Spence quickly agreed. "He's my crack rider for sure; probably the number one ace here at this meeting and he is still wearing his bug. When he loses it, he will be Spence Stables number one contract rider. Matter of fact, wouldn't surprise me one bit to see him in one of those big stakes races this spring in Louisville."

"Is that where you'll be heading after this meeting?" Lowenstein asked.

"Naw, we'll be heading to Lexington first from here. Want to try my string against some of those platers there, maybe pick up a couple new nags and fill the kitty a little. Then I'll head to Churchill and see what them Eastern boys are sending down our way as competition. Not only that, I want Tommy to experience some of those roughneck bad boy jockeys from that New York circuit, just so he knows what they're like in that league. Different bunch up East for sure."

"Amen to that, Kay. Always one or two of them manages to get killed every year, in spite of the cracking down the stewards are leveling. I hear they're handing out suspensions this year like candy. Them rough riders will either straighten up or they'll wind up being 'rough rubbers', mucking out stalls in their spare time. Now that is one viewpoint of the horse they definitely will not like, eh?"

"Right you are, sir, so very right you are," Spence agreed.

200

CHAPTER THIRTY-FIVE
Saint Patty's Day

"Well, not a bad day so far, son," Spence acknowledged upon Tommy's dismount after getting the nod from the judges' stand.

"Can't be a bad day today, sir. It's Saint Patty's Day, the most important day of the year!"

"Hmm," snorted Spence, "and here I thought Derby Day was the most important."

"If it wasn't for Saint Patrick and the luck of the Irish, then there wouldn't be no sense in racin' horses, sir."

"Now just how in Sam Hill do you figger that, boy?"

"Well, if it wasn't for the luck of the Irish, then the best horse would always win every race! With a little luck, then other horses can win sometimes. See?" Tommy grinned.

"Okay, okay, you little leprechaun. Back to the business of the day."

As Spence gave Tommy a leg up on Walter Mack, he told him in a very serious tone, "Now you know this hoss can beat this field, and it looks as if the public thinks so too. He's two-and-a-half to one. Keep him right behind whoever sets the pace and let him chase. He likes that, but if he loses his stride, take him back. I'm concerned about his right front and if he changes leads and he don't feel right to you, then don't push him. Got it?"

"Oh, don't worry, boss. Luck won't ever do lame any good, that's for sure."

Tommy started out in the fourth spot and had nine pounds on his closest competitor.

"Should be a walk-over," Tommy thought to himself.

Walter Mack was perfectly relaxed and focused on the moment. When Jimmy Milton hollered "Come on", it was a very good and smooth start. As predicted, the T.J. Brown horse, Phedoden, which was the odds-on favorite in the third hole, broke out in first place setting a very fast pace and trailed the leader by less than a length all the way around the first turn and into the straightaway. Suddenly, Tommy felt the horse hesitate when he switched leads and knowing something was not right, he immediately eased him up as the field all left them behind. Walter Mack threw his head up and down as if to say *"C'mon, what the hell you doing? Let's get going!"* but he just as quickly realized a tight pull when he stepped and he seemingly accepted what was going on.

"I was afraid of that," Spence confided to Tommy as they slowly cooled Walter Mack down and walked him back to where Cupe was standing, waiting to take the horse.

"That's okay, Cupe. I ain't riding in this next race. I'll just spend a little time here with my ole buddy and let him cool. You can just tell he's disappointed. He really had his sights set on that there Phedoden horse and on any other day, he'd a had him dead to rights. You saw how he let that eight-year-old come down on the inside on the stretch turn with a rush and then beat him going away? That's the exact path me and Walter here was plannin' on taking. Thank God we quit and didn't ruin him. He'll be fine with some treatment and a long overdue rest, won't ya boy?"

Walter just slightly shook his head and then reluctantly nodded and let go a snort.

"That's my boy; you'll be just fine. We'll tear 'em up in Lexington!"

"Tommy, these last two races today I'd like you to make into hot works for Gear and the Shop. Let 'em both out as soon as the dust clears. They need to be blowed out a couple times before getaway day. I want 'em strong and in shape when we get to Lexington. I'm little worried about Walter. His right front is still a little warm. He just might wind up bowin' that tendon. We need to keep a close watch on him. I hear the stewards want to see you after today's card is run," Spence added, almost as an afterthought.

"Fer what?" Tommy questioned.

"Prolly nuthin'," Spence calmly whispered. "Just gonna find out for sure what made you pull Walter up, beings as he was the two-to-one runner that let the ten-to-one nag go by. That's all! You know, with the likes of Pock being around again, and his reputation fer trying to fix race outcomes, it's just their job to follow up on things unexpected, that's all. Ain't nothin' to worry about. Just tell 'em what happened when he tried to change leads."

"Guess they'll also wanna know how come I was trying to blow the saddle cloths off all the other dogs in these next two races too, when I work Gear and the Shop," he laughed.

"Doubt that, Tommy but I'll bet your old tout buddy will wonder what got into them, for sure. Maybe I'll just spread the word around that you been seen hoppin' them horses with something. Wouldn't that just stir up somebody's pot?"

"Oh, oh," Tommy muttered in a very serious tone as he dug into his pocket. "Guess I better get shed of these things then, huh?" he added as he and Spence stared down into his palm at the several sugar cubes he carried from the backstretch kitchen. They laughed all the way back to the barn.

Spence was pleased with Tommy's efforts and showing in the fifth and sixth races of the day. He guided High Gear to a second-place finish in the mile plus 20 yards contest in a time of 1:40. The track was fast and Gear stayed in close pursuit of the winner Dimitri, who set a very fast pace from the start and led wire to wire. Second place money amounted to $100, good enough to pay off some feed bills. In the last contest of the day, Tommy managed a time of 1:44 and four-fifths for the mile and 50 yards distance, again finishing second for a $70 portion of the purse. Lady Jane Grey set a good pace from start to finish and shook off Beauty Shop in the last dozen yards to win. Soon after leaving the paddock for the barn, the messenger from the racing stewards showed up, summoning Tommy to the top floor of the clubhouse "for a few questions."

"Tell 'em everything you know, boy," laughed Spence. "And tell 'em I send my best."

Tommy did just as he was told and the stewards answered, "Be sure to let that old codger know that we realize that he sent us his best! Son, you have been a joy for us to watch this meeting. You have a good seat, good balance, patience, ability and a good handle on what race ridin' is all about. We've watched your progress and you are on course to become one of the best, so long as you keep a level head, integrity, keep your weight and avoid the corruption and the reptiles, like that apprentice tout fella. What's-his-name? He's always up to no good and to tell the truth, he's no good at it, either!"

They all laughed at Pock's expense and Tommy was relieved how much they were on to that trouble-maker.

"Boy, I hope you realize that you're under the wings of one of the very best trainers and conditioners of jockeys in this entire country and he thinks an awful lot of you too, son. Don't let him down."

"No sir, not me. I'll never let Mr. Spence down. It's just like he's my own sire, and I'm his colt. I know I'm comin' from good stock and it's up to me to develop into a champion like him and I will always be fair and square, just like I was raised to be. May I ask, uh, what was it you wanted to talk to me about, sirs?"

The stewards glanced about at each other and then Mr. Fitzgerald answered simply, "We just did, son. We just did! As you know, when an animal performs in a race in a manner we find unexpected or unusual, we are required to investigate what may have occurred to have caused such an outcome. You know, like were the horse drugged, or the race fixed, or was it due to rough riding? Things like that. We could see why you pulled Walter Mack up so abruptly. This ain't our first day on the job but we had to go through the motions just to keep everything fair and on the up-and-up. That's all, son. Now back to the barn with you, and have a successful season out there."

"Yessir, and thank you Mr. Fitzgerald and Mr.Shelley, sir."

"So? What was that all about, son?"

"Just like you said, Boss. Nothin'. Nothin' at all! They just had to follow-up on why I pulled Walter up but they already figgered it out. It was nothing, just like you tole me."

"They're good folks, up there Tommy," Spence added. "They ain't the enemy or a bunch of ogres like folks like to make them out to be. They are only concerned that horseracing stays clean and above board and safe and fair to everyone involved. Kinda like the parish priest back home, looking out for the interests of all his parishioners. The stewards are the authority and they deserve the respect and cooperation from everybody within their fold. It all comes down to checks and balances, just like everything else in life. If you can learn to respect authority and play by the rules early on as a young boy, then you will never have any problems in life at all and that's a fact, son. Just give it a chance. Ain't at all any different from what they wrote down in your bible. Same thing!"

"Yep," Tommy grinned. "Fair and square!"

CHAPTER THIRTY-SIX
Spence's Crack Jockey

It was Thursday morning and Tommy was busy at his chores early in the day. He was enjoying his status as Kay Spence's crack jockey, but he still missed Harry. Now Tommy had to accept his new roles as mentor and teacher of L. Woods, his new underling apprentice and Spence's latest project. At 85 pounds, Spence recognized great potential in this boy if he could just manage to keep upright on the sky-side of the beasts he would be assigned to ride. The horses paid no mind to this featherweight. They acted as if no one were on them, probably because that was how it felt to them. On several occasions, Woods was even swatted off the horse's back by its tail, just as if he had been a common horse fly, only a little heavier but Tommy enjoyed teaching his new subordinate, because it helped Tommy to keep refreshed on the fundamentals of race riding for himself, and consequently on top of his game. Today, Tommy was particularly proud because Woods actually won his first race as a Spence apprentice the day before and that made it an overall good day for the stable.

As Tommy entered the tack room, he noticed a copy of the day's *Daily Racing Form* strategically left lying on one of the feed barrels, opened to a specific page. The headlines read:

"KAY SPENCE SADDLES THREE WINNERS"
Horses from His Stable Win Half of Havana Card---Close and Interesting Racing

HAVANA, Cuba, March 19---The Spence stable was much in the limelight at Oriental Park this afternoon, horses from that establishment winning half the card, U Twenty-Three, Blondel and Sky Man were the successful trio, the first named being the property of W.W. Darden, but is trained by Kay Spence. U Twenty-Three's victory came in the second race and was easily achieved, while Blondel and Sky Man won by small margins in whirlwind finishes. In the Blondel race F.D. Weir's Earnest set a fast pace to the last eighth, where both Blondel and Lackawanna passed him, the former getting the decision in the final strides. The finish of the fifth race was even closer and more exciting, Sky Man having only a nose margin over Sevillian, which in turn was but a neck in advance of Jake Schas, and the latter only a nose to the good of Dalrose. U Twenty-Three and Blondel were ridden by the promising apprentice T. Murray, who has come to the front with rapid strides since coming here this winter.

Warm weather and a fast track made conditions ideal for a good day's sport, and the large crowd that came to Oriental Park was not disappointed, the majority of the races being well contested, with the finishes close and exciting...

....At the conclusion of the races this afternoon a ruling was handed out which brought the suspension for thirty days of jockey Bullman, besides a fine of $100, for insubordination. The further entry of the horse Ambrose will also be refused."

As he put the Form back down, he thought to himself, *"I wonder if Virginia ever gets to read these racing news papers back home?"*

Little did he know she was keeping a very active scrapbook on him and reveling in his progress and success. She was saving articles from the local newspapers and from any *Daily Racing Form* she would find at newsstands or neighbors would leave on her front stoop.

"Hmm," Tommy thought out loud. "I wonder why they didn't mention that Woods was the winning rider on Mr. Spence's other winner? Reckon when you're a bug boy to a bug boy, you just ain't much count." Tommy just went on about his duties for the morning, not giving the article any more thought.

Had he read down a little further, he would have seen a small blurb that announced what would probably turn out to be the most significant event in the history of Kentucky horse racing, and definitely the most important event in the history of Latonia Race Track and its future; both of which would significantly impact his own racing career. The headline read:

"M.J. WINN TAKES OVER LATONIA TRACK"

CINCINNATI, O., March 19---Colonel Matt J. Winn, vice president and general manager of the Kentucky Jockey Club arrived in Cincinnati Tuesday and formally took possession of Latonia in the name of the new owners. He was met by President Harvey Myers and general manager John Hackmeister, who took him to the track and turned over the properties...

...Harry Breivogel came on from the east and met Mr. Winn here and will be the second in command at Latonia. Breivogel is well known here, having worked at Latonia only a few years back, and was a newspaper man prior to that time."

With Matt Winn taking charge of Latonia, along with the Lexington track and Churchill Downs, a new era of professional horse racing was about to embark in Kentucky. It would define what the sport had long since been seeking, that is, professionalism, respect, entertainment, industry, careers, and longevity and it would re-establish

Kentucky as a national leader in the sport and in Thoroughbred breeding and production. It was to be Kentucky's brand before the concept existed. Looking back, this is where Kentucky's Unbridled Spirit began! Thanks to Matt Winn, it all came together.

When Winn took the reins, they were not looped around his wrists. They were full out, with no restraints. He immediately committed to purses of nothing less than $1000 at Latonia in the upcoming meeting and he was determined to put the Latonia Derby on an equal footing as the Kentucky Derby. His intention was to integrate the best of the eastern industry with the best of the western industry in order to establish truly national competition. And the way to accomplish this, of course, was to make it worthwhile to all the owners and trainers. He was quoted in the March 29th, 1919 edition of *The Thoroughbred Record*: *"Now that all the Kentucky tracks are under one ownership and one management," said Colonel Winn yesterday, "there is a chance to give an extra inducement to owners of Derby horses. Of course it is too late to announce any such innovation this year, but for next year I propose to add $5,000 for the winner of a race for Derby horses who may win at Lexington and then go on to win either the Kentucky Derby at Louisville or the Latonia Derby at that track. Another added inducement will be $10,000 for any horse that may win both the Kentucky and the Latonia Derbies, or $15,000 for any one that may win the Lexington, Kentucky and Latonia Derbies."*
He envisioned the Kentucky triumvirate as the Lexington Derby at a mile and a furlong, followed by the Kentucky Derby at a mile and a quarter, and then the Latonia Derby at a mile and a half, "which is the only real Derby in America." He went on to further state that he felt confident that next year, the Kentucky Derby would boast $25,000 added money and the same for the Latonia Derby. Winn added, "With a $10,000 added purse for a Derby at Lexington and with the entry fees added to the three purses and $15,000 in addition offered for any horse who may win all three events, there will be a chance for any horse who can take the trio to win $100,000." Matt Winn was talking "Triple Crown" lingo before there officially was a Triple Crown and he was on the right track, for sure.
Over the next couple of weeks, Tommy and Spence kept hard at it, picking up wins here and there, enough to meet the bills, but nothing fantastic. Tommy spent all his leisure time reading the newspapers and track publications and racing papers as he could get hold of them. He was eager to get back to the states and begin the racing season there, first at Lexington and then to Churchill and Latonia, the very three tracks that Matt Winn was counting on to revive Kentucky racing to exceed the national standards. Tommy was excited.

Tommy again found his name appearing in the *Daily Racing Form*, dated Saturday, March 29, 1919. It stated: *"Racing at Oriental Park today (March 28th) was of the spectacular order, even though the fields were made up of mediocre racers. The finishes in all six races were close and hard fought, with the results in doubt until the winning numbers were hung up. Plain Bill (Murray up) had only a nose margin over Hatrack in the opener, while Callaway got up in the final strides to beat Golden Chance by a neck in the following race. Gaffney Girl (Murray up), favorite in this race, finished absolutely last."*

"Another tight fit came in the third race when the long shot Croix d'Or just lasted long enough to score by a neck over Mike Dixon (Murray up), after having led throughout. Miss Ivan (Murray up) won the easiest victory of the day when she prevailed over Lucky Lady in the fourth and incidentally made it a double for Kay Spence, Plain Bill being his other winner.

"… Jockey T. Murray carried off the riding honors of the day with two victories and one second."

The next day, Tommy produced another win and another second. On Sunday, March 30th, he had a mount in six of the seven races, but could do no better than third place in two of them. Monday, March 31st, saw Tommy riding in all six races on that day's card, pulling down a first and two third place finishes but the real thrill of the day came when Tommy got a hold of Mr. Spence's *Daily Racing Form*. There was an article entitled, "Thirty Leading American Jockeys" that read: *"Little Tommy Murray had a whale of a time at Havana last week and in riding the winners of nine races put himself firmly in the leadership of the jockeys of 1919. C. Robinson is reported to be about ready to resume riding, but even if he does so with a fair measure of success in the saddle, he will find it difficult to overcome Murray's lead of nine winning mounts."* A chart followed the article, and listed in first place was Tommy Murray with the record of 251 total mounts, with 52 first-place, 30 second-place and 26 third-place finishes. His overall win percentage was .21.

CHAPTER THIRTY-SEVEN
April Foal!

Tuesday morning dawned and brought with it the month of April. It was finally getting around to get-a-way day, and the anticipation was palpable all along the back side and stable areas.

"Mr. Spence, Mr. Spence!" shouted Tommy as he ran down the shed row of their stables. "Come quick, come quick, Mr. Spence!"

Tommy kept running up and down the row shouting at the top of his lungs. Finally, out from one of the stalls came Spence, "What in tarnation is all the hollerin' and screamin' about, boy?! Is the place afire or something? What the hell's the matter?"

"It's Lucky Pearl, sir. She's down in her stall and she's a foalin'."

"What?!" shouted Spence as he commenced to running down toward all the commotion. "Why that's dang right impossible. She can't be foaling! Why she ain't even ever been bred! Impossible, impossible. You're daft, just plain daft!"

"I'm telling you sir, she's birthin' a young'un and I done throwed a blanket over the foal. Come quick!"

When Spence arrived at the stall, sure enough, there was Lucky Pearl lying in the stall with a blanket beside her covering what appeared to be a quivering baby. Spence flew into the stall and grabbed the blanket away from the supposed foal and there was the 85-pound apprentice Wood, laughing uncontrollably as he and Tommy kept shouting "April Fools! April Fools!"

At first, Spence could not even gather himself. He was out of breath, sweating, and obviously beside himself. As he looked around the stall, it became apparent that he was piecing things together, but that he wasn't finding any humor or satisfaction in any of it. After what seemed an eternity, he finally spoke.

"Get that horse out into the paddock and rub her down thoroughly. Then, you better be meeting up with me in the winner's circle with her, and then we will talk!"

By this time, Woods was back under the blanket. When Spence left, he peeked out from under it and said to Tommy, "Wow, he scared me! I ain't never seen a man that mad what didn't kill or whoop up on somebody. Did you see how he was chomping and frothing? He looked like a crazed stallion!"

"Ah, don't get all in a tizzy, little buddy. He ain't gonna do nothin' to us. He was plain old fooled, pure and simple and he knows it. If he's mad at somebody, then it's at his own self, not us but just to make sure, I think I'll go out and win these first two races for him, especially the second race, on Lucky Pearl."

And that's exactly what he did. Plus, he finished up the day with two more first place rides and one second. The only race he did not ride in that day was the fifth race, the Ecuador Handicap, which another Kay Spence horse won. Spence went with jockey J. Howard in the race because Hodge was assigned to carry 119 pounds. With Tommy at 98 pounds, Spence didn't want that much added lead, so he went with the heavier jockey and less lead. The headlines of the next day's *Daily Racing Form* read:

"GREAT DAY FOR K. SPENCE STABLE
Kentucky Turfmen Win Three Races At Havava---Old Hodge Runs a Brilliant Race

HAVANA, Cuba, April 1.---The Kay Spence stable was much in the limelight at Oriental Park this afternoon, the Kentucky turfman furnishing three winners --- Lucky Pearl (Murray up), Zoie (Murray up) and Hodge (Howard up) --- while Whippoorwill (Murray up) finished second in the seventh. Hodge's victory came in the feature of the afternoon, the Equador Handicap at three-quarters of a mile, in which he carried top weight of 119 pounds. Hodge was ridden by J. Howard. He trailed the leaders to the stretch turn, where Milkman left a slight opening next to the inside rail. Howard was quick to take, and pushing up on Hodge fought it out with Milkman all through the homestretch and the finish was a head to the good. The three-quarters was run in 1:12 and marked an excellent performance on the part of the old horse (Hodge was eight years old at the time, and technically, a horse isn't really a horse until he is past five years old. Up until he is five, he is still a colt. Same for a female; a filly until after her 5th birthday, and then she is officially a mare).
...Senor A. H. Diaz, whose stable is particularly strong in two-year-olds, furnished the winner of the opening race, a dash of half a mile, in the colt Douglas Fairbanks (Murray up), which made it a runaway affair and won in easy fashion by four lengths from Queen-Gaffney.

After reading that article, Tommy put down the paper and shouted out over to Kay Spence who was running dry bandages up the two front legs of Jack Snipe.

"Wow," he said. "Yesterday is gonna be hard to beat, ain't it?"

"Well, it damn sure will be with an attitude like that," shot back Spence from behind the stall wall. "I ain't a takin' all this time doctoring these two horses up so's you kin doubt their ability to run today."

"Naw, sir, I ain't doubting these ol' boys' ability to run. I'm just thinking out loud that it's gonna be hard to match yesterday's results."

"There ya go agin' boy! Doubt, doubt, doubt will keep you out, out, out! Remember what I always told you, son. You will ride each race as good as you will let yourself ride."

"Well, okay, then," he fired back with just a little more than a touch of pressured irritation in his voice. "I'm just gonna boot both of these two old fellas home to the winner's circle. You'll see!"

Spence just kept on wrapping, head down, and a huge, quiet smile across his stubbled face.

The next morning, a copy of the *Daily Racing Form* was lying on top of the feed barrel as one entered the tack room. The headlines read:

FOUR WINNERS FOR JOCKEY T. MURRAY
Kay Spence Adds Two More Victories to His Long Score

HAVANA, Cuba, April 2.---The Program at Oriental Park this afternoon was made up of a series of selling races, a majority of which were at sprinting distances. The fields were small, but spirited finishes marked the day's sport. Kay Spence furnished two winners in Solid Rock (Murray up) and Jack Snipe (Murray up). G. Sulley scored his first victory of the meeting when Past Master came from behind in the stretch run and beat Frozen Glen by a length in the second. Another driving finish came with the running of the third, when Buster Clark (Murray up) wore down the tiring pacemaker, D. C. Girl, and beat her by half a length...Jockey Murray rode four winners...

Tommy also had two second place finishes on the day's card. When he went to bed that night, he felt pretty good about himself but he couldn't get it out of his mind what Spence had said to him just the day before, "You will ride each race as good as you will let yourself ride." As he fell off to sleep, he told himself, *"Tomorrow, I'm gonna ride as good as I will let myself ride, again, and see if he is really right and knows what he is talking about."*

Sure enough, out of seven races on Thursday, April 3, 1919, Tommy had won four of them, placed second in another, and third in two others. The *Daily Racing Form* for Friday, April 4, 1919, wrote on the first page headlines:

FOUR MORE WINNERS FOR T. MURRAY

HAVANA, Cuba, April, 3.---For the third day in succession, jockey Murray rode four winners. Besides his winning mounts today Murray had one second and two thirds to his credit.

There was a decided improvement to the sport today, the fields being composed of a much better class of horses than those which participated in the racing of Wednesday. Keenly contested races were in order, and the finishes in the majority of them were close and hard fought.

That evening, Kay Spence was working late in the barn and had just settled down into his favorite hay bale lounge chair in the tack room to begin reading through his accumulating papers and mail that had to deal with the conclusion of the Cuba meeting and the final preparations and duties pertaining to the upcoming move from the island back to the states. He was interrupted by Tommy's knock on the door frame.

"Come in, son. What's on your mind?"

"Well, Mr. Spence, I'm feeling real nervous and jittery inside, and I reckon it's because I'm so excited about getaway day and going back home to Kentucky but then I think, naw, it ain't because of that. It's because I'm scared."

"Scared? Well for heaven's sakes, boy, whatever are you scared of?"

"Well, I, uh…well you know how I just pulled off a hat trick three days in a row, sir?"

"Yes Tommy, believe me, I am well aware of that. Just like every horse player here in Cuba and back in our country is aware. They all have heard your name by now."

"Well, I'm real scared about the next time I ride and I don't pull off a hat trick, or I don't even win one, er jist git a second, er a third place. Then what happens?"

"Well, whadda you mean, 'what happens?' Why nothin' happens. You jist get back on that horse the next day and you try again. Nobody expects you to win races every day, son. If they did, then they ain't right and you don't need to be foolin' with them. Any good owner or trainer knows he ain't gonna win every day. Why that's just how horse racing is. Pick up that paper right there and look at that chart showing the leading riders in the country. Now who's the current leader?"

"Well, I am. It's me, sir."

"Right, Tommy. You are the current leader in the country. Now follow the line by your name over to the next column to the right. Now, tell me, what does it say your win percentage is?"

"It's point one nine, sir"

"Right, point one nine. Now that says that the winningest jockey in the country at this particular time, wins nineteen races out of every hundred horses he rides in a race. Now, if that's the case, do you really think there is anyone in this business who would expect you to win four races every day?"

Tommy quietly chuckled a sigh of relief, while acutely aware of the lump in his throat getting bigger and bigger.

"You know, Mr. Spence, someday I hope I get to be as smart as you are. Thank you, sir."

And off he went, just as that lump jumped over into Spence's throat.

So, the next day, the 98th day of the 100 day meeting came and went and sure enough, Tommy did not get another hat trick but he didn't ride poorly either. His first place finishes in the last two races of the day did wonders for his confidence, and his happy and excited mood as well. Saturday saw two second places and a third. As soon as the final race was completed, Spence and his crew attended all the horses and then he instructed them all to start packing the trunks and equipment. The entire backside and barn area took on an almost festive holiday spirit and feel. Everyone was busy and cheerful and talkative and laughing; hugging and kissing and shaking hands and exchanging goodbyes and good wishes. It was a joyous atmosphere that lasted long into the evening.

Before Tod Sloan perfected his signature riding stance (still used today), this is how jockeys sat on their mounts, 1909.

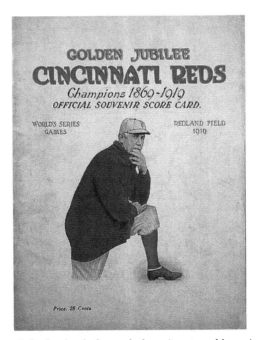

Some of Tommy's boyhood pals dreamed of growing up and becoming professional baseball players for the Reds. Tommy dreamed of becoming a jockey.

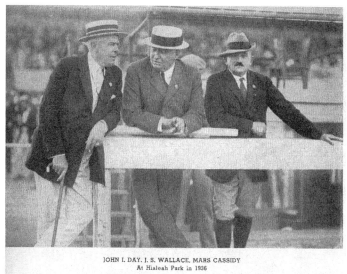

JOHN I. DAY, J. S. WALLACE, MARS CASSIDY
At Hialeah Park in 1936

Renowned starter Mars Cassidy (far left) at Hialeah Park

Unloading a horse off a rail car at Latonia. The railroad ran behind the grand stand.

Famous African-American jockey James "Jimmy" Winkfield

Jockeys waiting to weigh out. They would weigh out before the race and weigh in after the race.

Kentucky bootleggers made up for alcohol availability during prohibition.

The Prohibition Movement put a real damper on horseracing entertainment.

Pancho Villa and his gang

Princess Doreen was the most successful horse trained by Kay Spence and broke the 40-year record for wins by a mare held by Miss Woodford.

Hall of Fame Jockey Roscoe Goose, one of Tommy's friends and mentors.

Tommy's nemesis, jockey Earl Sande, on Gallant Fox, the 1930 Triple Crown winner.

Regret, the first filly to win the Kentucky Derby (1915)

Old Rosebud, one of Tommy's favorite horses to ride. Old Rosebud won the 1914 Kentucky Derby in a record time which stood until 1931.

Jockey Isaac Murphy

Tod Sloan developed the modern jockey riding stance in the late 1890s.

Mack Garner on Blue Larkspur. Mack was a long-time friend and mentor of both Tommy and Harry.

Matt Winn

E. Sande on Zev. Despite Sande's rough and tumble style, he was a very sought after jockey by the Eastern owners and trainers and consequently found himself astride many stakes winners.

Charley Kurtsinger (left) was a good friend and cohort of Tommy. He eventually rode the son of Man o' War, War Admiral, to the 1937 Triple Crown and Horse-of-the-Year.

Jockey Laverne Fator was a very close friend of Tommy's in the 1920s. He would become the top money winner for both the 1925 and 1926 seasons.

Tommy's friend Willie Knapp aboard Exterminator after winning the 1918 Kentucky Derby. Exterminator went on to win 50 first places out of 100 career starts.

Sande, aboard Milkmaid, placed second in the 1919 Kentucky Oaks behind Tommy and Lilian Shaw's winning effort.

Tommy loved to look through all the different turf good catalogs that Kay Spence kept handy in the tack room. They helped him learn all the different aspects involved in horseracing.

The racing in Tommy's day in Lexington took place at the Kentucky Association Track. Present day Keeneland didn't open until 1936.

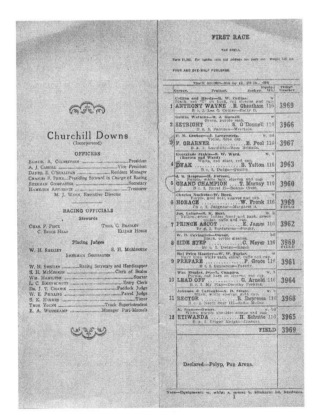

Official 1931 Churchill Program (with Tommy Murray)

Oriental Park Program

Serenest1 with Harry Lunsford aboard in the 1918 Churchill Downs' winner's circle.

Juarez Racetrack – Racing in Mexico was a popular winter racing location until the warring factions and gun fighting made it too uncomfortable and dangerous to continue.

Latonia Racetrack Program, 1921 - Program lists T. Murray, H. Lunsford, and L. Lyke in the sake race. Despite regularly competing against each other, they were very good friends.

Ad for Churchill from the 1919 American Racing Manual

229

Ad for Latonia Jockey Club in the 1919 American Racing Manual

230

Ad for Oriental Park in the 1919 American Racing Manual

*The Daily Racing Form was and still is the definitive and authoritative daily
publication in American Thoroughbred horseracing.*

THE AMERICAN
RACING MANUAL

1919

A Book of Reference for Persons Interested in Affairs
of the Running Turf.

Contains All Racing Records and Statistics for the Entire Year 1918. Three
Speed Tables as Used by the Handicappers of Racing, with Direc-
tions for Application. Bookmaking Percentages. American Track
Records. Track Speed. Comparative Speed Records. Win-
ners of Important Stakes. Brief History of the Leading
Sires Since 1870 and Table of Winnings of Their
Get. Great Races of England, France and
Australia. English Betting Rules. Method
for Pari-Mutuel Calculations, Etc.

PUBLISHED BY
DAILY RACING FORM PUBLISHING CO.
441 Plymouth Court, Chicago, Illinois

*The American Racing Manual was and still is the definitive and authoritative yearly
summary report in American Thoroughbred horseracing.*

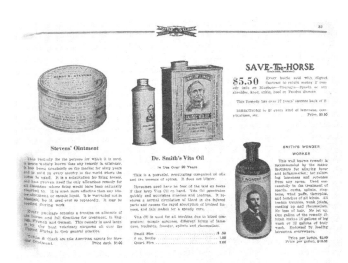

*Horse meds – page out of a veterinarian supply catalog showing some of the many horse
preparations available during Tommy's racing days.*

Johnny Loftus on the 1919 wire-to-wire Kentucky Derby winner, Sir Barton. The race was Sir Barton's very first as a maiden.

Albert Johnson aboard American Flag, Mao o' War's first champion son. Albert was a friend and colleague of Tommy and Exterminator's regular jockey.

Clarence Kummer was also a close friend and cohort of Tommy. Here he is aboard Man o' War.

One of Tommy's main nemeses was a tout who Tommy felt preyed on innocent track patrons and gave wagering and racing a bad name.

Snapper Garrison was the late 19th century jockey who was known for his famous riding style of "coming out of nowhere" to win victories in a come-from-behind finish.

Kay Spence and his entire stable of horses and staff traveled to Havana Harbor from Louisiana and from there to Oriental Park in Marianao by train.

CHAPTER THIRTY-EIGHT

A Sad Getaway Day

Sunday morning arrived quickly. Here it was, the 100th and final day of the Havana, Cuba meeting; clear, sunny, and 75 degrees. Just a perfect day for getaway day. To Tommy, the time there had seemed to drag on and on, while at the same time the whole meeting was over in a flash. It all seemed very surreal and strange, but Tommy was still out on the track early, exercising and breezing certain of the Spence string. He finished by giving a brief blowout to each of the Spence horses which would appear on today's card. After all the workouts were completed, Tommy helped with the hot walking, rubbing, bandaging, feeding and watering and whatever else was left to do. As he was getting ready to make his way up to the Oriental Park clubhouse to attend the final Mass of the race meeting, he was called into the tack room by Kay Spence.

"Son, sit down. I need to speak with you."

"Yes, sir. What is it? You look...well, you look..."

"Looks like I been crying, Tommy? Is that what you were wanting to say?"

"Yes, sir. That's how your eyes look, and your face looks sad. What's wrong, sir? What happened?"

"Well, Tommy, a good friend of ours got hurt in a race a couple of days ago up east, and...and...he died last night."

"Oh no, sir! Not Frankie, please, not Frankie! I heard he took a spill up in Maryland. Not him, please, Mr. Spence."

"I'm sorry, son. Yes, it was Frank. Turned out he fractured his skull. He got trampled by some of the horses when he went down. Never woke up. They done everything they could to save him."

By this time, Tommy was sobbing so loudly, he couldn't even hear what else Spence was trying to say. He just sat there, bent over into his own lap, sobbing and snorting, almost wailing. Spence went over and held him. Neither one spoke for a long time.

Frank Robinson had been an icon in the jockey profession. He was admired by all, trainers, owners, fans, track officials, and everyone who ever came in contact with him. To the veteran jockeys, he was a friend and cohort, but a strong competitor and a go-getter. He was honest and fair, and didn't have a crooked bone in his body. That is why the touts and the race fixers avoided him. He was much more to the younger boys of the business. To the apprentices and the track workers, he was a mentor and a hero. He, for sure, was this to Tommy. Frank was one of the top leading jockeys for the years 1916, 1917, and 1918. His yearly win percentages hovered at .20 to .22. It was sad to learn that his percentage for 1919 was .20 and that was for a total of just 20 races.

Sadly, there would be no more. When Tommy hung out at Latonia as a young boy, Frankie would always come up to him and spend time and conversation with him, encouraging him to pursue his dreams of becoming a jockey and working real hard toward that goal. He taught him to be fair and honest and to treat everybody with respect and courtesy, but to never let anyone bully him or force him into doing something that he didn't think was right or he didn't want to do. He was like a big brother and to Spence, he was like the older son

When Tommy finally looked up and spoke, he said in broken phrases, "Frankie always told me...to always watch out...for the other riders...because, if you was ever to git hurt...it wouldn't be because...of something you'd a done to yourself...it would be because of one of them making a mistake...or doing something stupid. He would say, 'a good jockey never kills his self...it's always a bad jockey that does it!'"

Tommy and Spence took a long time getting their composure back, but they managed eventually and they spent a long time just sharing memories of Frank with each other.

It was just after noon, and Tommy had no doubt already missed the celebration of Mass up in the clubhouse but he got up and quietly headed up to the small chapel room up there so he could light some votive candles for his dear friend Frank and spend some time praying and reflecting. As he left the room, he was clutching his rosary and his Saint Patrick medal. Tommy didn't utter a word, but Spence knew where he was headed and knew he would be back in time for post time of the first race.

Come post time for the first race, Tommy was more composed, but still a bit preoccupied. He and Laverne Fator, who was also a friend of Frank's, spent some time alone in the jockey house just talking as they prepared for the first race of the last day of the Havana meeting.

"Tommy, we just gotta go on. That's what Frankie would tell us. When we get out there on that dirt on top of them power plants, we just gotta stay alert and aware of everything and everybody around us and ride smart. We're all wanting the same thing, to be the first to cross that wire and there ain't very much time to do it in. Them other jocks sure ain't concerned about nobody but themselves and their horse so you better always ride smart."

When Tommy got back to the paddock after that first race, Spence helped to unsaddle Walter Mack.

"Looked a little undecided and skittish out there, son. You alright?"

"Yeah. I'm fine. When I heard 'come on', I forgot all about Frank and had my mind on winning but when Walter broke, he broke bad; had a slight stumble on his right front. That's the leg he hurt couple weeks ago and Laverne had Weymouth Girl out in front so quick and setting such a fast pace, I didn't urge Walter on much at all. I just let him do what he felt comfortable doing and it obviously wasn't winning a race today. He didn't seem to be favoring it while he was running, but he wasn't running all that hard. We need to check him out good anyways, just in case."

Spence was glad to hear Tommy talking business to him. He was very concerned for the boy earlier in the day.

Laverne and Tommy were side by side in the post parade for the second race. They were still talking as they were getting lined up. Most importantly, they were smiling and cutting up with each other this time. Spence was glad to see that. After all, this was getaway day, and it's supposed to be one of a jockey's and a trainer's favorite days of the year.

"Well, Laverne! My turn to win one now," laughed Tommy as he was placed in the first post position and Laverne led down to the fifth spot.

"We'll see about that!" Laverne shouted back.

Tommy was right. He was the one heading to the winner's circle this time.

In the end, it turned out to be a very fun getaway day for the two boys. They seemed to just swap wins back and forth all afternoon. They concluded their 1919 winter meeting season with three first-place wins each.

"That'll be two hat tricks to go, please." Tommy shouted over to the judges' stand as he and Lavern walked arms over shoulders back to the paddock area.

"See you boys back in the states," one of the judges shouted back.

CHAPTER THIRTY-NINE
Most Successful Meeting Ever

Tommy was up bright and early the next day and running on the track in his flannels, sweaters, and rubber suit. It concerned him that he was three pounds over his riding weight of 97 pounds in one of his races the day before. So, while he had the extra time, he planned on working on that problem.

Packing up and tending to the horses was the order of the day for the boys and the stable hands. Every one of the horses had been carefully prepared for the train car trip back to where they would load on to the steamship back to New Orleans, having been fed wet, cooked mashes twice a day for two days. Then, this morning each was dosed with two ounces of powdered aloes in linseed oil, a good twenty-four hours before the actual loading. This was one of Spence's routine preps for the prevention of shipping fever in his horses (Collins, 1959). Spence spent the better part of the day in the clubhouse. Even though the track was dark, the activities and the number of people in the clubhouse and business offices were about the same as any other race day, maybe busier. There were a lot of loose ends to tie up and a lot of paperwork to finish and sign. There were fees and bills to settle up, checks to cash, winnings to collect, ownership papers to review, and transportation and animal transport plans to finalize. Just a lot of things to attend to before anybody could actually get away on get-a-way day.

When Spence finally got back to the barn later that afternoon, he brought with him the latest editions of the *Daily Racing Form* and *Thoroughbred Record* to read. He also wanted Tommy to read them as well, and when they were finished reading them, Tommy could cut them up for his scrap book. One of the articles on the first page read:

HAVANA MEETING COMES TO AN END
Large Crowd Sees the Final Day's Sport of Long Winter Season of Racing at Oriental Park

HAVANA, Cuba, April, 6.---The racing season of 1918-1919 of the Cuba American Jockey Club at Oriental Park came to an end today with the running of an excellent program of seven races. A great gathering turned out anxious to participate in the sport of the closing day. Racing conditions were ideal, the weather clear and warm, and the track in perfect condition. Stirring contests were in order and much enthusiasm was in evidence. The consensus of opinion was that the meeting just brought to an end was the most successful ever held at the Marianao course, and it was the belief that the one to be held next year would be even greater. During the meeting nine track records were either equaled or reduced. Which was the champion racer among the older division was a matter of different opinion, but it was conceded that Orestes, the most popular Thoroughbred of the Diaz stable outclassed the others and there was no question that Senor Diaz has some of the best material among the two-year-olds. Jockeys Murray and Fator were in great form today and rode six of the seven winners, each having three to his credit...

...On Tuesday morning a special will pull out for Maryland...

...The Kentucky special will pull out the following day and will be made up of horses owned by Kay Spence...

A little further down on the same page appeared the following article:

THIRTY LEADING AMERICAN JOCKEYS

T. Murray continued his meteoric career at Havana track last week by riding the winners of fifteen races and placing himself twenty-one winning mounts in advance of his nearest pursuer, C. Robinson. The lad will have sterner opposition when he comes to this country to ride, but competent judges say he is a real comer, who shows all the qualifications for making a star jockey...

"Go ahead, son, cut those papers up and put 'em in your books. You should be proud of your accomplishments this winter," but being the concerned father-figure he was, Spence just had to add, "But don't let it all go to your head, son. You're gonna be up against a whole bunch of jockeys who are just as good or better, when you get back to the states. It's a whole different game from here on out. A lot of these fellas here at this meet won't get another mount until next winter. If they work at all, it will be the county fair circuits and in the bull rings out west. Once you get out of Havana, there are no guarantees whatsoever."

"You mean I can't ride for you anymore, Mr. Spence?" Tommy asked pathetically.

"Of course you'll be riding for me, son but if you want to advance to the big show, you'll have to impress one of the big show trainers or owners who will want to buy your contract from me. I ain't one of the big show trainers. I like it just where I am - at the top of my game in my own league. It's more of a challenge to me to test my abilities in the claiming race circuit, to choose horses. I think may have potential if they got away from their current conditioners. I really ain't the kind of trainer who can work for owners who win by buying the best horses for the most money. I like to mold something out of nothing, so to speak. I like to say, 'now there's a horse that could be a good one with some work', or 'there's a boy who could be a good jockey if I could get hold of him for a while'. That's how I like to play the game."

He continued, "But with you, Tommy, it's different. I think you have a good chance of competing and making it in the big show but mind what I say! There's traps and snares and temptations and false promises all along that road to the big show and there's greedy and dishonest slugs everywhere, waiting to prey on you at the first sign of weakness or discouragement. You've touched a slug before, haven't you? They're slick! Slick as hell so you just have to remember all of your comin's up and that's everything you've learned from your ma and pa, and your Catholic church, and your Seckatary Hawkins stories, and from me and Harry and from Frank, and all the other mentors and teachers you have come to respect and emulate over the past few years. Just ignore and keep away from all the Pock's you will encounter in the future. There's a bunch of them out there and they are all the same and easy to recognize."

"I've run off the mouth long enough," Spence concluded. "Now let's see what is ahead for us, eh?"

Tuesday came and went in a flurry of activity as the first special loaded the racing stock and equipment that was headed to the Maryland tracks for the opening of the 1919 racing season for the Eastern circuit. Tommy hung out at the train observing in awe the monumental yet very meticulous task of boarding all of that very valuable horseflesh and accouterments. What seemed to be overall mass confusion was in fact just multiple pockets of manageable and controlled confusion, each lending its part to the whole, which gave the appearance of total chaos. Most of the horses were easily led up the loading ramp into the car, but, as is the case when lining up for the start of a race, there were those fractious individuals who didn't want any part of that train car. Tommy especially enjoyed watching the tried and true procedure in dealing with these horses. The grooms and stable hands were all skilled in these problem loads, and they all gathered at whichever car was having the difficulty and stood in a half circle around the problem animal, awaiting the count. On the count of three, they all positioned themselves under the horse and literally carried it up into the car, but to the horse it must have seemed like being thrown up into the car because it happened so fast and the horse hardly had time to react. The most impressive part of it all was the fact that there was seldom any injury to man or beast. The day's edition of the *Daily Racing Form* ran this article:

Racing Statistics Of The Long And Successful Winter Meeting Of
THE CUBA-AMERICAN JOCKEY CLUB

The winter meeting of the Cuba-American Jockey Club, which began at Oriental Park December 7, 1918, and came to an end April 6, 1919, embraced 100 days of racing, during which time 626 races were run and $349,015 distributed in stakes and purses. The daily average money distribution amounted to $3,490. Despite an unusually long spell of rainy weather and a layoff of eight days on account of the general strike that tied up transportation, the meeting is said to have been the most successful held at the beautiful Marianao course.

Kay Spence won the lion's share of the stakes and purses, his horses, winning with uniform regularity, accounting for fifty-six races and $29,195 in stable earnings, placing him at the head of the winning owners, Frank Weir has every reason to feel satisfied with his trip to Havana, his horses accounting for $17,005, while Senor A. H. Diaz enjoyed the most successful season since he entered the sport, his stable ably trained by W. McDaniel, earning $13,285. [Spence finished with a total of 56 first place wins; 34 second place wins; and 37 third place finishes, which put him in the money 127 times; Weir had 25 firsts, 15 seconds, and 18 thirds (58 times in the money); Diaz totaled 22 firsts, 11 seconds, and 12 thirds (45 times in the money). Indeed, a most impressive record for Kay Spence.]

CHAPTER FORTY
The Kentucky Special

Finally, Wednesday arrived and the Kentucky special left Marianao and Oriental Park with the Spence stable and associates on board.

"Now, this is what I call getaway day, Mr. Spence," Tommy said with a huge sigh of relief. "When do you think we'll get to New Orleans, sir?"

"My God, boy! We just sat down on the train and you're already askin' when we'll be there! It's the same thing as when we came here, only in reverse. We take this special to the end of Cuba, then board the steamship to New Orleans, and then another train from New Orleans back to Kentucky," Spence explained. "When we get to Louisville and get the horses all settled in and doctored, then you can be off to Covington for a visit."

"Louisville?!" Tommy exclaimed. "I thought we were going to Lexington to race?"

"That's right, son. We are. But with thirty-five horses in our string right now, I made sure to book barn space in Louisville before that meeting started so's I would be sure of getting' it. I got a feeling that there are going to be a lot more horses coming down from the east this year to the Church than there is stall space to house them. I could only arrange for fifteen stalls and they are down at Douglas Park. I'm leaving nine of the horses right here in Havana. Tex Brosier is keeping them here for me and will keep them in top shape come next winter's meet. One of them I'm leaving is Walter (Mack). I want him to rest up a whole season so he can get back to his real form next meeting down here. I'm leaving Miss Ivan and Terrible Miss here too, along with Zoie and Unar. The other ones staying behind are Solid Rock, Elga, and Shiro. Oh, and Froglegs. He's the one I bought at the paddock auction fire sale the other day, after the meeting concluded.

"Fire sale?" questioned Tommy. "I don't remember them having a fire? Where was it?"

Spence belly-laughed his response, "No, son, there wasn't no fire anywhere, thank God. Fire sale is just slang for white elephant sale."

"What?" cried Tommy. "I know some of them nags ain't no faster than an elephant, but I still don't get it."

"Have you ever heard of a rummage sale?"

"Oh sure I have. The ladies at church have one every year and my mother used to love them. They sell stuff they don't use anymore and somebody else pays them money for it so they can spend in on the stuff that another lady doesn't want. We kids would just swap stuff. It's quicker and easier."

"Well, son, a fire sale is the exact same thing as your mother's rummage sale and I got Froglegs for $100 cash. The only difference is that I'll probably have to fire a couple of places on his legs and feet before he can ever be able to start training."

Spence continued, "As I was saying, the barns at the Church have been booked out for months. Remember that special that left day before we did, going to Maryland? A lot of those trainers are going to run at Bowie and then on to Harve de Grace and then they will be shipping their horses to Kentucky for the big stakes races that will be coming up at the Kentucky tracks. Remember what I told you about Matt Winn a while back and how he is going to make the Kentucky tracks the best ones anywhere? Well, this is where it all begins and you're gonna be right in the middle of history in the making! The Lexington meeting is only for thirteen days and I'm just sending Foster Embry, Sasenta, and Miss Burgomaster to that meeting. I'll have a few more that I'm training for other owners already there. This is gonna be a good chance for you to cut your own teeth on racing that's up a notch or two from what you've been used to so I plan on getting you on some other horses that you ain't so used to and ride against some different jockeys."

Racing in Louisville, KY

CHAPTER FORTY-ONE
Hello, Louisville

On Tuesday, April, 15, the Spence Stable and associates arrived in Louisville. The first page article in the *Daily Racing Form* for the 16th read:

"The stable of Kay Spence, the largest money winning establishment at Havana last winter, reached Douglas Park yesterday in good condition. The horses have had a strenuous campaign and will be given a much needed rest. Jockey T. Murray, the stable's rider, who headed the jockey list at the Havana meeting, has gone to his home in Covington for a brief visit."

Tommy paged through his scrap book while waiting for his train home to pull away. He read an article dated April 9, 1919 in the April 10th edition of the *Daily Racing Form* that ended with news about Harry, entitled:

MCLEAN HORSES ARRIVE AT DOWNS

Louisville, Ky. April 9---Harry Lunsford, the stable's contract rider, who has been spending several weeks at his home in Covington, reported to trainer Schorr, and is now engaged galloping the stable's horses.

"Darn, I wish we could have gone home to visit at the same time. Now he's back in Louisville and I'm just leaving," Tommy thought to himself.

On the train ride from Louisville to Covington, Tommy tried to sleep, but he was just too excited. He didn't realize how homesick he really was until he started recognizing the scenery and landscape along the Licking River, going through White Villa and through Ryland Lakes, where a lot of the rich and well-to-do from Cincinnati and Covington have their smaller summer vacation homes. A lot of them frequented Latonia when the race meetings were being held. It's a very pleasant ride from Ryland and up Decoursey Pike into Latonia, once you make it up that first hill. As the train continued through the huge Decoursey Yards, Tommy became more and more excited because he was seeing places he was familiar with and places he had been and played with his school chums and neighborhood friends. He even recognized places and things that he read about in his favorite Seckatary Hawkins stories and adventures. Only they had different names in the newspaper stories.

The train then reached the Great Crossing at the far west end of Latonia where a total of 17 railroad tracks converged and intersected before being switched onto the correct tracks for their final destination. From here, Tommy had a good view of the northern end of the oval track which was the final turn. He could see the back stretch and the barns, already showing some human and equine activity. Heading on towards Covington, through the rest of Latonia, he could look right straight down the final stretch and see that giant three-spired clubhouse on the right and the judges stand on the left in the distance. With his eyes fixed on this site, he could even hear the roar of the crowd and feel the pounding of his heart in his chest cavity and whooshing in both ears. He was spellbound for a time, but had no idea of the name describing his condition and the way he was feeling.

Finally, the train was in sight of the Covington Depot on Pike Street. He didn't have much baggage along. Everything fit nicely in a burlap oats sack, tied at the top with a length of strong white cotton standing bandage material. As he flung the bag over his shoulder, the only real weight in the bag that he could notice was that of his scrap book, which was becoming a fairly good sized tome. Down the two steps of the boarding stoop, he headed toward the steeples of the Mother of God Catholic Church, which filled the skyscape. After lighting a votive candle there in thanks for arriving home safely, he proceeded westward through the various ethnically oriented neighborhoods until he came up on the heartwarming sight of Saint Patrick's Church. Now, he was home. On down to Second Street to his family home he ran, not even realizing that he was running.

As he ran up onto the wooden front porch, he thought, *"Home at last! If only mother could have been here!"*

Oh my! What a wonderful reception and welcome he received from his brothers, sisters, friends and extended family! They were all there to celebrate his return home and the great success he had enjoyed over the winter. Tommy could just not control his feelings, even though he practiced not crying over and over in his head hundreds of times on the train trip home. He thought of himself as finally an independent young man, but for the moment, his manhood façade failed him miserably and he was still just a little boy again, longing for his mama.

Tommy's brother Joe was standing half way up the staircase as all the hoopla was going on. The grin on his face was enough to show how proud he was of his next youngest brother.

"Tommy!" he hollered. "Look up here a minute."

As Tommy's gaze followed the command, his expression immediately reflected his emotion. There at the top landing was Virginia, the most beautiful sight he had ever experienced. She was all dressed up in her best church gown, all decorated in gingerbread lace and fresh flowers adorned her wavy brown hair. Both of them welled up as one descended and the other ascended what to them had to be the stairway to heaven. After a period of staring into each other's eyes and clutching each other's hands, they finally kissed. Right smack on the lips! It was actually the first time they had ever done that and everyone could tell it was just a magical moment in their lives, one that neither one of them would ever forget.

Tommy's sister suggested, "Let's give the love birds some time to themselves and all gather out on the porch for refreshments. We have freshly squeezed lemonade and pound cake with real butter and sugar icing, just for this special homecoming. Tommy will be here as long as he wants and we can all visit with him."

"But Tommy is back here in Kentucky in order to race," interjected Joe. "He'll be going to Lexington, and on to Louisville, and then back here to Latonia. Isn't that the plan, Tommy?"

"Sure is. That's it exactly. I have to be in Lexington next Thursday for the opening of that meeting. Mr. Spence already has me a train ticket for Wednesday's special from Latonia to Lexington. He said there will be a lot of horsemen and patrons on the train, so I shouldn't have any problem getting to where I need to be."

The happily re-united family spent the rest of the evening on the porch catching up. Virginia insisted that Tommy sit in the swing with her just like he always wanted to do in the years past. Joe rocked in his rocker nearby and listened for hours of Tommy's experiences in Havana. His sister saw to it that there was plenty of lemonade available, but she couldn't for the life of her get Tommy to eat anything.

"Honey, that was such a long and tiring trip. Surely you could use a little nourishment. Just let me prepare you a little something."

Tommy looked over at Joe's girth and laughed, "Sis, from the looks of Joe over there, I'm afraid if I was to eat any of your cooking now, I'd never make weight for the Lexington meeting but thanks all the same!"

Everybody got a big kick out of that statement, but Sis could only tisk in pity as she shook her head back and forth.

The next six days were filled with a wonderful array of visits and day trips, spending time with family and friends who Tommy hadn't seen for the past six months. It wasn't really all that long a time that he was away, but it was a different person returning from the one that left the last winter. Tommy came back a young man. He was much more mature and confident of himself. He obviously developed self respect, integrity, and a work ethic. The pride his siblings and extended family had for him was clearly worn on their faces when they were with him or talking about him. Tommy may just have been the very first person of his generation from that small but closely knit Covington neighborhood to have had the chance and opportunity to pursue the American dream but it was far too early to tell. The planets were all in the correct alignment. It just depended now on the path the shining star would take.

All of this was oblivious to Tommy, however. He may have come back a different person, but he was not really aware of it. Deep down he felt that he was the same Tommy Murray that he had always been, except for the fact that he was blessed doing what he loved most, riding horses.

Postcard of Lexington Association Track in Kentucky

CHAPTER FORTY-TWO
Lexington, April, 1919

Tommy arrived at the Kentucky Association Track in Lexington early Thursday morning, April 24, 1919, without a hitch. Spence was hoping the boy would be in good physical shape and weight on his return. Tommy didn't know it, but this was just another one of Kay Spence's little tests that he gave to his boys. If Tommy came back in good shape and in the correct weight range, then Spence would know that he was truly set on the goal of success in the profession. Spence purposely gave Tommy no standing instructions for his visit home but he passed with flying colors without even knowing that he was being tested. He ran several miles every morning and again every evening while he was away and his diet consisted of one piece of toast in the morning, and then fresh fruits and vegetables during the day. Avoiding the tempting fare of his sister's table each day actually required lighting a votive candle every morning in St. Patrick's church followed by a special prayer. It took a lot of will power and faith, put he persevered and it showed! Spence couldn't have been more pleased.

"Tommy, listen up. Some of Jefferson Livingston's stable arrive here yesterday with his trainer Jack McCormack. Jack stopped me last night as I was leaving and he joined me at the diner, because he said he wanted to talk to me. He told me that Jefferson liked the way you were riding down in Havana and that's why he put you on a couple of his horses. Well, he's got Major Parke down here to Lexington for this meeting, and he's got high hopes that this horse will persevere and improve enough to be a real Derby contender. He wants you to exercise and work him down here. If the two of you click, he may consider putting you on him for a couple of races here. Listen son, this is a great opportunity for you. You have a good chance to get picked up by a stable down here this spring, and this is the first indication. You know, Livingston has quite a barn full of contenders. I hear he's got his heart set on winning the Derby as well as the Oaks."

"I thought he had Willie Crump riding first call for him Mr. Spence? What about that?"

"Well son, you know, you can't put all your eggs in one basket. It's the same reason a horseman wants more than one crack horse in his barn."

"Well, Boss, I wanted to tell you this anyway, and now it's even more fitting. My best girl, Virginia, said she loves me. I told her that I planned on coming down here to Lexington and then to Louisville to make her very proud. I told her that I was doing it just for her, and that I wouldn't let her down and when I got back to Latonia, I would save enough money so me and Virginia could get married and raise us a family and be real comfortable, maybe even rich enough to travel all over the U.S. racing and live like rich people."

Spence laughed his customary gut laugh and responded, "Tommy, that is the best set of plans I ever did hear and we are puttin' that plan of action into place starting right now!"

Spence patted Tommy on the back. "But before we get down to brass tacks, I want you to read this article in today's *Form*. Take it back to our barn with you and go ahead and get settled in. The program today starts at 2:15. In the first race, you'll be on one of the Williams brothers' horses and Willie will be on one of Livingston's. In the third race, we got you on his filly, Lillian Shaw, who has been training real good so far this spring. It's the Danville Purse, an allowance race for three-year-old fillies and there's about ten of them slated to run. It should be a good test for the Kentucky Oaks next month."

Tommy set up his cot in the tack room next to Spence's stalls, unpacked his bag, and made up his bed. He read with excitement and adrenalin producing anticipation what the *Form* had to say about the Lexington meeting:

"What promises to eclipse in brilliancy any former opening of Kentucky racing is in prospect tomorrow when the sport will inaugurate the control of the Kentucky Jockey Club over the historic course formerly conducted by the guiding spirits comprising the Kentucky Racing Association."

He read on with enthusiasm about Colonel Matt J. Winn and his plans for the future for Kentucky racing. Tommy had actually met and talked with Mr. Winn back in Covington just a few days ago, when they both had made a visit to the Latonia track. Tommy was there just to see how things looked and to visit any old friends who may have been there. Mr. Winn was there purchasing a home in Covington at Fifth and Garrard, and to make inspections of the conditions of the entire Latonia plant in order to direct what future work would be needed to be accomplished before the return of the fall meeting there. As president of the Kentucky Jockey Club, Winn was in charge of the tracks in Latonia, Lexington, and Louisville, each one playing a very integral part in the quality and the growing prestige of Thoroughbred racing once again in Kentucky.

Running behind the Latonia property was the L&N Railroad tracks, which facilitated convenient transport of horses to the Lexington and Louisville tracks. Behind that ran 3L Highway which provided the convenient motor car roadway that linked the three tracks.

Tommy got a little rush of big head, remembering how Mr. Winn actually came up to him at Latonia and began talking to him and addressing him as "one of my jockeys" to his entourage of followers that day. Tommy's girl, Virginia, had another cousin, named Jimmy Sorrell, who dated Matt Winn's niece, and Tommy made sure that Mr. Winn was aware of that relationship. He just figured that every little bit could only help him to reach his goal as a leading race rider and he saw no reason to miss out on this particular opportunity.

The article went on to state that there really wasn't a huge influx in the number of horses that showed up for the meeting; total was right at 600 head but it did stress the fact that the quality of horseflesh this year was far superior to the normal turnout:

"Always regarded as a testing ground for future greats, the Lexington track will this year be particularly so on account of the numerous highly regarded two-year-olds that will try conclusions, and their performances will be observed with particular interest by the racing element in all parts of the country. The three-year-old brigade will also be the cynosure for the critically observant, not alone because of their Kentucky Derby prospects, but because of their possible chances in lesser engagements in which they may figure."

The first race of the first day of the Spring Meeting 1919 of 13 days went to post at 2:24 p.m. Willie Crump was in the first post position on Jefferson Livingston's six-year-old Prince of Como. Tommy started in the fifth spot on the Williams Brothers three-year-old, Linden. The field of five was at the post for one minute when starter A.B. Dade hollered "Come on." Prince of Como took the lead at the very first and held it for the entire race.

"Showing great speed, he raced into a long lead at once and, holding sway for the entire distance, won in a canter," reported the next day's *Daily Racing Form*.

Tommy's horse, starting on the outside getting off in third place, but fell back to last place to save ground until the three-quarter pole, when Tommy rode him hard, *"saving much ground when coming into the stretch, finished fast and gamely through the stretch."*

Tommy and Willie chatted with each other on the way back to the finish line and clubhouse area, and as they were approaching the winners circle.

Willie chided, "Oh, this is where I get off, ole buddy," laughing and slapping his left thigh.

"Don't make too big of a mess in there, Willie, 'cause I'll be using that circle next," hollered Tommy as he headed to weigh in.

Willie Crump was the first call jockey for the Livingston stable and he was up on another of Livingston's horses in the second race as Tommy sat one out. Willie finished out of the money while Tommy was busy putting on the Livingston colors back at the jockey house. As Spence had told Tommy earlier, he and Livingston had discussed putting Tommy on his good filly, Lillian Shaw, just to see how things went here in the spring in Kentucky. Tommy was already familiar with the horse, having been on top of her in Havana a couple of times. She seemed to respond more to Tommy's style of hand riding than she did to Willie Crump's (It is interesting to note that Willie Crump was a left-handed jockey, which at the time was an oddity, indeed. A blurb in the *Daily Racing Form* for Monday, February 5, 1917 had this to say: *"Jockey Willie Crump, the little apprentice lad riding in such brilliant form at New Orleans, is left-handed and a turf critic says that 'when he is guilty of rough riding it is because the horse swerves when he whips it left-handed, according to his own version, but they never seem to swerve when he does not have to outgeneral some other rider in a close finish.'"*). Besides that, Willie had a few more pounds than Tommy who currently tipped the scales at 99 pounds.

Willie had actually just returned to race riding earlier this past winter racing season after an extended period of inactivity. *"Ed Moore brought Crump to the races and signed him to an iron-bound contract. After leaving here the winter he was so successful, Crump slumped into wretched form and dropped almost into obscurity as other good boys forged to the front. It was said at the time Crump could not get along with his contract employer, Ed Moore. In fact, Crump, according to the story, refused to do any more riding for Moore, and Moore, by refusing to sell his contract, automatically kept Crump off the track, though compelled to pay him. Crump went to work in a New York shoe store, but since Moore has decided to sell his contract, has decided to resume the saddle."* (*Daily Racing Form*, 12/18/18.)

The article went on to say: *"NEW ORLEANS, La., December 17.---Willie Crump, the left-handed jockey, who was a riding sensation down here several winters ago, again will be seen in the saddle here. Crump's contract has been sold to*

Jefferson Livingston, and Crump will ride the Livingston horses here this winter. John McCormack is training the Livingston string."

The third race of the day was an allowance race for three-year-old fillies called the Danville Purse. It was worth $550 to the winner and there were 10 entries vying for the purse. The track patrons that day had decided that Regalo would come off the most popular choice to win, with Legotal being the second pick. Lillian Shaw was not a favorite, with odds of 6,225-to-100. The April 26th, 1919 edition of *The Thoroughbred Record* had this to say about the race:

"The Danville purse, the third race on the program, one of six furlongs, brought forth a rather classy field of ten, amongst which were the Debutante Stakes winner, the rather diminutive Regalo, the Spinaway Stakes heroine Passing Fancy, a very attractive bay daughter of Ormondale and Passan, Edwards dam, and half sister to Colin by Hamburg; Legotal, winner of four races this season; Madras Gingham, and six others, amongst which was the ultimate winner, Lillian Shaw, a chestnut daughter of that handsome stallion Fair Olay and Early Love by King Eric. Legotal was first to show and led her field up the back and over the hill, only to be caught and passed by Regalo, which an eighth out appeared a certain winner until Lillian Shaw, in no wise discomforted by a slow beginning, ranged alongside. It was all over in a couple of strides, the daughter of Fair Play proving altogether too much for Regalo. This performance was, to my way of thinking, by far the most impressive of the afternoon. The Livingston filly may or may not be quick off the mark, but the style in which she tackled Regalo was irreproachable and the latter's collapse can only be attributed to her having met a more worthy antagonist. In Lillian Shaw I feel assured Mr. Livingston has a filly of more than ordinary merit, thoroughly level headed and game and one which will run any distance in reason and an Oaks victory may not prove beyond her; anyway I must have her on my side for the Ashland Oaks next Tuesday— [signed]Exile"

"You did good out there, son," Spence greeted Tommy back at the paddock. "Livingston's really got his heart set on that filly winning the Oaks in May but I just don't know. She's sure got some good competition agin' her. Whad'ya think, Tommy? Did she have any left?"

Tommy grinned, "She sure did, sir! Could'a run her around the track again if I wanted. She just come on as much as it took to win, as if she knew she should save herself for another time. I think she knows what's coming up in May and she's gonna win it all. I can just tell when I'm on her. She's a gamer."

"Well, you made a good showing on her today. Now you know, Livingston's probably gonna put Willie on her next Tuesday for the Ashland Oaks, just to see how he handles her against that same bunch. He's not worried about what his horse can do, he's just trying to decide if he wants a right-handed or a left-handed monkey up on top of her. We'll just have to wait and see. Meantime, you spend some time with her every chance you get, make sure he sees you there, and always give him a hard-grippin' right handshake," he chuckled.

CHAPTER FORTY-THREE
Who Will It Be?

When Tuesday arrived, sure enough, Livingston had Willie Crump up on Lillian Shaw for the Ashland Oaks. Tommy knew what Livingston was doing by changing jockeys. It was a common occurrence at every track and with every owner and trainer. They were looking for the best combination of horse and rider but for some unexplained reason, Tommy felt funny about it this time. It was as if he had 'ownership' somehow in Lillian Shaw and indeed he did, albeit emotional ownership but he couldn't distinguish it from real personal or physical ownership. He tried to explain his feelings to Spence, but couldn't quite find the right words.

Spence just laughed, "Son, you and that filly is just bonded, that's all. Why she'll probably feel the same way today with Willie up and not you. Let's just watch the race real close and see how she runs. Then, you tell me if you think things would have turned out different if you were up."

The day was rainy and the track wet. Tommy was riding Port Light for P.A. Houde in the first race on a heavy track. They went to post at 2:15 and by 2:18 Tommy was scraping about two pounds of mud and sand off his face, chest, and pants. Squeeler, the eight-year-old favorite, was driven hard from the start and lead all the way to the finish, while Port Light raced in closest pursuit the entire length in second place. Eventually, in the last sixteenth, Port Light tired and Squeeler pulled away.

In the next race, Tommy had a breather and Willie Crump was up on another Livingston horse and managed a $4.40 show payout on Starview in a match for two-year-old filly maidens. Next up was an allowance race for three-year-old fillies. Light rain continued and added to the already heavy track, causing four of the scheduled ten entries to scratch. Tommy was up on Lady Fair Play at six to one odds, while Tommy's nemesis in the year's jockey percentages standings, Cliff Robinson, was aboard Dancing Spray, at 2.5-to-1. Willie Crump was on a long shot, By Right. Tommy must have already had enough mud in his face for the day as he and Lady Fair Play showed the most speed and led wire to wire, winning five lengths ahead of the second place winner Dancing Spray. Tommy laughed and shouted something to Cliff from the winner's circle as Cliff dismounted and shed himself of several pounds of mud. It was hard to tell if he was laughing or not, but Tommy sure was.

As they planned earlier, Kay Spence and Tommy were going to get a good vantage point and watch this next race very closely.

"I don't know how she'll do in this slop," Tommy said to Spence.

"Me neither. Don't even know if she's ever tried it in the mud," Spence answered.

The turf writer for *The Thoroughbred Record*, working under the pen name EXILE wrote of this next race as follows:

"...After this came the paddock inspection of the runners for the Ashland Oaks, which afforded Regalo and Lillian Shaw a chance to renew hostilities. Soggy track conditions precluded any intelligent attempt to forecast the winner. Often have I heard it stated that a good horse can run in any kind of going; take it from me, this is a mistake; some horses can, while others cannot run in the mud. Big feet, mule feet, it does not matter, no one can guess them until they are tried. J.H. Rosseter's Passing Shower, on account of track conditions, declined the issue and this left only five to go. Regalo looked all the better for her previous outing, but the strongly fancied Delico did not altogether please me. Lillian Shaw looks strong and able, and the bay War Tax is a filly of fine size and pleasing appearance. Off they go, to a good start, Regalo at once assumes an easy lead, bouncing along after the fashion of a rubber ball, evidently well suited by the condition of the track. There is nothing more to be said, it was Regalo's heat from start to finish. Delico raced forwardly in second place for a time, but was overtaken and passed by Lillian Shaw when half the journey had been run. For a second Lillian appeared to be about to repeat her previous performance, but it was not to be; soon Lillian was seen to be floundering and she was repassed in the stretch run by Delico. The latter, however, was quite incapable of making any impression on Regalo, who won at her ease by a wide margin. Should by any chance the track proves to be muddy on the day set for the running of the Kentucky Oaks, Regalo, on her today's performance, will come in for strong support."

"Well son," Spence leaned over and said. "What's your take on it?"

Tommy was still running the finish through his mind one more time and with an analytical tone and expression responded, "She's the perfect lady and she don't like gittin' muddy and I surely can't blame her for that! If I ever get another chance to get up on her, I guarantee you, her face won't get muddy!"

Little did Tommy know at that moment that in as little as four days hence he would indeed again be aboard Lillian Shaw, due largely to what can only be explained as fate or maybe good luck. Even though Willie Crump was Livingston's first call jockey, the filly's owner just couldn't help but notice that Lillian Shaw liked Tommy. She seemed more at ease when he was straddling her than when Willie was on top and he noticed how she perked a bit every time Tommy came to visit her and fool with her but he also considered the fact that maybe he was just imagining that the two of them had some unexplained chemistry so he sought out Kay Spence to have him evaluate his suspicions.

"Funny thing you are asking me that question, Jeff," replied Spence. "Cause I, too, have seen it, plainer than that big schnoz on the boy's face. Yep, them two got some chemistry goin' on. Ain't no doubt about that at all. That horse is all he ever talks about, but more like she's his girlfriend. It's like he's love struck or something."

They both laughed, but there was no denying the fact.

"Kay, listen, if you ain't got plans for your boy in this Saturday's third race, I'd like to put him up again on my filly. Willie's been a good rider for me and all, but he ain't her good rider. The race is an allowance race for three-year-old fillies and it looks like it could turn out to be a prep race for the Oaks. Another reason is the fact that Regalo won't be runnin' in it because the Gallahers got her entered into the Blue Grass Stakes, which happens to be the very next race and that makes Lillian's chances even better."

Spence quickly agreed and said, "Why don't you just go on over now and tell the boy the good news. He'll be your friend forever, and that's a fact!"

The next three days seemed more like three weeks for Tommy. As soon as his duties were completed each day at the Spence barn, and his chores and exercising were done, he was over to the Livingston Stable spending time with Lillian Shaw. He and Willie had always been good pals and colleagues, and there certainly weren't any bad feelings brewing in Willie's case over this current arrangement. As a matter of fact, they even compared riding notes and strategies from Tommy's other two wins on her and Willies recent third place finish just a few days before. Time seemed to pass a lot quicker as the two boys sat in front of Lillian's stall door talking as she stuck her head over to eavesdrop.

When Saturday finally arrived and Tommy and Lillian Shaw paraded out to the post, it was hard to tell which one showed the most confidence. They were to start in the fourth spot in the field of five, and the bettors in the full capacity crowd decided that Lillian Shaw would receive the third best odds. That small detail phased neither horse nor human. The Lexington Form Chart in the Sunday edition of the *Daily Racing Form* spelled out the race in this way: "*Went to post at 3:30. At post one minute. Start good and slow. Won handily; second and third driving. LILLIAN SHAW, lucky and saving much ground on the turns, ran into a good lead after going five-eights, but had to be ridden hard for a time in the stretch to outstay IWIN. The latter, much the best, suffered repeatedly from interference and was forced wide frequently by LADY FAIR PLAY, but finished gamely and would have won with a clear course. THE COLLEEN BAWN saved much ground on the last turn and made a fast finish. DELICO had no mishaps. LADY FAIR PLAY set the early pace, but tired badly after swerving out at the half-mile.*" A two dollar bet on Lillian Shaw paid $7.20 to win.

Lillian Shaw led her own way to the winner's circle. She knew where she was going and she looked very accomplished and proud as she transported Tommy along with her. When Tommy got the nod, he dismounted and as he headed to the scales, he rubbed Lillian's face and said to her, "See girl? I promised you no mud in your face." Lillian bobbed her head seemingly in agreement.

The thrill and pageantry of the win was short lived, however, as all eyes were trained on the next race, the Blue Grass Stakes. This $2,500 added allowance stakes race for three-year-olds was populated with all Derby contenders and one of them was the filly, Regalo. So far in the history of American racing, there had been only one filly to have won the Kentucky Derby, and that was Regret in 1915 (In the year 1919, this fact was notable, but really wasn't that significant or astounding because there had only been 35 previous Kentucky Derbies and it wasn't surprising to Thoroughbred racing enthusiasts that a filly couldn't win against the boys. Today, in 2011, there have been only two other fillies to have accomplished that feat in 136 attempts, Genuine Risk in 1980 and Living Colors in 1988. This does not preclude that fillies cannot compete successfully against their male counterparts, because they do so all the time. It's just that by the time all the contenders for the big Triple Crown events have floated to the top each year, not very many of them are the fillies and it all boils down to purely physical reasons: overall strength and endurance and lung capacity. The same law of nature holds true for every genus and species. There are always exceptions to the rule. In the case of the Kentucky Derby, there have been three exceptions out of the 136 chances).

This next event was to be the fifth running of the Blue Grass Stakes, and it had come to be considered a pretrial for the Kentucky Derby. The odds for the race clearly indicated that the patrons of the full house Lexington track that day felt that the filly Regret was not to be the favorite. As a matter of fact, there were two colts ahead of her favored to win but she was still picked over four other colts. The race was best described in a separate article in the next day's edition of the *Daily Racing Form* under these headlines:

"*REGALO'S STRIKING RACE---Defeats Many Derby Candidates in Fast Time Easily --- Now Looms Up as a Dangerous Figure in the Race Itself*"

The article goes on to say: "*LEXINGTON, Ky., May, 8. --- Another Kentucky Derby factor loomed up in most promising style this afternoon, and it is not beyond possibility that another filly's name will be added to the roster of winners of the much coveted Louisville event, for Gallaher Bros. Regalo, by her sparkling triumph in the Blue Grass Stakes, contested by most of the formidable Kentucky Derby contenders, excepting Eternal, Billy Kelly, Vindex, Sir Barton, clearly demonstrated that she is the superior of the band that made the race with her this afternoon, and on her showing must hold a place of consideration for chief honors in the Derby running next Saturday.*"

"The race, however, thoroughly exploded the Derby pretensions of St. Bernard, whose recent pair of victories caused him to be regarded with more than passing consideration; American Ace, which showed positive sprinting qualities only, and brought into notice Pat Dunne's much-campaigned Under Fire. The latter ran a fine race and may improve on it at the added distance that the Derby is run over."

"His close proximity to Regalo at the finish, however, was due to Jockey Murphy's action in having eased the Gallaher filly up to little better than a canter in the last sixteenth, for at this stage she had the victory won and was commandingly in advance.

"The earlier stages of the race were dominated by American Ace, which sprinted into a good lead at once and showed the way to St. Bernard and Sennings Park, his closest followers, Regalo heading the second division, with Under Fire far back. There was no noticeable change in the running for the first three-quarters, but just before reaching the lower turn St. Bernard gave way and Regalo began making play for the lead. An extra effort on her part readily gave her command, and before the last eighth was reached she was five lengths in the van. American Ace retired in the stretch, and soon after Under Fire made his challenge, which caused him to displace Sennings Park, but the filly was too good for him and she won in hollow style. The time of the race, 1:51 3/5, marked a splendid effort, considering that the track was not in its best, though regarded as fast."

"The splendid racing offering, coupled with the ideal conditions, was responsible for bringing to the Kentucky Association course this afternoon by far the largest gathering that has ever witnessed the sport in this locality. Every available inch of space in the grandstand was occupied and the overflow jammed the lawns and paddock to the crowding point. The betting pavilion was a seething mass and the mutuel equipment totally inadequate for the accommodation of those speculatively inclined...."

"Well, son," Spence concluded, "That's that! Looks like Regalo is headed to the Derby and that means we don't have to worry about her in the Oaks. Now we gotta convince Livingston that you're the one that needs to be up on her for that victory!"

"But Boss," Tommy objected, "Willie is his contract jockey."

"That may be my boy, but you are Lillian Shaw's jockey, and Livingston knows it. Won't take much convincing though. Ol' Jeff knows plenty about horses and riders. C'mon son, you got two more races to win today. Let's get you back to the jockey house and I'll see you in the paddock."

And win he did. Tommy took his mounts in the sixth and seventh races of the day to the finish line first. Besides giving Spence a win on Plain Bill which paid $17.60 on a $2.00 mutuel, he also chalked up two more wins ahead of Cliff Robinson to maintain his lead as the winningest jockey of the year. Overall, it was a very good day for one Tommy Murray.

With just three more days remaining for the Lexington meeting, all talk was concentrated on the opening of the Louisville meeting of nineteen days duration which would feature the running of the 45th Kentucky Derby in the fifth race of opening day. Oh, how Tommy wished he could be one of the exclusive riders chosen for one of those equine champions of 1919! What an honor and thrill that would be! Just 15 out of the hundreds and hundreds of jockeys in the entire country would be granted the elite status of having a Derby mount.

As he dreamed and fantasized, he clutched the St. Patrick medal around his neck that his mother had given him and he remembered what she had always told him: *"Tommy, the only thing that can keep a person from fulfilling his dreams is himself."* She would tell him, *"You are blessed with the strong will and backbone of your Irish background. If you want something bad enough, you will get it with hard work, determination, perseverance, and the will of God. No one will just give it to you."*

He went on about his duties and chores as usual, but with a more pronounced spring in his step.

"What's with you today, boy?" Spence leaned over the stall door and asked.

Tommy was sitting on a bale, going through his scrap book, "Nothin' particular. Why do you ask Mr. Spence?"

"You just seem to be more energetic or something today and when ya get that-a-way, you sing to yourself and boy, I have to tell you your singin' just ain't that good. While you was out there running, these here horses were having a fit from them awful sounds!"

"Don't really know. Guess I'm getting excited about get-a-way day and going to Louisville and seeing the Kentucky Derby on Saturday. I ain't never seen one, you know?"

"Yes, I know, Tommy," Spence grinned. "They say the best place to see the Derby is from a saddle!"

"Well, someday, sir, I'll let you know," said Tommy in a very matter-of-fact and confident way.

Spence chuckled, because he knew for a fact that the boy would someday keep his word. "Let's get ready for the afternoon, son. You got five races coming up and your buddy Cliff has four today and you know he's on your tail now for total wins!"

"I know," Tommy retorted, "but I aint a-gonna let him catch me, no way!"

The day wasn't that spectacular as far as Tommy was concerned. He finished out of the money in all but one race which he won in a very hard drive in the end after a poor start. That win, however, was more significant than it seemed. Corson was a three-year-old colt owned by W. W. Darden and trained for him by Kay Spence and depending on how this horse looked in this race was to decide whether Darden would take the chance of entering Corson into the Kentucky Derby. He won by a head over Cantilever, who beat the third place finisher by a head. *The Thoroughbred Record* had this to say about the race:

"Corson, the best furnished horse in the sixth race, was overlooked, and besides was off all in a tangle when the start was effected. However, by diligent perseverance and the persuading application of the raw hide, Jockey T. Murray induced the chestnut to be on the premises as they raced through the stretch. The leaders, Cantilever and Cacambo, both had enough ere the finishing line was passed and Corson won in a hammer and tongs set to." (5/10/19).

Corson's form was exceptional and his heart was huge, and that was enough for Darden. This might be his only chance ever to have a horse in the Derby. Spence knew all along that Darden would do it if Corson won, but he never let on to Tommy and if Corson was entered, then it was Tommy who would be up. He didn't want to put any pressure on the boy, and he just wanted to see Corson run his own race. Spence knew it was a long shot, but long shots have placed before and he wasn't going to wager more than the obligatory two-dollar ticket for souvenir purposes for Tommy. For the time being, Tommy would be kept in the dark about this matter.

Next day, Cliff Robinson picked up two more wins to Tommy's one win and one second. Unfortunately, the second and third places don't fit into the equation of win percentages for jockeys but one good thing for Tommy was the fact that his win and his second was for owner Jefferson Livingston. Willie Crump, his regular jockey, wasn't entered in any of the seven contests that day, but Tommy didn't know the reason for his absence.

That night, as Tommy and Kay Spence were packing things up in preparation of getaway day, Spence told Tommy, "Son, I had a long talk with Livingston's trainer today. He likes you a lot and he is going to recommend to Mr. Livingston that you get the mount on Lillian Shaw for the Kentucky Oaks. He was real impressed with how you handled her in the other races, while she just didn't show the same kind of flair when Willie was up on her. Now, mind you, Willie is still Livingston Stables' number one jockey, so he has a bit of a say in the decision, but Jack McCormack is of the mind that he will have no objections, unless not being able to ride in the Oaks is one, and in that case he will convince him that he really has no objection, because if Livingston don't win races, then nobody gets paid. He did not have a winning year last year, and he doesn't want to repeat it this year."

CHAPTER FORTY-FOUR
Exterminator

Tommy was excited with the dawning of May 8th, even though it was rainy and dreary, because it was get-a-way day and because he would get to watch Exterminator run a race. He knew an awful lot about Exterminator, but never saw him in person. Tommy looked to the horse as a role model or mentor. Nobody at first had faith in the horse. They said he was not very royally bred and then they castrated him because he supposedly was unruly, but truth be known, they cut him so his poor breeding wouldn't be propagated. His owner, Willis Sharpe Kilmer, bought him only as a running companion for his crack Sun Briar's training regimen. Kilmer never had anything good to say about the lanky gelding, that is, until his prince became the pauper, and the pauper became the 1918 Kentucky Derby winner. Tommy would dream that he too would transcend his Covington street urchin background and become a famous rider who would win the Kentucky Derby and the Belmont Stakes and the Preakness all in the same year and rise to the pinnacle just like Exterminator had done. He loved and admired that horse without ever having seen him.

Tommy placed fourth in the first race of the day and then promptly spent the next two races at Exterminator's barn, spellbound and entranced most of the time there. He was just inspiring to the boy and Tommy benefitted from the experience. The fourth race was the tenth running of the Camden Handicap and would be worth $2,310 to the winner. The track was declared muddy, and boy, was it ever! Two of the four entries slated to run were scratched, which just left Exterminator and Midway in what quickly became a match race.

The *Daily Racing Form* described the race as follows: *"Went to post at 3:46. At post 1 minute. Start good and slow. Won easily; second driving. EXTERMINATOR raced into the lead in the first quarter and held MIDWAY safe for the entire race, but was shaken up in the stretch, only to come away near the end. MIDWAY ran well and made a game finish."*

It was apparent that something inspired Tommy, because he rode very well in the next three races, taking a third place, a second place, and winning the very last race of the Lexington meeting with Kay Spence's good four-year-old, Woodthrush.

"...and so ended Lexington's 1919 spring meeting. A meeting made memorable by the huge and enthusiastic attendance. Visions, visions, yet again, some time in the future I see Lexington's beautiful, well appointed, commodious race course, somewhere in the county of Fayette. When, ah when? [signed] EXILE" (*The Thoroughbred Record*, 5/10/19).

CHAPTER FORTY-FIVE
Kentucky Derby 1919

"A record Derby in more ways than one was this year's Louisville's big racing attraction. Never was there such a crowd, the dimensions of which reminded me of Epsom and of Flemington. A vast surging mass of racing enthusiasts, which, prior to the running of the big race, were to be found eagerly discussing the merits or demerits of the Derby contestants and afterwards the whys and wherefores of the success of one and the failure of others. A record Derby also because of the fact that two horses in the same ownership finished first and second, and also for the first time in its history the spoils fell to a sportsman who hails from the land of "God save the king and heaven bless the maple leaf forever." So wrote EXILE in the May 17th, 1919 issue of *The Thoroughbred Record*, describing the 1919 Kentucky Derby.

Friday, the 9th of May, witnessed the largest influx ever of train cars into the city of Louisville, Kentucky. There were trains from everywhere. The largest majority were from Lexington, transporting horsemen of every category and description as well as over 1,200 horses, all headed either to Churchill Downs or Douglas Park for stabling. Mass congestion was the order of the day. Trains carrying patrons from Cincinnati, Chicago, Maryland, New York and other major cities were arriving hourly. It didn't matter that there were no accommodations for this mass of humanity. They just kept coming and coming. Many of the rich and elite from the Wall Street ilk and the big steel and oil magnates had their own private train cars to live in, fully stocked with all the necessities and the servants to handle and prepare them.

Spence and Tommy and the other stable workers all arrived with the Spence string of horses, and unloaded at Douglas Park, where their barn and stalls were reserved. It took the entire day to sort things out and get settled in. As usual, Tommy bedded down in the tack and feed room, making his bed on the bales of hay with his mother's coverlets. This was home for him and he could not settle in until he was set up in his usual manner. He opened his copy of the day's *Daily Racing Form* to read about tomorrow's Derby. Mr. Spence was still up at Churchill, taking care of all the necessary registrations and other paperwork. There wasn't much in the Form about tomorrow's Derby, mostly stuff about the past Lexington meeting and the upcoming New York racing. He also read about how all the Derby contenders from the East who were already settled in at the Church were working in their Derby trials. It said there were 15 entries, but they weren't listed. He figured Mr. Spence would have a copy of tomorrow's form with him when he got back and would tell him what races he was entered in. Tommy fell asleep.

Very early next morning, Tommy was up and about, getting an early start on his chores. All the activity this early in the morning was very unusual, but very contagious and exciting.

"This is Derby Day morning," Tommy thought to himself. *"It feels just like Christmas."*

As he was making his rounds to all the stalls housing Mr. Spence's string, he came up on Corson's box and was most surprised to see Mr. Spence putting bandages on Corson's front and back legs.

"Well, good morning, sir," greeted Tommy. "I didn't expect to see you up this early in the morning. You must have had a late night last night."

"Naw, Tommy. I wasn't up late. You just fell asleep extra early. It was hardly dusk out."

"Why are you bandaging up Corson, Boss?"

"Well, Tommy. It's like this. I need you to breeze him this morning, and the earlier the better," Spence replied as he kept to his task.

"How about right now, sir? Ain't gonna get any earlier later."

They both laughed at Tommy's wisdom.

"Right now is just perfect," responded Spence. "Soon as I finish here, let's get him out to the track. Get your tack, son. Now, I want you to limber him up real good. Then breeze him for three-eighths, while I clock him. I want to see what he can do in this slop. If it's anywhere decent time, then we're gonna blow him out for a quarter mile. Pay particular attention to his footing and his recovery."

"Wow, Boss," Tommy opined. "Sounds like race day orders, sir."

"Well, they are, son. Darden done went and dropped Corson's name and the two-hundred fifty dollars into the box and he's officially entered in the Derby."

"What?" squeaked Tommy.

"Yep, Darden done put him in the Derby for this afternoon," replied Spence with a sigh. "But don't get all set on it, Tommy. I expect we will scratch him right before the race."

"What for? Then why put his name in if you're planning on scratching him?" Tommy demanded.

"Now, hold on a minute, son and let me explain. Now I ain't hundred percent sure we will scratch him. We need to see how the day pans out with all this rain and mud, and who eventually runs and who don't run. Come post time, if it looks favorable, we may keep him in it, if enough of the big dogs drop out. If not, then I ain't for risking Corson's health just to say he run in the Derby. It's already to his favor that he was entered into the Kentucky Derby, because that is what people will read and remember about him in the future, when it comes time to put him

264

out to stud. They ain't gonna remember he was scratched and if they do, they'll just think it was because of the slop and not because of his class. Get it?"

"Yeah, I guess so," answered Tommy. "That ain't cheating, is it, Boss?"

"Why hell no, son. It's just playing the odds and advantages. It'll look good on his record and it'll look good on your record too, Tommy."

"How's that, sir?" Tommy inquired.

"Just wait until later this morning, son, when the *Form* comes out and the programs for the day get printed. Right there in big bold print it will say 'Corson.....Owner : W.W. Darden....Jockey: T. Murray'. Somewhere down below, it will say 'Scratched: Corson' but that won't be in bold print and it ain't something people will remember either. All they remember is the winner's name and most of the time they even forget that come next Derby Day. So as of this moment, son, Corson is one of the entries in the 1919 Kentucky Derby, and Tommy Murray is his jockey of record. So, enjoy the moment. Believe me, it will happen again and it will be for real. I knew for a while that Darden might do this, but I didn't want to get your hopes up high and then have to let you down in such a way. But let me tell you this much. There was never a time he even gave it a thought to have another jockey up, and that's the God's honest truth."

As they entered the track in the rainy, dreary darkness, Spence spoke, "Son, you know as well as I do that Corson is in no way a mudder. He don't like runnin' in it and he hates it on his face. Now in this field of fifteen horses, there's at least ten of them that's up a class or two from Corson. Now that's a lot of mud we would be asking him to eat fer no good reason, wouldn't ya say?"

Tommy looked up and smiled, "I'd say, boss. I'd say."

"Now let's get you and him out there in the slop and get in a good work so all these touts and railbirds can do their clocking and contemplating. Besides, I think Corson will enjoy the attention and the exercise."

Spence went to the rail and Tommy and Corson hit the mud.

By the time the three of them returned to the barn, it was just beginning to show some daylight. The rain continued in a light but steady drizzle. Puddles were forming in the hoof prints everywhere a horse had recently trodden. There was still bounce in the track, but how long it would hold up was dependent on the Kentucky spring showers. The May flowers be damned was the general consensus in the backstretch kitchen. As Tommy and the boys attended Corson after his workout, Kay Spence left strict orders to withhold his food and water until further notice. He was on his way to the Church for the stewards/owner/trainer meeting with respect to the running of the forty-fifth Kentucky Derby. Tommy, with his fingers crossed so tightly that they were losing their feeling, snuck into Corson's stall for a little pre-race bonding and fellowship.

"What do you think, ole buddy? You up for the mud?"

He snorted a definite 'no' and lightly nipped Tommy on the shoulder.

"Good enough for me, my friend," Tommy whispered.

When Kay Spence returned, he had with him the Saturday edition of the *Daily Racing Form* and he promptly handed it over to Tommy.

"Here, son," he said. "Look it over real good. I didn't get a chance to read it yet."

Tommy immediately dug into it and read it cover to cover. The article on the front page mirrored what Mr. Spence had been saying all morning long. There were a group of genuine contenders and there was a group of outclassed dreamers, of which class Corson was one. On page two, was another article entitled *"Historic Kentucky Derby Race"* and it included the morning line odds. Tommy read on and came upon the name 'Corson'....his breeding listed as Ivan the Terrible --- Frogmore...Jockey: T. Murray...Trainer: K. Spence...Owners: W.W.Darden...Colors: White, brown belt, red cap. It also listed post positions and odds. Corson was post position number four with odds of 100-1. Vulcanite (no jockey named) was in post position number seven, also with 100-1 odds. Clermont, with N. Barrett up, got post position number 12 with 200-1 odds. Noted just below these listing, it was written: *"Corson, Vulcanite and Clermont are doubtful starters."*

Tommy finally conceded to the inevitable. He was not to run in this Kentucky Derby, but he damn sure would be included in the 1920 running!

The steady rains subsided by the time the first race took place. However, the heavy track persisted and played a deciding hand in many of the events. A lot of Tommy's long time cohorts and friends were present at this meeting. Harry Lunsford was here, as was Mack Garner, E. Pool, J. Howard, Willie Crump, and many others. Even Cliff Robinson, Tommy's main nemesis in the overall yearly winning percentage standings race but they were not enemies, they were cohorts and colleagues. Sometimes they would scrape in the jockey's room, but most likely the true physical battles occurred on the track, and most of them in the final stretch, vying for the finish line.

Tommy's first contest of the day found him astride Bon Jour, the good filly of E. B. McLean, in which he ran a disappointing fourth place. He might have had third place except for being blatantly cut off at the half mile mark. In the fourth race, The Seelbach Hotel Handicap, the warm up stakes race before the highly anticipated Kentucky Derby, Harry Lunsford aced out Tommy for first to cross the line, as Tommy took second place in a commanding battle of strength and stamina. *"Drastic was hard ridden for the entire race and, saving ground when coming into the stretch, outstayed Jim Heffering in a game finish. The latter showed high speed from the start and would have won, but for swerving out in the last eighth"* (*Daily Racing Form*, 5/11/19).

Tommy hurried to the saddling paddock for the next race, the 45th Kentucky Derby. He was outfitted in a brand new set of silks, representing the stable of W. W. Darden. He was splendid looking and proud at the saddling enclosure and thoroughly enjoying the moment when the dreaded announcement came, declaring the scratch of three separate entries, all due to the heavy and sloppy track conditions. Even though he knew what was to transpire, he still felt the disappointment of missing his chance for destiny. Sadly, he meandered back to the jockey house to change into J. Lowe's colors for the seventh and final race, after witnessing a Kentucky Derby win by a maiden. Sir Barton had never won a race until today, and it was the greatest race of all! This brought a smile to Tommy's face, to witness a Derby win for a maiden horse. There were two more races on the card for the day, and Tommy was glad to see that Harry was able to win one of them and place second in the other. The Louisville summer meeting was officially underway and would run for 19 days, ending with the 1919 Kentucky Oaks for the fillies.

CHAPER FORTY-SIX
A Matt Winn – Win Situation

Besides witnessing a three-year-old winning his maiden in the Kentucky Derby, Tommy was also to witness another 'first' at Churchill Downs. This had been the first Kentucky Derby that the general public had not been permitted free admission into the infield to watch the race. For 44 previous years, those who could not afford the price of admission into the clubhouse were granted a vantage point to see the race because it was felt that every Kentuckian was entitled to witness the most prestigious equine event in the world, regardless of their financial state.

This year, however, there was such a turnout of paying patrons that benches, accommodating five thousand people were set up in the infield next to the fence and directly across from the grandstand. Matt Winn was quoted in *The Thoroughbred Record* as saying: *"It is hard to give a correct estimate of the number of persons who were at the course this afternoon, but an idea can be gleaned from the fact that nearly 20,000 programs were sold. There is only one reason for the big crowd to witness the Derby this season, and that is that racing has taken on added interest for the masses and will have its patronage as long as conducted on high-class lines"* (5/17/19).

As Tommy read this, he thought to himself, *"Mr. Spence sure was right about Mr. Winn. His aim was to save horseracing here in Kentucky and clean it up so it would become a respectable sport again, and it looks like he done it!"*

Tommy also read that Matt Winn had been present for every one of the 45 Kentucky Derbies run. *"And I just saw my very first,"* thought Tommy. *"From now on, I'm going to watch every one too!"*

There was a little poem at the bottom of that same page which Tommy thought was the very best poem he had ever read. So he carefully cut it out and pasted it into the first page of his scrap book. The poem was called Derby Notes and it was written by James Whitcomb Riley:

I love the Hoss from Hoof to Head,
From Head to Hoof and Tail to Mane.
I love the Hoss, as I have said
From Head to Hoof and back again.

I love my God the first of all,
Then Him that perished on the Cross
And next my Wife and then I fall
Down on my knees and Love the Hoss

Kay Spence got back to the barn later than usual that night. He had been renewing old acquaintances and visiting with old friends and cohorts. There were a lot of them present for the Derby, and many more from the eastern concerns than usually showed up. Spence looked upon this new interest in the Derby as a boon for horseracing as a whole. He was impressed with what Matt Winn and the Kentucky Jockey Club was doing.

"If the money's there, then the horses will be there. And if the horses are there, then the players will be there. And if the players are there, then the money will be there again for another round," he was thinking to himself as he checked on the horses.

Tommy was busy tidying up the stalls and putting fresh bedding down.

"Hey, son," he hollered into the stall Tommy was working in. "Glad you're here. I got some things to tell you about."

Tommy poked his head out, "I'm all ears, Boss."

"Come out here and sit down a minute," Spence suggested. Tommy sat down on a straw bale that was up against the stall door. "Son, I ran into Jefferson Livingston down at the clubhouse. He's down here from Chicago for the Derby and he's planning on staying here a few more days to look over his horses and tend to business. We got to talking about the Kentucky Oaks on the last day of the meeting here, and about his filly's chances. I flat out told him that her chances were very good if not better if he'd just put you up on her for the race!"

"You did? You said that to him?" Tommy couldn't believe what he was hearing. "What'd he say, Boss? What'd he say when you told him that?"

Spence grinned a little and answered, "Said that McCormack's been telling him the same thing, and that he usually depends on his trainer to decide stuff like that. So we should be expecting to hear from Jack fairly shortly. Said he'd like to watch you work her early in the morning if you had time. I told him that I would make the time for you and how does 5:00 a.m. sound? So that should fit nicely into your plans for success, shouldn't it?"

"You bet it does, Mr. Spence. Thank you! Thank you so much! I'll never be able to repay you for all you've done for me. I just can't believe it. This is the best thing that's ever happened to me. I wish mother and father were still around. They would be so proud and happy."

By this time Tommy's joy and excitement had turned to a steady flow of tears, but he couldn't stop smiling.

"I feel like a day when it's raining but the sun is still shining, Mr. Spence," he said as he was speaking in broken sobs.

"Well, just don't slop up the track, son."

After Tommy gained back his composure, Spence continued, "That ain't all the news, my boy. There's an article in the *Daily Racing Form* today that says how successful the Lexington meeting had been despite all the wet weather and it mentioned that you 'finished at the top of winning jockeys, having two more than Cliff Robinson, your nearest rival'. I also heard that Regalo had suffered a bad cut to one of her hind legs in today's race which probably accounted for her poor showing. And they're saying it will probably 'necessitate a slight let-up in her training.' So I don't have no idea if the Gallaher boys was planning to get her into the Oaks or not, but this might just quell those thoughts. You sure don't need to be up against her in the Oaks, now, do you?"

"Right now, I'd race Man o' War and Exterminator both and beat 'em outright, Boss! That's just how good I feel right now," Tommy assured.

The next two weeks were a fun and entertaining time for the boys as they all were relatively good friends in the first place, and they were enjoying the competition each other had to offer, both in the matches themselves as well as the competition to work for the different trainers and owners and secure the most favored mounts. Besides Tommy and Harry, there were Willie Crump (Jefferson Livingston's main contract rider), Mack Garner, Cliff Robinson (Tommy's challenger for highest win percentage of the year), J. Morys, J. Howard, E. Pool, O. Willis, S. Boyle, J. Thurber, and many others, but in the heat of battle out on the track, your only friends were your own skill and smarts and the 1,200 beast between your legs. Everything else out there was against you.

Early on the stewards had made it perfectly clear that they would tolerate no rough riding or bad horsemanship at all. Trouble makers would spend the rest of the meeting behind the rail. The May 13th issue of the *Daily Racing Form* reported that: *"Jockey J. Groth was suspended for five days by the stewards for his rough riding in the Debutante Stakes when he interfered with Busy Signal."* The same issue reported too that: *"Jockey Frank Murphy was the first to draw the first dose of discipline by the stewards for insolent and rebellious conduct toward the starter. For this offense he was suspended for ten days, the starter previously having suspended him for three days, will make his vacation a thirteen days' period."*

During this time, Ogden Stable had been trying to negotiate Tommy's contract from Kay Spence, but they just couldn't seem to come to terms. Spence placed a price on the boy that had thus far exceeded any known agreed-upon price for any jockey. As it turned out, Spence had other things in mind, when he negotiated to Jefferson Livingston second call on Tommy and sold his contract to W.V. Thraves: *"W.V. Thraves, wealthy oil man, has secured the transfer of jockey T. Murray's contract, but Kay Spence will have the boy in charge for the next two years, as he has contracted for that period to train the horses that W. V. Thraves is accumulating…Second call on the rider has been signed to Jeff Livingston for the Kentucky spring meetings, ending at Latonia"* (Daily Racing Form, 5/14/19).

One week later, in the May 21 issue, the *Daily Racing Form* wrote: *"The transfer of jockey Robinson's contract was consummated this morning, and he entered the employ of Lester & Henderson, racing under the nom de course of the Ogden Stable, at once. The transfer price for the rider's services is the highest ever paid for a similar transaction."*

Elsewhere in the same issue, it was noted that: *"the Ogden Stable scored its initial Kentucky success when War God cantered home in advance of the others, and it incidentally furnished jockey Robinson with his first winning mount for his new contract employer."* He beat second place Clermont by half a length after a gamely stretch run under a hard drive by Tommy.

That very same issue of the *Daily Racing Form* also reported that: *"Jockey T. Murray was suspended for five days by the stewards for rough riding in the fifth race, having interfered with Spring Vale in the stretch."* That report, however, turned out to be premature after a meeting with Tommy and the other jockeys in the race. The foul leveled against Tommy by Spring Vale's jockey Barrett just couldn't be substantiated and the suspension was rescinded. Neither did the official call even hint at interference. It read: *"At post one minute. Start good and slow. Won easily; second and third driving. MARIE MAXIM moved up steadily and, saving ground when coming into the stretch, overhauled SPRING VALE in the last sixteenth and drew out near the end. SPRING VALE showed the most early speed and finished gamely, but tired in the last eighth."* Tommy's horse paid $18.90 on a $2.00 bet and the winner took home $900 in this allowance race for two-year-olds, the Jeffersontown Purse.

"Good work out there, ol' buddy," Harry told Tommy back at the jockey house. "How'd you convince the stewards that you didn't interfere?"

"Simple, Harry! I didn't interfere," Tommy shot back.

"Come on, man! What'd you do? Grab his saddle cloth? Lock legs? Smack him across the nose with your bat?" Harry insisted.

"I'm tellin' you, Harry. Only thing I done was to feed that nag my mud all the way down the stretch. I didn't touch that horse or that rider and I got plenty of witnesses to back me up." Tommy said.

"Then why the foul call? Why the interference?"

"Don't know Harry. You'll have to ask Barrett." Tommy explained. "Now I have to get changed for the next race and it looks like Barrett is, too. Go ask him."

"Maybe I just will," Harry said. "I just might do that."

Sure enough, Harry went over to where Barrett was getting ready for the next race. Tommy could see them talking, but couldn't hear a thing. They were still talking when the bugle called for the jockeys. Out in the paddock while Kay Spence was giving Tommy the leg up onto Hodge, his trusty eight year-old campaigner, Harry came up to them and whispered, "Why you sly dog, you! Little Tommy Sweet Water! Would never pull any tricks, huh?"

"Now what's that all about, Harry?" Spence demanded.

"Oh, nothin', sir. It's just that our little apprentice here is finally learning a little horse sense, that's all."

"Well," Spence interjected, "horse sense ain't never hurt anybody no-how. Now let's get on with this race."

That night, after helping Kay Spence apply the standing wraps on his horses' legs and before turning in, Tommy confided in his boss and mentor.

"Mr. Spence?" he hesitantly uttered. "I want you to know that I didn't do anything illegal out there today in that race. I didn't interfere with Barrett's horse and I don't know why he called a foul."

"Well, I do," answered Spence. "He lost a race he should'a won and he needed somebody to blame it on so his trainer wouldn't chew him a new asshole! That's what! I saw the race and I saw that move of your's clearly. Son, that was just masterful race riding, changing leads like that so your horse would kick up dirt into Spring Vale's face. I was watching him purposely keeping to your left so any dust you kicked up would miss him if you were to overcome him, but changing leads like you done when you done it, sure peppered his ambition to keep running that route. That was nothing less than perfect! Now, on to bed with you. We got a busy day ahead, and it's gonna be here sooner than you think."

Spence wasn't kidding. The next day began at 4:15 a.m. Tommy spent the first half of his morning breezing Major Parke and Lillian Shaw for Jefferson Livingston's trainer, McCormack.

272

CHAPTER FORTY-SEVEN
Just Believe in Yourself

In the Tuesday, May 27, 1919 edition of the *Daily Racing Form*, the thirty leading American jockeys were listed according to their overall win percentage. Tommy Murray headed that list but the report opined:

"Jockey T. Murray's hold on the leadership of the American jockeys for the current year was seriously menaced during the past week. C. Robinson, by riding seven winners, while Murray was only riding two, almost overtaking the latter. At the end of Saturday's racing, only four winning mounts separated Murray and Robinson, and if the latter maintains the form he has displayed lately, he will overhaul and pass the leader..."

In the first race on that day's card, however, Tommy was on a mission. As he came from far back in the field in the final quarter guiding Kay Spence's Leap Frog to a spectacular finish, ultimately passing into the lead and winning over Miss Procter and Hopeful but by the end of the day, his additional place finish and show finish was overshadowed by Robinson's three victories, resulting from his "superior riding," according to that day's Form.

"Did ya see how ole Clifford handled that pompous Sande?" Harry asked Tommy. "Why he just flat tracked her down in that slop and gave Sande a dose of his own nasty medicine at the wire, even after that bastard tried to run him through the fence. Hot damn, now, that cocky son-of-a-bitch knows he's in Kentucky! And we can ride any kind of race he wants, clean 'er rough. It's his choice. When he comes to our house, by God, we're the boss!"

Harry just went on and on as Tommy continued on to the jockey house with the ranting Harry right on his heels.

"How come you ain't sayin' nothin'? Weren't you glad ole Cliff gave Sande some overdue comeuppins?" Harry asked Tommy.

"Damn it, Harry!" Tommy bloated out. "From where I was sittin' I didn't see nothin' but mud balls and twats. I wasn't even sure I'd be home in time to watch the next race take off."

"Well, damn good thing you ain't in this next race," Harry chided. "Gives you time to get ten pounds of mud off your body and ten more pounds of lead out your ass."

With that remark, Tommy flung his tackle at Harry while striking him on the back of the neck with his bat.

"Now that's the ticket, boy! You gotta hit that son-of-a-bitch real fast like, so' nobody sees it. Just like ya just done to me. 'Course I'm gonna take ya down and leave ya like a pile of horse shit right there on the track...all steamy and drawing big green flies!"

"Go on with yourself, Harry! Get the hell outa my way. I gottta get dressed for my next race."

The third race on the day's ticket had Sande, Tommy, and Clifford Robinson all competing for something different. Sande had a point to prove to these uncouth Kentuckians and, of course, Tommy and Cliff had plans of their own for this foreigner which was to send him packing back to the East Coast tracks empty handed.

When Sande emerged from his mount unscathed and perfectly unblemished while Clifford and Tommy trailed the pack from start to finish and were unrecognizable in their gooey mud plasters, however, Tommy started to feel a little worried and intimidated by this Sande. Oh sure, for years he had heard about this guy and what a great race rider he was, but he had never seen him in person before, much less compete against him, but Tommy knew all about him. Back when Harry was first an apprentice jockey, riding in the Mexico winter meeting, Earl Sande was also a noted crack apprentice. As a matter of fact, he was Harry's major nemesis just as Cliff Robinson was Tommy's this year. Tommy had a much higher number of first place rides than Sande did, but Sande had a higher win percentage, which was the number of first place finishes in the number of races started.

Tommy, by far, had ridden in many more races than Sande but Sande was getting mounts on a higher class horse and was winning in more prestigious stakes races in the Eastern circuit and the Eastern horsemen had always held the Western tracks, trainers and jockeys in a much lower regard than themselves and their associates. It was painfully apparent that this Earl Sande fostered this same disregard for Kentucky jockeys. He wore custom tailored pin striped three piece suits to the track and drove a monstrous brand new Packard coupe that was supplied for his personal use while in Louisville. Tommy swore that he had to be sitting up on a soap box to see over the steering wheel, but he could never figure out how his feet reached the pedals. Of course, he could never figure out how Sande's legs would find their way to an opponent's mount, without falling off his own horse either.

"This guy is nothin' but trouble," Tommy muttered to Clifford on their way back to the jockey house.

"No doubt in my mind," Clifford quickly responded. "He's takin' wins away from me that I need in order to catch your record, and I ain't real happy about that!"

The next day, though, Cliff Robinson made considerable gains on Tommy, by winning three races and placing second in another that Sande won. Tommy could manage nothing better than one second place and one third place finish and Harry came up with the same numbers for the day. The good thing for Harry was that the second place finish he had was in the St. Matthew's Handicap for $1,600. Cliff Robinson riding for his contract stable, Ogden Stables, won the race. They were both very pleased to have held Sande to a third place finish, especially since the field only consisted of just three horses.

That night, back in the Spence barn, Kay approached Tommy who was in the feed and tack room diligently paging through Spence's collection of *Daily Racing Forms*. He was so preoccupied that he didn't even see or hear Mr. Spence enter the room.

"What 'cha studying there son?" Spence boomed, breaking the deafening silence which was followed by a startled shriek from Tommy.

"Holy Mackerel, Mr. Spence! Ya just scared the Holy Ghost out of my soul and back to Latonia!" Tommy shouted.

"Sorry, son, but you weren't nowhere in your body either! What's got hold of your attention so much that you can't see or hear?"

"I'm looking up all of Sande's past racing charts and all his accomplishments. I wanna know just exactly why he thinks his shit don't stink!"

"Ha, boy!" Spence laughed. "You ain't gonna find that out looking in them Forms. You have to get inside his head to find all that out and that'll be quite a job considering the thickness of that boy's skull."

"So, do you know him very well, Mr. Spence?" Tommy asked.

"Reckon I know him as well as I'm a gonna want to, son! You see, he was apprenticing 'bout the same time I was apprenticing Harry, back in 1916 and 1917. Sande apprenticed under a fella named Doc Pardee, out in Arizona in them outlaw circuits. Doc Pardee was just one of them rough 'n tumble cowboy horsemen who travelled the county fair horse racing circuit. Sande had gone about as far as he could in the junior league leaky roof circuit out west, so he hooked up with Doc who had a higher quality of horse flesh in his stable. Sande got to be the number one rider in this jungle track circuit and eventually Doc Pardee did what was best for the boy and his career. He sent him to New Orleans with a letter of recommendation to an old friend of his, Joe Goodman. He said Joe would see to it that he got his chance to show his stuff to the big racing guys. He was still considered too tall to be a top-notch jockey, with a very real potential for weight problems, considering his frame but he had a riding style like no one could duplicate. He was able to get his lanky body perfectly in balance and parallel to the attitude of the horse, which put his face up into the horse's neck, almost buried in his mane and he whispered to his mount and hand rode him to victory after victory."

Spence continued, "But he had another very strong quality. He knew and orchestrated every low-lying trick in the book of rough riding, and he learned from the very best circuit riders in his survival-of-the-fittest background. He had tricks that none of our boys were even aware of. He had only one goal in mind, and that was to become the all-time greatest jockey in Thoroughbred racing and that would be by hook or crook, by God!"

Tommy went on, "Well Harry warned me to keep a close eye on him at all times because he would do about anything necessary to beat you to the wire."

"Harry should know, Tommy. He had enough encounters with that boy. That's for sure. You see, in 1918, there were only six outstanding jockeys in the entire country to ride one hundred or more winning mounts. Frankie Robinson, God rest his soul, led them all with 185 first-place wins. After him, Larry Lyke had a total of 178 first-place victories. Third place for that year was you-know-who. Yep, the rookie apprentice Earl Sande with 158 first-place finishes. Now all of his wins didn't come on major tracks like the other boys, but they still counted as wins. And that what really pissed off Harry, 'cause he placed fourth in the standings with 155 wins, but his winning percentage came out to 18% versus Sande's 22%. Boy, I'll tell ya, Harry and Sande had some humdinger battles back then at Latonia and at the Church. They were two top dogs fighting for just one bone. I can tell you right here and now, though, Sande got mounts on way better horse flesh than Harry got, and Harry just never saw the justice in it. Harry had probably 150 more races than Sande had in 1918, but Sande had the better horses but despite that, Harry placed in the money 51.2% of the time, to Sande's 50.9%. Not much difference percentage wise, but very telling considering Harry's larger number of races rode! It's all in that book right there you got in your hand. Read it for yourself."

Spence went on to say, "And Tommy, I feel real bad about it, cause it's totally my fault, but the reason Cliff is catching up with your record is because I can't get on the same quality of horse flesh that he is getting on over at Ogden Stable. You could'a been their contract rider, you know. You were their first choice, but I purposely put such a high price on you, that they declined, which is what I was hopin' they would do. I was very selfish and I wanted to keep you under my wing as long as I could and that's exactly what I done when I sold you to Thraves. You're his number one contract rider, but I'm his trainer and it's a two-year deal. Then here, Ogden went ahead and shelled out more money to get Robinson than I was askin' for you."

Tommy was almost teary eyed again and said, "Boss, please don't feel that way. I am much happier being with you another two years than I would be by winning the best record for jockeys and that's the God's-honest truth," as he crossed himself and wiped his eyes on his sleeve.

The book Spence was referring to was his 1919 edition of *The American Racing Manual*. It told the numbers story all right, but it sure didn't tell everything that went on in order to get those numbers. It told how many races Sande won in 1918, but it didn't tell all the tricks he pulled to get those wins. Harry knew all those tricks too, and Tommy remembered when Harry tried to make him listen and learn them.

"Now I see that Harry was tryin' to help me out," Tommy thought to himself, *"so I would be prepared to look out for myself and know how to react to all that rough ridin' when it was comin' my way. Here I thought Harry was just trying to teach me how to cheat. Damn! I'm stupid…and naïve."*

He remembered reading in this same edition some time ago that Kay Spence was the number one leading trainer in the United States for 1918, but he never mentioned it in his presence.

He looked back at Mr. Spence and inquisitively asked, "Who was the better jockey that year, Boss? Harry or Sande?"

"Whoa, boy! Now that's a tough one, it is! If you look through that book and other racing rags and then dig through all them New York magazines and newspapers and such, then your mind is made up for you that Sande is the better jockey and they all agree that he is going to get better and better until he becomes one of the foremost jockeys of all times. But when you know Harry like I do and know what a determined hard worker he is, and you recognize the natural, God-given talent he has, and his perfect balance and gentle touch, and his kind heart and deep respect and love for animals and people alike, and his fair and honest conscience and judgment, well then you'll know that Harry is. Now that's not saying that Sande is an inferior race rider. No he's got talent and smarts and precision and excellent racing skills and judgment too, just like Harry does. But son, I've seen his kind of personality and demeanor a thousand times before. He's just going to let his popularity lead him into believing that he is a star and that's just going to put more and more pressure on himself to maintain that status, and he'll be on a collision course toward failure. He'll have lots of money, which will get him lots of dames, and he'll hook up with lots of high rollers and gamblers and the rich and famous New York and East Coast socialites, and then come the alcohol and drugs and hopping horses and fixing races and then divorce, going bankrupt, losing grace, doing time or getting murdered, and if not that, then hopping a box car back to Idaho where he will either drink himself to death or commit suicide. It's his kind of antics what's killed Frankie Robinson back in April. Son, when you're a 100-pound man, balanced on your tiptoes with your center of gravity out ahead of your hand grip, on a 1,200-pound animal running about 35 miles an hour, trusting that all that PSI force won't shatter one of those four fragile china-doll ankles of not only your beast, but also all the beasts in front of you, then you sure as hell don't want to see no idiot rodeo cowboy with a death wish pulling' his shenanigans and putting' your life in danger just so's he can pull off another win at all costs, just to keep his ego in check, now do ya? That's my answer. I pick Harry."

As Spence turned to leave Tommy to his research, he concluded, "Tommy, first race tomorrow you'll have a chance to show Sande what kinda race rider you are. I have no doubt in your ability and talent, son. Believe in yourself and don't you harbor any doubts either."

With that, the door closed and Tommy turned off the light and wiped another tear from his cheek.

CHAPTER FORTY-EIGHT
A Budding Rivalry

Early next morning, Tommy was up and at it. There were two more days until the Oaks and getaway day. He was concentrating on getting his weight down a couple of pounds, so after his usual morning exercising rides and a good gallop with Lillian Shaw over at the Livingston compound, Tommy put on his Irish wool sweaters under his rubber suit and took to the track on his own two legs. He ran a mile and a quarter twice, pretending he was actually running the Derby, even though his horse had been scratched right before the race but he felt confidence and determination taking hold of him this morning, guiding him in his physical preparation for the upcoming Oaks. His mental preparation had already been launched in last night's heart-to-heart with Mr. Spence. After his run, he checked his weight at the scale house and then cleaned up and changed. He ran in to Harry on his way back to Spence's barn.

"Well, what's the weight today, Tommy," Harry inquired.

"Three," Tommy shouted back, obviously pleased with himself. "I was five yesterday!" (When jockeys referred to their weight, they seldom used the 'hundreds' portion of the total. Thus, if a jockey weighed 105 pounds or 109 pounds, he would simply refer to his weight as 'five' or 'nine', respectively. So, Tommy was pleased with his progress of getting to 103 pounds, down from 105 pounds the day before). "My horse today is assigned 100 pounds, so I'll come in two pounds over. That's better than five over."

At the call to the post for the first race of the day, Tommy got the leg up from Spence, on a Thraves' entrant. As far as riding instructions, Spence simply told Tommy, "Sande's horse is the favorite, but you got the better horse. When the barrier springs, let him go and don't look back. Marse John knows exactly what to do and so do you! Don't even give Sande a second thought. He just doesn't have enough horse to beat you."

Tommy was in the fifth post position and Sande was the number eight. Cliff Robinson was number 11. When the barrier sprung, Tommy was first to bolt and took the lead position immediately. Sande tried to work his way through traffic but had to go outside to do so, eventually getting from fourth place into second. From then on he was merely chasing Tommy and Marse John, who crossed the wire in a canter, winning it by six lengths and paying $9.40 straight.

As Tommy was entering the winner's circle, Sande hollered out, "Next time, Murray!"

Tommy smirked and shouted back, "Get the dirt off your goggles. Maybe you'll see me next time!"

Spence was really enjoying this budding rivalry, but dared not show it, thinking to himself, "Now he's finally feeling the real confidence, the kind that will make a decided difference and give him the edge he's been needing."

Spence and Cupe walked Marse John out of the paddock area and back towards the barn as Tommy practiced his new cocky victory walk. Luckily, not many people saw it because it was a bit awkward.

"That too will need some polish," Spence chuckled to himself.

In the third race that day, from a field of 12 entries, Tommy managed a second place over Sande's third place driving finish. Harry placed seventh and Cliff Robinson wound up eleventh. Tommy was leading the entire race until the very finish when the odds on horse overtook him for the win but Tommy was still pleased for beating Sande out for second and of course keeping Robinson from getting another win ahead of him. Harry wasn't too disappointed because his horse, a 25-to-1 longshot, at least finished seventh out of 12.

Cliff came back to win the next one as he eased up his 4-to-1 Bellsolar until the final stretch when he let out a notch or two to overcome the quickly tiring odds on favorite Clermont. Sande's horse which left from the last post position and quickly found third place by the quarter pole ran hard to gain first place at the half mile pole, but then suddenly quit and finished dead last by five lengths. Tommy didn't fare much better as he was almost thrown at the first turn, but he recovered to beat Sande. In the fifth, Robinson and Sande combined to turn the tables on Tommy with a second- and third-place finish respectively, as veteran Mack Garner took the favorite, American Ace, wire to wire, finishing in a canter. Tommy pulled up in seventh place in the field of nine horses.

Sande took the sixth race from Tommy at the half mile pole when he overtook him and Tommy's horse just quit at that point. The last race of the day was a 12 horse affair in which the two favorites were taken down by longshots in a three-year-old and upwards claimer. Sande's 3-to-1 Rookery could get no closer than fourth place, having been challenged by Tommy's 23-to-1 five-year-old Tanlac which ended up second place finisher.

As the boys were in the jockey house changing out of their racing colors, Tommy just put his work clothes back on because he was heading back to the stable for his afternoon chores and daily visits with the horses in their barn. Earle Sande emerged in a custom tailored three piece Searsucker suit with a starched white shirt, cuffed sleeves with diamond cuff links in the form of a Thoroughbred's head, and a silk hand tied bow tie, accessorized by a bone handled walking stick and a white, ribboned straw skimmer hat.

"Let me through, boys. Don't want any of your dirt and sweaty grime getting on my duds. The dolls like me best when I'm all pressed and smellin' sweet."

Nothing but cat calls could be heard throughout the jockeys' room as Sande swaggered to the door. Before heading through the doorway and down the stairs, he spun around on the balls of his feet and took a short but prolonged bow, tipped his hat, and said: "My name is Sande, and I'm fine and dandy/Got more going than sugar candy/Fillies by day, and dames by night; and they all agree I'm pretty handy."

"Why that cocky son-of-a-bitch", Tommy said to Harry, but loud enough for everyone in the room to hear.

"What's the matter, Murray?" Sande shouted. "You don't like it when class riders show up at your leaky roof meetings and still outride your best Kentuckians with the lowest claimers in the barns? You Irish Catholics need to stick to whisky drinking and womens' work. Leave the horse riding to us boys who know how to handle these beasts. You are much more fitted for farm labor and stable work."

As Sande sauntered down the steps to his fancy car and admiring public, Tommy hurried to the window above his waiting automobile, and as Sande was just about to enter the car to entertain his waiting guests, Tommy grabbed the flip tank and dumped it out the window onto the car and the unprotected Sande with the wish that he enjoy the warm meal. Sande disrobed and entered the car as the driver headed over to his barn where the grooms and rubbers were still bathing the horses, and made them stop everything in order to clean off the automobile.

If this wasn't a gauntlet thrown, then it wasn't anything. Sande saw and felt the challenge from this low rent Irishman and country bumpkin, and he would not forget. Ever!

CHAPTER FORTY-NINE
Day Before The Oaks

The next day was the final race day before Oaks Day and getaway day. The morning broke with excitement which continued all through the day. Some of the excitement was the anticipation of leaving this meeting and heading to Latonia for the next. Some of the stables already had cars loaded with their string stock; others were just beginning to pack up and make arrangements for transport. The rail cars were full today and promised to be full for the next couple of days. Only those stables with a true Kentucky Oaks contender remained in full bloom. This was to be the race of all recent races. The Eastern owners and trainers and jockeys were all here for this reason, this race. That was the only reason Earl Sande was even in Kentucky - just to win the Oaks for Commander J.K.L. Ross on his good filly Milkmaid.

The boys pretty much decided the evening before when Sande made his grand exit from the jockey house that he was not going to show off very much the next day. They held Sande to one second place finish and two third-place finishes. Harry wound up with a second place and three first-place finishes for the hat trick. Tommy managed one third, two seconds, and one first place finish. Cliff Robinson came away with a first and a second. Sande wasn't a very happy person in the jockey house that afternoon.

"Just wait until tomorrow," Sande warned. "I'll show you the difference between a Commander Ross horse and one of your beat down Kentucky brood mares. Guaranteed! If you want to leave this track with any dignity after tomorrow's Oaks, then put your money on Milkmaid. Just as sure a thing as the sun coming up in the East in the morning, Milkmaid will end her journey from the East right there in the West's winner's circle."

"He is really a burr under my saddle cloth," Tommy said aloud as Sande walked away. "We really need to shut him down tomorrow, so he thinks twice about following us to Latonia."

Harry agreed. "Don't worry about a thing, Tommy. I've had my fill of him for several years, and I aim to make his trip to Kentucky one that he will never forget or fess up to. When he gets back to New York and Maryland, it'll take all he's got to forget Kentucky. We'll see to that!"

The next morning, they were all reading the Saturday, May 31, 1919 edition of the *Daily Racing Form*. In it, was this article:

"The first spring meeting held at Churchill Downs under the auspices of the newly-formed Kentucky Jockey Club will come to an end today with the running of the Kentucky Oaks as the main attraction of an interesting closing-day program. The Oaks has a history as old as the Kentucky Derby, having been first run in 1875 and

continued each year since without interruption. It annually brings together the best three-year-old fillies of the west, often augmented by the best of the east. The latter is particularly true this year, Commander J.K.L. Ross sending Milkmaid to Kentucky especially for this race. This peerless daughter of Peep O' Day was a slashing good two-year-old and has proved herself the best of her sex in the three-year-old division in the east this spring, her sparkling victory in the Pimlico Oaks, entitling her to that consideration. However, Milkmaid will find worthy opponents in the Oaks with such as Regalo, Looking Up, Lillian Shaw, Bellsolar, Paris Maid, Lackawanna, Delico and Dancing Spray among the starters..."

"You're damned right she'll find worthy opponents," mumbled Harry as they read along, "And they're all sittin' right here, right now!"

As they paged through the Form, Harry shouted, "Hey, lookey here! An article about Major Parke's win yesterday. Here, Tommy, read it out loud."

Tommy took the paper and began, "'Hot weather, a fast track, a grand outpouring of devotees of racing, were prominent features of the afternoon at Churchill Downs today. The racing was worthy of the occasion, although marked by some incidents not in the contemplation of the assembled thousands. For instance, the main race of the day, the Memorial Handicap at three-quarters of a mile, brought abundant backing for Rancher, Blackie Daw and Courtship, with Rancher the favorite, but a neglected son of Dick Welles, Jefferson Livingston's Major Parke, at long odds, spoiled all calculations by taking the race himself. The finish was bitterly contested, Major Parke winning by a short head from Rancher, with the latter a neck in front of Blackie Daw, Courtship a close up fourth. Blackie Daw was unlucky, and with a clear course would probably have won....'"

"Yeah, and if bull frogs had wings they wouldn't bump their ass so much," said Tommy, in a personal commentary directed toward the newsprint in his hand.

They all had a hearty laugh as Tommy flung the copy of the Form onto a nearby hay bale.

"Let's see what they write in tomorrow's edition after I show Sande and Milkmaid what real Kentucky racing is all about," Tommy calmly announced to whoever was listening.

Harry responded reflexively, "Hey, don't forget you all got me to deal with too before you go dreamin' of the Oaks record books! I ain't nobody's patsy either. Sande and I go way back, competing against each other for Apprentice of the Year in 1918. He's got nothin' on his mind now but revenge and retaliation. Poor guy's gonna get another dose of Kentucky education, just in time to get to Latonia to further his education."

"This is getaway day and I've got a mount in every race. What better way to end a great meeting," Tommy announced as he headed back to his barn to retrieve his Irish woolen sweaters and rubber suit. "I gotta make weight for today. See you fellers at the barrier."

At 2:29 p.m., Tommy lined up in the tenth position in front of the barrier. The field of 12 was sent away to a slow but good start after three minutes. Star Baby, starting from the eighth position, Cliff Robinson up, showing the most speed from the start, raced into a good lead at once and just lasted long enough. Arthur Middleton, Tommy's horse, lost much ground by being forced to race wide and finished with a great rush, only to get beat by a neck.

The second race of the day, a claiming race for maidens, three-year-olds and up, found Harry dominating a field of 12, to win. The Form's description of the race credited Harry with "getting away forwardly and benefitting with a good ride and raced into the lead and, being hard ridden for the entire way, outstayed Brunette II to win by a neck". Both Clifford and Tommy finished way out of the money. The third contest of the day was an allowance race for three-year-olds and upward for a purse of $1,200. Out of the field of five horses, Willie Crump managed to bring the 9-to-1 Livingston horse to victory, narrowly defeating by a neck Harry Lunsford on the good horse Leochares, of the J.F. Schorr stable. Third place was taken by Cliff Robinson aboard the Ogden Stable five-year-old Grundy. Again, Tommy placed out of the money.

The fourth race, The Oakdale Handicap, a $1,200 purse for two-year-olds, found Tommy astride Miss Bo-Peep, a Kay Spence trained horse, in the six field event. The race was hard run with the first place horse winning easily and second and third driving. Tommy's horse was simply outpaced and finished last, Tommy being three pounds overweight.

The time for the main event of the day's slate was upon them. Sande on Milkmaid was the clear favorite at about 1.35-to-1. Tommy and Lillian Shaw was actually the fourth favorite, behind Looking Up (C. Robinson up) at 4.5-to-1 and Regalo at 4.55-to-1. According to the *Daily Racing Form* line notes, they went to post at 4:45 and were there for four minutes. Milkmaid was lined up in the first post position and Lillian Shaw in the third spot. The start was good and slow. Lillian Shaw got away well and benefited by a good ride, followed the early leaders closely and drew out decisively in the last sixteenth. Milkmaid moved up fast after going a half mile and took the lead, but gave way when challenged by the winner. Dancing Spray ran well, but tired after disposing of Looking Up. Bellsolar was going fast at the end. Paris maid was away slowly. Looking

Up raced into the lead but quit badly. Delico was caught in a jam and fell. Lillian Shaw paid $15.20 to win.

The Sunday, June 1, 1919 issue of the *Daily Racing Form* had this to say: *"Louisville, KY., May 31. The forty-fifth renewal of the Kentucky Oaks, which had its decision this afternoon and featured getaway day at Churchill Downs, brought to the post the best collection of three-year-old fillies that has, in the aggregate, ever contested for the much coveted race. Its running developed several incidents, including the fall of Delico, the overthrow of the highly regarded pair, Milkmaid and Looking Up, and the glaring attempt of jockey Sande on Milkmaid to impede Lillian Shaw from passing his mount, but the finish found the Jefferson Livingston representative triumphant in easy style, and by her good performance fully entitled to the $4190 net to the winner. Milkmaid landed in second place and Dancing Spray headed the others in third position. The mile and a sixteenth was run in 1:45, a highly creditable achievement in itself considering that the winner carried her full weight—117 pounds. Milkmaid was at all times the favored one, with Looking Up, another eastern comer, and Regalo next in demand. Lillian Shaw also had an extensive following."*

"Hal Price Headley's Dancing Spray and Looking Up raced out as a team after rounding the first turn and continued to show the way until after passing the half, where Milkmaid made a play for command and displaced the others in a flash, but Lillian Shaw also moved up rapidly at the same time and when straightened away in the stretch, began her challenge. Milkmaid still seemed to be going well, but seemingly being short. Sande found her tiring and it was then that he began reaching out for Lillian Shaw's bridle. Unsuccessful in his first attempt he made another reach but again failed to hold it. Murray, on Lillian Shaw, then moved out a little and in the last sixteenth drew away decisively, Milkmaid outstaying Dancing Spray."

"…The stewards took note of Sande's attempt at foul riding and after the finish of the final race they announced that he had been suspended for sixty racing days. Sande tried to deny having sought to impede Lillian Shaw, but all the stewards witnessed the action, as well as the placing judges under the stewards' stand and many spectators. Sande is said to have retarded Blackie Daw also by taking hold of his bridle in the Memorial Handicap yesterday."

Tommy proudly took up residence in the winner's circle after receiving the nod from the judges. He was joined there by Harry and Mr. Spence and all the Jefferson Livingston staff members. Livingston himself was unable to attend the Oaks. Willie Crump, Livingston's top call jockey was there and one of the first to congratulate Tommy. After all the ceremony and photograph making, Tommy checked Lillian Shaw over from head to tail, with very special attention paid to her mouth, neck and shoulders and any other area that he recalled was violated by Sande's rough riding shenanigans. He felt each lower leg individually, checking for any tenderness or heat. Satisfied that she was fine, he turned her over to her groom after having a few private words with her. The horse took it all in as if she knew exactly what she had accomplished that afternoon, and strutted away with her groom, back to her barn.

Tommy wanted so much to confront Sande right there and then, but he had to make it back to the jockey house to change his silks for the last and final race of this particular meeting. By the time he got back to change, Sande had already donned his expensive three piece suit and left the track in his expensive motorcar. Tommy snickered to himself as he walked out for the last race. He knew now that he was ready to ride with the 'big boys,' and in any venue, on any track, East or West. He graduated from rookie to journeyman professional that afternoon. He had no doubts that he would have a mount in the 1920 Kentucky Derby and he couldn't wait for his next opportunity to meet up with Earl Sande so he could thank him properly for topping off his final educational lesson in professional race riding.

EPILOGUE

In the overall history of American Thoroughbred racing history, there are some key factors involved in this story about Tommy Murray, along with some key phrases, names, situations, and issues of the times. The title *A Flash in the Pan* is what most accurately describes the career of my grandfather. In flintlock muzzleloading rifle terminology, a flash in the pan describes what takes place when the trigger of a fully charged flintlock rifle is squeezed, and the flint strikes the steel of the face of the frizzen to create the necessary sparks to ignite the very finely granulated priming powder, only resulting in the ignition of the powder in the pan without igniting the main charge in the rifle via the touch hole. A flash of smoke occurs, but no discharge of the rifle. So too, Tommy's career had already peaked when the trigger was pulled, and his most notable accomplishments took form in the pan and not in the main rifle charge.

He was basically an orphan taken in by a race track and raised by a very wise and celebrated bush league horse trainer. They bonded like a father and son, and each made the other very proud and fulfilled. Tommy learned his trade and earned his status by starting at the very bottom and working very hard to advance his way up into a very competitive trade, one filled with outside obstacles at every step of the way. The horse racing business was on very shaky terms in this particular time (late 1910s-early 1920s). Gambling, organized crime, prohibition, national mores, war, pandemic disease and death, poverty and economic depression all negatively impacted the future of horse racing in the United States.

In many ways, Tommy's career as a professional jockey mirrored the career of Sir Barton, as a professional Thoroughbred racehorse whose claim to fame was being the very first American Triple Crown Winner. However, since the term Triple Crown wasn't established until 1923, Sir Barton finished the 1919 racing season without the official accolades and title. The amazing thing about his accomplishment was that he won the three major points of the Crown, plus one other important stakes race, all in the matter of just 32 days. As a matter of fact, his very first win as a maiden was the Kentucky Derby and just four days later, he won the Preakness Stakes. In between the Preakness and the Belmont, he took first place the Withers Stakes, and next he won the Belmont stakes, setting a new track record for the event. These accomplishments led to his being named the Horse of the Year for 1919. By 1920, he was just another also-ran.

Tommy's accomplishments in 1919 were equally astounding. In a total of 832 mounts for the year, he had 157 first-place finishes, 103 second-place finishes, and 109 third-place finishes for a winning percentage of 0.19. He finished the year as the second winningest jockey in the nation, finally being outlasted by his year-long nemesis, Clifford Robinson. Tommy won the 1919 Kentucky Oaks, beating the top fillies of the eastern stables and trainers, and overcame a stretch duel of the blatant rough riding tricks of the famous Earl Sande. He landed a mount in the 1919 Kentucky Derby to compete against Billy Kelly and Sir Barton, but was scratched just before post time. His brush with fame and destiny was just that, a brush but at least he made it to the big league of his dreams. He made a name for himself competing against the very best horses and jockeys of the times. He knew all the major owners and trainers. Just like Sir Barton, his flash in the pan came early on, but he dedicated his whole life to horse racing and continued on the track in some capacity or other, giving it his all until the very day he died.

Is horse racing just a game of luck? Try these statistics on for size. Kay Spence was the number one trainer in the country in total number of wins for 1918, 1919, and tied for number one for 1920. Harry Lunsford was the fourth winningest jockey for both 1918 and 1919. There's much more to this game than luck.

Grandpa died on January18, 1963. I was 13 years old at the time. To this day, I have never seen as many flowers and arrangements as I did at his funeral. They were from all over the country, and from the biggest names in horseracing and they all had a horse or horseshoe motif. There were an abundance of red roses.

When I was young, grandma didn't talk much about him. Neither did my mother or his other three children. Whenever he was referred to in a conversation at a family gathering, it was always concerning a funny story or one in which other names were dropped. My uncles and my great uncles always would come up with stories about his track career and exploits, but they never spoke of him as a father or husband or family man. My mother, the eldest child, would reminisce about her very early life, when "things were going good." She could vividly recall the many trips to New Orleans for race meetings in their own private train car, just the three of them, plus her own nanny. After the other children came along, things apparently were no longer "going good." Hard times, alcohol, spousal abuse, leaving home, things like that were always hinted at, but never presented to me as fact. All I know is that eventually he and grandma were estranged but they never divorced.

The paucity of details that I gathered from overhearing (yes, I was definitely a little pitcher with big ears) family conversations were, of course, biased and one sided. Never did I hear his side of the story. When I was the only grandchild, grandpa made me a small black leather wallet, highly decorated and tooled, with my name stamped diagonally across the front. It said "DONIE", misspelled but obviously a labor of love. I still have that wallet. Now, I have this book. Mom would say,

"He had friends in every bar and at every track in the country. Everybody loved him!" But things were different at home. I wasn't told the details, nor do I need to know them. Trying to compare early 20th century family relations and behavior to 21st century standards is just an exercise in futility.

From what I pieced together, his life would make the perfect black and white "B" movie for the late 1950s and early 60s television. Mickey Rooney, Humphrey Bogart, gangsters, Elliott Ness, alcohol bootleggers, the syndicate, Newport, Kentucky all come to mind at once. His was the very life story which made dime store novels.

In a 1946 newspaper article when he was 48 years old and working as a jockey valet at Churchill Downs, he told reporter Marvin Gay of the Cincinnati Times Star the difference between modern jockeys and the jockeys in his day: "They are made too quickly," he opined as he shined a pair of boots. "When I was broken in by Kay Spence, I walked horses and cleaned out stalls for a year before I got on a horse. Now some of the kids are riding in less than a year's time." His love and enthusiasm for the horses and the game was no less in his valet years as it was in his active jockey years.

Another newspaper dated June 18, 1950 carried an article about him. Entitled FORMER STAR JOCKEY, VALET at ASCOT PARK, and dated AKRON, June 17, 1950: *"Fame in the sports world can be very fleeting and Tommy Murray, jockey valet at the Ascot Park races these days, can vouch for that."* This was the year I was born. I guess I am his biggest fan.

The article continued: *"Thirty years ago there wasn't a horse player in the country who did not recognize the name –T. Murray. He was the jockey sensation of the day. His slam-bang stretch duel in the Kentucky Oaks of 1919 at Churchill Downs was the talk of the fans. His riding opponent was the immortal Earle (sic) Sande. The same year Murray was the nation's second ranking rider. Jockey C. Robinson beat him out by six winners. At Ascot Park there are not a dozen persons who even know that Murray ever was on a horse. And there probably isn't even one race player who recognizes him as he carries jockey equipment to the paddock and then from the track after the races."*

DUEL WITH SANDE

"Murray rode at practically every race track in America and Canada. He rode such famous horses as Old Rosebud, Busy Signal, owned by the late Edward Riley Bradley, and the notorious bad actor, Flags, owned by the Whitney stable. Of his famous ride in the Kentucky Oaks, Murray says: 'I was on Lillian Shaw, the winner, and Sande was on Milkmaid, which ran second. Coming down the stretch he grabbed my saddle and I took my stick and half beat him to death. We had a ding-dong battle that afternoon.' Murray rode in the 1920 Kentucky Derby and finished ninth on Bersagliere. His horse got away in front but quit after a half mile. He rode his first race at old Douglas Park in 1918 when he was 17, and quit in 1932 when he was 31. He is now 49, married and has two boys and two girls. His home is in Covington, Ky."

QUIT FOR GOOD

"Murray spent a year in Uncle Sam's mechanized cavalry during the war and became a jockey valet four years ago. He weighs 128 pounds as compared with his former jockey weight of 107. Although he is around horses every day, Murray doesn't have a desire to ride them. He says: 'There isn't a man alive who has enough money to get me back on a horse. The day I quit riding, I quit for good. I'll bet I would have a hard job today just trying to stay on a horse's back.'"

Except for the year in the U.S. Army as a teamster in the mechanized cavalry, he worked at the track in some capacity or other his entire life up until 1963, one week after his discharge from the Veterans Administration Hospital in Cincinnati for some sort of surgery. He was found dead in his room in one of the dive hotels in the slums of Cincinnati. Most of his gear and money was missing. All that was left was his camelback traveling trunk which wound up in grandma's basement. It sat down there for a long time. I was always fascinated by it and by him, probably because of all the mystery created by the family's reluctance to talk about him.

This historically accurate novel is the result of many years of research into the career of the jockey Tommy Murray, and the business and game of horseracing in general in the second and third decades of the 1900s, in the northern Kentucky area of Covington and Latonia, the famous horseracing tracks comprising the 3-L circuit (Latonia, Lexington, and Louisville), and the winter racing haven of Oriental Park, in Havana, Cuba. I am convinced that the Tommy Murray depicted in these pages is an accurate representation of the man; dedicated, driven, focused, extremely gifted and talented, kind, loving, tender-hearted, emotional, gentle, and a role model. He was a good Catholic and a better horseman. This book is merely a record of his legacy which has lain dormant and hidden from the public for far too many years. His milestone accomplishments during the 1919-1920 Golden Age of Racing, in my mind, qualify him for a spot in the National Horse Racing Hall of Fame. Consider this book to be his nomination form.

GLOSSARY

Acey Deucy---a style of race riding in which the jockey adjusts the right stirrup shorter than the left to improve his balance in the turns encountered during the race.

Across The Board---a bet placed on the same horse to win, place and show. A $2.00 bet 'across the board' will cost the bettor $6.00.

Added Money---prize money added to the purse money by the racing association, the track, owners, trainers, or other entities, thereby increasing the total prize money for the particular race event.

Agent---a person who arranges and manages a jockey's riding assignments.

All Out---when a horse extends himself to his utmost and maximum potential.

Allowances---officially sanctioned and approved reductions in the weight a horse is required to carry in a race. Most common are weight allowances for apprentice jockeys (bug boys). An apprentice jockey with less than five professional wins can be allowed up to a 10 pound allowance. After the fifth win, the allowance drops to five pounds until the fortieth win after that or the one year anniversary from the apprentice's fifth win. At this point, the apprentice 'loses his bug' and becomes a journeyman jockey and receives no other weight allowances. There are also races that have allowances for fillies running against all males, and age allowances for three-year-olds running against older, more mature horses.

Allowance Race---a non-claiming race in which weight assignments and other conditions are assigned by a racing secretary in accordance with stipulations posted beforehand, calculated from data of previous purse winnings, performances, and number and types of wins.

Also Eligible---a horse officially entered, but not permitted to run unless another horse or horses are scratched or vacancies are created for some other reasons.

Also Ran---a horse having competed in a race but did not finish in the money.

Apprentice---an amateur jockey riding under the aegis of a licensed trainer who has not yet boarded the necessary number of winning mounts within the specified amount of time. Also called a *bug boy*, because of an asterisk which appears next to his name on the racing program.

Apprentice Allowance---the weight concession granted to a horse being ridden by an apprentice jockey.

Apron---the area between the grandstand and the track.

Baby---a two-year-old, especially in the early part of its second year.

Baby Race---a two, three, or four-furlong race for two-year-olds, early in the year. A *baby* is a two-year-old, especially in the early months of the year.

Backed---a horse which has recorded a large number of placed bets is said to be 'backed'.

Backstretch---the straight part of the race track on the far side, across from the finish line and the stands. This is the geographical center for the incidences of fouls and interferences since it is the furthest from the judge's stand. The stable area is located behind this portion of the track. Considered by many to be the pulse of the racing community for the current race meeting. Considered by others to be the slums and skid-row of the event. Interpretation solely depends on one's status and point of view. Also called the *Backside*.

Back Up---to noticeably slow down in a race.

Bad Actor---a fractious horse that misbehaves at the post.

Bad Doer---a horse with a poor appetite or refuses to eat.

Bandage---strips of cloth wrapped around the lower leg of a horse for support and protection from injury.

Bang-Tails---colloquial jargon for horses; from the practice of bobbing or tying short of their tails.

Barrier---the mechanism for starting a race. It was a netting stretched across the starting line which sprung upward upon its release by the official starter, indicating the start of the race. Now refers to the mechanized starting gate.

Bat---one of several names given to a jockey's whip. The term was more popular with sports writers than with jockeys.

Bear In---running toward the inside rail instead of in a straight direction or course.

Bear Out---running toward the outer rail instead of in a straight direction or course; especially on the turns.

Beef---slang term for a complaint or protest made by a jockey against another jockey for the commission of interference of some kind during a race. A public declaration of a personal complaint of one jockey against another for an alleged offense.

Bell---the signal that announces the beginning of a race and the termination of placing wagers.

Bend---any of the turns on a race track.

Big Apple---a major racing circuit. Initially big apple referred to a horse racing track or plant, getting its name from the oval shape of an apple, and 'big' meaning one of the major tracks or plants. Believed to have been coined by the black African American stable hands and groom, to refer to major New York racing tracks. Eventually, in a non-horse racing sense, it came to mean New York.

Bit---a horizontal bar connecting both sides of the bridle, that fits in the horse's mouth. It is made of stainless steel, aluminum, or rubber and is used to guide and control the horse.

Blanket Finish---an extremely close finish; so named because the finishers were so close that a blanket could cover them.

Bleeder--- a horse that bleeds during exertion or a heavy workout. The bleeding is usually from ruptured blood vessels in the nose, but it could also be from pulmonary edema, which is bleeding in the lungs from ruptured capillaries in the lung tissue. Some horses are dosed with Lasix before the race to prevent this from occurring.

Blind Switch---caught in a pocket behind or between other horses that impedes or prevents any further forward progression.

Blinkers---a fabric hood with cups sewn into the eye openings which blocks any peripheral visual distractions the horse may experience, keeping its visual field focused straight ahead.

Blister---a counter irritant applied externally to a body part of a horse to ease pain or to treat an ailment.

Bloodline---the family tree or pedigree of a particular horse which traces the maternal and paternal line all the way back to one of the three original Thoroughbred sires (Darley Arabian, Godolphin Arabian, or Byerley Turk).

Blowout---a short, quick, two or three furlong hard gallop exercise and final workout in order to limber a horse before a scheduled race. When and how long the blowout is done depends on each individual trainer and the condition of his horse, usually a day or two before the horse is scheduled to race. Back in the 1920s, they blew the horse out the day of the race.

Blow the Turn---when a horse does not corner properly going into the turn and runs wide, losing a lot of ground, as well as the race.

Bobble--- a bad break at the barrier or starting gate caused by the racing surface giving way as the horse makes its break, causing the horse to duck its head to maintain balance in order to prevent going to its knees.

Bolt---a sharp break toward the left or right side by the horse.

Bomber---a winner at high odds; a long-shot winner.

Book--- a stallion's *book* is the number of mares scheduled to be bred by him in a given year. A jockey's *book* consists of the mounts and dates a jockey or his agent has arranged or agreed upon.

Bottom Horse---the horse that draws and starts from the outside post position.

Bottom Line---a Thoroughbred's lineage on the female side of the family tree; the maternal pedigree.

Bounce---an unusually poor showing following an unusually good one.

Bow a Tendon---this was always my grandfather's worst fear. When the tendons running down the back length of the cannon bones of a horse become strained, sprained, swollen, inflamed, or otherwise injured from excessive repetitive overuse, such as the stress of racing, they tend to take on a bowed shape and never fully recover or straighten back out, thus rendering them inefficient for the horse to run at full potential.

Boxed in---trapped behind or between other horses in a crowd with no feasible way out (see Blind Switch).

Brace (or Bracer)---a rubdown liniment used on a horse after a race or a workout.

Break---the initial departure from the barrier or starting gate at the beginning of a race.

Breakage---the money the track keeps after the payoffs are rounded to the nickel or dime on the dollar, resulting in a little extra profit for the track.

Breakdown---refers to a horse that suffers a serious injury while running.

Break Maiden---winning the first race of one's career. Refers to a horse or to a jockey.

Broodmare---a female horse used for breeding purposes.

Breeze---to work out a horse at a vigorous competitive speed, without peaking its maximum potential.

Bucked Shins---inflammation along the front of the cannon bone, occurring most frequently in younger horses.

Bug Boy---an apprentice jockey. The name originated from the asterisk placed in front of the name of the apprentice jockey on the racing forms.

Bullet Work---depending on a trainer's individual methods, a contender in a major stakes race is given one all-out major workout generally within a week of the scheduled race, in which the horse is pushed to its maximum performance.

Bull Ring---the smaller race tracks around the country that are less than a mile in circumference with the resultant shorter and sharper turns.

Bush Tracks/ Bushes---non-endearing names given to half-mile racetracks.

Butcher---an unscrupulous trainer who will drug an injured horse and knowingly risk further injury or breakdown just in order to run him.

Buzzer---usually a battery powered electrical device hidden in the saddle or the whip or any other piece of the jockey's equipment that delivers an electric shock to the horse intended to urge the horse to shift to the next gear. Also called *a wire* or *a battery*.

Calk---a projection on the bottom of a shoe which gives greater traction while running, especially on wetter surfaces; similar to a cleat.

Chalk---the favorite in any given race.

Chalk Players---bettors who wager their money exclusively on the favorites.

Chart---a written narrative of a race describing the position and margin of each horse at certain designated points or distance increments in a race, along with other pertinent data such as age, weight carried, owner, trainer, jockey, odds, conditions of the track, purse, type of race, length of time at the start, pay-off prices, previous performances and details of last previous race.

Change Leads---while running in competition, a Thoroughbred reaches out and digs in with either a dominant right or left front foot. Changing leads means to get the horse to switch to the opposite front foot to pull with, thus giving the horse a boost in energy. A jockey will usually try to get the horse to change leads at the top of the stretch when he senses the horse is tiring out.

Checked---pulling up of a horse momentarily because of being cut off or in tight quarters.

Chestnut---the horny growths on the interior aspect of each of a horse's legs. No two of these growths are ever the same and are therefore an identification marker for every horse. Also called a "night-eye".

Chute---an extension of the track into a straight stretch to allow for the running of a shorter or longer distance race than the actual length of the track.

Claimer---a horse that usually or only runs in claiming races.

Claiming Race---a race in which all the entrants have a pre-established purchase price at which any other registered owner or trainer at that particular race meeting may buy that particular horse by submitting a written claim at said price into the claim box ten minutes before the race is run. In the case of two or more claims being submitted for the same horse, the winner is determined by a "shake", which is a lottery of numbers assigned to each claim. The numbers are shaken up and the winner picked in one draw. Claiming races make up the overwhelming majority of all the total races run each year at all the tracks across the country.

Classics---the traditional and established most important races in a certain country. In the United States, there are three classics: the Kentucky Derby, The Preakness, and the Belmont Stakes. Altogether they make up the Triple Crown. There are also a number of classic graded prep stakes races which are important to encounter on one's way to the Classics.

Clerk Of Scales---the race track official whose responsibility it is to weigh each jockey and his tack before and after each race to insure that the proper required weight assigned to each horse is accurate and correct.

Climbing---the running action of a horse in which the horse is actually abnormally high instead of reaching out with each stride.

Clocker---the person who measures and records the length of time of a horse's workouts and races.

Closer---a horse that runs better toward the end of a race. A closer is a horse that prefers to "come from behind" or "from off the pace."

Clubhouse Turn---the first left hand turn in the race track; the turn closest to the clubhouse.

Colors---the combination of designs, insignias, colors and their placement on the jockey's riding uniform that identifies the particular horse's ownership and stable.

Colt---a male horse under the age of five which is anatomically intact (not castrated).

Company---the collective class of the horses in the field of a race; the class of each individual horse in the field.

Condition---to train a horse. A conditioner is the same as a trainer.

Condition Book---the written compilation which describes the requirements, eligibility and parameters of each race that is to be run at that particular track by the track's racing secretary.

Condition Race---an individual race which carries certain requirements and mandatory standards which each horse must meet in order to compete. For example, the race may be declared for three-year old fillies who have never before won a race.

Conditions---the circumstances under which a race will be run, such as: distance, track surface, purse, and eligibilities.

Conformation---a horse's overall physical structure and build; its skeletal and muscular make-up and characteristics, the combinations of which reflect the performance potential of that particular animal.

Contract Rider---a jockey that is under contract or retained by a certain trainer, owner, or stable.

Cooling Out---the process of restoring a horse's condition back to one of normal resting-state vital functions and core temperature after an exhaustive physical workout or race, usually by closely monitored walking and passive exercise.

Corn Cracker---slang term for a race horse.

Coupled---two or more horses running as a single unit betting entry.

Crack---an adjective used to describe an exceptional horse or jockey.

Cribber---a horse that clings to objects by its teeth and sucks air into its stomach (also called a Wind Sucker); considered to be a behavioral dysfunction of the animal.

Cup---the trophy presented to the owners of the winning horse.

Cup Race---a distance race of one and a half miles or more.

Cup Horse---a horse trained and qualified to compete in long distance races.

Cuppy Track---a term to describe the surface of a race track that gives way or breaks down under the placement of a horse's hoof. Also used as an observation or excuse a trainer may use in explaining to the owner the poor performance of his horse in a race.

Cushion---term used to describe the very top layer of a track's surface. Ideally, it is resilient, springy and supportive with good memory.

Dark Track---indicates that there is no live racing that day; a day off, which is usually a Monday.

Dam---the broodmare, or mother, of a horse.

Damsire---the sire of a broodmare (also, Broodmare Sire).

Dead Heat---two or more horses finishing a race in an exact tie.

Dead Presidents---gambler's or bookie's slang term for paper currency.

Dead Track---surface of a track that has no resiliency.

Dead Weight---additional weight assigned to a horse in the form of static lead weights placed in the blanket. Unlike live weight, added dead weight will definitely slow a horse's speed.

Declare---to withdraw a horse from a race ahead of the scratch time.

Disqualification---same as it is in any sport or contest. In horse racing the decision comes from the stewards' ruling following an objection or inquiry into a possible infraction of racing rules.

Distaff Race---a race for fillies, mares, or both.

Distanced---finished a race far behind the winner.

Driving---term used to describe the effort of running by a horse being vigorously urged on by its jockey.

Drop---to move down a class. A potentially dangerous move if dropped down a class only in order to have a greater advantage of winning, because it increases the possibility of the horse being claimed away from the current trainer or owner.

Dropped---same as foaled; having given birth.

Early Foot---describes a horse that shows its best speed immediately, especially as it breaks away from the barrier at the start.

Eased---deliberate slowing or restraint of a horse by its jockey to conserve strength and energy or to avoid harm or injury.

Easily---the running performance of a horse without any outside urging from the jockey or challenge from the rest of the field.

Eighth Pole---a vertical pole on the inside rail marking the distance of one furlong, or one eighth mile, from the finish wire.

Entry Fee---the money paid to enter a horse into a stakes race.

Exercise---regularly scheduled and preplanned workouts for both horses and jockeys in order to keep in tip-top competitive shape.

Exercise Boy---one whose job it is to put a horse through its preplanned early morning workouts; usually an aspiring jockey.

Evenly---neither losing nor gaining speed, position, or distance in a race.

Even Money---a bet or wager at odds of dollar to dollar.

Extended---forced to run at maximum speed and effort.

Extra Weight--- more weight carried by the horse than the conditions of the race require (also, "added weight"), usually due to an overweight jockey.

Faltered---describes a horse that was in contention early in the race, but loses ground toward the end. It describes an effort that is worse than 'weakened', but not as bad as 'stopped' or 'quit.'

Farrier---person who makes, fits, and applies horse shoes and performs hoof and foot care; a blacksmith.

Far Turn---the second left-hand turn on the oval track; the turn after the backstretch.

Fast Track---surface of the running track is dry, hard and even; not much or any give or spring. T he footing is even. The fastest running times and track records usually occur on a fast track.

Favorite---the horse on which the largest amount of money is wagered in a race.

Fence---usually refers to the outside rail along a race track.

Field---the combined total number of horses starting in a race.

Filly---a female horse under the age of five years.

Fire Sale---an auction sale of portions or all of a stable's horses held in the paddock on the last day of a meeting, open to the registered owner and trainer participants at the meet. Horses that have proved undesirable and unproductive for one stable can be obtained by another horseman for relatively inexpensive prices. Also refers to a drastically lowered claiming price placed on a horse before a race for the sole intent of liquidating that horse from one's string.

Firing---treatment of a leg injury or malady by applying a hot searing instrument directly to the problem area to promote healing.

Firm---on a turf course, the equivalent of a fast track on dirt.

First Turn---the first left handed turn or curve encountered on a track (also, Clubhouse Turn).

Flank---the side or thigh of a horse.

Flatten Out---term applied to a horse that is exhausted and completely spent toward the end of a race, manifested by the appearance that his head and body are in a straight line as his head goes down while running.

Foal---newly born male or female Thoroughbred until weaned.

Founder---(a nautical term) that has come to mean any chronic changes in the structure of a horse's foot that can be linked to laminitis. It basically involves the 'sinking' and rotation of the coffin bone further down into the foot.

Founding Sires---most Thoroughbreds can trace their lineage back to one of these three stallions: Darley Arabian, Byerly Turk or Godolphin Barb.

Fractional Times---clocking the horse's speed at the standard parameters of a quarter-mile increments either in a race or in a workout.

Fractions---same as above.

Fresh---a well-rested horse.

Front Runner---a horse that takes the early lead and sets the pace for as long as he can.

Furlong---an eighth of a mile. Furlong is a 14th century English measurement of length and distance equal to 220 yards. Keeping an old tradition, most horse racing tracks in the U.S. and U.K. are 8 furlongs (one mile) long. There are many popular 6 furlong (3/4 mile) races as well. The Kentucky Derby is a 10 furlong (mile and a quarter) race. The Preakness is a slightly shorter 9.5 furlong (mile and three-sixteenths), while the Belmont Stakes, the last leg of the U.S. Triple Crown, is the longest at 12 furlongs (mile and one half).

Gait---term for the various types, descriptions and methods of ambulation in a horse, such as walk, trot, canter, gallop, run.

Gallop---the gait of a horse that is a fast canter; (v) to ride a horse at that speed.

Gamely---description of a horse performing with spirit, fortitude, resolution, and courage.

Garrison Finish---a victory by a come-from-behind horse in the style made famous by turn-of-the-century jockey Edward "Snapper" Garrison.

His ability to come from behind and snatch victory in the last jump made his name a part of horse racing's vocabulary.

Gelding---a fully castrated or neutered male horse.

Get---the progeny or offspring of a horse.

Getaway Day---the final racing day of a meeting.

Girth---the leather strap that secures the saddle to the horse by encircling the entire midsection of the horse; also, the measure of circumference of the horse's midsection.

Going---the overall condition of the racing surface. Dirt courses are usually rated as follows: Fast, Good, Slow, Muddy, or Sloppy. Grass courses are rated as follows: Firm, Good, Heavy, Yielding, or Soft.

Going Away---approaching or crossing the finish line while still increasing the lead margin.

Goo---mud.

Good---condition of the track that is between slow and fast; footing is firm, but moisture remains in the strip.

Good Bottom---a track that is firm under the surface, even if that surface is wet or sloppy.

Good Doer---an eager eater.

Grab A Quarter---racetrack jargon which means that a horse cut one of its front feet with one of its hind feet in the act of overstepping or overreaching while running.

Granddam---grandmother of a horse (also Second Dam).

Grandsire---grandfather of a horse. Also, the sire of a horse's dam.

Groom---a person who works for a trainer or a stable that personally cares for a horse. A groom usually cares for the same assigned horse(s). The groom is responsible for the overall physical appearance of the horse and to take the horse to and from the paddock area before and after the race.

Half Brother (Half Sister)---two horses that share the same dam, but have different sires.

Half---half-mile; the time 'to the half' is the fraction of time expired after one half mile of racing.

Half-mile Pole---the vertical pole on the inside rail marking the distance of four furlongs remaining to the finish line.

Halter---to claim a horse in a claiming race.

Halter Man---a horseman who claims another man's horse in a claiming race.

Hand---a unit of measurement in determining the height of a horse from the ground to the top of the withers. One hand is equal to four inches.

Handicap Race---one in which horses known to be faster are assigned additional weight by the racing steward or track handicapper to carry, intended to equalize that advantage over the other horses, thus providing each horse the same chance of winning; (v) to study a horse's vital statistics and past racing records in order to effectively predetermine the winner of an upcoming race.

Handily---a manner of comparative easy victory not requiring any corporal prodding, urging or encouragement from the rider or his whip. Racing with moderate effort, but more effort than breezing.

Hand Ride---encouraging and urging a horse along by use of the hands only, without kicking or using the whip.

Hang---failure to negotiate a move or advance at a particular point in the race.

Hardboot---a horseman of the old school.

Hard in Hand---riding with a tight rein

Hat Trick---for a jockey, winning three races on one day's program.

Head---the measurement of margin between two horses equivalent to the length of a horse's head.

Head of the Stretch---the end of the final turn approaching the straight portion of the track before the finish line.

Heavy Track---the surface of the running track which is wet, but still has spring and support and does not give way to the weight of the horse. Not as wet as Sloppy and wetter than Fast; similar to muddy, but slower. Footing is sticky.

Highweight---the horse assigned to most weight in a handicap race.

Hock---the hind leg joint, comparable to the human ankle.

Homestretch---straight part of track from the final turn to the finish line.

Hopping---the administration of a stimulant drug such as cocaine to boost the energy and performance of a horse, or of a sedative such as morphine or heroin to slow down the performance of the horse. The practice was quite common and openly used in the early days before the advent and demand for honest and professional competition.

Horse---an intact ungelded male five years old or older.

Horseman---the term used throughout the industry to describe a well respected trainer, owner, or official who is a true professional and steward of all aspects of the sport.

Hot Box (also "sweat box")---a sauna of sorts in which a jockey is completely encapsulated except for his head, in an enclosed environment of heat and steam in order to lose a couple or a few pounds of weight before a race.

Hot Walk---walking a horse by hand or a machine to cool down after a race or workout.

Hot Walker---person who walks horses to cool them down right after a workout or a race.

Hung---description of a horse that is tiring, but still holding position.

Icing---standing a horse's legs in a bucket of ice or the application of ice packs to the legs to control swelling and inflammation.

Impost---the amount of weight assigned by the track handicapper to a particular horse in a particular race intended to even out each horse's chances for winning.

In a Ruck---horses racing in a group with no clear leader.

Infield---area defined as and comprised of the space within the inner rail of a race track.

Infield Racing---same as turf racing.

In Foal---synonymous with pregnant mare.

In Hand---the horse is running under moderate control of the jockey and not at its best pace; running under restraint.

Inquiry---before declaring a race official, a review of a race by the stewards in order to determine if any infractions of the rules had occurred. Before the advent of filming races, this was accomplished by personally interviewing the jockeys directly involved in the alleged infractions.

In the Bridle---a horse that is eager to run.

In the Money--- finishing first, second or third in a race and recipient of the corresponding prize money.

In the Right Key---in a good mood; an agreeable disposition; responding well to jockey's commands.

Irons---stirrups

Jam---a congested pile-up as horses run together during a race.

Jockey---the rider of a horse; race rider; 'monkey'; 'boy'.

Jockey Club---formed in 1894 and based in New York, it is the organization responsible for keeping the national registry for Thoroughbreds in North America.

Jockey Fee---the sum of money paid to the jockey for riding a horse in a race.

Jog---slow, easy gait.

Judge---the racing official(s) whose responsibility it is to witness and view the race's finish and declare the results.

Juiced---a horse that is running on performance enhancing drugs.

Juice Trainer---a trainer who uses unapproved drugs on his horses to make them run better.

Juvenile---a two-year-old horse.

Jungle Circuit---term used by Charles E. Van Loan in his 1917 book _Old Man Curry_ to describe the second and third grade horse racing tracks and participant horses, trainers, and jockeys. A step below and inferior to the leading professional tracks. Also called "the leaky roof circuit."

Lame---the inability to walk, gallops, or run normally due to pain, swelling or injury.

Laminitis---a potentially fatal condition of inflammation and ischemic changes in the laminae between the horny section and the vascular portion of the hoof, which, if untreated, causes severe pain and lameness resulting in failure to thrive and progressive deterioration of the overall health of the animal, eventually requiring euthanasia (also known as Founder, Foundering).

Lead (or Lead Pad)---the weights a horse is required to carry in addition to the weight of the jockey and tack to make up for any discrepancies in the amount the horse is assigned to carry.

Lead---a strap or rope attached to a horse's halter; to coax a horse to follow in a walk by use of a strap or line attached to the halter.

Lead, left or right---the front leg that is left to hit the ground. Ideally, a horse will race on its left lead in the turns (all the turns are left hand turns in an American racecourse) and in its right lead in the straight-aways.

Lead Pony---a horse or pony that heads up the post parade from the paddock to the starting area; also a horse or pony that accompanies the Thoroughbred to the post for the start of a race and also back to the paddock after the race is run.

Leaky Roof Circuit---the minor tracks; 'bush' tracks; county fair tracks; the minor leagues for horse racing.

Leg Up---to help a jockey mount his horse; also refers to the jockey assigned to ride a particular horse; also to condition and build up a horse's speed and stamina by working the horse.

Length---the distance from a horse's nose to its tail; generally about eight feet. It is generally accepted that a Thoroughbred can run a length in one-fifth of a second (five lengths per second) at racing speed. It is also the measurement used to denote the distances between horses.

Live Weight---weight carried by a horse in the form of the weight of and carried on the jockey. Live weight is balanced over the axis of the center of gravity of the horse and has little negative effect on the speed of the horse.

Lock---racetrack jargon for a "sure thing" winner.

Longshot---a horse that is not highly regarded to win by those placing the wagers, making the odds and consequently the payoffs much higher if the horse wins.

Lugging In or Lugging Out---terms to explain the action of a horse as he veers to the left (lugging in) or to the right (lugging out) during the running of a race. This is usually due to the horse tiring out, shying away from the applied whip, or some kind of injury, pain, or discomfort.

Lunge---refers to a horse's rearing up or abruptly plunging forward.

Maiden----a horse (male or female) that has never won a race. Also refers to jockeys who have not yet won their first race.

Maiden Race---a race for horses that have never won a race.

Make a Bid---action of a horse attempting to take the lead in a race.

Marathon---traditionally a race that was two miles in length or longer. Now any race over a mile and a half.

Mare---a female horse five years of age or older; or female horse of any age that has already been bred.

Mash---a hot or cold moist mixture or concoction of grain, oats, sweet feed, bran, other feeds, and added supplements that are fed to a horse.

Match Race---an intentionally arranged race between just two horses.

Middle Distance---any race that is longer than a sprint and shorter than a marathon in length. In most countries, a middle distance race was defined as being between a mile and a sixteenth and a mile and a quarter. In contemporary times, it is generally defined as equal to or longer than seven furlongs but equal to or shorter than nine (one and one eighth miles).

Miler---a horse that runs its best race at or near the distance of a mile.

Milkshake---an illegal mixture or concoction fed to a horse to make him run faster.

Miss the Break---breaking slowly from the starting barrier and behind the rest of the field.

Money Rider---a jockey who excels at placing in the money in high stake races and highly sought out by owners and trainers.

Monkey---slang term for jockey. Not a derisive or degrading term. Sometimes referred to as "monkey on a stick."

Morning Glory---a horse that performs better in morning workouts than he does in competition in an actual race in the afternoon.

Morning Line---the odds given on each horse after the morning workouts, but before the actually racing begins.

Mudder---a horse that actually runs well on a muddy track.

Muddy Track---racing surface is soft, wet, holding water; horse's feet sink below the surface. Footing is deep and slow.

Mudlark---a horse that loves to run in the mud and generally performs well in the mud; a superior mudder.

Mutuel Field---horses grouped together as one betting entity.

Muzzle---the nose and lips of a horse; also an appliance placed over the mouth to prevent the horse from biting or eating.

Near Side---the left side of a horse; the side on which the jockey mounts the horse.

Neck---an arbitrary unit of measure in horse racing equal to the length of a horse's neck; approximately one quarter of a horse's length, or two feet in length.

Nerved---a procedure by which a nerve is surgically severed for the purpose of eliminating any pain while running. This in not accepted standard practice and is illegal in most all jurisdictions.

Nightcap---the last race on the program for the day.

Nod---lowering of the head; also winning by lowering the head at the wire.

Nose---the smallest arbitrary unit of measure in horse racing that a horse can win by; usually only inches.

Oaks---a special stakes race for three-year-old fillies, patterned after old English racing tradition.

Objection---a complaint levied by a jockey against another jockey, or one lodged by a patrol judge or other official. It is called an "Inquiry" if lodged by an official.

Odds---the chances of a particular horse winning a particular race based on the pari-mutuel wagering of the general public. Payouts are based on these numbers.

Odds On---betting odds of less than even money.

Official---a race is not official until the results are confirmed by the racing stewards. Also, a judge, steward or other designated administrative personnel given authority to make decisions.

Off Side---the right side of a horse.

Off the Pace---a horse that is lagging behind in the early stages of a race.

Off Track---a track with a wet running surface that is anything other than Fast (Dirt) or Firm (Turf).

On the Bit---refers to a horse that is eager to run.

On the Board---a horse that finishes among the first four.

On the Ground---suspended from riding.

On the Nose---a bet placed on a horse to win only.

On the Shelf---refers to a horse that is taken out of training and competition due to some kind of injury or adverse physical condition.

Opening---that long-awaited micro second opportunity to slip between and past two or more horses (also referred to as "Light").

Open Race---a race that does not restrict eligibility and every horse carries the same weight.

Out---an outing; same as a start; a race. The number of outs a Thoroughbred has in a race meeting means the same as the number of races he ran.

Out of the Money---finishing worse than third.

Overland---running wide for the entire race on the very outside, avoiding the other horses, but covering a longer distance.

Overnight---the list of entries for the upcoming racing day.

Overnight Race---a race for which competing horses must be entered less than three days before the race is scheduled to run.

Over-Reaching---the toe of the shoe of a rear foot strikes one of the forelegs on the heel or back of coronet causing injury to the horse.

Overweight---the extra weight carried by a horse when a jockey is unable to make the required weight assignment for the horse.

Pace---the speed of a race.

Pacesetter---the early leader in a race.

Paddock---the enclosed area where the horses are saddled and contained until the post parade and the start of the race.

Paddock Judge---official in charge of the paddock staging area and the saddling procedures.

Pari-mutuel---the form of wagering, first developed by the French, in which those who are making the wagers are betting against each other and not against the 'house".

Pastern---area between the fetlock (ankle) and the hoof (foot).

Patrol Judges---track officials who observe the progress of the race from various vantage points around the track.

Photo Finish---a finish that is so close, the winner must be determined by reviewing a photograph of the contenders as they cross the wire.

Physic Ball---given to a horse that has a very poor appetite in order to clean out his intestinal tract. Most physic balls contain 40 to 60 grains of calomel mixed with aloes and other ingredients.

Pill---small numbered ball used for drawing post positions.

Pinched Back---a horse that is running in very close quarters and is forced to back off.

Pinhook---The act of purchasing a horse at auction with the only intention of reselling it and not training, running, or breeding it.

Pinhooker---a person who engages in the act of pinhooking.

Pipe Opener---a fast work-out that is a furlong or two longer than a blowout.

Place--finishing a race in the second position.

Place Bet---a wager on a horse which pays off if the horse finishes first or second.

Placing Judges---the track officials who decide the official order of finishers for a race.

Plater---term for a claiming horse; also track jargon for a farrier or blacksmith.

Plates---the varied number and styles of shoes used on horses in racing.

Pocket---a situation or position of being completely blocked by the horses in front and along sides.

Points of Call---certain distance parameters in a race at which point the running positions of the horses are recorded and indicated in a chart. Final point of call is at the finish line.

Pole---distance markers permanently placed around the track, usually every 1/16th of a mile apart, which mark the distance to the finish line and not the distance from the starting point.

Pool---the sum of money wagered on a dedicated outcome. For example, the 'place pool' is the total amount of money wagered to place (come in third).

Post---the starting point of a race; or the starting position assigned each horse for the race.

Post Parade---the single file line up of horses going from the paddock to the starting line.

Post Position---the assigned order (going from the inner rail outward) in which each horse is lined up at the starting line.

Post Time---the pre-scheduled time for the start of a race.

Prep (or Prep Race)---a workout or a race used to prepare a horse for a future, upcoming race.

Prop---refusing to break at the starting line; makes no effort to run; also, abruptly stopping during a full run by extending the front legs straight, or "putting on the brakes".

Proud Flesh---a skin growth or lesion comprised of an exuberant mass of fungal granulations.

Public Trainer---a trainer who is not exclusively employed by one stable or owner and who accepts horses from a number of owners.

Pull Up---to slow a running horse to a stop during or after a race or a workup.

Pull Up Bad---a horse that is lame after a race or quits during the race because of lameness.

Pull---to 'pull a horse' means the jockey intentionally impedes and prevents the horse from winning.

Punter---an older English term meaning *gambler* which found its way into American racing jargon; a horseplayer.

Purse---the total prize money, to which owners do not contribute, offered for the winners of a race.

Put Down---to euthanize an injured horse on the spot on the track the injury occurred. Also, "Destroyed".

Quarter Crack---a hoof irregularity in the form of a small crack running from the coronet longitudinally down the wall of the hoof.

Quarter Pole---a vertical pole on the inside rail marking the distance of two furlongs, or one quarter mile, from the finish wire.

Rabbit---a fast running horse with little chance of winning that is entered in order to establish a fast pace from the start for the sole purpose of tiring out the rest of the field early in order to benefit its stablemate's chances of winning.

Racing Secretary---the track official who draws up the conditions of the races and assigns the weights to the horses in the handicapped races.

Rail (inner and outer)---the barriers that mark and outline the inner and outer periphery of a race track. Also called the fence.

Rail Runner---a horse that prefers to run its race along the inside rail of the track.

Rake Down the Socks---to win all the money.

Rank---a horse that refuses to relax or settle; constantly fighting the rider.

Rate---restraining a horse early on in order to conserve energy for the end of the race.

Refuse---when a horse will not break from the starting barrier or gate.

Reserved---deliberately holding a horse off the pace in order to conserve energy.

Reins---leather straps connected to the bit and used to guide and control the horse.

Reining In---holding back firmly on the reins in order to keep a horse from running all extended and at his maximum.

Ridden Out---refers to a horse that wins under a vigorous hand ride but is not being whipped.

Ride Short---using shorter than normal stirrup leathers.

Ridgling---a half-castrated male horse or one with one or both testicles absent from the sac.

Riding The Rail---hugging the inside rail to save distance and ground covered.

Ringer---a similar looking (or altered) better quality running horse that is substituted in a race for a lesser quality horse for the purpose of cheating to win larger pay off at higher odds. A very common form of cheating in the early days of professional horse racing and around the end of the 19th and turn of the 20th century, both at minor and major tracks. Virtually impossible today.

Rogue---an ill-tempered horse.

Rollers---shoes that are purposely smooth and altered in order to make a horse run poorly. They are beveled and rounded at the toes and heels to prevent the horse from getting any traction. A technique used in fixing a race

Romp---running or winning without exerting much effort.

Route---race distance of a mile or longer, as opposed to a sprint.

Router---a horse that performs well in distance races.

Rubber---a stable employee in charge of rubbing down a horse after exercising or racing; also called a Swipe.

Ruled Off---permanently suspended from a track and its privileges for some serious infraction of the rules.

Rundown---to suffer abrasions on the heels caused by contact with dirt and sand from the surface of the track.

Rundown Bandages---padded bandages on the rear legs to avoid the friction burning, abrasions, and scraping of the heels as the horse is running.

Running For Sweeney---a phrase which originated in horse racing and meant that the race was fixed or a fix was on. Also adopted and used in other sports to indicate that some form of extraneous dishonesty or cheating was occurring that would manipulate the final outcome of the contest. Also used to mean the avoidance of something dangerous or illegal (Sweeney being the stereotypical Irish policeman).

Running Horse (or Running Nag)---nineteenth century slang for a venereal disease.

Run-Out-Bit---a specially designed bit used to prevent the horse from veering to the outside (or inside).

Saddle Cloth---a cloth placed under the saddle which displays the number of the horse's post position and usually the name of the track.

Savage---to bite another horse or a person. In the heat and excitement of a close race, a horse may reach over and savage another horse's shoulder or hip.

Scale of Weights---official tabulation (adopted by the Jockey Club) of the weight formulas assigned to each horse, based on the age of the horse, its sex, the distance to be run, and the time of the year. The official track handicapper uses this formula to assign the necessary weight each horse is to carry in each race during that track's particular meeting.

Schooling---acclimating a horse to break from the starting barrier or gate by repetitious sessions of practicing; also practice sessions that stress other racing fundamentals.

Scraped the Paint---pushed up so close to the rail that the horse figuratively could have taken some of the paint off the fence. To squeeze through a very narrow slot between another horse and the rail to gain position. Used to describe a very daring ride.

Scratch---to withdraw an entry from a race; usually this is determined and initiated by the track stewards or the track veterinarian.

Second Dam---the maternal grandmother.

Selling Race---same as Claiming Race

Set Down---when a jockey is suspended by the track stewards; also, Taken Down and On the Ground.

Sex Allowance--- fillies and mares are allowed three to five pounds (depending on age and the time of year) reduction of weight when racing against males.

Shadow Roll---a cylindrically rolled piece of lamb's wool placed across the face half way between the eyes and nose which prevents the horse from seeing it shadow.

Shank---the rope or strap attached to a horse's halter or bridle by which the horse is led.

Shed Row---stable area on the backside. Rows of barns. Also the dirt path that encircles a barn (shed row).

Shake Down The Persimmons---to win it all.

Shipping Fever---a condition in horses manifested by lethargy, dull coat, change in demeanor and behavior, and an elevation in temperature by a degree or two, as a result of confinement in a train car and the anxiety producing changes from the usual ordinary daily routine and activities and eating habits.

Short---not up to full potential; lacking necessary conditioning.

Show---finishing in third place in a race.

Show Bet---a wager placed on a horse to finish in the money...first, second, or third.

Shut Off---trapped in a pocket; unable to improve position (See "Boxed In").

Silks---the identifying costumed uniform (jacket and cap) worn by the jockey while he is riding in a horserace. The silks, or colors, are the unique identifier for each particular stable or owner.

Sitting Chilly---term used by jockeys that means being patient and laying back, not using the horse up in the early part of the race.

Sire---the father of a horse.

Sixteenth Pole---a vertical pole on the inside rail marking the distance of one half furlong, or one sixteenth mile, from the finish wire.

Sloan, Tod---the jockey from the late nineteenth century who developed and made famous the current jockey style and form of race riding. Because of his unusually short legs, his nickname was 'Toad' which he later changed to Tod. It was because of his short legs that he had to raise the stirrup level higher up on the horse which resulted in his new and unusual riding stance.

Sloppy Track---running surface is covered with puddles of water, but the surface is still hard. Not yet Muddy. Footing is splashy but even.

Slow Track---running surface of track is wetter than Good, but not yet Muddy and thick.

Snug---mild restraining hold on the horse by the jockey.

Solid Horse---a contender.

Sophomores---refers to three-year old horses. They are called sophomores because they are in their second year of eligibility for professional racing.

Spit the Bit---when a horse quits running against the bit, most often indicating fatigue.

Splits---same as fractions; fractional times.

Sponge---(v) the act of secretly placing a piece of a common stable sponge or other foreign body up into one nostril of a horse before a race with the intent of obstructing the horse's airway, thus decreasing his lung capacity, causing him to run poorly.

Sprint---a race that is less than a mile in length. Generally, sprints are five, six, or seven furlongs.

Sprinter---a horse that has all speed to compete in races under a mile, but has no staying power for those over a mile.

Stakes Horse---a horse of such proven quality that it is classed and capable of running such races.

Stakes Race---a type of race in which the owners are required to put up a fee in order to enter their horse, thus giving them a 'stake' in the race. Many stakes races are graded I, II, or III, with Grade I attracting the best quality horse, Grade II a lesser quality, and so on. It is the Grade I and Grade II stakes races which are the building blocks and stepping stones to the Classic Races. Non-graded stakes races also feature exceptional quality horses, but of a lower classification. Some stakes races are by invitation and require no fee.

Stallion---an adult male horse over five years of age that has not been castrated.

Stall Walker--- a horse that moves about his stall and frets rather than rests; nervous; unsettled.

Starter---the track official responsible for getting the horses lined up at the barrier and getting them off at an equal and fair advantage.

Starter Race---an allowance or handicap race restricted to horses that have started for a specific claiming price or less.

Stayer---a horse with the proven stamina, strength, and heart to race long distances.

Steadied---a horse being taken in hand by the jockey, usually because of being confined or impeded in close quarters.

Steward---one of three official judges and arbiters overseeing each sanctioned race meeting held during the Thoroughbred racing season in the U.S. The stewards are given the responsibility of monitoring all human and equine conduct and behavior during the meeting and the authority to enforce all racing laws, rules, and regulations; having the power to levy fine, revoke licenses, suspend and disqualify owners, trainers, jockeys, grooms, valets, stable hands, horses, or strings of horses.

Stick--- the jockey's whip; also called 'bat'.

Stickers---shoes that have cleats or built-up rims designed to improve a horse's footing on a slippery, slick track surface.

Stifle---the next joint above the hock in the hind leg, comparable to the human knee joint.

Stockings---white markings from the hock to the hoof.

Stooper---a person who picks up discarded tickets after the races are run in hopes of finding one that is redeemable for cash.

Stretch---the final straight portion of the race track leading to the finish line.

Stretch Call---the position of the horses at the eighth pole.

Stretch Runner---a horse that finishes fast in the stretch.

Stretch Turn---the final bend in the track leading into the straight homestretch and finish line.

Stride---the distance covered after each foot has touched the ground once.

Stuck Horse---horses that are sore, or lame, or poor performers entered into a race for the sake of padding the field. The track management and trainers are full aware and close-lipped about it. It's up to the horseplayers/handicappers to find out on their own.

Stud---a male horse used exclusively for breeding purposes.

Suckling---a Thoroughbred not yet weaned from its mother.

Surcincle---a girth that secures a saddle to a horse.

Suspension---the punishment for some infraction of the rules of racing or rules of the track, denying the offender the privileges of the racetrack for a specified amount of time. If the person is permanently suspended, he is said to have been Ruled Off.

Swipe---another name for one who rubs down horses.

Tack---the various equipment used by both horse and jockey for the purpose of riding in a competitive racing situation. The weight of the jockey and the tack is counted toward meeting the weight assignments given each horse for each individual race.

Tackle---the earlier term for tack, meaning the necessaries, accouterments, apparati, and equipment needed for the proper performance of a task or an activity.

Taken Back---restrained to conserve energy for a late run.

Taken Up---a horse pulled up sharply by its jockey, usually because of dangerously tight quarters or a jam.

Take the Corn---to win the race and take the money

Tight---a horse that is ready to race.

Tightener---a race or workout intended to get a horse to its ultimate desirable level of fitness and competitive ability.

Tongue Strap (or Tongue Tie)---a strap or tape bandage used to tie down a horse's tongue in its mouth to prevent it from obstructing the airway and choking while running.

Top Line---a Thoroughbred's genealogy and breeding record on its sire's side.

Top Weight---the highest weight assigned or carried in a race.

Tout---a track regular who provides 'hot tips' to those willing to pay for his services.

Track Bias---a racing surface that favors a particular running style or position.

Trial---a workout.

Trip---a summary of a horse's race.

Triple Crown---in the United States, the Triple Crown consists of winning the Kentucky Derby, the Preakness Stakes, and the Belmont Stakes. In England, the 2,000 Guineas, the Epson Derby, and the St. Leger.

Turf Course---the grass track usually located on the inside oval of the larger dirt track. In the United States, most races are run on dirt, while most races in Europe are run on grass.

Turn Down---an added protrusion on the bottom of a horse shoe in order to improve traction.

Twitch--- a loop of rope attached to the end of a stick which is placed around a horse's nose and upper lip and twisted, used for curbing and controlling fractious behavior in the horse.

Two Minute Lick---to gallop the distance of one mile in two minutes time.

Under Punishment---horse being whipped and driven hard in an effort to cross the wire first.

Under Wraps---horse being held back in tight restraint by its jockey in a race or workout. Also refers to exercising a horse wearing a blanket or lighter fabric covering. Also, covering a horse with a blanket immediately after a vigorous workout while being cooled down.

Untried---not yet raced or tested for speed and endurance. Also, a stallion that has not yet bred a mare.

Unwind--- to gradually taper off a horse's training program in order to rest the horse.

Up---term used to indicate the name of the jockey riding a particular horse, e.g. "Lillian Shaw, Murray up." Also used as the command indicating that it is time for the jockeys to mount their horses and head for the starting barrier.

Used Up---a horse that is thoroughly exhausted and spent.

Valet---a track employee who takes care of a jockey's clothing and tack and assists the jockey in dressing prior to a race, paying particular attention that the jockey and his tack meet the assigned weight requirements. He also assists in saddling the horse.

Vice---any undesirable habit or behavior of a horse.

Walkover---a race that scratches down to only one starter who simply gallops the required race distance in order to satisfy the requirements of the rules of racing to be declared the winner.

Warming Up---a pre-race gallop.

Washy---a horse that breaks out in a pre-race nervous sweat.

Weanling---a young Thoroughbred not yet one year old.

Weaving---a swaying side-to-side motion of a horse in its stall. Also, the act of threading the way through the other horses that make up the field in a race.

Webfoot---a mudder.

Weigh In---recording the jockey's weight with his tack after the running of a race.

Weigh Out---recording the jockey's weight with his tack before the running of a race.

Weight-for-Age Race---a race in which horses are assigned weight to carry as determined by the official scale of weights.

Whip---a leather instrument a jockey utilizes to strike a horse in the flanks to encourage more speed and fight. Also called a stick; a bat; a gad.

Whoop-de-doo---a riding style that focuses on getting the lead immediately and run as fast as possible with much whip action and little effort at rating.

Win---coming in first place in a race.

Winded---a degree of labored breathing after a race or a workout.

Wind Gall---a soft tumor on the fetlock joints of a horse.

Wind Kicker---a very fast race horse.

Windsucker---a cribber (see).

Winter---to spend the winter or off-season away from racing, usually at the owner's main horse farm or winter quarters.

Wire---the finish line.

Workout---exercising a horse at moderate to extreme speed for a predetermined distance.

Work---an exercise session on the inside of the track for a horse in training for an upcoming scheduled race which is clocked and published for the general public's knowledge, in which the horse is asked to perform at a maximum level. Not necessarily a bullet work.

Wound Up---the condition of a horse that's fit and ready to go to racing after an intensive regimented training period.

Yearling---a one-year-old Thoroughbred.

SUGGESTED READINGS & BIBLIOGRAPHY

Ainslie, Tom. *Ainslie's Complete Guide to Thoroughbred Racing.* 1968. Trident Press, a division of Simon and Schuster, Inc. New York.

American Thoroughbred Breeders Association. *A quarter Century of American Racing: Silver Anniversary Supplement to The Blood Horse of August 30, 1941.* Lexington, Kentucky.

Arcaro, Eddie. (as told to Jack O'Hara). *I Ride To Win.* 1951. Greenburg: Publisher. New York, N.Y.

Auerbach, Ann Hagedorn. *Wild Ride:The Rise and Tragic Fall of Calumet Farm, Inc., America's Premier Racing Dynasty.* 1994. Henry Holt and Company, Inc. New York.

Blanche, Ernest E. *Off to the Races.* 1947. A.S. Barnes & Company. New York.

Bowen, Edward L. *Masters of the Turf: Ten Trainers Who Dominated Horse Racing's Golden Age.* 2007. Eclipse Press/Blood Horse Publications. Lexington, Kentucky.

Boyd, Eva Jolene. *Exterminator: Horse Racing's Beloved "Old Bones".* 2002. Thoroughbred Legends. Eclipse Press/ The Blood-Horse Inc. Lexington, Kentucky

Claypool, James C. *Old Latonia Race Track (1883-1939).* Northern Kentucky Heritage. Vol.VI No. I. Fall/Winter 1998. The Kenton County Historical Society. Covington, Kentucky.

Claypool, James C. *The Tradition Continues: The Story of Old Latonia, Latonia, and Turfway Racecourses.* 1997. T.I.Hayes Publishing Co. Fort Mitchell, Kentucky.

Collins, Robert W. *Grooming Horses*. 1959. The Blood-Horse. Lexington, Kentucky. Reprint 1971. The Thoroughbred Record Co. Lexington, Kentucky.

Collins, Robert W. *Race Horse Training*. 1938. The Blood-Horse. Lexington, Kentucky.

Cristgau, John. *The Gambler And The Bug Boy*. 2007. University of Nebraska Press. Lincoln and London.

Daily Racing Form. *The American Racing Manual: 1919*. 1919. Daily Racing Form Publishing Co. Chicago, Illinois.

Drape, Joe, editor. *To The Swift/ Classic Triple Crown Horses and Their Race for Glory*. 2008. The New York Times Company. New York, N.Y.

Dodds, John W. *Everyday Life in Twentieth Century America*. 1965. G.P. Putnam's Sons. New York.

Engelhard, Jack. *The Horsemen: The Thoroughbred Racing World from the Other Side of the Rail*. 1974. Henry Regnery Company. Chicago.

Faulconer, J. B. *The Keeneland Story: A Quarter Century of Racing in the Finest Tradition*. 1960. (No publisher information).

Gillham, Lisa Curtiss. *Images of America: Latonia*. 2009. Arcadia Publishing. Charleston, S.C.

Haskin, Steve. *Horse Racing's Holy Grail: The Epic Quest for the Kentucky Derby*. 2002. The Blood Horse, Inc. Eclipse Press. Lexington, Kentucky.

Hildreth, Samuel C. and James R. Crowell. *The Spell of the Turf*. 1926. J. B. Lippincott Company. Philadelphia.

320

Hollingsworth, Kent. *The Kentucky Thoroughbred.* 2009. The University Press of Kentucky. Lexington, Kentucky.

Leerhsen, Charles. *Crazy Good: The True Story of Dan Patch, the Most Famous Horse in America.* 2008. Simon & Schuster. New York.

Maturi, Richard J. *Triple Crown Winner: The Earl Sande Saga, Tragedy to Triumph.* 2005. 21st Century Publishers. Cheyenne, Wyoming.

McCormick, Gene. *The Blue Collar Thoroughbred; An Inside Account of the Real World of Racing.* 2007. McFarland and Company Inc., Publishers. Jefferson, North Carolina

Menke, Frank G. *Down the Stretch: The Story of Colonel Matt J. Winn as Told to Frank J. Menke.* 1945. Smith & Durrell. New York.

Moore, Bob. *Those Wonderful Days: Tales of Racing's Golden Era.* 1976. Amerpub Company. New York.

Murray, William. *The Right Horse.* 1997. Doubleday. New York, N. Y.

Peyton, Richard, editor. *At the Track: A Treasury of Horse Racing Stories.* 1986. Souvenir Press, Ltd. 1987 edition, Bonanza Books, distributed by Crown Publishers Inc. New York.

Robertson, William H. P. *The History of Thoroughbred Racing in America.* 1964. Bonanza Books. New York.

Scanlan, Lawrence. *The Horse God Built: The Untold Story of Secretariat, The World's Greatest Racehorse.* 2007. Thomas Dunne Books. St. Martin's Griffin. New York.

Schulkers, Robert F. *The Cazanova Treasure: Seckatary Hawkins.* 1921. Seckatary Hawkins Co. John G. Kidd. Cincinnati, Ohio.

Seckatary Hawkins: Original/The Rejiment Stories. Volume I of II. 1918. Charles R. Schulkers, Publisher. 2011.

Seckatary Hawkins:Stoner's Boy. 1921, 1926. Charles R. Schulkers, Publisher. 2011.

Self, Margaret Cabel. *The Horseman's Encyclopedia.* 1946, 1963, 1974. Arco Publishing Company, Inc. New York.

Scatoni, Frank R., Ed. *Finished Lines: A Collection of Memorable Writing on Thoroughbred Racing.* 2002. Daily Racing Form Press. New York.

Shoemaker, Bill and Barney Nagler. *Shoemaker: America's Greatest Jockey.* 1988. Doubleday. New York.

Shoop, Robert. *Down to the Wire: The Lives of the Triple Crown Champions.* 2004. Russell Dean and Company. Everson, Washington.

Simon, Mary. *Racing Through The Century: The Story of Thoroughbred Racing in America.* 2002. BowTie Press. Irvine, California.

Squires, Jim. *Headless Horsemen: A Tale Of Chemical Colts, Subprime Sales Agents, And The Last Kentucky Derby On Steroids.* 2009. Henry Holt and Company. New York.

Horse of a Different Color: A Tale of Breeding Geniuses, Dominant Females, and the Fastest Derby Winner Since Secretariat. 2002. PublicAffairs. New York.

Surface, Bill. *The Track: A Day in the Life of Belmont Park.* 1976. Macmillan Publishing Co., Inc. New York.

Thornton, T. D. *Not By A Long Shot: A Season at a Hard-Luck Horse Track.* 2007. PublicAffairs. New York.

Von Borries, Philip. *Racelines: Observations on Horse Racing's Glorious History.* 1999. Masters Press. Chicago, Illinois.

Wall, Maryjean. *How Kentucky Became Southern: A Tale of Outlaws, Horse Thieves, Gamblers, and Breeders.* 2010. The University Press of Kentucky. Lexington, Kentucky.

Watman, Max. *Raceday: A Spot on the Rail with Max Watman.* 2005. Ivan R. Dee, Publisher. Chicago, Illinois.

APPENDIX A

TOP 25 OWNERS FOR 1918

Owners	1st Place	2nd Place	3rd Place	Winnings
Ross, J.K.L.	64	52	57	$99,107
Macomber, A.K.	50	41	32	$95,264
Whitney, H.P.	33	30	16	$70,309
McClelland, J.W.	11	13	9	$60,865
Coe, W.R.	36	36	31	$58,228
Williams Brothers	77	49	44	$55,831
Wilson, R.T.	28	35	35	$50,527
Kilmer, W.S.	12	11	16	$50,303
Widener, J.E.	29	30	29	$42,269
Clark, P.A.	13	10	5	$42,111
Sanford, J.	21	12	21	$37,087
Bradley, E.R.	30	44	34	$37,087
McLean, E.B.	29	28	23	$35,905
Polson, W.F.	24	19	25	$34,710
Brannon, B.J.	27	26	16	$33,011
Livingston, J.	34	46	42	$32,807
Brighton Stable (George Smith)	27	12	16	$32,389
Quincy Stable (J.F. Johnson)	28	24	24	$29,253
Miller, A.	13	15	8	$30,039
Loft, G.W.	21	24	24	$29,253
Weir, F.D.	37	19	31	$27,594
Applegate, W.E.	12	4	4	$26,741
Carman, R.F.	25	26	18	$26,176
Hildreth, S.C.	26	30	16	$26,117
Spence, Kay	44	39	30	$26,001

TOP 25 TRAINERS FOR 1918

Trainers	1st Place Wins	Winnings
Spence, Kay	58	$35,303
Bedwell, H.G.	53	$80,296
Williams, P.J.	51	$32,875
Perkins, W.	49	$55,658
Weir, F.D.	47	$53,092
Clopton, S.A.	45	$28,988
Fitzsimmons, J.	44	$42,777
Burttschell, W.A.	43	$32,881
Arthur, J.	42	$34,696
Carman, R.F.	41	$41,575
Musante, F.	41	$32,312
Karrick, W.H.	40	$65,675
Martin, W.F.	38	$25,094
Jennings, W.B.	36	$79,443
Bressler, A.R.	35	$26,488
Odom, G..M.	34	$36,752
Hildreth, S.C.	31	$31,759
Schorr, J.F.	30	$37,599
Goodman, J.B.	29	$22,197
Herold, F.A.	28	$22,888
Healey, T.J.	27	$48,878
Goldblatt, M.	27	$23,737
Boden, J.	27	$21,356
Hirsch, M.	26	$34,169
William, R.D.	26	$22,936

TOP 25 JOCKEYS FOR 1918

Jockey	Mounts	1st	2nd	3rd	Unplaced	Win %	Winnings
Robinson, Frankie	864	185	140	108	431	.21	$186,595
Lyke, Laverne	756	178	123	108	347	.24	$201,864
Sande, Earl	707	158	122	80	347	.22	$138,872
Lunsford, Harry	850	155	167	114	414	.18	$125,708
Ensor, Lawrence	508	117	81	72	238	.23	$17,240
Howard, J.	607	106	67	68	366	.17	$64,395
Walls, G.	568	95	89	77	307	.17	$95,993
Rodriguez, J.	580	77	68	71	364	.13	$57,773
Kummer, Clarence	439	69	66	69	235	.16	$73,305
Connelly, Danny	591	67	76	77	371	.11	$63,941
Johnson, A.	541	59	83	73	236	.11	$56,497
Schuttinger, Andy	317	58	46	29	184	.18	$146,969
Pauley, R.	224	56	33	38	97	.25	$11,810
Smith, F.	375	55	46	49	225	.14	$37,417
McAtee, L.	409	54	37	53	245	.13	$48,732
Gentry, L.	407	50	48	40	269	.12	$43,533
O'Brien, W.J.	278	50	41	38	149	.18	$47,147
Mooney, J.	418	46	49	57	266	.11	$36,232
Simpson, R.	359	44	41	36	238	.12	$46,893
Kelsay, William	369	44	32	56	237	.12	$41,205
Collins, A.	623	42	75	57	449	.07	$31,699
Garner, Mack	297	42	49	44	162	.14	$37,987
Taplin, E.	304	41	41	27	195	.13	$46,564
Rice, T.	362	39	44	59	220	.11	$31,145
Pitz, J.	292	38	37	32	185	.13	$86,946

TOP 25 HORSES FOR 1918

Horses	Age	Starts	1st	2nd	3rd	Unplaced	Winnings
Eternal	2	8	6	1	0	1	$56,137
Johren	3	22	9	5	3	5	$49,156
Exterminator	3	15	7	4	3	1	$36,147
Cudgel	4	17	9	4	1	3	$33,826
Billy Kelly	2	17	14	2	0	1	$33,783
Dunboyne	2	6	3	2	0	1	$32,030
War Cloud	3	15	5	2	2	6	$25,100
Jack Hare, Jr.	3	13	8	2	2	1	$23,815
Roamer	7	16	6	6	2	2	$21,950
Hannibal	2	12	3	2	1	6	$19,725
Colonel Livingston	2	22	9	7	4	2	$19,623
George Smith	5	8	4	2	2	0	$18,550
The Brook	5	14	9	2	1	2	$17,410
Motor Cop	3	12	6	2	3	1	$16,810
Sweep On	2	15	4	3	2	6	$16,751
Elfin Queen	2	7	4	1	0	2	$15,936
Lord Brighton	2	17	6	2	2	7	$15,161
Naturalist	4	17	9	1	4	3	$14,942
War Pennant	2	11	6	1	1	3	$14,020
Hollister	4	24	9	6	3	6	$13,358
Hauberk	6	26	9	5	4	8	$12,623
Bet	5	19	4	5	0	10	$12,506
Slippery Elm	5	23	10	1	3	9	$11,735
Sunny Slope	3	11	6	1	2	2	$11,263
Corn Tassel	4	26	8	6	5	7	$11,237

APPENDIX B

TOP 25 OWNERS FOR 1919

Owners	1st Place	2nd Place	3rd Place	Winnings
Ross, J.K.L.	64	41	34	$209,303
Hildreth, S.C.	61	32	15	$169,075
Whitney, H.P.	46	41	16	$92,308
Glen Riddle Farm (S.D. Riddle)	14	4	8	$87,876
Widener, J.E.	30	22	21	$65,054
Parr, R.	45	36	36	$61,457
Coe, W.R.	38	40	28	$55,928
Wilson. R.T.	23	26	16	$48,185
Loft, G.W.	28	30	27	$45,617
Spence, Kay	67	42	51	$40,080
McLean, E.R.	22	15	8	$39,201
Macomber, A.K.	18	15	19	$38,655
Weir, F.D.	29	36	42	$37,921
Kilmer, W.S.	17	14	12	$36,604
Clark, P.A.	12	8	12	$35,171
Ogden Stable (D. Lester & S. Henderson)	19	16	19	$34,965
Forman, G.W.	31	30	23	$32,572
Williams Brothers	33	28	38	$32,491
Bradley, E.R.	28	21	22	$32,380
McClelland, J.W.	25	16	10	$31,714
Polson, W.F.	25	33	37	$31,679
Goldblatt, M.	27	13	15	$29,563
Gallaher Brothers	19	19	16	$27,836
Diaz, A.H.	33	20	16	$27,757
Garrison, C.M.	3	5	4	$27,715

TOP 25 TRAINERS FOR 1919

Trainers	1st Place Wins	Winnings
Spence, Kay	96	$67,352
Bedwell, H.G.	63	$208,728
Burttschell, W.A.	62	$54,121
Hildreth, S.C.	60	$123,986
Karrick, W.H.	48	$67,582
Arthur, J.	41	$38,261
Garth, W.	37	$53,884
Hirsch, M.	35	$47,864
Goldblatt, M.	35	$35,740
Harmon, T.J.	34	$27,526
Weir, F.D.	33	$41,617
McDaniel, W.	33	$27,757
Dunne, P.	30	$38,906
Garth, L.W.	29	$40,161
Fitzsimmons, Jimmy	29	$38,287
Smith, R.A.	27	$30,296
Short, W.	26	$36,071
Schorr, J.F.	25	$43,196
Simons, A.	25	$31,040
Goode, J.M.	25	$25,521
Staton, F.W.	25	$16,880
Brannon, B.J.	24	$26,267
Neusteter, H.	24	$24,617
Clopton. S.A.	24	$15,520
Healy, T.J.	23	$48,185

TOP 25 JOCKEYS FOR 1919

Jockey	Mounts	1st	2nd	3rd	Unplaced	Win %	Winnings
Robinson, Clifford	896	**190**	145	126	435	.21	$201,282
Murray, Tommy	832	**157**	103	109	463	.19	$140,562
Fator, Laverne	606	**129**	105	83	289	.21	$213,051
Lunsford, Harry	639	**100**	84	80	375	.16	$96,394
Thurber, H.	722	**85**	110	88	439	.10	$107,098
Kummer, Clarence	399	**82**	59	61	197	.21	$137,809
Sande, Earl	346	**80**	67	58	141	.23	$126,042
Butwell, Jimmy	449	**77**	80	60	232	.17	$78,615
Rice, T.	462	**71**	82	75	234	.15	$78,986
Ensor, L.	334	**70**	45	41	178	.21	$116,044
Boyle. S.	468	**67**	54	49	298	.14	$76,853
Loftus, Johnny	177	**65**	36	24	52	.37	$252,707
Gamer, Mack	449	**61**	92	59	237	.14	$70,002
Connelly, D.	447	**59**	61	61	256	.13	$58,353
Ambrose, Eddy	343	**59**	58	46	180	.17	$101,791
Mooney, Jimmy	539	**59**	54	55	371	.11	$47,586
Johnson, Albert	409	**59**	51	52	247	.14	$63,994
Kelsay, William	383	**58**	55	49	221	.15	$69,089
Wida, S.	476	**56**	57	70	293	.12	$45,833
Pool, E.	327	**55**	38	49	185	.17	$70,894
Hamilton, H.	356	**53**	42	39	222	.15	$58,689
Nolan, T.	329	**52**	51	48	178	.16	$61,010
Schuttinger, Andy	220	**49**	43	21	107	.17	$68,911
Coltiletti, Frank	292	**49**	24	60	159	.17	$43,757
Burke, H.J.	394	**48**	37	47	262	.12	$34,045

TOP 25 HORSES FOR 1919

Horses	Age	Starts	1st	2nd	3rd	Unplaced	Winnings
Sir Barton	3	13	8	3	2	0	**$88,250**
Man o' War	2	10	9	1	0	0	**$83,325**
Mad Hatter	3	7	4	2	1	0	**$54,991**
Purchase	3	11	9	2	0	0	**$33,710**
Vexations	3	4	2	1	0	1	**$27,930**
Be Frank	3	14	3	3	3	5	**$27,315**
Billy Kelly	3	19	9	7	2	1	**$26,563**
Exterminator	4	21	9	6	3	3	**$26,402**
Royce Rools	4	21	10	2	2	7	**$22,940**
Midway	5	13	3	2	3	5	**$22,065**
Miss Jemina	2	12	8	0	1	3	**$20,055**
Hannibal	3	10	5	0	3	2	**$19,291**
Naturalist	5	15	8	4	1	2	**$19,259**
The Porter	4	15	7	2	2	4	**$19,226**
Constancy	2	13	5	3	2	3	**$19,194**
On Watch	2	13	5	3	0	5	**$18,447**
Milkmaid	3	14	8	2	2	2	**$18,067**
Lucullite	4	17	9	3	2	3	**$17,137**
Thunderclap	3	19	7	4	5	3	**$16,981**
Cudgel	5	11	4	3	4	0	**$16,462**
Bonnie Mary	2	7	3	2	0	2	**$15,600**
Slippery Elm	6	30	9	10	6	5	**$13,950**
Courtship	5	22	5	5	1	11	**$13,765**
War God	4	18	6	2	4	6	**$13,487**
High Cost	4	24	10	5	3	6	**$13,300**

APPENDIX C

TOP 25 OWNERS FOR 1920

Owners	1st Place	2nd Place	3rd Place	Winnings
Whitney, H.P.	76	61	44	$270,675
Ross, J.K.L.	118	115	64	$250,586
Glen Riddle Farm (S. D. Riddle)	22	10	8	$186,087
Parr, Ral	44	26	30	$114,838
Bradley, E.R.	38	32	25	$94,067
Salmon, Walter J.	25	21	18	$91,223
Hildreth, S.C.	36	18	17	$82,649
McLean, E.B.	38	30	33	$76,049
Wilson, R.T.	45	36	30	$74,319
Coe, W.R.	21	30	16	$69,692
McClelland, J.W.	31	18	21	$67,360
Loft, G.W.	31	21	12	$64,429
Sunnyland Stable (Robert A. Smith)	27	32	19	$64,410
Kilmer, W.S.	15	6	5	$63,300
Widener, J.E.	26	30	23	$59,372
Baker, R.L.	27	21	38	$58,473
Thraves, W.V.	32	32	35	$57,614
Skinker, J.R.	42	33	26	$52,309
Williams Brothers	42	35	36	$48,906
Clopton, S.A.	47	42	32	$48,210
Arthur, J.	31	37	34	$47,446
Weant, W.C.	48	53	55	$47,085
Hendrie, G.M.	24	24	16	$47,075
Greentree Stable (Mrs. P. Whitney	23	25	21	$44,115
Quincy Stable (J.E. Johnson	23	19	19	$40,148

TOP 25 TRAINERS FOR 1920

Trainers	1st Place Wins	Winnings
Clopton, S.A.	74	$152,312
Spence, Kay	74	$94,674
Bedwell, Harry G.	73	$175,023
Burttschell, W.A.	65	$73,090
Perkins, W.	60	$75,552
Weant, W.C.	54	$53,405
Garth, William	51	$123,065
Fitzsimmons, James	50	$76,475
Healy, Thomas J.	49	$78,023
Arthur, J.	48	$63,926
Davis, H.E.	41	$21,575
Schelke, F.	41	$61,125
Rowe, James	40	$155,434
Schorr, J.F.	37	$73,951
Hildreth, S.C.	36	$81,149
Hirsch, Max	36	$76,420
Major, E.E.	36	$17,175
Buxton, C.	36	$56,679
Waters, T.B.	36	$16,795
Carter, William A.	34	$28,830
Graham, B.E.	34	$21,670
Short, W.	34	$41,819
Walker, W.	34	$25,815
Crippen, G.W.	33	$13,365
Baldwin, J.S.	33	$18,795

TOP 25 JOCKEYS FOR 1920

Jockey	Mounts	1st	2nd	3rd	Unplaced	Win %	Winnings
Butwell, Jimmy	721	152	129	139	301	.21	$216,742
Ensor, L.	372	116	77	42	137	.31	$192,244
Coltiletti, F.	665	115	132	101	317	.17	$195,110
Rodriguez, J.	706	114	126	107	359	.16	$1770,581
Lyke, Lawrence	489	111	81	62	235	.23	$175,464
Kennedy, B.	604	110	106	99	289	.18	$140,874
Carmody, J.	541	106	88	82	265	.20	$77,306
Sande, E.	355	102	80	56	117	.29	$228,231
Duggan, C.	631	100	87	90	354	.16	$53,350
Roberts, J.	581	96	85	77	323	.17	$70,287
Kummer, Clarence	353	87	79	48	139	.25	$292,376
Wilson, F.	560	86	80	68	326	.15	$105,249
Thurber, H.	410	84	58	57	211	.20	$78,855
Mooney, J.	693	83	76	98	436	.12	$113,201
Fator, E.	499	82	73	63	281	.16	$76,610
Wida, S.	653	80	105	100	368	.12	$90,912
Murray, T.	419	79	67	46	227	.19	$68,876
Hinphy, W.	537	78	62	75	322	.15	$47,635
Dominick, J.	358	75	65	48	170	.21	$41,935
Yeargin, G.	373	74	68	84	347	.20	$63,774
Thompson, Charles	330	72	64	55	139	.22	$29,475
Morris, L.	446	71	70	64	241	.16	$123,655
Ponce, C.	429	69	64	76	220	.16	$78,872
Richcreek, A.	599	68	98	89	344	.11	$96,823
Stack, G.	517	68	63	58	328	.13	$76,703

TOP 25 HORSES FOR 1920

Horses	Age	Starts	1st	2nd	3rd	Unplaced	Winnings
Man o' War	3	11	11	0	0	0	**$166,140**
Exterminator	5	17	10	3	2	2	**$52,405**
Tryster	2	6	6	0	0	0	**$49,925**
Boniface	5	26	11	9	3	3	**$47,565**
Cleopatra	3	15	6	5	3	1	**$46,731**
Paul Jones	3	13	4	2	2	5	**$44,636**
Leonardo II	2	4	4	0	0	0	**$36,078**
Careful	2	17	12	1	0	4	**$34,383**
Dr. Clark	3	16	7	4	1	4	**$32,681**
On Watch	3	22	10	5	3	4	**$30,743**
The Porter	5	13	6	2	3	2	**$28,044**
Minto II	6	21	7	5	5	4	**$27,695**
Upset	3	6	2	3	0	1	**$26,969**
Wildair	3	17	5	5	4	3	**$26,196**
Prudery	2	8	5	2	0	1	**$25,650**
Cirrus	4	14	6	5	0	3	**$25,196**
Sir Barton	4	12	5	2	3	2	**$24,494**
Irish Kiss	5	18	8	2	5	3	**$24,197**
Blazes	3	19	6	3	2	8	**$23,994**
Mad Hatter	4	20	9	3	4	4	**$23,834**
John P. Grier	3	10	6	1	2	1	**$23,817**
Paul Weidel	3	16	9	2	0	5	**$22,635**
Baby Grand	2	28	12	6	4	6	**$20,188**
Woodtrap	6	39	11	7	7	14	**$19,304**
Bondage	6	34	7	8	8	11	**$19,261**